God's Fires

Ace Books by Patricia Anthony

COLD ALLIES

BROTHER TERMITE

CONSCIENCE OF THE BEAGLE

HAPPY POLICEMAN

CRADLE OF SPLENDOR

GOD'S FIRES

God's Fires

Patricia Anthony

ACE BOOKS, NEW YORK

cop. 1

GOD'S FIRES

An Ace Book
Published by The Berkley Publishing Group
200 Madison Avenue, New York, NY 10016

The Putnam Berkley World Wide Web site address is
http://www.berkley.com/berkley

Make sure to check out *PB Plug*,
the sciencefiction/fantasy newsletter, at
http://www.pbplug.com

Book design by Maureen Troy

First Edition: April 1997

Library of Congress Cataloging-in-Publication Data
Anthony, Patricia.
        God's fires / by Patricia Anthony.
            p. cm.
        ISBN 0-441-00407-5
            1. Portugal—History—Alfonso VI, 1656-1683—Fiction.
        2. Inquisition—Potugal—History—Fiction. 3. Portugal—Church
        history—Fiction. I. Title.
        PS3551.N727G63 1997   96-31430
        813'.54—dc20   CIP
Printed in the United States of America

10 9 8 7 6 5 4 3 2 1

To Evelyn Anthony,
a career woman who read to her daughter.
See where it got us, Mom?

God's Fires

Day 1

FORNICATION. IT WAS NOT A SIN HE EXPECTED HER TO CONFESS. NOT HER. Not She of the Three Hairy Moles. Father Manoel Pessoa's gasp tasted of Dona Inez: a reek of stale goat cheese and decomposing sardines. The resulting cough saved him from laughter, or from shattering the silence of the church by blurting, "Sainted Jesus! With whom?"

He longed to know, of course. And then he ached to share this amusing news with Father Soares. He was tempted to look up to see if some miracle had caused the moley trinity to disappear from her nose, mouth, and chin.

He stared at St. John's painted toe, instead. To be sure, this was no ordinary confession—his rear propped against a cold stone shelf, the statue an intercessor between them. Yet Dona Inez had uttered the words which ensured her anonymity and his silence: "It has been five days since my last confession." He searched furiously for a way around that.

"Are you all right, Father Inquisitor?" she asked. "Your trip has not exhausted you into a *gripe*? Or made you spend too long in the sun?"

"No, no. Please. Tell me more." A name, he prayed.

"They come at night," she told him. "And wake me from sleep. They put their hands on me, and lay me on an altar where they lift my skirts."

Doubtful. Simply imagining Dona Inez with her skirts up made Pessoa's eyes water. "An impure dream. Make a good Act of—"

"Not a dream!"

The interruption shocked Pessoa mute.

"A man," she said, "who is maybe an angel, comes in to where I am lying. He is tall. Taller than the others, and he is so bright that it hurts to look. He asks me questions which are hard to answer, and which make me fear for my soul. He has a long *pau,* and he sticks it in me. Would an angel do that, father? Does a dream have the power to give you pain? I beg him to stop, but he refuses. He puts his hand over my eyes, and he kisses me, and tells me to sleep. When I awaken in the morning I find blood between my legs."

As Jesuit, Father Pessoa had been taught to question. What Dona Inez confessed caused him to ponder the *paus* of angels. Surely if God set angels higher than man, their *paus* would be huge. Ah. Now there was a deadly thought.

She said, "I have seen the little Castanheda girl with the angels, too. She lies on an altar of silk. Her skirt and her blouse are gone, her shift pulled up. The angel lies on top of her, and makes her groan."

"Are you talking about Marta Teresa da Penha Castanheda?"

"Yes, Father Inquisitor. She has led this angel into temptation, and has caused him to fall from grace. Conversion never took with that family, you know, and Moors capture their men with love potions. Now the angel is crazed with lust and cannot help himself. He sticks his *pau* wherever, whenever. May we have an *auto-da-fé,* please? I think a girl who seduces an angel needs burning."

Father Pessoa had watched the Castanheda girl grow. Just this summer, she had become ripe for plucking. Were he an angel, he would fall for her. He imagined himself, skin aglow, his *pau* huge, Marta groaning beneath him.

He huffed, irritated by his own lust, by Dona Inez's dream, and of deciding whether or not to shrive her. "I shall question the girl, of course. Is that all?"

Dona Inez propped an elbow on St. John's sandaled foot and leaned over, breathing onion-and-rot effluvium into Pessoa's face. "She swears it is the Virgin Mary. But I have seen with my own eyes and I tell you, saying a creature with a *pau* like that is the Blessed Mother can only be heresy."

Abruptly Dona Inez was up and gone, leaving a doppelgänger of her odor. Father Pessoa eased a kink out of his back and genuflected.

His self-imposed circuit ride, which began six years earlier as dull pain, was now a toothache of sameness: the small heresies, the interchangeable towns, the litany of edicts. Once he yearned for absolute knowledge; now a comfortable bed and a roast chicken would do.

Through the narrow Romanesque windows of the church, he saw that the sun was setting. Already vespers. By the time he got to the rectory, Father Soares, who had not been informed of his arrival, would have eaten every scrap of dinner.

He picked up his cloak and his wide-brimmed hat, and walked out through the front doors. The late-summer air was sweet. Sheep moved like dingy clouds across a firmament of gray-green hills. A cork tree gathered the westering sun in its dense branches. His donkey, Felicidade, stood in the yard below, head down, tail swishing. Pessoa's buttocks still chafed from Felicidade's spine. No remedy for it; and no hope of salvation. When his horse died, the Holy Office hadn't the money to send him a replacement.

Somebody needed to bugger someone soon in his district. Have congress with a cow. He wouldn't mind sending a sodomizer to the provincial tribunal at Mafra. Wouldn't mind confiscating the man's horse and a little money. Inquisitors before him had become rich. Now the Holy Office lacked even the means to send him a secretary and an armed guard. Ha! They would see. One day he would be set upon in the hills and be assassinated.

He jammed his hat on and limped, sore-legged, down the steps. The secret to life, Pessoa had discovered, was timing; and he was habitually late—late for dinner, late for the Inquisition, birthed thirty minutes slow. His twin, João, received the title and the estate. Manoel inherited eight year's study of the law and an ass misnamed "Happiness."

The loud, heartfelt "Praise God, stranger!" sent him fumbling for his dagger.

It was Magalhães, the tailor. The bald man moved closer, squinting. "Ah! But it's only you, father. Time to read the Edicts already? You see the signs in the sky?"

"Sorry?"

"In the sky!" The tailor pointed upward, as if Pessoa might have difficulty locating it. "At night. Burning crosses."

"Um."

"I take it for a good sign, although maybe not. God doesn't translate, does He, at least to an ignorant man such as myself. The Castanheda girl talks to the Virgin, though, and the Virgin explains things, but women are known to gossip, *verdade*? When you figure out the signs, perhaps you will tell us, because the women keep the Virgin's talk a secret." The tailor wandered off, pulling on his ear.

Troubled, Father Pessoa watched him go. *Not here. Not this. Better a sodomite, Domine.*

Clucking to Felicidade, Pessoa led her down the hill, around the corner, and down a row of whitewashed houses. At the richest house, he stopped.

Senhor Castanheda himself opened the door to Pessoa's knock. His swarthy face fell. "Ah," he said. "I thought you would come." The lamps in the entranceway were lit. Over Castanheda's broad shoulder, Pessoa could see a mahogany-and-gold crucifix and a garish painting of El Cid. A war trophy? For surely Castanheda dared not champion the Spanish—not after killing so many for Portugal's independence. And why the Cid? Did he admire him for fighting for Muslims, or for being the consummate Christian warrior? It was elegant, this choice of art, one that the Holy Office would always suspect, but could never fault.

Castanheda opened the door wider. "Please."

Pessoa, imagining a curved Moorish dagger between his ribs, smiled, thanked him, and waved the offer away.

"If you have come to arrest my daughter—"

"O, no! No! Nothing so official, really. I simply want to talk to the child."

Castanheda called, "Marta! Father Inquisitor is here!"

Little Marta came, doe eyes downcast, hands together as if in earnest prayer. Senhor Castanheda propped his arm against the doorframe, a brawny barrier.

Pessoa bent and tried to peer into her face. "Hello, Martinha! Hello! How are you? Good to see you again. You remember me? Father Pessoa? Of course you do. I come into town four times a year just so the old men can fall asleep during my reading. Well. Imagine this!" He clapped his hands softly. "It seems that I came into town today, and people are saying that you have seen the Blessed Mother."

She stood, meek and silent.

"Ah. I see. It's a difficult thing to talk about, miracles. You know, Martinha, I'd like to see the Blessed Mother. I've always wondered if she's pretty."

Marta raised her head and Pessoa's heart stopped. The girl was ethereal. Her huge eyes were aglow, as if angels had touched secret places in her. She said, "Would you like to see?"

A growl: "Marta—"

"No, *papai*. It's all right. He can't hurt me." She ducked under her father's sheltering arm, and ran lightly down the short steps into the street.

Not *won't hurt me. Can't hurt me. He can't hurt me.* Apprehensive, Pessoa looked at Castanheda. The man was regarding his daughter, tears trembling on his lower lids.

"Hurry! Hurry!" Marta called, and her voice echoed along the narrow road. "Come see before the light fails!"

Pessoa left Felicidade at the steps and followed. Marta ran, skirts billowing, dark hair loose, gilded by dying sun. Stiff from his journey, he limped after, from cobblestones to clay, from glimmering village to brassy meadow. And at a lone olive tree beyond the edge of town, she stopped.

"See?" she cried in triumph. "Her power is too much for living things."

The top of the olive tree was blighted. Marta grasped Pessoa's hand and pulled him, stumbling, to a circle of dead grass.

"Here is where she appears to me," Marta said, her eyes alight. "Feel the power? Like a tingle up and down your arms and in your stomach?

Hear the buzzing in your head? She speaks to me, and her voice is like water over rocks, like a wind through branches. O, she is so beautiful. Come. Kneel, father. Kneel with me and pray."

He tried unobtrusively to get away, but she pulled him down beside her and turned. "Here in this place of glory . . ."

He froze. Those eyes, huge and dark. He closed his own and felt the whisper of her breath against his cheek.

". . . confess your sins," she said.

KING AFONSO CARRIED his Italian spyglass with him everywhere. Three days ago he had peered through it to see people on a balcony making love. The day before, a woman beating a child. The day before that, a man beating a woman. Because kings should make everything right, Afonso had called for his soldiers. By the time the guards arrived, the beatings were over, and try as he might, Afonso couldn't remember which house, which woman, which man.

Sunset turned the Tejo's pewter to flame, and a caravelle, perhaps back from India, perhaps from Brazil, tacked its calm burning waters. Afonso liked ships. They brought him things: African slaves who sang and danced and grinned; leopard-skin drums; banana and papaya trees which bloomed for a while, and died of homesickness.

He adjusted the focus to bring the quay into view. With much hand waving and officiousness, the caravelle docked. Behind it, weary fishing boats bobbed home. He lowered the glass, shivering as summer sun abdicated the castle. He saw daylight retreat from the crowded homes of the Alfama below, and watched Lisbon's blue chill return.

"Lights!" the king cried, and a servant sprang to the candles. The dark frightened him. The dancing shadows the candles threw made him anxious.

Tucking his spyglass into his belt, he left the room, shuffling down corridors, through smells of damp and mildew, past iron-banded oak doors.

He ran, boots slapping an uneven rhythm on stone. He counted rooms on his fingers. ". . . four. Five." Reaching the limit of his numbers, he returned to "one," then started on the other hand. ". . . two. Three!" With a whoop, he pushed the latch. The second-third door swung open.

The room was bright with candles. Dom da Fonte started, and drew his sword. Pedro leaped to his feet. Bishop Días clutched his pectoral cross.

"Ha!" Afonso laughed. "I am King Sebastião, and you are my prisoners!" Fumble-fingered, he drew his own sword, his new one. "Fall down on your knees and beg for my mercy!"

Dom da Fonte sheathed his weapon and retreated behind the desk. "Get that away from him."

"Afonso . . ." Pedro warned.

Afonso cried, "Death to the coward who dares not fight!" He swung his sword. Without meaning to, he struck a gold chalice, and it fell, chiming, to the floor.

The bishop ducked farther into the cushions. Da Fonte backed another step and ran a hand through his graying hair. "Who in God's name gave him that blade?"

Afonso pointed the tip downward and struck a wobbly, although heroic pose, one such as he had seen on a tile mural at Estoril. "The Flemish ambassador. And it is a fine one, with words writ on it. And its edge is very sharp."

From his hiding place in the cushions, the bishop laughed. "A plot. Didn't I tell you the Flemish hate us?"

"Put the sword away," Pedro said.

"But I am King Sebastião, Pedro. And you are Muslims."

No one in the kingdom had a voice as gentle as Pedro's. "It is time to put the sword up. Come here. You've been eating chocolate again."

After four tries, Afonso slid the blade into its sheath. He went to his brother, standing before him toe-to-toe, a measuring distance. Just this winter, Pedro had grown until he was almost as tall as himself. His voice was beginning to deepen in fits and starts, as Afonso's had two years before. Each day, Pedro looked more and more like their dead father.

Pedro hummed a *fado* as he dipped the edge of a linen napkin into a goblet. He sang softly as he scrubbed Afonso's lip. Afonso tried to escape, but Pedro held him fast. "No one will give you presents if you're dirty. Stop squirming! I wetted the napkin with Oporto wine, just the kind you like."

"You're hurting me."

"Am not."

Afonso liked the way Pedro spoke, the way he always sounded sure of himself. "Do you want to see my spyglass? It's from Italy!" He took it from his belt.

Pedro ran his hands over the silver scrollwork.

"Silly Pedrinho," Afonso said. "You aren't using it right. Put your eye to the tiny end, and things look close. Put your eye to the larger end, and they look far away. Bring it to the window. You can see the people in the Alfama just like God can!"

Pedro looked at the bishop, who smiled a funny smile and shook his head.

"You don't have to ask the bishop's permission, Pedro. Castelo Melhor says he's just a Jesuit whoremonger, and you're the brother of a king, after all."

They laughed: the bishop and Pedro and Dom da Fonte. The bishop laughed so hard he choked, and spilled his wine.

Afonso's insides went jittery when people laughed and he didn't understand. To make the sick feeling stop, he bounced up and down on his toes. "Come, Pedro. Please? The view is finer from the battlements, but the window will do. You can look down on people, and no one knows you are seeing them! I have watched men piss in the streets. I have seen women lift their skirts for money."

He pulled Pedro to the window. Da Fonte followed, grumbling. "So he likes to watch whores, does he. I was wondering when he would discover what his cock is for. Ask him if he has managed yet to stick it into that French bitch of his, or if he needs someone to show him which end is for what."

Pedro pulled free. "Stop, Afonso! Stop tugging!" Afraid and hurt, Afonso backed up.

Then Pedro turned to da Fonte. "Damn you," he said between clenched teeth. "Stop."

"If he gets that French whore with child—"

"Get out," Pedro said.

"How *can* I get out of this? I'm pledged. Will you let that renegade count remove our heads in the square?"

"I said, get out!"

With a sigh, the bishop gained his feet. "I believe it's time. . . ."

Da Fonte came up until he was toe-to-toe with Pedro—not measuring, not playing. Da Fonte was so much older, taller, stronger. The two glared at each other like a pair of dogs. They were silent for so long that Afonso grew frightened. Then abruptly da Fonte turned and stalked out, the bishop at his heels.

Pedro looked so sad that it made Afonso sad, too. A king should make everything right.

"I know!" He clapped his hands. "Jandira has been reading me *Don Quixote*! I will go on a quest. And you will go with me."

At last a smile. Pedro reached up and brushed the hair away from his brother's face. "No one goes on quests anymore."

"Castelo Melhor said it was a wonderful idea."

"I imagine he did."

"We will tilt at windmills. There are windmills in the Alentejo, and Jandira says they whistle!"

Pedro stroked his brother's cheek. Afonso closed his eyes. Whenever the word *safety* was uttered, it was Pedro's warm hand that he thought of.

"You go," his brother said.

Afonso whispered, "I can't enjoy windmills without you."

"Castelo Melhor has ordered me to leave."

Panic thrust Afonso through, belly to spine. "No!"

"Only to Mafra. Only for a while."

"No!" Afonso dropped the spy scope. The lens shattered in a spray of thin glass. "You can't go!"

A guard rushed in from the hall. Pedro motioned him out.

Afonso wanted to run away, but he knew that the word *leave* would follow him through the door, down the hall, to the courtyard, and out into the night.

"Believe me, it is not my choice—"

"No! I am the king. And I say no." He held his cock tight and danced up and down, the way he did at court when there was no chamber pot and he had to piss. Pedro would go away like Catarina had gone away. He would disappear to the place his father and mother had gone. "Catarina went away and she never came back!" he wailed.

"Hush. Don't cry," Pedro said, but he was crying, too. "She is all right. Our sister is all right. She's just—"

"No!" Mucus ran from Afonso's nose. He sobbed so hard, he drooled. Kings should make things better, but planning was hard, and the world went by too fast. "She went away, and Castelo Melhor says she's dead!"

"The count means that she is dead to the country. She married England, and you are friends with France. He speaks in riddles sometimes, and thinks he's clever. You know that."

Everyone but Afonso was clever. "Why should I love France? What does France or England matter, unless they bring presents?"

Pedro threw his arms around him and put his lips against his ear. "I promise I'll come back."

Afonso held on to his crotch with both hands. He held himself until the good feeling stopped, until the ache that replaced it was as good as forgetting.

Pedro rocked him. "It's only for a while."

If Pedro went, the ground would open and Afonso would drop through the hole left in the world. "It is me you must obey, Pedrinho. I am the king."

"I know."

Afonso rested his head in the warmth of his brother's shoulder. "There are windmills in the Alentejo."

"Slay one for me," Pedro said.

W HEN PESSOA ARRIVED at the rectory, he found Father Soares
tending cabbages in the twilight.

"Damn you." Pessoa let Felicidade's reins drop. He whipped off his broad-brimmed hat and slammed it to the ground. "Damn you for a Jew, Luis!"

The gaunt old Franciscan looked up, terrified, blinking fast. "I . . . I . . ."

Pessoa snatched up his hat from the clump of turnip greens where he had thrown it. "Why didn't you send word? Do you expect me to receive divine knowledge? Have a vision myself? God in Heaven! Well? What do you have to say for yourself? Is there any dinner left?"

Still blinking, Soares pointed to the cottage. "Boiled potatoes—"

"Bloody Hell," Pessoa muttered, and walked inside.

Soares called after, "I'll see to your mount!"

"My ass!" he shouted back.

A candle sat guttering on the table, the perfect metaphor for Rome's *lux perpetua:* the Church, its light failing.

On a plate sat boiled salted cod, the fish so rancid that it brought back queasy memories of Inez. In a black three-legged pot, Pessoa discovered what the notoriously insatiable Soares had overlooked: a pair of mealy potatoes. Pessoa found a clean plate, a wooden spoon, and fished his dinner out.

"Cabbage with that?" Soares stood in the doorway, a bouquet of fresh-picked leaves in hand.

Pessoa gave him a dark look. He sat down so hard on the bench that his sore buttocks nearly sent him bolting to his feet again.

"Wine, then?" Soares asked.

"Yes, and may you die before my eyes of indigestion. Yes. Thank you so much. I'll have some wine."

Soares filled an earthenware jug from the cask. He brought that, and two fine black pottery mugs to the table.

Pessoa drank. "I come into town, and everyone is talking of crosses in the sky. Visions of Mary." He gave a *puh* of disgust. "I tell you, when children—children of *cristãos novos,* mind—order you to confess your sins . . ." Sensing the danger, he stopped himself. "You always have good wine."

"Mm. The best of the village. They coddle me, you know. The cheese they bring! *Quejo fresco,* white as lilies, and so moist that it quivers. Four entire *quejo frescos* I ate with my dinner. And the sausage—I must confess that it is beef sausage—probably the Olivieras keep to their Jewish ways . . . but, O Manoel, the sausage! They brought me two fine ones, their casings stuffed so full that when you roast them, they pop."

Pessoa took a deep breath and thought he could smell a lingering odor of sage and cured meat. His mouth watered. His stomach growled in anticipation. "Sausages? *Quejo fresco?* Where's the food you saved for breakfast?"

"All gone." Soares studied the crucifix on the wall. *"Mea culpa."* He spied the plate of codfish. "Ah! The *bacalhau!* Kitty, kitty, kitty!" Picking up the plate, he toddled to the door.

Through the doorway came a flood of cats. So many that, in awe, Pessoa stopped drinking. "More than last time."

"They multiply." Soares patted the striped, arched backs. "They go forth, yowling. Who am I to tell them no?"

Exhaustion made Pessoa's ears hum. He ate the final overdone potato and poured himself more wine. "How long has this been going on?"

Awash in a sea of cats, Soares looked up. "The kittens?"

"The heresy."

Soares stiffened. The plate was licked clean of fish, the cats already milling from boredom. "Who's to say it is heresy? Who's to say that the Castanheda girl is not another Teresa d'Avila?"

"I'm to say." Pessoa sat back. "Besides, you're gullible. If a rooster crows tomorrow, you'll think God caused it."

In the Franciscan's look was a hint of a smile. "Won't He?"

"Don't. I'm not in a mood. Did you encourage that girl?"

"No. Yes. Well . . . who knows? It might have been the Blessed

Mother, Manoel. It's possible. When Marta speaks of it, she convinces me. She is so transported. Have you seen her?"

"Girls get transported all the time. I transported a few myself when I was younger." Ripe little Marta. Angels with glowing *paus*. The thoughts brought on an unwelcome stirring, and he redirected his lust to where it belonged. "How is the Pinheiro woman?"

"The witch!" Soares waved a hand in annoyance. Cats bounded away. "She is possessed of the evil eye. Besides that, I hear she's well. From time to time she asks of you. I speak as a friend now: lie with her if you must, but don't look her in the face."

Pessoa propped his elbows on the wooden table. "All right, all right. To business. Let me point out the pitfall in Marta Castanheda's story: holy visions normally cause trees to bloom."

Soares looked crestfallen.

"We have a blighted tree, Luis. A withered circle of grass. So either this is a demonic apparition—which I would rather not investigate—or we have a lightning bolt, and a question I can leave to science."

"Um. I remember the night. A terrible storm."

"Good. And warn that father of hers to keep the girl silent. Can't he marry her off? She needs to be less transported, I think."

The last cat wandered away, tail proud and straight as a mast. Soares came and sat down on the opposite bench. In the hearth, the fire popped. Day died outside the doorway, and the air turned chill.

Pessoa scraped his spoon across the gritty, empty plate. The sound it made sent a shiver through him. "Listen to me carefully. I don't mind finding a little heresy, but this is dangerous."

A quick nod from Soares.

"This doesn't involve the penitence of *sanbenitos*. What I've heard today would call for relaxing to the flames. I'd rather not conduct such an *auto*."

"Agreed. More wine?"

The jug was empty. Soares rose to fill it again. Pessoa wiped his mouth. His hand felt awkward. His lips were numb. Suddenly the world seemed brighter. "O, well. The visions are probably just a summer malady," Pessoa said. "Don't you think?"

Soares poured his mug to the brim. "Yes. Drink up. I'm sure they'll be gone by winter."

In the dusk outside, swallows sang evensong; sparrows chittered as they flew to roost. Pessoa yawned. "Something amusing I wanted to tell you. What was it? Something . . . o, yes!" Pessoa took a sip of wine.

Eager, Soares sat forward.

"So I arrive in town." Pessoa lowered his voice. "And a penitent gives me an *auto da graça*. I'm not sure how it happens, but it turns into confession. And there we are, seated to either side of St. John. Should I take notes? Jail her? Shrive her? Come to think of it, I never told her to make a good Act of Contrition."

"Auto da graça," Soares decided.

"Then we'll say *auto;* but to be safe, I'll think confession. Now. The sin was fornication. Fornication from someone I knew . . . well, granted, if it was confession, she is therefore anonymous—but let me tell you I'm sure no one would fornicate with that, at least no one not possessed or blind or lacking the sense of smell. And she admits to fornication with angels! I prayed to God, please, please don't let me laugh, and by His mercy, I controlled myself."

"Lauda Dei. More wine?"

Pessoa belched—a belch that tasted of boiled potato. He slid his mug across the boards toward Soares.

Soares let slip "What else did Dona Inez say?" the instant before his eyes flew to Heaven and he crossed himself.

Pessoa clamped a hand over his mouth. Laughter began as a tickle in his belly—effervescent and scintillating as new wine. Then Soares snickered. Pessoa whooped and slapped his knee. They laughed until they were damp-eyed and gasping.

At the window, the last glimmer of light failed. Pessoa was lightheaded; tired, but restless. Glowing *paus* of angels. Marta Castanheda groaning beneath him. In his groin burned man's corporal and highly irritating *igne aeterna*.

He stumbled as he got up. "I think I'll walk a bit before retiring." He needed quenching, but Marta was too young, far too devoted.

Soares lifted his mug with his left hand, tossed a sloppy but sincere blessing with his right. "Don't look her in the eye," he said.

MONSIGNOR INQUISITOR-GENERAL Gomes came to a halt in the middle of his study. He wore a meditative look, one which in another man might have signaled piety; but young Father Bernardo Andrade recognized it for what it was: precursor to "Take a letter," or—

There. The second choice. A fortissimo fart that stank of that afternoon's onioned pork roast. Bernardo inched the incense brazier closer.

Then he noticed, with some alarm, that the pensive expression on Monsignor's face had not vanished.

"Take a letter," he said.

Bernardo chose the red leather journal. He dipped his quill into the ink pot.

"To His Grace Archbishop Vásquez of the Holy See, Seville, my fellow Dominican and esteemed brother in Christ, blah, blah, blah, I beseech your favor—insert some pathetic groveling here, Bernardo. You're so good at it—for it has come to my attention that Rome punishes Portugal's Holy Office due to the misguided allegiances of the Jesuits—"

A small, very small, voice at the door. "Monsignor?"

Bernardo looked up from his work. Monsignor whirled, all three chins uplifted and quivering.

The Cistercian friar was woeful. "I do so hate to interrupt, Monsignor Inquisitor-General, but Count Castelo Melhor has arrived and requests—"

"Tell him to wait!"

"Yes, Monsignor. Thank you."

"Get out, and close the door."

The friar's tonsured head bobbled. "Thank you, Monsignor. Thank you, I shall do so immediately. Thank—" He shut the door on his own apology.

In one swift move, Monsignor lifted his habit. "Quick. Bindings."

Bernardo put the quill down and retrieved a long strip of linen from a rosewood case. He knelt beside Monsignor's right thigh, and started the wrap where the tip of Monsignor's cock peeked shyly from under his prodigious stomach.

"Tightly, Bernardo," he said. "That young fool only respects power. It's the fashion, you know. God is unimportant. Secular power is all."

"Shocking."

"Always 'force of arms,' 'force of arms,' as if the boy alone defeated Spain, and God had nothing to do with it." He emitted a grunt as the linen compressed his solar plexus. "Busy following his own whimsies, with no guidance from the Church. He will burn in Hell for it."

"Yes, Monsignor." Bernardo wrapped Gomes upward in corpulent billows. Above the bindings, Monsignor's chest swelled with excess flesh. Then a frown of concentration. Bernardo stepped away just as Monsignor's rear gave an onion-scented bleat.

Bernardo held his breath. "Done," he pronounced.

Monsignor waved the smell away with his hem, then let the habit fall. "Announce him."

When Bernardo opened the door, Castelo Melhor, handkerchief pomade providentially in fist, mustaches a-quiver with indignation, pushed him aside. In passing, some sharp edge on the count's breastplate snagged the loose folds of his wool sleeve. Metal scratched his arm. Head lowered, Bernardo kept an obedient silence. The count, too far above Bernardo's station for sympathy, never looked back.

Castelo Melhor reached the center of the room and dropped to one knee. "Your servant."

Ah. Here at last was Monsignor's attempt at a pious expression: the eyes ostentatiously sweet, the mouth smug and as tight and pink as an asshole. With languid hand, he sketched a benediction. Before it was complete, the count bounded up. "Why did you use the *potro* on that French wine merchant?"

The sign of the cross became gesture. The monsignor pointed to the polished table and a burdened silver tray. "Candied orange? Sugared chestnut?"

Bernardo backed up and merged with the shadows. He sat down at his desk and pulled the green leather journal closer, opening it to a back page. He took up his quill. Under an illuminated *MP* for *Monsignor Peccati,* he drew flames.

The count slammed his helmet onto a mahogany sideboard, and the noise startled Bernardo so that his hand shook. Ink dropped off the quill tip to form a messy blot on the page. Three flames lost. Bernardo felt sick at heart. In penance, he offered a silent *gloria Dei.*

The count was ranting, ". . . all because he carried with him a few pages of Hobbes."

"What do you care for a wine merchant?"

"The man is third cousin to Louis's second-favorite mistress. France has complained, and rightly so. Louis asks why we can't control our clerics."

"Then ask why he can't control his Huguenots." Much to Bernardo's horror, Monsignor began furiously eating sugared almonds. Above the three unsalvageable flames of pride, Bernardo drew a tongue of flame for gluttony.

Monsignor was saying, "My dear count. Hobbes is on the banned Index. Haven't you read him?"

"Enough."

"How much, exactly?"

With a flourish, Castelo Melhor lifted his pomade and sniffed. Bernardo noticed a crust of sauce on the front of the man's steel breastplate. Did the man actually dine with his armor on?

"People explain it to me."

"Don't listen to rumor. Read the book. You think Hobbes legitimizes you, but in fact he legitimizes anyone with the strength to take over a country. So Cromwell had the right to behead Charles and, ten years thereafter, Parliament had the right to restore the monarchy. Think about that."

Castelo Melhor fell into a nearby chair, propped an elbow on the armrest, and nibbled on a fingernail. Bernardo noticed that it was a stalwart and much-bloodied soldier of a fingernail. Things did not go well at court.

"The French feel that we have used the wine merchant badly."

"Badly? Perhaps. But justly. Always justly. Bernardo!"

Bernardo came alert. "Yes, Monsignor?"

"Read the transcript."

The yellow book. Bernardo flipped pages. "Ah, yes. Here. Wine merchant Michel François Millet. I read, '. . . then he is ordered to be put on the *potro*. At the first tightening, he says, "Let me down, sirs, for I have done nothing." He is told to confess, and he says, "Of what am I accused?" At the second tightening, he says, "O stop. Have mercy. My arms hurt beyond bearing. Help me. Someone help me." He is told to confess, and at the next tightening—' "

"Yes, yes, yes." A brusque circling gesture. "More toward the end."

Bernardo flipped pages. ". . . Have pity, et cetera, et cetera, ah here . . . 'The doctor pronounces him fit, and states that the questioning may continue. The prisoner then cries out, "Something in my luggage. But I had nothing but clothes." He is asked to confess. He says, "Was there something in my luggage?" At the next tightening, he says, "The pages with the writing. But I only kept them to wipe myself with, sirs. I was indisposed, and used the pages to wipe myself, for I cannot read." The questioning is then halted. The inquisitor orders the secretary to write on a paper the words in French: "YOU ARE ORDERED BURNT," so that the inquisitor may show this to the prisoner. He does so, and when the prisoner does not start or pale, he is ordered released and the record noted that he abjured *de vehementi.*' "

Monsignor poured sherry.

Castelo Melhor gulped his down. "The man can hardly walk. He can't sit a horse."

"There was a doctor present. Two jurists. Myself, my secretary, the state executioner. What more do the French want? Had the idiot told us in the beginning that he was illiterate, it never would have gone as far. And you might warn your Sun King to read his Hobbes more carefully." Monsignor's eyes suddenly glazed: a visitation of sugared nuts. "Well, my son. I must to prayers, and you must to running the country. . . ."

Distracted, clutching his empty glass, Castelo Melhor got up. "I'm sending that little idiot Pedro to Mafra. I'm beginning to hear some gossip. I can't kill him publicly, unless I have proof. His sister would press England to invade. And I fear for my soul if I kill him privately. Or do you think I could be appropriately shriven for that?"

Monsignor's pious expression was gone. In its place was desperation. Bernardo sat up straighter. With a stouthearted attempt at nonchalance, Monsignor clapped the count on the back. "Remember that life is natural order, my son, from the hierarchy of heavenly hosts, to church, to king, to people. Only evil confuses things."

Castelo Melhor looked confused. He set his glass down, and Bernardo ushered him out.

When the count was gone, Monsignor put his hands on the tabletop, leaned his weight against it. His voice was strained. "Merciful God. Get me out of these bindings."

Bernardo came to his aid. He worked quickly, loosening the linen, hurriedly but neatly folding it, settling it in its case.

Behind him, in Monsignor's direction, came a loud agonized wind noise, followed by a series of tight squeaks.

"Shall I finish the letter, Monsignor?" Bernardo turned. The room stank of onions and sulfur.

The inquisitor-general stood, head down, in a near swoon. *"Miserie meum,"* he whispered. A dreamy look. Another horn blast, one that rose at the end, like a question.

Bernardo bent, picked up his books. "Will that be all, then?"

Monsignor's face was slick with sweat, his mouth open. Bernardo had seen that same fearful concentration on those sent to the *potro.*

"Monsignor? Will that be all?"

Clutching his belly, Monsignor shuffled away and collapsed on a cot. "Yes."

Bernardo bowed and exited. He took the long way back to his rooms, moving silently along the colonnade walkway, past the monks' cells. In an alcove near Mary's chapel, by a niche dedicated to Jesus and the children, he stopped, held his journals to his chest, and praised God.

For the choir was practicing for a society funeral to be held on the morrow; singing a requiem motet by Lassus. Bernardo closed his eyes.

Everything fell away: Monsignor's vanities, the polluted stench of modern politics, the weight of his own flesh. It seemed as if the pure voices of the children bore him up. His body lightened to unblemished spirit, his feet threatened to leave the ground.

"Deum de Deo, lumin de lumine," he whispered. He dared not speak loudly, dared not move, lest someone notice. Prayer was meant for dark closets, although the shadowed niche of statue children would do.

The voices drove splinters of ecstasy into him. He bled joy. *"Deum verum de Deo vero,"* he prayed, and it seemed as if beauty was piercing him, head to toe, with sweet yet unbearable pain. *"Genitum non factum, O, incarnatus est."* Dropping to his knees, he clutched the edge of the niche, and wept.

THE DEMONS WINE and Exhaustion conspired against Pessoa. First they made him dizzy, then they caused him to be lost. When he finally stumbled onto the right path and arrived at Berenice Pinheiro's house, he entered the wrong door and ran, belly first, into the fleecy flank of her burro. The animal snorted and stepped away.

Inside, beyond reach of gibbous moon or starlight, Pessoa was struck blind. He groped through blackness until he touched the rough surface of the stucco wall. At last he spied a glow—a promising orange strip. Through a gap in her curtain, he could see the coals of her hearth fire.

He waded through the straw, but impish Wine made him forget that Berenice's house was a step higher than the stable. His toe caught on a flagstone, and he sprawled through the curtain into the neighboring room. The impact knocked the breath from him.

A fast-moving shadow. Something thrashed his back. "Mary and Joseph!" he cried, crawling away.

A soft voice asked, "You?"

He rolled over. Bouquets of herbs dangled like bats from the rafters. The plain wooden cross he had given her hung dutifully above the fireplace. Berenice stood above him, broom at the ready. Her shift was thin. Through it he could see the glow of the hearth and the shadow of her small but luxuriant body: her legs—praised be—slightly parted.

He reached out and caught what he could of her: her toe. "Ah, Berenice. You transport me. You lead me into temptation."

She slapped him with the broom. He sat up, coughing and sneezing dust.

"You're drunk," she said, and knocked him down again.

Before he could orient himself, she splashed him with icy water.

"You dare come here stinking of the road, of that donkey?" Fury and determination made her his match. Tearing at buttons, she snatched his cassock over his head.

He spat water and tried to get away. She followed him with the bucket and brush. She scoured as he begged for mercy.

He upset a three-legged stool, fetched up in the corner, and put up his arms to shield his face. "You will give me a *gripe*, woman!"

The soap smelled of ashes and tallow and dog rose. She scrubbed so hard, it stung.

"Bathe once a week," she was saying. "That's a preventive, not the cause of illness. Didn't your St. John lead his flock to wash in the river? All your Bible talks of cleansing, yet one would think Christians die from getting wet. I tell you, you stink. Your churches stink. You live in filth like pigs."

He manacled her tiny wrists with his hands. "Don't say that."

Her body was so close that it was like sitting before the warmth of a fire. Her shift was damp, and it clung to the swell of her breasts, to the nubs of her nipples. He shivered, but cold water had done nothing to quench him. His *pau* stood at attention.

She wrenched loose. "So stake me," she said.

He snatched up her shift. They tumbled together to the floor. Too much wine; too long a trip. Five thrusts, and he released, leaving her rubbing against him in frustration.

He put his hand to her, but she pushed it away.

"Not like that," she said.

"But my stake is soft. My fire is out."

"We'll see." She wrapped him in a blanket that smelled of lavender. She combed his wet hair. She put her arms around him and told him that she missed him.

"Have you anything to eat?" he asked plaintively.

They sat across from each other at her table. She served him a Judaizer's meal: bread and salt, olive oil and herbs, hard cheese, purple-brown olives. She mixed his water with wine. As he ate he looked up, saw her looking back with eyes as remarkable as a Byzantine Madonna's.

He caressed her fingers, unintentionally anointing her with oil. "Dona Inez has seen glowing angels."

Berenice snorted. "Inez? That's in doubt."

"Yes, granted. But tailor Magalhães speaks of crosses in the sky. Little Marta Castanheda has seen the Virgin. Do you hear rumors like that?"

In her face he saw a quick flash of anger. "Who bothers to speak to a witch?" She went to kneel before the hearth, laying on fresh wood, poking at coals, her expression bleak.

He dipped the rest of the bread into the salt, into the oil, and went to sit at her side. "I only ask," he said, "because you told me that your angel glows."

Pine bark sizzled. A knot of oak caught with a blaze of yellow flame. "All angels glow," she said. "Everything glows."

"Tell me."

"You never wanted to hear it before."

"I was an inquisitor before. Now I am simply a man with a question."

"He's all I have," she said, resting her cheek on her bent knees. "And he is enough. I love him without stint, without boundaries."

Pessoa failed to see it coming. Jealousy stabbed him in the back.

"It was when I was sick," she said. "I told you."

He chewed the tough, oiled bread. When he was away from her, it was the sight of her body he thought of first. Then the touch of her skin. Then the clean, strawflower scent of her hair. Yet when he dreamed of her, he awoke to the tastes of olive oil and spices. "Yes, I know. But I wasn't listening at the time."

"You're a pig, Manoel. If you listened more carefully, maybe you'd find that faith of yours."

He tore off another piece of bread and sucked oil from his fingers. "Start from the beginning."

"I died," she said. Those large eyes were wistful. "And I went through a cave to another place. There was light there, all around."

"Inez says it hurts to look at it."

"Ha! Then I know she's not seeing angels. Because the angel light would never hurt you, never. Yet it pierces things. When I was back in my room, the light turned everything gold: the table, the stool, the iron pot. A man was with me, and he was all made up of light, and he said, 'You must go back now, Berenice.' O, you see, Manoel? He knew my name. He called me by my name. And he looked me in the face, and his eyes were kind."

When she fell silent, he tore his gaze from the hearth. Her cheeks glistened, her chin quivered.

"How long is his *pau*?" he asked, even though he feared the answer. How could he, a mortal, compete with a creature like that?

She looked up. "What?"

"The man of light. Does he have a long *pau*?"

She slapped his shoulder. "He has no *pau,* idiot. He's an angel."

"Doesn't he lie with you, then?"

"No, and no!" She hit him harder. She wasn't crying anymore.

"Well, if he doesn't have a *pau,* Berenice, I don't see the point of your fantasy. You had a fever dream—"

"A fever dream? A *fantasy*! Can a dream change you?"

He shook his head. "You didn't die, obviously. You're here, aren't you? You were lonely, so you've created a fantasy to keep you company."

"If it's a fantasy, then why do I still see colored edges to things?"

"The fever damaged your vision—"

"O? Then how can I tell illness from the colors? Answer me that."

"You merely think you tell illness by colors. You've been tending the sick all your life. You see other signs, and don't realize—"

"You're insufferable!" She shook him so furiously that she tore the blanket off him. "Little prick-proud man! Contentious, closed-ass Jesuit who thinks he knows the answer to every question!"

They fought for possession of the blanket, and in the end, he let her win. "Damn you." He got up. Cold, naked, he poured himself a mug of wine, drank it, then poured himself another. The cup was cracked. The glaze on her pottery was thin and cheap, the clay so poor that the texture of it set his teeth on edge. The cup nearly made him weep.

He took a deep breath. Her house smelled of burro and herbs and rain. From the direction of the hearth came a rustle of clothing. He felt her approach.

"I always thought I was ugly," she said.

He turned, surprised. "Why?"

"God bless, Manoel! Because people don't *look* at me."

"Don't be silly. That's only because they think you sour milk. Make them lose their babies. Give them running sores. It has nothing to do with being ugly."

Her jaw set: a dangerous expression. Why was she so annoyed? When they made love, he always looked her in the face. He never forgot.

"The Church teaches that evil is ugly."

Ah. Now he understood. "I was taught to question, of course, but this is not to say that a bit of ecclesiastical simplification is wrong. Really, Berenice. Don't look at me so. I didn't make the doctrine, but it serves. In fact, I concede the Dominicans and Franciscans this one point: if ordinary men start to distrust their place in the universe and are not taught the Jesuit skill of answer, what can they do but become embittered? I imagine there are far more English with poor digestions than there are Portuguese. That's what the Inquisition's for."

"So the Inquisition was created to produce better digestion."

Her gaze was frighteningly direct. He yearned to look away, but didn't dare. "Well, I paraphrase, but . . ."

A quick and entirely unexpected move. She grabbed him by the *pau*. He froze, fearing that he had been mistaken all these years, that reason was wrong, superstition valid. He was terrified suddenly that she was a witch with enough supernatural strength to rip his *pau* out by the roots.

"Tell me I'm pretty," she said.

"What?"

Her dark eyes didn't waver. Her hand moved up and down his shaft. "Tell me I'm pretty."

"Well, of course you know . . ." But perhaps she didn't. "Berenice," he said softly, and touched her cheek. "You're really very . . ." She dropped to her knees and took him in her mouth. He gasped and closed his eyes. The fire was suddenly lit, his stake ready. "God. God."

Another greedy pull, and she let go. Laughing, she led him to her pallet. "Now," she said.

Soon ecstasy made her cry out. She clung to him tight. And when he, too, was done, they lay exhausted together, her stroking his back. He drank more wine, although he knew he shouldn't. The wine made him drowsy, and it seemed like a dream when she said, "I see colors in you, Manoel. Blue like the sky, for questions. A buried golden treasure trove of faith. And a line of red lust at your edges, just for me."

He drifted in the slow current of her voice. Bewitched, he fell asleep in her touch. Hours before dawn, she awakened him, kissed him, and told him it was time to go.

Day 2

BERNARDO AWAKENED WITH A START, THINKING HE HEARD THE MATINS bell, knowing he was late. He slipped out of his nest in the covers and into the numbing chill of the corridor. Standing unshod on the stone floor, he saw that the monastery was quiet, the votive candles in a niche across the way standing guard. His frightened heart slowed.

Lauda Dei. Only a dream.

Picking up his sandals, he scurried barefoot down the corridor, making no noise in passing. Inside Mary's chapel he bunched his habit so that belly and groin were bare, but the back of his legs covered.

He prostrated. The cold was always a shock. His teeth chattered. The floor sucked the heat from him and left his heart quivering in his chest. His *pau* shriveled.

Not that lust plagued him. Bernardo did not lie with women as Father José Renato was wont to do. And he did not seek out other men, as Friar Coelho. Nor did he feel the need to abuse himself under the blankets, as did Jorge or Jeronimo.

"Sanctus, sanctus, sanctus," he whispered.

He lay the way he had when he had accepted his vows, cheek to floor, feet together, arms outstretched, as if seeking crucifixion from the stones. His cock shrank more. His testicles tried to burrow into the warmth of his pelvis. And as the engine of lechery diminished, holy ecstasy came awake. A spot at the root of him tingled.

"Dominus Deus Sa—"

Wait. Was that a sound in the hall? Bernardo caught his breath. Someone would walk in and discover him here. He listened, his pulse racing. Mortification should be secret between penitent and God. Not loud and brash like Friar Carlos's self-scourging.

The monastery kept its silence. *"Pleni sunt caeli . . ."* He closed his eyes and the sensation in his groin spread. It melted ice. Contraction became aching, infinite expansion.

Knowledge didn't cause the Fall as Monsignor believed. Monsignor was a modern man, one who believed that doubt was more evil than lust. Bernardo knew better. Just as Eve led Adam into temptation, women tricked men. He had seen strong schoolmates weep for love; seen soldiers come raving back from war, their cocks rotted from the English disease, their minds gone. That was the consequence of sin.

". . . et terra gloria tua." His breath came faster. His mouth opened. The tingle shot upward, impaling him with joy. *"Osanna in excelsis."* He bit his tongue to keep from crying aloud.

He arose, steadying himself on a pew. Bone and muscle hummed as if he were the tuning fork, and God the music master.

Bernardo would forgo breakfast and his midday meal today in penance for awakening late. Before retiring, he would say ten Pater Nosters and ten Ave Marias. Lust was not his sin, nor gluttony, nor pride, nor greed, nor sloth. He was guilty of small transgressions. The kind one could always make right.

The matins bell rang.

He genuflected. On his way from the chapel, he paused at the Madonna and Child. When he was sure no one was watching, he rose on tiptoes and kissed the rosebud lips of the baby Jesus.

CATS MEWED. SOMEWHERE farther away, roosters crowed. And much too close for ear's comfort, Soares sang. Pessoa lay, indisposed by yesterday's wine, his face turned to the wall. He tried not to listen. The song was of a maiden who jumped the fire on St. John's eve.

"Lavender thistles, thistles, thistles . . ." A loud resonant gong sounded. Soares had dropped the iron pot, ostensibly by accident. Pessoa knew it was a hint, and he didn't move. If he stayed still, his head wouldn't throb. Soares would think him dead, and go away.

". . . under her pillow, oh, yes, her pillow."

Pessoa remembered the end of the song. Instead of dreaming of her future husband on St. John's eve, the girl saw herself wrapped in the arms of Death. A sad ditty. Pessoa couldn't help picturing little Marta Castanheda as the maiden.

"She knelt by her be-e-e-ed, and said her rosary as any good girl should."

Cats meowed discordantly. Pessoa's head throbbed, a guilty sentence handed down by last night's wine. He tried to remember what day it was, but his attention wandered.

"On St. John's eve," Soares sang.

A litany marched through Pessoa's consciousness, keeping time with the headache: *Lacrimosa dies illa* . . . What day *was* it? He'd left Montemuro two days before. No. Three days before.

"On St. John's e-e-e-eve . . ."

And three days before was . . . what? O. Tuesday, the day of Montemuro's fair. His head hurt from thinking, and so he let his mind ramble again. . . . Marta Castanheda opening her almond eyes, her face wearing the languid look of a woman with her suitor. Pessoa imagined waking with his arms around her, imagined himself smiling back.

Qua resurg—

Pessoa's heart stuttered. The requiem. That's what he was reciting. He nearly bolted from his cot. The rectory was silent now. Soares must be standing behind him, waiting, probably praying that he arise.

"Manoel? One of my flock has brought us fresh bread and Spanish cherries."

The requiem. What did *that* mean? Pessoa was not a superstitious man, but still, it seemed ominous to awaken thinking of the requiem, and imagining himself as Marta Castanheda's Death.

"Manoel?" Soares's voice was louder. "Manoel, please."

Pessoa rolled over, hiking the blanket over his shoulder. The straw mattress rustled. Leather and wood squeaked.

Soares peered at him, concerned. "You look afright."

"Mm. A touch of *gripe*. A bit too much of the road."

"Ay!" The old Franciscan lifted his arms skyward. "I warned you not to look! Now you'll be impotent. You'll have hemorrhoids and strange fevers."

Pessoa ran his tongue over his teeth. His mouth felt mossy. He closed his eyes, and felt himself drifting off. "That's right," he muttered. "Sleep in."

"You can't! I've laid out your vestments. The Mass has already been announced. Aren't you going to be co-celebrant?"

Miserere nobis. The last Thursday of the month. Time to read the Edicts.

PEDRO WASN'T IN his rooms. Afonso looked for him under the bed and behind a tapestry of the victory at Batalha. "Pedro?" Arms out, fists clenched, nightshirt flapping, he ran his brother's room in circles until he was dizzy and his breath came quick. "Pedro! Stop hiding!"

Afonso returned to the hall, where a guard came to clanking attention. "Where is my brother?"

"Gone to Mafra, sire."

A moan climbed Afonso's throat. He slapped both palms to the guard's breastplate and drove him into the wall. The man went down on his knees, babbling apologies. Afonso stumbled down the steps, pushing aside chambermaids and footmen.

He heard Jandira call his name. He didn't stop. He knocked a char sprawling, sent a tide splashing from her bucket.

Down a back hall, through the kitchens, through smells of coffee and onions and cinnamon and blood, past cages of squawking game hens and hamstrung, gutted stags. He ran awkwardly, staggering and panting. His own weeping blinded him. He struck hip against table, knocked shoulder against pots. As he passed, cooks screamed, chars fell to their knees. Butchers dropped cutlery.

"Sire!" Jandira called.

Afonso gave vent to an alarm that was more grief than name. Then out the shadowed archway, into the sunny cobblestone courtyard, past hills of carrots, mountains of cabbages, potatoes piled like stone cathedrals.

And there was Pedro, astride his Barbary gray stallion. He was surrounded by soldiers and nobles, and Bishop Días walked at his side.

"Pedro!"

In his saddle, Pedro turned.

Afonso slid on the dung-slick cobbles.

"Pedro! Wait!"

The gray shied, tossed his head. Pedro drew in the reins.

When Afonso reached his brother, he wrapped his arms about his leg.

"O, Afonso. What are you doing out here in your nightclothes? It's cold. Where are your shoes? Come, let go of me, and I promise I'll get down. Jandira? What is he doing in his nightclothes?"

Hands gently pulled Afonso back. When Pedro dismounted, Afonso fought free to kneel at his brother's feet.

Gasps escaped from the lips of the nobles. A surprised grunt came from the bishop. Even the honking geese hushed.

Pedro tried to lift him. His voice was quiet. "Don't. Don't do this."

Afonso clung to his brother's belt. "I will give you my kingdom if you stay."

"I pray you, my liege." The bishop's voice was strained. "Please get up."

Then Jandira was there, smelling of vanilla. Her robes were a swirl of color, her face the hue of wet cork. "That's right. We'll pray, won't we. Won't we, bishop? We will kneel and pray for the king's brother's safe journey." She knelt, took hold of Pedro's tunic, and pulled him down with her. The nobles and equerries dismounted. All around the battlements, guards went to their knees.

Bishop Días looked confused until Jandira tugged the cuff of his wide sleeves and said, "Our Father . . ."

Jandira made the bishop remember his prayer. "Ah, yes. Our Father, um . . . Our Father, protect Your son Pedro on his short—I must say very short—journey to Mafra, ah . . . and keep your servant the king safe from harm. Amen."

"And now Pedro may go," Jandira said.

Afonso grabbed his brother's tunic. Pedro tore loose.

Jandira put her arms around Afonso to stay him while Pedro leapt onto his saddle, agile as a cat. The nobles and equerries, too, took to their mounts. The bishop flung *benedicto* after *benedicto* at them as the courtyard echoed with Afonso's shrieks.

Afonso heard the clop-clop of horses' hooves recede. He saw Pedro glance over his shoulder and wipe his eyes.

Jandira was saying something, but Afonso was wailing too loudly to hear. He held his arms out to Pedro. He rocked back and forth until the stones rubbed his knees raw.

"Did you hear me, my liege?"

On the opposite side of the courtyard, gatekeepers sprang to the ready. The huge castle doors swung open. Pedro was merely a spot of color among the rest.

Afonso rocked, keeping his eyes on the place where Pedro was disappearing, and taking world and light with him.

"Listen to me, my king!"

Afonso turned and looked at Jandira: the three decorative scars on her right cheek, the three on her left.

"I said, tomorrow we can go on a quest to Mafra."

"O? O!" Strange how, as relief flooded him, his eyes streamed even more. "A surprise. Will we surprise Pedro?"

She grinned. Between her lips he saw a flash of her white teeth. "By Mary and St. George, sire. I imagine we will."

DON'T DRINK WATER atop a bad head from wine. Pessoa knew that, but he had been thirsty. Now the wine from the night before was making him drunk anew. Early in the Catechumens, sometime after the Gloria, he dozed off. The missal nearly fell from his lap, and he snapped awake just in time to stay its slide. Soares was reading from Ezekiel.

Pessoa drifted. Vaguely he heard Soares's voice and the response from the congregation. He opened his eyes, hoping he had looked prayerful. It was time. He stood and made his way down the altar, stopping to genuflect. That's when Berenice's foreign spices hit him. Nausea sapped the strength from his legs.

Behind him feet shuffled, clothing rustled. There was a scattering of coughs.

With a mighty surge of will, Pessoa braced himself and lunged to his feet. He pulled the altar cloth off square, nearly knocked over the chalice. A well-trained altar boy stepped forward to discreetly set the chalice aright.

Pessoa turned, breathed deeply, and staggered up the three stairs into the pulpit. "Friends . . ." he said, and spread his arms. A wave of vertigo struck. He gripped the carved sides of the pulpit. The church pitched like the sea.

In the front row sat Dona Inez and her moles: *Pater, Filius, et Spirito Sancti.* Marta's love-starved fantasies would disappear once she married. Pessoa would see to it personally that Berenice was satisfied. But Inez . . . O, Inez. Even if called to serve, he could not.

God help him. He was going to laugh.

He ducked his head, took the Edicts from his pocket, and began hurriedly to read. "The Holy Office in Braga calls upon all obedient Christians to seek out heresy. Here are the signs: those among you who do not eat pork or shellfish, those who bathe and change their bed linens before feast days . . ."

The church was overly warm. He fought a yawn. ". . . who are engaged in the smuggling of books which are on the Index, who read of such books . . ."

He rushed headlong toward the Credo, muttering as fast as a petitioner reciting a novena. Every year the Edicts grew. When he had started his rounds, they took fifteen minutes. Now they could last an hour. And then he would have to sit through General Intercessions, co-celebrate the Eucharist, and assist with Communion. What if he told everyone *"Ite, Missa est"*? Would the congregation rise like good sheep, and leave?

Pessoa skipped fifteen pages, neatly editing superstition and adultery, to read the final sentence. "So I bid you, stand and say."

In his six years through Quintas, only two people had ever stood, and they stood at the same time: Magalhães, to admit having said that adultery was no sin; and Magalhães's wife to accuse her husband of the same crime. In fact, it was Magalhães's *sanbenito* that Pessoa's eyes locked on as he raised his head. The linen shift, red cross already fading, hung from a rope at the back of the church.

Below it, Gregorio Neves stood, scratching his cheek.

"Do you have a confession?"

He shook his head.

Pessoa's heart sank. No. Not Berenice. "Then do you have an accusation?"

Another shake.

Pessoa took a steadying breath. "Then why are you standing, my son?"

The farmer shifted his weight to his other foot and mumbled something.

"You must speak up, Gregorio."

Neves shrugged. "Well, I don't know that it's confession, exactly. Or an *auto da graça*. I don't even know that it is important, father."

"Yes?"

"But I was reminded of it by the reading today."

"Go on."

"And I thought, well . . ."

"Say it!"

Neves grinned broadly, nodding around at the congregation. "Ezekiel's wheel set itself down in my potato field."

BERNARDO FINGERED HIS rosary as he walked; careful to step around last night's garbage and a fresh pile of dung. The street was narrow, packed with wealthy, jostling mourners.

"Behind the horses," Monsignor whispered. "That Jesuit planned this."

Bernardo lifted his eyes. Ahead of the wood-and-glass hearse and the matched black geldings with their ebony plumes, he caught a glimpse of Días's miter, the upheld cross, and a white thread of smoke. Beyond, he saw startled faces in windows, heard the noise of hurriedly slammed shutters, heard the warning cry move from house to house, "Funeral! Funeral!"

"He's laughing at us, Bernardo."

A clean whiff of incense ran a gauntlet of garbage, perfume, and body odor to reach him.

"Well he may play with us." Monsignor nodded at a stray noble and a woman in rich widow's weeds. "But Días would do best not to tease our count. That boy is wicked," he said with relish.

A well-fed, smug hog—that's what Monsignor resembled. True piety was the contorted face of the crucified Christ, eyes raised to heaven. Holy pain uplifted the soul. Bernardo sometimes saw it happen on the *potro;* and for a lucky few who found God when their feet were put to the coals.

Bernardo himself was still exalted by the Lassus motets. He felt so light, in fact, that it seemed his feet barely touched the cobbles. A rebellious grumble from his stomach brought him back to earth. He had skipped breakfast and his midday meal: a whisper in God's ear.

"Wicked," Monsignor said again.

Up the cobblestone streets they went, around corners so tight that the pretentious four-horse team had to be led. Wooden shutters banged like cannon. A whore mistress in a bawdy house shrieked more loudly than the funeral drums, telling her girls to get up, get on their feet, before Death mistook their sleeping.

"The English disease," Monsignor said in an aside. "That's what he died of."

Bernardo nodded.

"Died stark, raving mad, they say. And blind. No telling how many he gave it to. Our beloved slave merchant Villas enjoyed boys and women both. Traveled to Brazil, to Africa, to France. Spread his joy about; although it must be understood, Bernardo, that he never confessed to me."

"Completely understood, Monsignor."

"The same amorous leanings as our count, I might add. I should not be surprised if Castelo Melhor has much mortality to ponder today."

Just behind the spire of Días's miter was a flash of polished steel, a blood spill of velvet cloak. Bernardo wondered if the count had cleaned the crust of sauce from his armor.

"Too bad we need that boy. He simply cannot keep it from rising to attention."

Monsignor's face was puffy. The almonds had evidently kept him awake. Yet his eyes were sharp; and although Bernardo had bound him tightly just prior to Mass, he had yet to exhibit discomfort. Robust health, a society funeral, and an opportunity for gossip. The inquisitor-general was having a good day.

The procession wound through the iron gates of the cemetery, past plain Romanesque crosses and graceful Baroque angels. Monuments rose in ranks like the spears of a quiet, marble army. At the Villas crypt, they stopped. Family wept as pallbearers took hold of the coffin. Amid the obligatory mourners—the acquaintances and business partners and non-celebratory clerics—quiet chatter droned.

Bernardo watched the knot of black-robed activity at the crypt: the sway of a censer, the sign of the cross. He spied only one spot of color: Castelo Melhor, his breastplate shining, plumed helmet in hand. Días was accustomed to the practices of the elite. He spoke the graveside service so quietly that he didn't disturb the background of subdued babble.

The bishop suddenly raised his head. His voice rang over the gather-

ing. ". . . good man here interred. He should be remembered for his gen-
erosity. His kindness. Roberto Villas truly gave unto others. . . ."

A strangled noise. Monsignor hid his face in his kerchief. When time
came to make the sign of the cross, he was still snickering.

Then the ceremony was over. "Such a tragedy," an elderly and distant
cousin of the House of Bragança said, shaking Monsignor's hand. "A man
struck down unexpectedly in his prime."

Monsignor made sympathetic noises. Bernardo fingered his beads.
By the crypt, Castelo Melhor and Bishop Días were talking. The bishop
was smiling; the count was not.

The royal cousin left just as an attractive woman seized Monsignor's
hand in a death grip. "A blessing that his suffering is finally over." Her
voice, Bernardo noticed, held a vibrato of anxiety and a falsetto grief.

Monsignor murmured agreement. The crowd began to disperse.
Bernardo watched Castelo Melhor stalk over, pulling at a mustache.

"Do you know what that traitor Jesuit said?" the count demanded as
he reached them.

Mourners turned, expressions eager. Monsignor told him, "Keep your
voice down."

The count raised a French pomade shaped like a black chrysanthe-
mum. The stick was wound with purple ribbon, and trailed appropriately
funereal streamers. Bernardo could barely credit it: the breastplate's sauce
stain was intact.

Castelo Melhor sniffed loud and long. "The pig! He said Afonso told
him what I call him in private. He looks at me, all wooden-faced, and asks,
since he wrote up the peace with Spain, and I say he is a whoremonger—
what does that make me?"

"Mm."

"Too brazen. They're hatching something. And have you heard that
Afonso knelt at his brother's feet this morning, and offered him his kingdom?"

Offered the kingdom? That flew in the face of God's order. Bernardo
wanted to hear more, but Monsignor's attention drifted.

"If Afonso would only consummate his marriage," the count said.

"Get a son by her. Yet they lie together, and he is limp, and when he is told what he must do, he weeps. Why, the girl's not so repulsive as the Flemish royals I've seen. Perhaps I could—"

That snagged Monsignor's roaming interest. He raised an admonishing brow.

"Or perhaps not." Castelho Melhor lifted both pomade and nose skyward. His expression turned so thoughtful that Bernardo wondered if he was passing gas. Suddenly he looked down. "Hm. A piece of interesting news. Some of my soldiers in Setúbal say they have seen shields in the sky, with angels standing on them. My men said they sing with odd voices, like crickets. A chorus of angels, as if God has put a blessing on our undertaking. What do you think of that?"

Bernardo's heart stopped. *Sanctificatur nomen tuum.* He clutched his beads so tightly that his nails dug into his palm. O. He would do anything to see God's angels. To hear that singing.

"It means you should limit your men's wine." Monsignor huffed. Clutching his missal to his chest, he turned and started down the hill. "Really, Bernardo. Soldiers seeing shields in the sky. Hearing angels sing. As though God would speak to just anyone."

PESSOA PLANNED A quiet after-Mass trek to the potato field and then a well-earned nap; but Marta Castanheda caught him leaving with Neves.

"I am to go with you. The Blessed Mother told me to stand witness," she said.

Pessoa, who had struggled against misery all morning, relinquished the battle. His forced smile drooped. "No, Marta. You cannot. I think the Virgin knows what happens without your having to tell her."

Their discussion caught the attention of some who were leaving the church. Magalhães and his wife drifted over. "Put on your hat, father," the tailor said. "The sun is bad for the head."

Pessoa's head pounded; but wine, not sun, was the culprit. In the bird-loud morning the congregation milled, chattering and laughing, freed from the long-winded ritual of the Edicts. From a nearby hill came the clank of goat bells, the baaing of sheep.

Duarte Teixeira and his family stopped at Pessoa's shoulder. "A good reading this morning, father," Teixeira said, as if he had not, as Pessoa longed to do, dozed through the entire Mass.

"Merely the voice to God's words."

Teixeira's handshake was excruciatingly earnest. He squeezed so hard that bone grated bone. He pumped in rhythm with Pessoa's headache. "You keep us in line, father. I listened well: adultery, fornication, superstition." Abruptly Teixeira leaned forward to eye him sharply. "Do *you* listen well?"

"Sorry?"

"The stories, father. Appearances of the Virgin. Crosses in the sky. Can angels visit women and get them with child? Tell me. Is that superstition or not?"

Teixeira's wife snatched the hat from off the head of her eldest daughter and batted her husband with it. "More respect," she hissed.

And that's when Pessoa noticed the girl's swollen belly. *Misereri nobis.* To see signs in the sky was one thing, but to declare a birth *ex virgine . . .*

Marta fingered her rosary. "Would that I had been the one so visited."

"Wait!" Pessoa held up a warning hand.

No use. Teixeira's voice rose. "Visited. Yes. The girls are visited by the boys in the next village, and cannot keep their skirts down. Then you, Marta Castanheda, help them make up angel stories about it."

"I only tell you what the Blessed Mother tells me, Senhor Teixeira. I did not get your daughter with child. God did."

Time for a quick *addicere.* "Well, well, well," Pessoa said, lacing his fingers. The grip prevented him from slapping Marta's too accessible cheek. "Perhaps you are right, Marta, since He is Lord of all, and any birth, therefore, would be truly His. But let us calm ourselves, shall—"

"Blasphemy." Teixeira was red-faced. Maria Elena, gravid with God or with shame, was sobbing.

They had attracted a crowd. At its periphery stood Senhor Castanheda and his eight-year-old son, both looking as if they had heard this all before, and knew where it would end. Near them stood the useless, if apparently sympathetic, Soares.

"Silence! No more!" Pessoa said. "You cannot judge what is blasphemy. Marta is a young girl, Senhor Teixeira, and zealous. In her zeal, it is perfectly understandable that she thinks she talks to the Virgin Mother, and the Blessed Mother to her. Is that not the case, Marta? But I must admit to you, my girl, that out of everyone in all the world, the living saints, the nuns, even those born into authentic Christian homes, I find it hard to believe the Mother of God chooses little Marta Castanheda as her messenger."

With one swift glance, Marta took his measure. "I do not know why the Virgin chose me, either, Father Inquisitor. She tells me her bidding, not her reasons. You are more dedicated to her service. Perhaps you could tell me why she did not select you."

His cheeks burned. *Maledictus.* Couldn't anyone control her? Pessoa saw the answer in Senhor Castanheda's face. He was obviously afraid for his daughter; yet the burly war hero was frightened of her, too.

"All right." Pessoa waved an arm. "All right. It is pointless to be uplifted at Mass, then stand outside the church afterward to gossip and to quarrel. Neves. I wish to see you. Everyone else, go home." He stalked down the clay road toward Neves's farm, his angry steps raising dust. At the bend he slowed to look back. Marta was at his heels, Neves two paces behind. The rest of the town—Soares included—followed at a cautious distance.

"Go home!" Pessoa ordered.

They halted. Some looked at their feet. Some studied the roadside trees.

"By the power of the Holy Office, I command you to go home!" O *libera me, Domine.* Idiotic for him to have used the mightiest weapon in his arsenal. Without the Holy Office, Pessoa was unarmed. He didn't have the courage to check and see if he had impressed the crowd into submission. Head down, stride purposeful, he scattered a flock of grazing sheep. He trudged up a manure-scented rise and down the other side. He lifted the hem of his cassock and forged a watercress-fragrant stream.

Beyond Neves's modest hillside of mustard was a potato field. What Pessoa saw there brought him to a sudden halt. In the center of the field was a circle, as clear as Marta's circle of dead grass. The vines were alive—but potatoes were swelling from the earth in a mockery of Judgment Day.

Neves said, "Grown this large in a single night! I looked out and saw the wheel spinning, and a lance of light from it. I woke my wife. I crossed myself. It was so bright, the rooster woke and crowed."

A rooster crowing in the dark of night—the most somber of all death omens. And the bloated potatoes in Neves's field caused Pessoa to wonder what monster grew in Maria Elena's womb. Too much of the supernatural to repudiate, even for a Jesuit. He broke into a sweat. His voice shook. "You mistook what you saw, Gregorio. You awoke with your mind befuddled by sleep. There was a storm outside, and lightning."

The townsfolk had caught up with them. Magalhães, his wife, and his four children wandered the rows, marveling. Sleepy bees hummed through the mustard-scented air. Senhora Teixeira walked the circle of potato plants slowly, hand in hand with her waddling daughter.

Marta said, "I think it was Archangel Michael, announcing the birth."

Pessoa couldn't breathe. His throat closed so tightly that it seemed the pressure would stop his heart. "If you will both just stop to consider, you will see it had to be a storm, as I've said. . . ."

Neves shook his head. "I don't know, father. I've seen a lot of storms. This is the first cloud I've seen spin or glow like that."

Marta agreed. "I've seen the angels, myself, Senhor Neves, and they are so bright, so beautiful."

"No. I'm afraid you are both mistaken. A lightning strike has caused a disease in the field, don't you see? Look. Can't you see how swollen and tumored the potatoes are? How can you believe this ground sanctified when the earth itself seems to be spewing the diseased things forth? Really, Gregorio, they look quite unhealthy. They should not be eaten, lest they cause—"

"Chest high!" Magalhães called. Next to him, Maria Elena, waist-deep in potato vines, hand resting serenely atop her belly, was beaming.

Neves shouted back, "I'm thinking to make this a shrine. Charge visitors to see it—"

"Damn you!" Pessoa threw his missal at him. Neves backed up so quickly that he tripped and fell. "Safer for you all that you clean your souls of this heresy!" Pessoa should have been better prepared for the gasps, for the hurried signs of the cross.

In the fell silence, Soares bent and picked up the missal as gently as he might have lifted one of his kittens. He dusted it with his sleeve. "Manoel?" he said quietly, and went to him. "You dropped this."

The leather cover was soft from a lifetime of handling; the seams worn and split. As the Church had ordered, Pessoa memorized and pondered it, and still had not found faith. Yet habit had made it a living part of his hand.

Pessoa slipped the missal into his pocket. He was trembling. "Neves?"

"Yes, Father Inquisitor?"

"Plow this field."

AFONSO WANTED TO take the *Quixote* and his copy of Camões. "You will read to me."

Jandira was seated next to him on the Turkish rug in the middle of his room. "Every night, my king. Will we take the Swiss compass, also? So we can find our way?"

"Yes." He watched as she wrapped the compass in cloth and put it into the chest. "And don't forget to pack the golden bell Salvador de Sá gave us, so that I may ring for you."

She wrinkled her nose.

"It makes a pretty sound."

"Pretty. Can you tell the difference, my king, between screaming and singing?"

A trickster's question. Because he was not clever enough to guess the answer, he rocked back and forth until the scrapes on his knees stung. "A joke?"

"I don't know, sweetling."

She looked so sad that he grabbed her hand. "I will tell you a joke, Jandira. When is a book not a book?"

A man's voice came from the doorway. "When?"

Castelo Melhor was standing in the shadows. The French girl was beside him. He was wearing a forest-green velvet tunic sewn with gold thread, and the girl had on spiderweb-fine lace. "Are you not going to finish the jest, sire?"

"No." Afonso picked up a marble globe and tried to wrap it in a handkerchief; but he was shaking, and the silk was too airy and fine.

"It began like a good jest."

Afonso rocked again. "The world is round," he said.

Suddenly Castelo Melhor was squatting beside him, his velvet sleeve brushing his arm. Afonso felt trapped in the count's heat. Castelo Melhor's perfume reeked of ambergris and flowers. "Yes, my liege," the count said. "The world is round. I have a present for you."

Afonso looked at the floor, but caught sight of Castelo Melhor's hands: the short powerful fingers, the dark veins, the scar running up the wrist and into the sleeve.

"We go away tomorrow," Afonso said. "Jandira and my soldiers. All my soldiers. We will camp in silk tents, and tilt at windmills, and Jandira will read me about Esmeralda."

"Ah. Where do you go, sire?"

"To—"

"—the Alentejo," Jandira said.

Afonso was afraid to look up. The silence in the room was huge.

"The Alentejo?" Castelo Melhor asked.

Jandira was trying to warn Afonso about something, but he wasn't smart enough to know what it was. His hand shook. The globe dropped onto the stone.

The count picked the world up and turned it over. "Ah, sire. It seems you have chipped India. But I have a new plaything for you."

Two playthings. Carved dolls. The count put them on the rug, just short of Afonso's lap.

"From your colonies in Africa, sire. Yoruban, I believe, although perhaps Jandira could tell you best."

Afonso laughed and held them up. "Look! Presents!" Such funny presents. The male doll's *pau* was as long as his arm and as thick as his leg. The dugs on the woman sagged as far as her knees.

"Said to promote fertility, sire," Castelo Melhor said. "Isn't that right, Jandira?" He squeezed her knee. "Answer me, um? At least look me in the eye. Bashful? Surely not bashful—not a mongrel bitch whose father was whelped by a slave and a miner with too little to do. And whose mother, I might add, wore only a breechcloth and climbed trees."

She pushed his hand off her.

He put it back. "A true bastard daughter of Brazil." He rubbed his hand up and down Jandira's leg so slowly that it made Afonso want to stare and yet not look, all at the same time. "See who I brought to visit?"

Out of the corner of his eye, Afonso saw the count gesture to that French girl. When she sat down on the rug, Afonso clambered to his feet.

"Sit *down!*" At the count's bellow, the guards at the door flinched. The three servants who were packing, froze.

More gently, he said, "Come. Sit down, sire. For God's sake. Don't tremble so. You look like a beaten dog. See? Your queen pines for you."

She was sad, but Afonso didn't think she was sad for him. He wondered if she missed her family.

"She doesn't speak," Afonso said.

The count rolled his eyes. "She speaks French."

"Her words are all wrong."

"But you are married, my king. You don't have to speak to put it in her."

"She frightens me when she does not speak."

Castelo Melhor said something to the French girl which was neither

Portuguese, nor Spanish, nor the language that priests use. She answered with a shrug.

"See?" Afonso said.

"This needs no speech, sire." The count unfastened the front of the lace shift and drew it back. The French girl's breasts were twin bumps not much bigger than his own. She sat, face lowered, shoulders hunched. The count put his forefinger under her chin and lifted her head. "What pretties."

The French girl's eyes were squeezed shut. Her cheeks were bright red. Tears streamed her cheeks. Afonso wanted to make her stop crying, but he didn't know how, so he made a fist and pounded his thigh.

Jandira said, "Don't, my king."

A moan came up his throat, filled his mouth, and did not want to stop. He hit his leg harder.

Jandira rose. "Cover her, my lord. You upset him."

Afonso danced in place while the French girl wept. She wept silently, and those strange quiet tears made Afonso's stomach feel funny, and so he began to cry, too. He always made a great clamor when he cried, that's what Pedro said.

"Cover her!" Jandira ordered.

Castelo Melhor pulled the lace bodice to. He grabbed Jandira's wrist and jerked her off her feet. Afonso had seen men kill, and so he recognized the hard killing gleam in the count's eye. Castelo Melhor leaned over until there was but a knife blade's distance between them. He whispered, "Guard him well on his journey, my brown lady, for without issue, Afonso is all that stands between Portugal and civil war."

Jandira turned her face away. "He is not interested."

The count snatched his purse from his belt and threw it, clanking, into her lap. "Teach him an interest," he said.

P ESSOA AWOKE NEAR vespers to find a covered plate waiting on the table. The rectory was silent but for the snapping hearth where a fire was dying to embers. The room was empty even of cats.

He arose. The front door stood open. Outside, sunset buffed the rocky hills until they shone like brass. No cow lowed, no donkey brayed, no bird sang. Pessoa was overcome with senseless fear: that the Rapture was more than fable, that God had turned His back, and everything in the world had gone away.

Heart in his throat, he walked outside. Soares was at a table under a bower of grapes. Cats sat on the benches nearby, attentive as a choir. Soares was telling them the story of Daniel.

Pessoa longed to stand and listen, but at the sight of him, cats bounded away. Soares stopped preaching.

As always, he'd broken the magic. "Tomorrow we begin an informal inquiry, Luis. You will serve as my notary, and you will take down what I tell you to write—no more, no less. There are no other ecclesiastical lawyers to form a *consulta da fé,* and I do not intend to ship the accused to the provincial tribunal at Mafra—my point is, in fact, not to call any of this to the tribunal's attention. So. All the accused are to abjure. We will see to that. Agreed?"

From a safe distance, cats watched him with harvest-moon eyes.

"For God's sake, Luis! We keep this between us. Do you agree?"

Soares nodded.

"Good. You will speak with Cândido Torres. He will act as my familiar. Tell him to strap swords on some of his field hands and to arrange for a jail. Assure him I will find some way to recompense him." Pessoa ran out of breath. When air came into his lungs, it came with an anxious, snicking jolt. Someone nearby was burning hardwood, and the fragrant smoke reminded him of Evora, and how clean the fires in the *praça* smelled before flames reached flesh.

Memory stuck in his throat, and he coughed to clear it. "To be frank, since I cannot afford to ignore such a public heresy, I intend to strike as much fear into your parishioners as I am able—enough fear to silence them all. If we are careful, when the Holy Office finds out how I have proceeded, the most that can befall either one of us is a reprimand for stupidity. But we must do something. I will not risk imprisonment over a townful of overheated imaginations and loose tongues."

The old Franciscan sat rigid, his gaze lowered to the tabletop, while a pair of kittens batted and chewed the ends of his rope belt.

Pessoa said, "I'm not hungry, but still, thank you for saving me dinner."

He walked away fast, past the stables, down the hill to the granite fountain where a boy was watering a sorrel mare, through an olive grove and a gray-green stand of pungent sage.

His steps slowed as he reached the church and the ruins of the old rectory—its roof fallen from an earthquake.

Moors still farmed the Algarve when the church and rectory were built. *Ventum est.* Only a year after its construction, God found fault with the priest. *Factum est.*

Because of superstition, the town had never rebuilt the rectory. Never cleared the rubble. *Dictum est.* Berenice once said that for God to make Himself heard to Pessoa, He would need to crush him under a slate roof, too.

The sun lost its grip on slippery heaven and sank beneath the waves of the hills. The road went blue, the shadows violet. In the village warm lights appeared in windows.

He passed an alley, and a woman singing a *fado* as she took her clothes off the line. He smelled dinner on a dozen tables: salt cod and pork and cabbage. His boots slapped a lonely rhythm on the cobbles. From the houses came snatches of conversation, the clack of plates, the clang of pots.

He wound up a hill, down another, turned into a narrow, twisting path, slowing nearly to a halt at the laughter and raised voices issuing from the town's inn. Should anyone have seen his attentiveness, his measured tread, they would have thought he was gathering evidence. It was fellowship he longed for.

Up an alley, down another short street, then he stopped at a sign shaped like a coat that read: ALFAIATE. He sighed, turned at the iron railing, and took the four steps down to the door. At his knock the youngest girl answered, and curtsied.

Although it was not obligatory, Pessoa took off his hat. "I wish to see your father," he said.

She led him to the back room, past bolts of Egyptian cotton and English linen and Alentejan wool. The family was in the quarters at the back of the shop. They were eating dinner. Magalhães put his knife down when Pessoa halted in the doorway, hat in hand.

Magalhães's wife stood. "José Filipe has been good. I swear it before God."

The little tailor was deaf as a post. His eyes were weak. Still, he must have known the dark figure who stood in the shadows, must have known why Pessoa had come. The man's cheeks went pasty. "Some chicken?" His voice sounded hollow. "No, no use refusing—I insist."

Gently, Pessoa said, "José . . ."

"Catarina!" Magalhães ordered, his gestures, his eyes, wild. The eldest girl stood. "Quickly, girl! Give Father Inquisitor the breast meat, some fava beans. A dish of that sweet rice—"

Louder now. A harsh shout: "José Filipe Magalhães!"

The wife grabbed Pessoa's arm. "O, please! He would never—he knows he had but one chance. He—"

Pessoa jerked free and tossed the words over his shoulder, "Search your heart." He wasn't quick enough. Before he could reach the front door, he heard Magalhães's cry.

Day 3

Afonso proclaimed that it was not proper to take a carriage to a quest, and so they brought Doçura to him. As the sun rose and the last of the wagons were packed, Jandira took him to the busy courtyard and lectured: he was not to go before the banner carriers, yet no one else was allowed to ride before the king. Too, no one must ride beside him except his flanking guards. There was much to remember.

Jandira tucked Afonso's peacock-blue cloak over his shoulder. She buffed a smudged spot out of his steel breastplate. She asked if he was comfortable.

Since awakening hours before dawn, Afonso had been impatient to start his journey. Now satin and armor trapped the morning heat. Afonso's boots pinched him. Sullen, he shrugged.

She smoothed the feathers of the helmet he had tucked in his arm. "Remember: don't smile overmuch," she told him. "And don't wave to the crowds so fiercely that you forget to watch where you are headed. Doçura is well trained, but still . . ."

The little chestnut mare nuzzled Afonso. He gave her carrots that he had stolen from the kitchen. Doçura never mistook finger for tidbit; neither did she shy at sudden noises. Afonso rarely feared her.

"I will be riding right behind you," Jandira said. "And if you become uncomfortable, or forget what to do, look to me or to the captain."

The captain of the guard stepped forward and asked if he was ready; and Afonso said that he was. A footman boosted him into the saddle. Two grooms fit his boots snugly into the stirrups, and the procession started through the gates.

The drummer's beat was lost amid the clatter of hooves on stone. Afonso forgot what he had promised Jandira. He forgot the princely lessons that his father had taught him. Excitement caused him to stand up in the stirrups and peer eagerly about.

Banners flapping, the procession wound through the Chão da Fiera, and down a street named for homesickness. Vendors and pedestrians ducked into doorways. Wives and children popped curious heads out of windows.

Afonso called, "Hallo! Hallo!" He shouted so loudly that Doçura pricked her ears and quickened her walk. His flanking guards looked on in alarm.

Laughing and waving, Afonso followed the banner carriers down the hill, turned with them at the sea-and-mud smell of the Tejo and its fleet of parrot-bright skiffs. He followed the bloodred and grass-green flags through the jostling mob at the fish market, where the captain of the guard began barking orders. Soldiers with pikestaffs cleared a path.

"King! It is the king!"

Children gawked. Women curtsied. Men swept off their hats. In the glorious, golden morning, Afonso held on to his helmet and the reins with one hand. Thus precariously balanced, he stood up in the stirrups and waved. Beyond the canvas roofs of the market, he saw wonders: fishermen spilling baskets of silver-plate flounder; hawkers sorting ribboned eels; mussels dangling in their seaweed like purple-black grapes.

They turned north, toward the business district of the Baixa. In the huge *praça* that housed the gold traders, commerce paused. Flower vendors looked up from their stalls. Merchants lifted their heads from their outdoor café breakfasts.

Afonso didn't realize the morning had gone awry until Doçura came to a stop—until he saw shock in the faces of the people around him. His flanking guards reined quickly so as not to outpace their king.

Castelo Melhor, dressed in crimson, was approaching the procession face front. His white Andalusian stallion was in a high-legged prance, tail held proud as a flag.

The only sounds amid the facades of the money houses was the echo of a single horse's hooves on stone, the chime of golden bells on a crimson bridle.

Before that blinding whiteness, that radiant crimson, Doçura's chestnut coat seemed mousy, and Afonso's peacock-blue satin plain.

Doçura saw the stallion coming, lowered her ears, and backed. Afonso dropped helmet and reins and, before he could fall, wrapped both hands around the saddle's pommel. The captain of the guard kicked his own horse forward and put a calming hand on Doçura's bridle.

Ten meters from Afonso, the white stallion foundered. It went down fast, Castelo Melhor tumbling with it. Gasps rose from a hundred throats. Afonso squeezed his eyes shut. Only the crowd's oohs and aahs coaxed them open again.

The stallion hadn't fallen at all. He was bowed, one knee and his soft dark muzzle touching the cobbles.

Castelo Melhor, still seated, swept off his hat. "Your servant," he said.

"What a pretty horse!" Afonso cried, then felt foolish saying it.

With the stallion still curtsied, the count dismounted. He offered the reins. "A gift."

The captain of the guard's cheeks went sallow. He turned, round-eyed, to Afonso.

"Such a pretty, pretty horse." The stallion's neck was thick, his mane silken and long. His white was brighter than sun on sea foam. Afonso wanted that clever stallion more than anything. More than his spyglass. More than his Flemish blade. If he had that horse, Afonso could be a champion better than Don Quixote, he could be as brave a king as Sebastião had been, or even his own father.

Suddenly Jandira was there, nudging her sorrel forward. "But good my lord count—a wise king does not take the battle mount from his bravest warrior."

The count's smile went sour. He jerked cruelly at the bridle. With a wild jingle of bells, the stallion lunged to his feet. "A good slave," he said, "should mind her place."

"Indeed. And a slave's place is with its owner. Just as your horse, too—"

"For God's sake! This is not my battle mount."

"Yet so cunningly trained."

Castelo Melhor looked past her, to Afonso. He held out the reins again. "My liege. Give me this pleasure."

Jandira answered, instead. "I don't understand, my lord. Why did you not use this as your battle mount? The stallion is so handsome and your clothes so fine, that the Spaniards would have fallen on their faces before your splendor, and the war more easily won."

The count blinked.

She turned to Afonso. "Please, sire. It would be unseemly to accept such a gift from someone to whom Portugal owes so much. Won't you order your loyal subject count to mount his pretty and ride with us? Wave your hand thus, and he will obey."

Afonso did as Jandira said. Castelo Melhor's face flushed as red as his tunic. After a hesitation, he flung himself into the saddle.

The captain of the guard let out a long breath. He gently pried Afonso's hand from the pommel and pressed Doçura's reins into his palm. Once more, the procession started on its way, the count now riding stirrup to stirrup with his king.

"It is a surprise to see you, sire. I thought you would cross the river," the count said, "seeing as you go to the Alentejo."

Confused, Afonso looked over his shoulder at Jandira.

"The king dislikes boats," she said. "So we ride to Santarém, and the bridge."

"Mm. A long ride."

"Yes, my lord. A long ride. But the king has his leisure."

Castelo Melhor turned around in his saddle. "I see my lady rides astride her horse. Does she feel the need of something between her legs?"

Afonso turned, too. Jandira was staring straight ahead, at nothing.

A laugh from the count. "Something large and hot."

Then they were past the Baixa. Women leaned out of second-story windows to watch the procession. As if aware of the scrutiny, the white stallion tossed his head. Bells chimed. A touch of the spurs and he pitched back and forth, back and forth: a gallop as easy as a wooden rocking horse, as slow as Doçura's walk.

Once more, Castelo Melhor turned about in his saddle. "I shall ride you again, my lady. Take my spurs to you, and make you bolt."

Jandira paled.

"I will tilt at windmills!" Afonso cried, to stop Castelo Melhor from alarming Jandira. Part of Afonso wanted to hurry to his journey, part of him longed to return to the castle. The count had stolen the splendor from the day.

Abruptly, Castelo Melhor pulled the stallion to a half-rearing halt. "Yes, sire. You tilt at windmills while I stay to safeguard your kingdom."

And the people listening, cheered.

A SHAKE OF HIS shoulder awoke Pessoa. Mid-morning sun was pouring through the open window. A square of whitewashed rectory wall blazed in a headache-inducing *fiat lux*. He rolled over on the cot. Soares was looking at him.

"Magalhães is here."

Pessoa sat up, rubbing his eyes.

"I have bread and cheese and coffee."

By the smell of it, the coffee was burnt. Pessoa pulled his nightshirt over his head, put his feet to the icy tiles, and groped for his undershirt and cassock.

"Manoel? Eat before you talk to him."

Pessoa lost his place in the cassock's long row of buttons. *"Maladictus,"* he whispered, and set about buttoning again.

"You see?"

"What?" When Soares didn't answer, Pessoa raised his eyes. The old Franciscan was skeptical and frowning. *"What?"*

"You see how you are, Manoel, before your breakfast?"

Pessoa got to his feet, still buttoning. "Easy for you. Plain comfortable robe, rope belt, sandals. The same church, the same house, the same pot day after day to piss in. Cats. *Salva me.* You even have the company of cats. Luis? Where are my boots? What did you do with my boots?"

Soares gestured toward the hearth. "You begged for this mission, as I recall—not that I do not cherish your occasional company. But I've noticed about you a morning's ill-temper." Pessoa's black boots, soles patched and repatched, leaned tiredly against a bench.

Pessoa drew himself upright. His cassock was only half-buttoned and it flapped open, exposing a gray and much-mended undershirt. He snatched the cassock closed. *"Mea maxima culpa,* Luis. I will be sure to mention my foul moods to my confessor."

"Not for your soul. But for Magalhães's peace of mind." Soares held a piece of bread-wrapped cheese and one of the fine pottery mugs toward him.

Pessoa sipped the burnt coffee with one hand, buttoned furiously with the other. In a corner, underclothes and nightshirts burst from his open saddlebags. Dirty plates sat atop the table. "Set up something away from this mess. That table in the grape arbor—"

"It looks as if it might rain."

"If it rains, Luis," he said with obviously overburdened patience, "then we will come inside." Stuffing a bite of cheese into his mouth, he spoke around it. "There is a journal in my bag. Find it. Get ink pot and quill. Here is what we will do: If you see me rest my chin in my hand, you will stop writing. Otherwise take down what he says verbatim—every slip in grammar, every graceless sentence. The Holy Office loves their notes. In fact if we are lucky, our little story will be lost amid the flood of trial records. Still, those Dominicans know confession well. We must tell the truth, but only so much. How long has he been here?" Pessoa finished buttoning. There was one buttonhole left.

"Just now arrived."

Pessoa sighed. "Good, good. And alone?"

"Yes. Quite alone."

"Then hurry and find paper and ink," he ordered, "before he loses courage and flees the kingdom."

Soares bent over Pessoa's bags. Underwear and nightshirts flew. Pessoa found the chamber pot and filled it. When he turned around, Soares was holding the journal, three quills, and an inkwell. Pessoa nodded and they walked outside.

Magalhães was seated at the table under a patchwork cloud sky. He was petting cats. When Pessoa approached, he arose. "I have been considering what you have said, Father Inquisitor."

Pessoa motioned Soares to sit, and noted that he had the sense to take a bench just out of the tailor's view.

Magalhães nodded fretfully. "Well. So. I have been thinking. I have not seen angels myself. Not that I believe there are none, mind. Never, never would I say such a thing. But I am a plain man, and no one an angel would wish to appear to. I have been taken in, it seems, by the idle talk of the town's women. And that is the way of women, is it not?"

Pessoa took a seat. Magalhães whirled to Soares, who stared impassively back.

Magalhães's tear-dampened eyes locked on Pessoa. His voice trembled. "Please, Father Inquisitor. Is it a sin to be mislead by lies? Is that heresy? The girls speak of visions, and Neves talks of signs, but I am a poor man. Not someone who hoards Moorish gold like Castanheda. And I am not a rich man who thinks himself above God, like Teixeira." His voice lowered. "But I can tell you about the heresies of others."

Pessoa rested his chin in his hand. Soares's quill paused.

A glitter of cowardice sparked in the tailor's eye. "Would that be helpful, father?"

In the silence, Pessoa could hear the reedy buzz of a circling horsefly; the hum of bees among the grapes. A plaintive meow.

Sweat ran down Magalhães's cheeks in fat drops, like tears. He wiped his palms on his coat, then wiped them again. At last the bald little tailor blurted what he had come so far to say: "Father Inquisitor, it pains me to tell you, but just this very morning, Maria Elena Teixeira killed her baby."

I T WAS AFTERNOON and the clouds were building, when the king's procession stopped to rest their horses. In an olive-tree-dotted meadow, amid grass as fine as rabbit fur, the royal cooks built a fire. They argued whether to serve pork in Madeira wine or cold slices of roast chicken.

Afonso was hungry. He asked for chocolate, and an equerry gave him an inlaid box of dipped walnuts. Carrying the candy, he sat on a rock beside a glassy ribbon of a stream. Two little boys who had followed from the outskirts of Odivelas approached. When the captain of the guard tried to send them on their way, Afonso, who in the court liked children best of all, called the pair to him. He gave them handfuls of sweets.

"Who are you?" one asked.

"I am the king."

The pair grinned at each other and shook their heads. They ate chocolate, and smeared their faces brown.

Jandira sat beside him. She threw an arm over Afonso's knee, and her touch made him feel bedtime safe, as good as before his nanny died and his mother went away.

By the wagons and the cookfire, furious voices rose. Jandira closed her eyes. "They will kill each other over a menu," she said.

One boy pointed. "She is a funny-looking lady."

Afonso looked at Jandira. He had not noticed the decorative scars in years. "O. That is because she comes from Brazil."

They whooped, and rolled in the grass like puppies. "Only monkeys come from Brazil."

Afonso noticed how her chin tilted, saw the look in her dark, liquid eyes. He thought of how the count had spoken to her, and how that had frightened him. He reached down and took her hand. "She is a beautiful monkey."

He felt her hand stiffen.

He said, "If you had only let me have the pretty white horse, Jandira, I would have made him bow to you. I could have been your champion, and you my Dulcinea."

She cast her gaze toward the distant olive groves, the slope-shouldered hills. "Sire, the count would not have given him to you."

"But he offered."

"Castelo Melhor offers many things he doesn't mean."

He lifted his head to the featherbed clouds. He took a deep breath and smelled rain. The idea of windmills tickled in his belly. It was easier to think of what lay ahead than of the bad thing which had begun the journey.

"I brought my Flemish blade," he told her, "I should have fought like Don Quixote. But I forgot I had it with me."

"Fought who?"

"Castelo Melhor."

Jandira's tears first startled Afonso. When they continued, they made him frantic. He clambered off the rock and sat beside her. "Jandira. I will battle dragons for you. I will kill him if you wish."

She pushed at him. "Never say that. Not where others can hear. The count will not hurt you, yet he must ever remind you of your place."

"But my place is as the king, and I can do anything."

The little boys laughed. "You are *not* the king. A king wouldn't ride such an ugly pony. The real king came by here yesterday, on a big gray stallion."

"Truly?" Afonso forgot Jandira's tears. He sat straighter. "Was he fair-haired? Like me, but thinner?"

They nodded.

"Astride a gray Barbary with a black mane and tail and one white sock to the knee?"

They nodded again, their lips pressed against a giggle; their cheeks brown with chocolate, red and puffed with laughter.

"That was my brother, Prince Pedro," he said proudly. "And I'm going all the way to Mafra to meet him."

"Not Mafra." They rolled their eyes, as if they had decided that Afonso was the greatest dullard in the world. "He wasn't going to Mafra. He rode west, toward the sea: the king and his nobles and lots and lots of English soldiers."

THE MAID OPENED the door to Pessoa's knock. Her hair was afright, her gown untidy. One look, and she slammed the door in his face. Pessoa could hear her retreating steps and her shout, "It's Father Inquisitor! Father Inquisitor's come!"

He waited on the stoop. The house fell silent. A misting rain began to fall. It beaded on the wool of his cassock. It wormed in glassy trickles down the varnished door. It darkened the stone stairs. He heard the lock click, saw the door open. The cook peered out. "Master says come in."

He stepped across the shadowy threshold.

"Wipe your feet." Inside was a rush mat and an ornately carved coat rack. The cook inspected him head to toe and, by her expression, found him lacking. She shoved her hand toward him. "Hat," she said.

He handed it to her. She threw it in the direction of the entranceway's chair. "Lunch?"

"Thank you, I've alre—"

"Right-hand room." She walked away, her skirts brushing his hat from its perch and onto the tiles.

Pessoa picked it up and took it with him.

He found Teixeira seated before a dying and cheerless fire. The windows were open, and the large, dim room smelled of rain. On a nearby table sat a miniature oaken keg and a glass goblet. Without looking up from his contemplation of the hearth, the man asked, "Brandy?"

Hat in hand, Pessoa halted at the side of his chair.

"Women," Teixeira said to the embers. "I live in a houseful of women, and all of them are silly as geese. When they stray, it is our duty to keep them to the path—we, as fathers. God gave us that charge, I think. And yet other men do their best to tempt them. Were we such men once?" He looked up, searchingly. "Manoel Pessoa? Were you ever such a man?"

The sullen fire snapped. A wood knot flamed a brief canary yellow. Outside the window, rain fell faster. "Are you admitting that the story is true?"

Teixeira's face hardened. He bellowed, "Sit down!" Then he said quietly, and with more circumspection, "Please. Sit. Have a brandy."

Pessoa cast around for a chair, found a proper straight-backed one, and dragged it before the hearth. When Teixeira neglected to pour him a drink, Pessoa found a clean glass goblet, filled it from the keg, and sipped. Apricot brandy. He had nearly forgotten the taste. The slick weight of glass in his hand brought back pampered memories of childhood. He licked the sugary liquor from his lips, and wondered how his brother was faring.

"Isadora!" Teixeira's roar was so sudden, so loud, that Pessoa started, nearly dropping the costly glass to the tiles.

The disheveled maid poked her head into the room.

"Something to eat, girl!"

A shy, "What?"

"How should I know what you have back there? Sweets. Nuts. Some of those cod cakes that cook makes. Something."

She disappeared as quickly as she had come, and the room plunged once more into the background silence.

"Stupid geese," Teixeira muttered darkly, and took a drink. "There was no blood."

"Sorry?"

"No blood, Father Inquisitor. And, from being present at the birth of animals, I know there must be blood. I looked. I made my wife show me chamber pots. I studied the laundry, the girl's bed." He gave a *puh* of disgust. "Women and their secrets."

Pessoa said, "You realize that this is a legal question, Duarte, not an inquisitorial one."

He shrugged.

Pessoa held the goblet up to the light, saw bubbles trapped in the glass like little silent rooms.

The maid brought a silver tray with neat ranks of cinnamon rolls, dishes of salted almonds, and a centerpiece of cold cod cakes. She left. Teixeira didn't eat. Pessoa didn't either. They filled their glasses again.

"Duarte?" Pessoa asked. "Would you like me to call a constable for you?"

The wind shifted. Rain splattered the granite sill. Outside, the world turned gray. Streams ran either side of the cobblestone alley. A cat huddled under the shelter of a washbasin.

"She says it was angels." Teixeira covered his face. His knuckles were scraped. His hand trembled. "I beat her and beat her, and still she said it was angels."

Pessoa put his goblet down and quietly left the room. Senhora Teixeira and the cook were waiting for him in the kitchen.

"Where is Maria Elena?" he asked.

The cook glared. Senhora Teixeira rose. "Who told you?"

Pessoa said, "Please bring her here."

Cook stalked from the kitchen. He heard her heavy footsteps on the stair.

"Who told you?" Senhora Teixeira asked.

Pessoa took in a breath that smelled of old smoke and stale food. The shutters were half-open, and rain beat in, wetting the floor tiles.

"May they burn in Hell for it," she said.

Slower footsteps came down. Pessoa turned, watched as the cook led Maria Elena inside. One eye was swollen shut. Her lip was split, her nose flattened.

"Child," he said, and put a hand out.

The cook steered the girl away and set her safely out of his reach.

"Has the herbalist seen to her?" he asked.

"Your whore?" cook shot back.

"Someone should see to her."

The two women stood, frowning.

He sat at the kitchen table. Across from him sat the girl, her long hair down, her head lowered. A crust of black blood ringed one nostril.

"She is still a virgin," Senhora Teixeira said. "Put your fingers in her, Father Inquisitor, and see for yourself. Don't gawk at me so! Go ahead! Or will you be like her own father and, given the evidence of your fingers, still not believe? Puh! How much proof do men want? Narrow-minded, all of you. And brat-spoiled. That is why the two Marys had only to see the rock rolled away, but the Apostles required a personal visit."

"Leave the room," he said.

Senhora Teixeira put her hand on her daughter's shoulder. Maria Elena didn't look up.

Pessoa said firmly, "Leave the room." He stared straight ahead until he heard the rustle of women's clothing, quiet footsteps, breathy worried whispers, and the click of a closing door.

The girl's hands plucked at a discarded crust of bread. He rested his own atop hers. She froze. "They took it back," she told him, "because I wasn't worthy."

He stroked her fingers. Her hands were pudgy with childhood. "Maria . . ."

"The baby was spirit, you know. Like them. Like the angels. I begged them to let me keep it, but I had sinned some way, father. And I don't know how."

He let her cry, and listened to the patter of the rain. Her brown hair was matted with blood.

When he tired of waiting, he asked, "Child? What did you do with the body?"

"I will see it in heaven," she said, "when I die."

He squeezed her hand. "Listen to me, Maria Elena. You lost your baby. Such things happen."

"I think I should die now. That is what I should do. I keep wondering if my baby is lonely without me."

She raised her head and stared out the window. It was hard to look at her—the single written page of her future; those illuminated wounds. "Say after me, child: *Dominus vobiscum. Ad sancta sanctorum. Et in terra pax hominibus. Laudamus te* . . . Please. Please say it with me."

"Laudamus te," she breathed.

She followed him, whispering, into the ascension, through blessed-be-Thy-name, into God's peace. And when they were finished, he arose and bent over her, gently cradling her head against him. He told her that everything would be all right.

Then he went out and down the corridor, brushing past the cook. He told Senhora Teixeira to come. Before leaving the house, he paused in the front room, and speaking to Duarte Teixeira's back, he told him that his daughter belonged to God and the Inquisition now, and Duarte was not to touch her.

Outside, he and Senhora Teixeira stood together in the gray drizzle. "I don't wish to hear talk of angels," he said. "Find the body. If the skull is crushed, let it be a civil matter, not mine."

Rain wet her hair and ran down her face in rivulets. "But there is no body," she said.

The late afternoon was chill, and when the wind blew, he shivered. "The court might have mercy, Dona Teixeira, if she has gone insane. Easier to enter that as a civil plea than to come before the Holy Office with it."

"The angels took the baby."

"Dona Teixeira . . ."

"They came in the house. I saw them." She shivered, too. "Bright, they were. And they never looked at me. And they went into her room, and later I heard her screaming."

"Listen to me carefully, for I dare not warn you more than once: the state is allowed to arrest only her. The Holy Office could take the other children. Yourself. Your house. If she killed her baby, let her go, and save the rest. And after all, if worse comes to worse, which would be easier on the girl: to hang, or to be consigned to the flames?"

The fine lace of her bodice had wilted in the damp. Her hair lay against her forehead in a cap of tiny ringlets. "Father Inquisitor, the proof lies a finger's length inside her. Why is it so hard for you to believe?"

His eyes fled hers. "You have two days," he said. "Make certain her story is ready."

AFONSO WEPT TO follow Pedro, but the captain of the guard dropped to his knees before him and said, "Forgive me, sire. We are but half a company, and ill armed. I am willing to die for your sake; but please, we must to Lisbon and gather more soldiers. If we do not, I cannot protect you from this terrible danger."

"Danger? But it is only my brother, and if there are English, my sister. I would show them my quest, and have them play games with me, and we could tilt at windmills."

Jandira said, "The weather! The weather is such a danger, is it not, captain?"

The captain knit his brows.

"I will speak for you, captain, if you are too timid to make such a request of your king. You fear *gripe*—do you not?—if your troops get wet in the rain. So, as the day is damp, the troops should huddle by their fires. We should not travel—neither to see Pedro, nor to return home, else many soldiers get fevered, and some die, and what would you and the king tell their mothers? Should not captains and kings make everything right?"

Somewhere by the sea his brother and sister were waiting. Afonso thought that if he rode far and fast enough, he could catch up with his mother and his father, too, and in that distant, happy land his father would be king again, a king over peace this time, rather than war. And Afonso could put the scepter down.

He peered longingly down the western road that led to the sea.

"Sweetling." Jandira lay her warm hand atop his own. "Can you cure the sick? Can you raise the dead?"

Afonso shook his head.

"Well, then." Jandira motioned for the captain to rise. "The captain will see to the soldiers' comfort, for if you cannot do these things, we must pitch our tents and stay."

URING INDIGO DUSK when the rain had blown clear and the sky was full of stars and tattered clouds, Pessoa went to Berenice. Her house smelled of straw and baking bread, of eye-watering unguents and bitter teas. She was at the hearth, where a flat loaf toasted on a slate, and an iron pot gave off an acrid, smoky reek. Her sleeves were rolled to her elbows. She was kneading something that was a noxious shade of green. He put his hat on her table, sat, and pulled his boots off, wondering: Did medicine ever fall into cook pot? Food into curative?

He was unbuttoning his cassock when she at last looked up, snorted, and looked away.

"What?" he asked.

"You make it too obvious that your *pau* needed a visit."

He pulled the cassock over his head and threw it onto a bench. In his gray, frayed undershirt he sat, rubbing the back of his neck. His muscles ached, not as if he had worked, but as if he was fevered. "I'm tired, Berenice. And this is the only place I can come," he told her, "where I needn't be a priest."

He watched the play of muscles in her slender forearms, the strength of her delicate hands. "Will you not greet me?" he asked.

She sat up, brushing her hair back from her forehead with a wrist. "Please, yes. Let me stop what I am doing, and spread my legs."

"I didn't mean that."

She went back to her labors. The glow of the hearth fire ruddied her cheekbones, shadowed her lashes. Each time he visited, he took memory away with him. Riding alone on the empty road, he would close his eyes, pluck a picture of her from his mind, and study it.

"I would not fault you, but did you give the Teixeira girl something to abort her baby?"

Her hands paused. She raised her head. The look in her eye frightened him, in the same way that a small, enraged dog would give him pause.

"She had no baby," Berenice said.

"I saw myself—"

"Duarte Teixeira called me to the house when the girl began to show. I felt inside her. She was intact."

Without his cassock, her house was cold. He made his way from the damp shadows and crept to the fire. He sat near her on the packed earth-and-stone floor. Berenice was kneading again.

"There is something more," he said. "I see it in your face."

A nod. "Her breasts were full. Her nipples darkened. And the colors told me there was life in her, yet not a life. I didn't know what to think."

"O Berenice. O please. Not angels. I am sick to death of angels."

She sat back on her heels and wiped her hands on her apron. Apparently the kneading was over. With her fingertips, she nudged the flat bread from the slate shelf onto a plate. "Will you dine with me?"

A single loaf. A bite of hard cheese on the table. Near that, two small roasted potatoes and a dish of some boiled wild greens. "No. But I'll bring you food on the morrow. The townsfolk overindulge—"

She got up, balancing the plate. "I would rather feel you in me, Manoel, than hear lies about your damned Christian mercy."

As she strode past he sighed. From behind him came an angry rattle of pottery. In the next room, her burro snorted and stamped restlessly in his straw.

"Commerce, then?" he asked. "Certainly you Jews understand money. Will you go there if I pay you? To the Teixeira house?"

He heard one loud clack, then silence.

"Bring your poultices and salves and needle and thread, Berenice. She has been beaten."

"Her father?"

"Yes."

"And does she bleed between her legs?"

"*Libera me!* As if I would look." He spun around.

She was chuckling. "Did you even ask?"

"It was not . . . Teixeira said sheets and chamber pots. Who knows? I suppose."

"Suppose?"

"He said no blood."

There. That impish smile. That is what he best liked to remember. "I hardly credit it, Manoel. You blush."

His gaze recoiled from hers. "Her own mother told me to put my fingers in her, Berenice. As if she were a sheep, and not a girl who . . . if I were of an age, I mean . . . And to be absolutely truthful, spirit ever wars with flesh . . . such as Marta Castanheda. At least when, *salva me,* she keeps her mouth shut. And do people not realize priests harbor desires? There she was, the *coitadinha,* all bruised; and yet here is the mother's offer. To my great shame, part of me—"

She fell on him so hard, she knocked him down. He might have thought her irate, but for the laughter. Her hand was up his undershirt in a way he very much liked.

He rolled atop her and pulled her skirts up. His own urgency surprised him. He thrust hard, harder. He put into her all of his day, so that at the end he cried aloud, never minding that the neighbors down the hill might hear. And in the lull after, he found that his *ovos* ached, and that he was too spent to move.

She stroked his face. Her fingers smelled clean and salve-pungent. Her breath held the odor of baked bread. He rested his head on her shoulder.

She grunted and nudged him off her. As they so often did, they had lain exactly where lust had seized them, her back to the flagstone floor. He thought that it must be in pleasure's nature, to bruise.

Before she got up, he grabbed her wrist and kissed it. Then she returned to her table and her meal. He crawled to her cot and settled her blanket about him.

"There is an herb for abortion, is there not?" he asked.

She raised her head.

"Well? Isn't there? *Deus gratia,* Berenice. I do not accuse, I merely ask."

"Yes," she said, and went back to eating.

"To me, she looked at least a month from term. You think? Perhaps someone else gave it to her. Does it work? Have you ever used the herb to abort someone?"

She broke off a piece of bread and dipped it in the boiled greens. "Only myself," she said.

For a moment his lips still wore the same puzzled smile, and the blanket that smelled of her felt safe, and her small house still seemed so familiar. Then his smile dropped and his chest emptied. Too late. Had he known . . . but still, would he have wept for his children?

"No, Manoel," she said softly. "Not yours."

That confession made him want to get up and pull on his boots.

"As much as we've lain together, your seed has never taken."

"Well." A short word. But by the end of it, his breath had failed. He lunged to his feet, pulled on his cassock, fumbled over buttons.

"It was when I was raped," she said.

His fingers halted.

"I was sick, you remember. And afterward, I was weak. It was hard for me to walk to the well, and impossible nearly to walk back. I liked to go in the evening time, when no one else was there, so I would not meet up with anyone who was afraid to look at me."

Beyond the drawn curtain came the swish of hooves in straw and the burro's contented whuffle.

"He came from the bushes and threw a sack over my head, and pushed me down. It happened five times, five evenings. It got so that I thought it better to die of thirst. He hurt me, because from behind that way . . . and not being willing . . . and he forced. But he never hit me, really. And it was over very soon. Probably he was terrified someone would see. And when I was stronger, he stopped."

From the burro came a long, sleepy sigh.

"Who?" She was eating again. His voice rose. "Damn you, who?"

Her eyes snapped to his.

"I swear I will bring the power of the Holy Office down on him, I'll—"

"Ask Luis Soares."

Breath exploded from him in a bark of laughter. "Luis? And you did not have the strength to push him off? That's doubtful. He is an old man. Even sick . . . And damn you! What I have said about priests, things I am ashamed to tell my confessor. Between myself and God, Berenice. Me. But not Luis!"

"It is a mortal sin."

"I know that. Who are you, a Jew, to—"

"Fornication and adultery. Not rape. Never rape. Your church teaches that it is not the hurt and the shame which are wrong, but only the putting in. Without marriage, always a sin—for whatever reason. Do you confess me when you return to Mafra, Manoel? Do you promise that you will never lie with me again? Do you say Pater Nosters and Ave Marias? Do you?"

And he understood. "O," he said.

Her face was crimson from more than firelight. "Do you skip meals and wear a hairshirt and scourge yourself? Do you weep and beg forgiveness for what your *pau* has done?"

His mouth moved long before he had the strength to speak. "Luis heard the man's confession."

She rose, clapping her knife to the table. "Get out." She brought his hat to him, shoving. He stumbled. "Get out!"

"Yes. Perhaps tomorrow?"

Slapping him savagely, striking anyplace her little hands could reach—face, shoulders, upflung arms—she drove him out the door and slammed it.

He stood there in the dark, dazed, unsure whether to be ashamed or indignant. When he was certain she would not open the door again, he walked off, tripping over stones and bushes, cursing in whispers as he went. He was halfway up the third hill when he noticed that the grass before him wore an eerie sheen, and that the foliage around him was casting shadows. The back of his neck prickled. His steps faltered. He turned in the direction of the light.

Brighter than the moon, larger than the morning star, luminous and eerily silent, it was the greatest glory in the heavens: God's white, pure fire. Pessoa sucked in a breath and told himself that the bright thing was merely tired vision, his own imagination, a fever of the brain. He rubbed his eyes. The star did not vanish.

A lance of green shot out, striking not two meters away. The hilltop meadow dawned a bright emerald morning. Pessoa howled and fell to his knees, babbling an Act of Contrition.

Then it was over. God's eye winked closed. Shaken, breathing in hard, fast whoops, Pessoa got up and looked around. There was no evidence left to show the star had ever been.

Ah. That was strange. But no sense panicking.

When his legs were steady, he crept to where the lance had struck. He saw grass, stones, a stand of blossoming meadowsweet. No proof of a dramatic manifestation. And as to his earlier fight with Berenice, well, the Lord—if in truth He existed—knew fully well that Pessoa confessed her. And even though Pessoa could not in good faith promise to stop, he knew his sin was not so grievous that it merited a fiery star and the accusing finger of God.

A comet. Perhaps oddly colored lightning. It was a hill, and lightning had a way of striking high places. Just an ordinary occurrence made extraordinary by his exhaustion. He would not worry anyone else about it.

Mindful to keep his head down, Pessoa sneaked home.

A SHOUT AWAKENED Afonso. Just the one shout, and the camp went midnight-quiet again. Rubbing his eyes, Afonso rose and left, stepping over the blanketed mound that was the sleeping Jandira.

The soldiers had emerged from their tents. As one, they knelt in the hush of the torch-guttering night, all facing east. Father de Melo was on his knees, arms outstretched, his face running tears.

Afonso had witnessed such a scene only once before, and that at a deathwatch. He looked east, too, expecting the ghost of his father.

He saw an odd star.

The thing did not wear a tail like a comet; and it was not orange and quick like a meteor. This star was radiant, blinding white, and it moved as if it were a ball that God had sent rolling across the darkened firmament.

High and higher it rose, drifting north. Soldiers and priest clambered to their feet to keep it in view.

The gathering of men stood, bound together by wonder: captain beside cook, cook by waggoner, scribe by pikesmen. The encampment was so still that Afonso could hear the torpid flap of royal velvet banners in the breeze.

The star grew distant and faint. Afonso watched it disappear into the ordinary stars that twinkled in the spaces between clouds. When it was gone, a buzz of conversation sprang up, some soldiers vowing that the star had gone into a hole God had made in the heavens, others insisting that they spied it still. "There! There!" They pointed eagerly. "Can't you see it moving? It travels through Cygnus."

Afonso stared until his eyes watered and he had to wipe them dry.

Then, where the star had disappeared, a bolt of emerald light connected heaven to earth. Afonso cried out with fear; but he was not ashamed, because the soldiers and Father de Melo cried out as well. And the captain of the guard dropped once more to his knees, and the cooks began crossing themselves.

The pillar of green vanished. Terrified babble arose. Father de Melo said in a reedy voice: *"Ecce Agnus Dei; ecce, qui tollit peccati mundi!"* And he began to pray.

Afonso noticed Jandira standing at his left side. "We go there," he whispered.

"Sire . . ."

"It was a sign. We must go to where the star pointed."

Soldiers were turning around now, to see who spoke.

Jandira shook her head. "I do not think . . ."

He raised his voice so Jandira would listen. He didn't intend to make the soldiers start nor did he intend to interrupt the father. "Please, Jandira. We must, don't you see?" Afonso said. "We must travel north, and we must do so at once. For God Himself is calling."

A KNOCK RESOUNDED on his door like thunder. Bernardo peeled the blanket back and, shivering, fumbled through the gloom of his cell.

A Cistercian friar stood in the corridor. In the dim glow of the man's lantern, Bernardo could see that his eyes were white-rimmed with alarm. "Another message."

The cheap whale oil in the lantern smoked, filling the air with a fishy reek. The air was cold, the hour late. Bernardo hugged himself to trap the dissipating bed warmth. Nothing stirred in the monastery, not even Filipe Câmara, who for sins acquired as a soldier, walked a nightly penance. The corridor to either side of the lamp glow was black void. The floor was icy, the air so damp that the friar's breath fogged.

"For Monsignor Gomes again." The friar shoved a cream-colored envelope at him. "And with the king's seal. The rider arrived in a rush, with his horse sweated and blowing hard. Please, father? Seeing as how the message cannot wait, and since Monsignor is most assuredly asleep . . ."

"A moment," Bernardo muttered. He turned and fumbled along the table for flint and candle.

Behind him: "Please, father? Can you?"

"Yes, yes." His groping fingers touched flint. With a snap and a spark, the wick began to smolder. Gently, he breathed life into the flame then, teeth chattering, he shrugged into his habit. His boots were where he always placed them: aligned with the edge of his cot. He sat and, in the clement light of the candle, pulled them on.

A shy voice came from the doorway. "Two king's messages in one day." The Cistercian poked his head into Bernardo's cell. "It must be a great matter."

Bernardo rose, straightened his robes, and brushed stray dust from his black wool sleeve.

The Cistercian asked, "What matter do you think?"

Bernardo dipped his fingertips into his washbasin, and combed water through his hair.

"Are . . . are you not going to take the message?"

One final habit adjustment, then Bernardo held his hand out. The Cistercian, with a relieved sigh, put the thick envelope in Bernardo's palm.

"Bless you, father." He left so hurriedly that the last word was an echo.

Shielding the flame, Bernardo picked up the rude pottery holder by one edge and walked out. A draft plucked at the candle. Impish shadows cavorted in its hectic glow.

"Kyrie eleison," Bernardo prayed, keeping his eyes lowered so that demon could not tempt nor fright; so that God would not think him proud.

Around a corner. Impenetrable Limbo lay ahead but for a remote nebulous glow. Another step, another, his eyes downcast, his pace slow but steady. That was the way to salvation. Bernardo strove, but what if, years ago, he had committed some forgotten but unforgivable sin, and all his labors were naught?

"Christe eleison."

Without raising his head, he peeked down the length of the hall. The glow was merely a small bank of candles which the choir had placed at St. Cecilia's feet. Her face was rosy. She wore a complacent smile. Were saints sure? Bernardo wondered. In their minds, was Heaven to be a certainty? Or did they dread night, too?

Rounding another corner, his own tormented shadow lunged, magnified in suffering. Bernardo imagined that he could feel the wild flurry of its passing.

"Kyrie eleison."

Did Monsignor never doubt—doubt not God so much as himself? The path to heaven was so narrow. So twisting. A wrong footfall, and . . .

He stopped before the carved oak door. Bernardo knocked. "Monsignor?"

Outside the ornate Manueline window a melon slice of moon peered behind clouds, casting paltry light over the gardens. Across the way was another window and a niche where St. Dominic stood, wrapped in a holocaust of candles.

Bernardo bent to the door, put his ear to it. "Monsignor?"

From beyond came a faint sound. Bernardo unfastened the latch and, holding his candle high, entered Monsignor's room. The inquisitor-general was still abed, but floundering about in the covers.

"Light." His voice was thick. "Make more light."

Bernardo lit the twelve candles in the silver candelabra. When he looked again, the monsignor was sitting up, yawning and scrubbing his hands over his sleep-rumpled face.

"Robe."

Bernardo took it from its place on the bedpost and settled it about Monsignor's shoulders.

Monsignor gave a phlegmy cough. "What?"

"Another message." Bernardo took the heavy envelope from the depths of his pocket and handed it over.

Monsignor sniffed, grunted. He hiked a hip. His brow furrowed in concentration and he passed descending-minor-key gas. With a fingernail, he pried the sealing wax loose. His eyes scanned the page. He sat back against his pillows and scanned the page again.

"Bring the candelabra."

As he had with the earlier message, Monsignor set the edge of the paper aflame, put it in the pewter dish he used for such things, and watched until it was ash.

Monsignor shrugged the robe from his shoulders. It fell to the floor. Bernardo picked it up, hung it on the bedpost, and straightened its folds. Taking up his candle, he started from the room.

"Bernardo?"

Hand on the latch, he looked back. Monsignor had dug himself under blanket and goosedown comforter until nothing could be seen but the soaring Alp of his belly.

"Yes, Monsignor?"

From the lump in the bed came a muffled whimper of a fart. "If it were not for my efforts, this country would be riding to Hell astride a governmental ass."

Day 4

CASTELO MELHOR'S CITY VILLA PERCHED ON THE BANKS OF THE TEJO and cascaded down the hill, its walls and patios brightened with flowers. Bernardo, careful to stay one pace behind Monsignor, walked through its brick-and-ivy courtyard, past the pots of geraniums, and to the massive mahogany doors. Monsignor lifted the knocker in a brass fighting cock's clutches and gave the plate three raps.

A footman answered. His eyes traveled from Monsignor, to Bernardo, and back to Monsignor. He said, "O."

"The count."

"Yes, Monsignor. Just . . ." A lifted hand. A nervous call into the depths of the house. "Senhor Farias!"

An answering mutter came from the quiet affluent world beyond. Through the clack of approaching footsteps, Bernardo could hear a lecture whose beginnings were swallowed in echo. ". . . must tell you, Sergio, tedious piece of dog shit that you are, that it is your duty to answer . . ."

Then, in the crack of the doorway, a surprised face appeared. "Ah." The *mordomo* regained enough composure to bow.

"The count," Monsignor said.

"Yes. Ah. Unfortunately, he is quite . . ."

"Home?"

"Well. One might say . . . Yes, I believe he . . . although perhaps not entirely prepared to receive—"

Monsignor pushed aside *mordomo* and footman. He strode into the house, Bernardo at his heels. The entry was done in the Moorish style, with twisting white marble columns and arches and so many windows that the glitter made Bernardo's eyes tear.

The *mordomo* wrung his hands. His face was luminous with panic. "Breakfast! We must set out a glorious breakfast for Monsignor. A cozy fire in the study. The best Brazilian or African coffee, whichever Monsignor would prefer. Pastries that will crumble in your fingers. Cream tarts that will melt on your tongue. Strawberries, apricots, plums in wine. All the best; the count employs a French cook."

Lowering his head discreetly, Bernardo sneaked a look out of the sides of his eyes. Monsignor was studying a rose alabaster statue of a nude couple who were far too intimately entwined.

"Sergio!" the *mordomo* snapped. "Inform our illustrious count that his excellency, the monsignor, is here. And as you do so, I will lead our two visitors—"

The footman started off across the gleaming tile, Monsignor right behind.

A panicked shout of: "Sergio! No!"

The footman halted too late. Bernardo had already spied which room he had been heading for; and Monsignor was on his way there, his huge head lowered like a bull's.

The *mordomo* trotted alongside, plucking at Monsignor's sleeve. "Sausages? Guava paste with an assortment of white cheeses?"

The huge room beyond was filled with sun. Behind a maze of couches, a fire blazed. On a nearby settee, a naked woman snored, an empty bridle in her hand. In the crack of her buttocks lay an orderly row of bonbons. Two nude boys sat at a card table, sipping coffee. When Monsignor stopped in the doorway, the pair looked up, blear-eyed and squinting. Their jaws dropped. Even under the rouge and the rice powder and the kohl, Bernardo could see their faces lose color. They scampered behind a nearby couch, quick as squirrels.

"Fried bread and honey!" the *mordomo* cried. "Brandied peaches! Currant-and-almond loaf!"

A man popped up from behind a chair, then dived so quickly that all Bernardo could be certain of was that he had been wearing a steel breast-plate.

The *mordomo* asked a dispirited question: "Would Monsignor care for lunch?"

On the other side of the couch a hand groped, and pulled down a fringed, embroidered tablecloth. From the same direction came Castelo Melhor's voice. "Farias? Perhaps you might show the most excellent Monsignor Inquisitor-General Gomes into the study and offer him a little something."

The *mordomo* sighed.

Bernardo peered through his eyelashes at the naked woman again. The bonbons had not shifted. He might have thought her dead but for the steady rise and fall of her back.

Castelo Melhor poked his head above the top of the couch. Under his breath he uttered an irritated, "Puh." He stood, wrapping the tablecloth about his waist. "Well. What can I do for you?" Chin up, he walked toward them, tripping over fringe. One leg was bare from the side of his buttocks down. Through the hair above his knee was a long angry scar, a memory of the Spanish wars. When Castelo Melhor reached the end of the settee, he halted.

With a gasp, the *mordomo* snapped up a nearby Persian rug and threw it over the woman and her chocolates. Bernardo wondered if she would die smothered, and move from dream into endless dream.

"I had a question," Monsignor said.

The count raised an eyebrow. "Really."

"Have you heard news of English soldiers marching near Lisbon?"

The count patted a mustache. He cocked his head to the side as if waiting for the remainder of the jest. He shifted his weight from foot to foot. "English."

"Unexpected, isn't it? Marching toward the sea. In the company of Prince Pedro. I received the information from a very reliable source, and so naturally I was wondering if you had received some announcement or declaration or . . . ." He gave a languid wave of his hand. "Whatever."

The count shifted his weight again. Bernardo wondered if he was in need of a chamber pot. "Soldiers." One small, disbelieving smile, then his eyes grew troubled, and his cheeks grew ashen. In a dead voice, he whispered: "Pedro."

C ASTANHEDA'S MAID ANSWERED Pessoa's knock and wordlessly ushered him in. She took his hat, hung it on the rack, then vanished into the gloom, leaving neither footfall nor echo in her wake.

Pessoa clasped his hands behind his back and paced. Reaching the mouth of the hall, he stopped to listen, but heard only a torpid hush—the peculiar silence of a house plunged into mourning.

He wandered the foyer, studied Castanheda's gaudy El Cid—a painting only a Moor could savor. Below El Cid was a fine rosewood table, upon it a Bible and a silver box whose top was a map of Brazil.

A man's voice spoke from the hall doorway: "Thieving, father?" Castanheda's muscular bulk loomed out of the shadows. His jacket was unfastened; his shirt hung out his pantaloons; at the knee his hose were soot-smudged. "Just ask. I would gladly give it to you. I would give you anything."

Pessoa set the silver box down. "I need to talk with your daughter."

"She is not here."

Pessoa forced relief from his face. "Fled, then?"

"Gone to see Maria Elena."

Easier to restrain the joy than the disappointment. "Ah, Guilherme. You must make an effort to control her."

"When you have children, you will gain the right of instruction. Come. I wish to show you something."

Castanheda left so abruptly that Pessoa had no time to demur. He followed through the shuttered darkness until they were deep in the lamplit bowels of the house.

Their destination was a musty study. On the desk stood a pewter holder with four candles. On the wall, pikestaffs and a halberd; a battered shield with a red fighting cock; and a faded green sash emblazoned with a golden medal rayed like the sun. Castanheda closed the door and, with a clang, shot the bolt.

Pessoa's pulse quickened. He inched to the desk and rested his hand near a filigree letter opener.

"Is stealing a habit with you, father?"

"Why have you called me here?"

In a soldier's deadly fluid move, Castanheda plucked down his shield. Pessoa snatched up the letter opener, and only then saw the hidden wall niche.

Castanheda said over his shoulder, "You put your faith in God, I see. You may have that. It's pure Moroccan gold. Or you may put the point between my ribs, if that sets your mind at ease."

Pessoa put the letter opener back, but let his hand linger.

From the depths of the niche, Castanheda brought out a teakwood chest. "What sort of father are you?" He slammed the chest down stunningly close to Pessoa's thumb. He twisted the lock. Inside sat a glittering pile of Spanish *reales* and gold ducats, so much wealth that Pessoa, incredulous, stepped away. Castanheda's dark look pursued him. "When have you cleaned milk puke from your clothes?"

Never. And never would. Pessoa's stillborn seed. "Put the money away."

"How many hours have you spent teaching someone the names of colors? Take the money," Castanheda said.

"I cannot."

"Buy yourself a decent horse, Manoel Pessoa. A saddle. A little comfort."

"I cannot take this from you."

"*Pôrra!* Am I not worthy? I have been damned by sniveling Dominicans and ass-licking Cistercians; and yet before each battle Jesuits petitioned God for me. What sort of father are you, who would turn his back on a son who disobeyed Rome for you, who slaughtered Spaniards when you asked? Damn you Jesuits to Hell for serving the Holy Office. For leading this country from one war to another. Take the money."

"Please, Guilherme. It is too late."

Pessoa saw a spark of rage that, had it caught, would have killed. Then the flame sputtered. Castanheda dropped his eyes. The room smelled of sweat, of long-dead fires. No, Pessoa was wrong. The house was shuttered not in preparation for grief; Castanheda had created a fortress.

"Tomorrow, two o'clock," Pessoa said. "I will send Cândido Torres. Marta is to—"

He whispered, "If not money, what? Tell me what you want."

Pessoa spoke to the candles, to the cold glittering coins. ". . . she is to appear and answer an inquiry. Speaking in general, Senhor Castanheda, it is always best for the accused to abjure. Privately, I admit that only a *de levi* is safe. An abjuration *de vehementi* carries with it death as punishment for relapse. Marta is young. And her heresy is grievous." He pursed his lips, toying with an ink-stained quill. "I believe it interesting, Guilherme, that although the Holy Office has the ecclesiastical power to pursue a fleeing accused, in practicality they have little means. This tidbit of information, as you understand, passes only between us."

Between them fell a sad taut silence, like that before battle. Through it, Pessoa could hear the slow march of Castanheda's breath. Suddenly the man hissed, "Damn you, Pessoa. You speak like a turd-tongued lawyer."

"Yes. That is exactly what I am."

Without raising his eyes, Pessoa pushed past, wrestled the bolt open, and stalked out of the house. It was only when he reached the street that he found he could breathe again.

He shoved his hat on his head and walked down the cobblestone road, away from the Castanheda house, away from the Teixeiras', away from it all. Townsfolk stared as he passed. Dishearteningly few called out good day. After two blocks he noticed a child trying to keep pace. When he recognized who it was, his feet—his heart—stumbled. Rodrigo Castanheda.

"Marta stole my toy soldier and put a dress on him and pretended he was a doll, and now she won't give him back."

Pessoa slowed to a stroll. "Did she."

"Uh-huh. She comes into my room all the time and steals things."

"I see."

They rounded a corner, where the smaller of the town's two bakeshops filled the street with the smell of warm yeast.

"She pulls my hair and yells at me, and breaks things and tells *papai* that I did it. She doesn't ever study her lessons, not like I do. And when the tutor asks her questions, she cheats."

Pessoa walked, nodding politely, past a street vendor and a trio of shopping women. They did not nod back.

"Is that enough, father?"

"I'm sorry?"

Rodrigo bounced excitedly on his toes. "Is that enough heresy to arrest her?"

Pessoa stopped dead.

"All you all right?" the boy asked. "You're not going to faint like Aunt Maria Perpetua?"

Pessoa laughed. When his legs were steady, he started walking again.

"I can stand on my head. Watch, father. Watch." The boy bent, propped his hands on the cobbles, and promptly tumbled ass over end.

Pessoa put out a hand to help him up, but the boy leaped to his feet. "Better against a wall." He shrugged. His hose had torn. His shirt was mud-stained at its hem. "I can stand on my hands forever. Better than Julio or Alonzo. And when I'm on my hands and I can't fight back, Marta pinches me. I pray for the angels to throw her into the pit, but it hasn't happened yet. If you sin, you're supposed to go to Hell, isn't that right, Father Inquisitor?"

Pessoa hoped he looked contemplative rather than entertained. "Well, Rodrigo, even though we may aspire to justice, one should not pray for another's damnation. I don't think that's quite right."

The boy shoved his hands into his pockets.

"Besides, this seems a matter for your earthly father, not your heavenly one. Why don't you talk to him?"

Rodrigo kicked at a pebble. Something in his eyes. Something. . . .

"Does he beat you? Your father?"

His shrug turned Pessoa's chest to ice.

More sharply: "Does he?"

Beyond a cluster of tile roofs gray-green hills hunched. Pessoa and the boy walked past a dusky-leaved stand of laurel, then a granite wall speckled with orange lichens.

"She makes him cry," the boy said.

"Who?"

"Marta. She makes *papai* cry."

Pessoa's thoughts floundered. "So he does hit your sister."

"No, no, Father Inquisitor. He promised *mamãe*. She said never hit my children, and he promised he wouldn't, and then she died. Sometimes *papai* gets so mad that he lifts his hand, but Marta starts yelling, 'There! There in the corner! Don't you see her?' and she's talking about *mamãe*, and she pretends she can see her, the way the witch did."

"The herbalist saw your mother?"

"Uh-huh. Big and bright as life, she said. It was when *papai* got sick, and everybody thought he would die of the brain fever because he was see-ing ghosts. The witch said she saw *mamãe* wearing a sky-blue scarf with gold roses, and *papai* said that was the scarf he bought for her in Spain. But he lost it, you see? No one but *papai* ever saw the scarf, so I think maybe the witch really sees ghosts. But Marta talks about visions all the time. She says she sees *everything*."

Pessoa halted. From down the winding street came echoes of a trick-ling fountain. A yellow strawflower bloomed in a crack in a stucco wall. "Never repeat that story," he said.

"But—"

"The story about the herbalist seeing the ghost. It would be a griev-ous sin, Rodrigo, to repeat that."

A cry went up from the next street. Approaching footsteps pounded. Pessoa wondered if it was God, coming to strike him down for his lie. Then from around the corner came a dark blur and a bruising collision of flesh. Pessoa staggered.

It was Castanheda. "You black-frocked bastard! Get away from my son!"

Hot wine-scented breath bathed Pessoa's face. At the edge of his vi-

sion he saw the glint of a blade. Something burned along his ribs. Pessoa
tried to cry out; but the street reeled and he toppled, warmth gushing from
his side.

Above him he could hear Rodrigo's pleading shouts of "No, no, *pai!*"
He heard other voices, too. "*Malandro!* See what you have done!"

"Trouble comes when you kill a priest. Bad as breaking a mirror."

Pessoa tried to rise, but he was weak. *Dice.* Say it. Say it quickly, before it was too late. Not the Act of Contrition, but a simple statement, long
overdue: *Credo.*

If God existed, He was feeling Pessoa's pain. He knew his sick fear,
and could cure it. I believe, Pessoa thought, and waited, anxious, for an answer.

A chiding: "Don't you remember when we had to have Spanish inquisitors, Senhor Castanheda? And no one could understand them when
they spoke? This one's not so bad."

Pessoa rolled over on his good side and looked up into a foggy circle
of faces. He opened his mouth to bid someone call Luis, but had not breath
to speak.

"Sugar water. That's all he needs. Quick, girl. Go bring the father—"

"A scratch. Seen worse in the war."

"You seen dead men in the war."

A chorus of laughter followed. Someone bent and gently pressed a
cloth to his wound. "Go home, Guilherme," the man said. "You've been
cause of enough trouble." Pessoa squinted to bring the face of the speaker
into focus. Cândido Torres.

Pessoa licked his lips. *Credo in unum Deum,* he thought, thought it
against all logic. Thought it so hard that it seemed he had cried it aloud.
Cold sank into him, bone-deep. Shivering, he held tight to Cândido's
sleeve. "Luis."

"No, just Cândido. What's the matter? You hit your head when you
fell?"

One God. *Patrem omnipotentem,* Almighty Father. Yet did He know
of milk puke and teaching colors? What sort of father was He?

Whether God or Hell existed, Pessoa could not take the chance, could not afford to die with mortal sins on his soul. "Call Luis. I need extreme unction."

"O, I don't think—"

"Call him! I feel Death's cold. Each breath comes labored."

"You're fearful," Cândido said.

"Of course I'm fearful, you misbegotten imbecile!" Pessoa bit his lip. Bad enough to die apostate . . .

"No. I mean that's how fear feels, father. Known it myself before a battle. Thought I was dying, too." Cândido grasped him by the shoulders of his cassock and hauled him to his feet. "Come on, I'll walk you home."

Afonso sought Him by torchlight at Caneças and Camarões; as the sun rose he asked for news in Almargem do Bispo. What seemed simple had become as perplexing as finding the end of a rainbow. Still he kept on, for it was not Castelo Melhor or Pedro who had been chosen. God had reached out to the least of His servants and said, *Come.*

He heard the moaning of the cows of Santa Eulália long before he saw them. Their pain tolled down the rounded hills, sounded in the grassy valley. At a bend in a stream he came upon the herd, udders swollen and leaking milk. And there was the rest of the fair: the Gypsies, wagonloads of carrots and parsnips, crates of chickens, live rabbits and their hanging dead.

In the fetlock-deep grass ahead of Afonso, the banner carrier reined his horse to a stop. The flanking guards halted. Merchants silenced their cries.

And when he had the crowd's attention, the banner carrier said, "The king."

Afonso kicked Doçura forward. "I come to ask your help."

Cloth merchant looked round-eyed to shopper, shopper looked to butcher, then everyone looked at Afonso, and he grew so afraid of their attention that he trembled.

There was a little boy with a spotted apple standing beyond the crowd. To make the words come easier, Afonso kept his gaze on him. "Last night there was a pretty star. And it traveled south to north, and when it reached some point, a finger of light came down."

The boy's eyes were brown and still. Heedless of worms, he took a great, cheek-stuffing bite of fruit.

Afonso asked, "Did you see it?"

The boy nodded, chewing.

Afonso grabbed the pommel of his saddle and dismounted. A guard came forward, but Afonso gently pushed the help away. He squatted until he and the boy were face-to-face. "You would not lie to me," he said.

From the gathering of shoppers, a woman came and stood watching.

Afonso spoke softly so that only the boy would hear. "I went on a quest," he told the boy. "Just like Don Quixote. And only a little while into it, God made me choose whether I would fight for good, and I chose wrong. Then God made me choose between my brother and Him, and I chose right. Because I love my brother very much, but all Portugal depends on me. So that's why I must ask you: did the star come here?"

When the boy shook his head, Afonso grabbed his arms. "Then where?"

The boy twisted in Afonso's grip and pointed to his mother. Her hands flew to her face. "What is it?" she cried. "What has my son done?"

"No. The star," the boy said. "The man wants to know where the pretty star went last night."

One by one, the merchants and the Gypsies and the shoppers and the boy's mother all turned and pointed. They pointed the same direction the boy had: up the stream, through a gathering of chestnut trees and oaks.

North.

CÂNDIDO HAD PULLED off Pessoa's cassock and settled him into his cot when Berenice poked her head in the rectory door. "Castanheda stabbed me," Pessoa told her.

Cândido looked to see who had arrived and, mindful of hexes, looked away.

Head lowered, meek as a nun, she entered. She knelt by the side of his cot. "You should have seen, Berenice," he told her. "Fierce and maddened, the man was. Totally unreasonable."

She pulled the blanket to his waist and began to peel off Cândido's wrappings. Pessoa ventured a look at himself. Beneath the blood-stiff cloth lay a scabbed welt. Surely that could not be all of it—not a wound that had felled him. He craned his head for a better look.

She pushed him down. She washed him with marigold water, and applied a poultice until the bitter herbs in it made his wound numb.

"I was minding my own business, can you imagine it? Doing nothing, Berenice—really nothing. A few moments before, I had actually tried to help him. Then the man attacks me right in front of a crowd, and no one cared enough to come to my aid."

Cândido crossed his arms. He cut a heroic figure, and postured as if he knew it. His quilted tunic was unbuttoned nearly to his waist. His collar ruff was loose. His kidskin boots hugged fashionably muscular legs. "Check his head, woman," Cândido said. "I believe he hit it when he fainted."

"Fainted? *Fainted?*" Pessoa's face flamed with rage. His head pounded. "Not likely! I slipped! And I tell you, had my heel not caught on a cobble—"

Berenice got to her feet and, carrying her basket, went to the fire. "I'll steep you some nerve tea."

"*Beata Maria!* It would help my nerves to know that that infestation of Dominicans in the Holy Office cared enough about my mission to send me an armed guard. Now see what has happened! I was forced to depend on locals who care not whether I live or die."

Cândido dropped his arms so fast that Pessoa recoiled. Hand resting on his sword hilt, he walked to the cot. "Guilherme and I will have a talk, father. From now on you should go nowhere without me."

Pessoa spent his sarcasm against Cândido's boots. "Oh, yes, or—who knows?—I might be stabbed."

"Exactly so. I'm glad you see it. Well, I'm off to see Father Soares and make the final prison arrangements." Cândido marched smartly out of the rectory.

A slice of afternoon brightened the open doorway. Light puddled on the floor tiles. Berenice came to him, holding a steaming cup. She knelt, lifted his head, and brought the cup to his lips. The tea tasted of mint and chamomile and bitters. It left a nettle prickle on his tongue.

He breathed in the musk of her skin, the lye soap smell of her clothes. He luxuriated in her warmth. "If I had died, would you miss me?" He rubbed his palm over the soft mound of her breast.

She slapped at him.

Her nipple was hardening. He teased it into an erect nub. "Would you?"

She let go his head, and he fell hard onto the pillow. He thrust his hand into her lap. "Close the door," he whispered. "Life is short. Lie by me and give me comfort."

She pushed at him. "Soares will be here. And Cândido with him. And then what?"

He tugged her blouse free, put his hand under, and dallied with what he was able to reach. "They're gone to arrange a prison. I ache for you, Berenice. Lie by me. Only your attentions can give me ease."

"Wait. All right. All right. Close your eyes."

Pleased, and more than a bit surprised, he obeyed. The quiet of the room was barely disturbed by a delicious rustle of clothing. He felt a tug at his blanket and the slide of dainty fingers across his belly. Warm, slick with grease, her hand slid over his *pau* and milked a groan from him.

"Ah." He shivered. His *ovos* felt in danger of bursting. "Ah. Faster."

Up and down her fingers went, root to tip. Blankets flapped. Anyone passing the door might glance into the rectory and see. "Ah yes. Yes," he breathed. "Harder." He was ready to explode, yet he held back, savoring the danger. His *pau* tingled. Tingled madly. Went hot, then cold.

His eyes flew open. Berenice slid her hand from out the blankets. The room stank of goose grease and pungent herbs. "That should help," she said.

He grabbed himself. His "stick" was dead as its namesake. "How could you?" he cried.

"So you can get some rest."

"Rest? I will lie in want for some little jot of pleasure."

She wiped her hands on her apron. "I visited Maria Elena."

He pulled on himself fitfully. The flesh between his legs seemed as though it belonged to another. "How long will this last?"

"You asked me to go, you remember?"

"My *pau* has died, Berenice. How can you talk of aught else?"

Her lowered gaze. That secret smile. The custody of the eyes the town's superstition had taught her. "Blessed are those that mourn."

"*Muliercula! Venefica!* How long?"

Her body shook with laughter.

"Here I lie . . . ah, perhaps it is here that you want me. I was told you visited Guilherme Castanheda after the death of his wife. You saw her ghost. Is that all you saw? Perhaps you met him at the well, and perhaps there was more seduction in the meeting than rape. Did Guilherme try to kill me for Marta's sake, Berenice? Or for yours?"

Berenice snatched his ear and twisted it hard. He cried out in pain. She put her face close to his—kissingly near—bitingly near. "What misery is yours, Manoel?" she hissed. "Fed by the Church. Clothed by the Church. Suckled at the teat of the Holy Office. A scratch along your side that would not make a child cry for long. All the while Maria Elena lies abed, her nose crushed, her ribs not scratched, but broken."

Her fingernail dug into his earlobe, but he didn't dare complain. Her eyes weren't hot and angry as he might have expected; they were cool and distant as the meat between his legs.

"She will die, Manoel." Berenice loosed his ear. The lobe was numb and cold; then the blood rushed back and it began, sickeningly, to throb. He wondered if, when feeling returned, the rest of him would feel the same.

"She will die all because from one day to the next," she said, "the girl has ceased to be virgin."

MORE GOOSE, FATHER Andrade?" the elderly Marquis de Paredes asked. Alerted, a footman stepped to the table, armed with platter and serving fork. The bird had been roasted in lemon and savory. Its skin was browned to a crisp. The slices oozed seasoned juices. A small mortification—Bernardo waved the offer away. For he had seen the message sent to Monsignor that morning: an appearance of angels not sixty kilometers distant. And if God heard Bernardo's prayer, Bernardo would see them, too. *Te igitur, clementissime Pater . . .*

"You barely eat." The marquis turned to Monsignor. "Look. The young father barely eats."

. . . per Jesum Christum Filium tuum Dominium nostrum . . .

Monsignor popped a forkful of chestnut stuffing into his mouth. "So by destroying the sovereignty of the Church, do we set ourselves up for Hell? Is *that* logical self-interest?"

"I don't really know," the marquis said in a voice as spidery as lace.

Bernardo closed his eyes and let the voices, the room, the world slip away. *Supplices rogamus . . .*

"Why doesn't he eat? Is it the goose? Is the goose poorly cooked?" The marquis patted Bernardo's hand.

The angels. God's light in the sky. *Caelestia replet laetitia.* Bernardo spoke into his napkin. "No, no. Quite tasty."

The marquis pulled the footman over, speared a slice of breast, and dropped it onto Bernardo's plate. The old man's smile was devilish. "Oh, yesterday was Friday, father. Fish, to be sure. Only fish. Pike and sturgeon and cod. But today, meat! If not goose, then the venison." He dropped the fork back on the platter with a clang and motioned to the footman. "Get the venison, and be quick."

Word of the wonder that the king and his soldiers had witnessed, the sight that had sent an entire company to its knees. A tingle shot from the base of Bernardo's spine—the same tingle that came to him during prostration. *Se libet. O memento me, Domine.*

"Hobbes," Monsignor said.

"Ah?" the marquis asked.

"The rule of Leviathan—French idiocy to follow where that madman goes."

"Ah."

Bernardo put his hands in his lap and dug his nails into his own flesh until the small pain cleared his mind. *Memento me.*

The footman arrived with the haunch of venison. The marquis carved two thick pink slices and put them onto Bernardo's plate.

"Eat," the old man urged. "Eat, father. Put some meat on those bones." He leaned toward Monsignor. "Watch this boy's chamber pot for worms."

Monsignor dropped his fork. "Castelo Melhor . . ."

The king and all his company, awash in that light.

The old man elbowed Bernardo from his reverie. "Vain as a rooster," the old man said. "Beard as thin as a boy's. He cuts hairs from his head and pastes them in that mustache of his, you ever notice? Mark my words— he'll go bald before he's thirty."

"It seems to me . . ." Monsignor raised his voice, snaring even Bernardo's attention. "My dear marquis!"

"Um?"

"It seems to me," Monsignor said, "that foreign ideas have turned the rest of Europe into a Babel of philosophies, everyone shouting at one another: Descartes and Hobbes. The English with their Calvinists. The French bedeviled by their Huguenots."

"Can't trust the French," the old marquis agreed. "You know that, father?" His face was translucent, as if his soul was bursting, luminous, from his skin.

Bernardo returned the old man's smile. Sun cascaded from the high windows, threw splendor across the linen tablecloth, the candelabras. Glory sparkled in the silver sugar bowl.

"Only God keeps us from anarchy, wouldn't you say?" Monsignor finished his plum sauce. The footman stepped forward and filled his plate again.

Bernardo marked it: three more flames for gluttony in Monsignor's ledger. Then his thoughts returned to the miracle and his hand trembled so, he had to set his wineglass down. The old marquis peered at him sharply.

Monsignor said in a voice loud enough to capture the old man's wandering notice, "The world is turned upside down. What are we—a noble unfairly stripped of his power, and a poor cleric stripped of his Vatican's solicitude—to do?"

"Perhaps we might—"the old man locked eyes with Bernardo. The sweet vagueness in them had disappeared"—revolt?"

THE VOICES OF Soares and Cândido awoke him. Pessoa's head felt stuffy, his mouth furred. Sensation had returned to his *pau:* a bothersome stickiness. He ran his tongue over his teeth and asked, "What o'clock?"

Cândido answered. "Past eight. You slept like the dead." He laughed. "You snored like a goat."

"Some dinner, Manoel?" Soares asked. "Rabbit stew."

Pessoa coughed and sat up. Night thickened at the open door. A lamp cast its ruddy light over the table: an iron pot, a triangle of hard cheese, the remains of a loaf. He saw Berenice's empty cup by his cot and memory of her smell, her touch, made his *pau* flex its muscle.

"We've already eaten, but we've left some for you."

Pessoa shook the sediment of Berenice's drug from his mind. He stood, wrapping the blanket around him to hide his *pau*'s enthusiasm.

"Prison's ready, Father Inquisitor." Cândido said. "You'll like it. We used the old inn, the one that burned. There's a room for the inquest. Below, you have stout iron bars, and we laid in good fresh straw for the floor. There are windows, even. Nice and bright. Father and I chased the rats out."

"Excellent. We will go to Castanheda's house on the morrow, sometime past two o'clock, and take Marta Castanheda into custody. Then we go to the Teixeira house, and take Maria Elena as well." Pessoa put on his undershirt and, seeing that he was covered, let the blanket fall. He turned. They were watching him.

Soares asked, "Will we not hold an inquiry, then?"

"Yes, Luis. As I have explained, we will hold some form of informal inquiry."

"Tomorrow is Sunday," Soares said.

Pessoa clapped hand to forehead. "O, Monday. Monday it is, then." He bent and rummaged in his bag for an extra cassock, found one, and dressed.

"Where are you bound?" Cândido asked. "See the prison? You can do that Sunday afternoon."

Pessoa turned, buttoning. "I thought perhaps a walk."

Soares, studying the tabletop all too intently, gathered bread crumbs with a fingertip.

"Wouldn't do that," Cândido said. "Your choice, though. Father Soares: I'm headed home before the wife locks me out. And Father Inquisitor: I'd ask myself if a dip in the oil pot's worth my life. If it is—so be it. I've felt the need as fiercely myself." Chuckling, he walked out the door.

Soares scrutinized his fingertip, then rubbed it clean with his thumb.

"Just a walk, Luis."

Soares nodded.

"I suppose I shall take my dagger." Pessoa took the sheathed weapon from his bag. The handle fit his palm as naturally as a Teixeira's glass goblet, as Berenice's breast.

"A lamp also?" Soares asked.

"Perhaps not." Whether in the safety of Berenice's house or unsafe on the road, it was best not to be seen. Pessoa cut a crumbling slice of cheese, took the rest of the loaf, and walked out into the night.

Above the black hills, sparkling heaven arched. Pessoa walked beneath the shelter of stars, through a nave of dark hedgerows and past orderly cabbage pews. Around one hill and up another, then beyond the edge of town and past intermittent farmhouses where lamplight gleamed from windows.

At the clotted dark by a grove of trees, he left the known quantity of the path for the surprises of the hillside. He stuffed the rest of the bread into his mouth and, lifting his cassock, climbed his way through the grass. Just over the lip of the hill, he stopped.

The windows were open in the small house below. In the glow of a lamp, he saw Berenice seated at her table, her head bent. She was studying a child's arm.

Pessoa sat on a boulder and watched her. The frame of the window formed a puppet play, a silent one. Berenice got up, walked out of sight. To her hearth? She came back with bandages and a knife. Then the child's mouth opened to blackness and her small arms flailed. The mother came forward to hold her down.

Berenice was more deft than Castanheda. One touch left a crimson splash on the child's arm.

Did she love him? Castanheda was everyday—a constant.

In the puppet-play window a mother, with lowered head, offered coins. Head lowered, Berenice accepted. How could the townsfolk not admire that exotic face? How could they help staring into those luminous eyes? Did Castanheda ever truly see? Even from that distance she had the power to stop Pessoa's heart.

The child and mother left, arm in bandaged arm. Their lamp cast a circlet of light along the road, as if they carried all world, all safety with them. Berenice extinguished her lamp and snuffed her candle to save it. He had forgotten to pay her, had never brought the food he promised.

She closed the shutters, and still he sat, studying the edge of hearth glow about the square where wood failed to meet wall. About him, constellations rose and set. Somewhere down the hill a dog yapped twice, then fell silent. The night smelled of bruised grass and sheep dung.

He rose, his knees creaking. The wound on his side was a sullen complaint. Lifting his hem, he stumbled up the dark hillside and started down.

There he stopped, for an apparition halted him. A radiant star shone as large as a plum. So bright—O dear God, so unexpectedly sweet—that he blinked back grateful tears. *Exultate.* The star shone its circlet of warmth onto the far hill—a spot of safety, just for him.

Silent and majestic, glory sailed near, filling the heavens with joy. *Ave.*

Ave. Not once, but twice He had shown Pessoa a miracle, that patient loving Father who wiped sin's milk puke, who taught all colors, who forgave doubt.

Unaccustomed humility felled him. Pessoa dropped to his knees. The star swelled until it seemed to be God Himself shouting: *Credis hoc?*

Credo. Belief tolled through Pessoa like a bell. He lifted his hands, his eyes streaming.

The star sailed over his beseeching fingers. He turned and watched it go. It shone wonder on Cândido's vineyards and lent splendor to a lacy field of mustard, before dashing itself loudly against the side of a hill.

L EST THE SCREAMS wake the monastery, Bernardo forced a cloth into Monsignor's mouth. He checked under the covers and gauged the temperature of the pig's bladder. The water in it was still hot.

"More senna tea," Bernardo urged. "And hold the pig's bladder closely."

Monsignor's eyes bulged. He spat out the cloth.

"Its heat relaxes the stomach."

Monsignor flailed, in his exertions catching Bernardo a stinging slap across the cheek. "Pray for me!" Monsignor cried.

"Shhh." Bernardo dipped a cloth into the brass basin by his chair, and laid it, cool and dripping, over Monsignor's forehead.

Monsignor flung it off. It hit the wall with a smack. "My confessor. Be quick."

"It is merely an indigestion."

Monsignor grappled for Bernardo's hand, held it tight. "Heed me. Take up your dagger—"

Bernardo tried his best to pull away, but Monsignor's grip was fierce.

"I beg you. Take up your dagger, Bernardo, and pierce my side. I pray you before God. Open me as a shepherd would a foundered sheep."

Bernardo dipped his free hand in the cool water and wiped the sweat from Monsignor's face.

"Let me die, then! Better the *verum corpus* God has promised. I beseech you. If you love me, you will open my stomach, lest I stab myself and be buried a suicide."

"Turn over. I'll rub your back."

With a whimper, Monsignor turned aside. Bernardo opened the jar of unguent, pulled the linen nightshirt up, and rubbed the brown, pungent salve into Monsignor's dimpled skin. He kneaded the meaty shoulders. He pressed his thumb into the loose-fleshed back, along the buried knobs of the spine.

The tincture of poppy had begun its work. Monsignor's thick-tongued plea stirred the candles on the nightstand. *"Domine, clamavi ad Te."*

Bernardo offered response: *"Et sanasti me."*

Neither healed nor soothed yet. Monsignor groaned, inarticulate and sonorous as a bullock.

The salve smelled of camphor and eucalyptus. The fumes pricked tears from Bernardo's eyes, so that when he blinked, the candle flames were magnified and all the darkness driven out.

Small daily wonders. Could Monsignor not see? Had gluttony and pride so dulled him? Bernardo worked, impressing charity into the skin, planting obedience.

He thought of angels; the king and all his company, struck dumb as Bethlehem's shepherds. *Memento me, Domine.*

"Like Luke," Bernardo said.

The large-pored flesh quivered, giving voice to another dull-witted animal moan. The candle flames fluttered, routing shadows.

"How like the story of the angels, when they said to fear not. And yet the shepherds, I'm sure, fell to their knees. There is naught else to do when in the presence of angels."

A sound at the door made Bernardo turn. Death stood in the shadows. It pushed back its cowl and Bernardo recognized the face, the tonsure. Friar da Costa held up a small lantern and said, "Still not asleep?"

Bernardo wiped his face with his sleeve, careful to keep the salve from his eyes. "The tincture of poppy settles him. Near morning, the senna tea should unstop his bowels."

"Deus gratia. For his moans down the corridors are terrible. In the darkness, it puts me in mind of a haunting." He chuckled. "And, *maxima*

gratia, my duties end at matins. I need not face the terror of that chamber pot. There is another message."

Bernardo's pulse quickened. He held out his hand. Next to him Monsignor let out a loud snick, then a snore.

Friar da Costa gestured with his chin. "For him. Given me by a soldier with orders that I put it in Monsignor's hand."

"My hand is Monsignor's."

"And your ears, too? For he will cuff them when he spies the seal is broken."

"Will you wake him? Or stay?"

With a snort of laughter and a wry shake of the head, the friar came forward and put the envelope into Bernardo's waiting palm. "I pray you note that the seal is intact."

Double swans. The old marquis's seal. Bernardo slipped the envelope into his pocket. "So noted."

Still the friar lingered. "For I fear the Holy Office, but I fear the nobles and the crown even more." At last he turned and, sandals flapping, made his way to the door.

When the friar was gone, Bernardo took the envelope from his pocket and split the seal. He opened the page and read.

O Castelo cairá.
Ora por nos.

Bernardo rose, took the letter to the candelabra on the nightstand, and set the thick ivory colored paper alight. He put it in Monsignor's pewter dish and watched it burn to ash. Neither kings nor angels, but Bernardo was not likely to forget the message:

The Castle will fall.
Pray for us.

THE CLAMOR OF the star's fall brought candles to burn in windows. Three ruddy sparks bobbed through the Torres vineyard, moving fast. Borne on the wind was the sound of hoofbeats and excited shouts: the voices of Cândido and his sons. They rode toward a burning coastline of grass, an orange archipelago in night's vastness.

Pessoa would have gone home, but the ruins of the comet drew him, its pull the lure of the extraordinary. Ahead, the three embers flew up the ebon slope. More shouted words, man's and boys', went astray amid the echoing hills. One ember drifted down the steep incline, gaining speed, to be lost momentarily among the trees. A wild crescendo of hoofbeats, and on the road below, Pessoa caught a glimpse of a lathered horse and an up-held lantern and a frightened face. Then Cândido's middle boy was gone, leaving questions in his wake.

Had the comet fallen on a house? Was someone hurt? Dying? Pessoa quickened his pace, for what did it matter if the fingers that anointed the forehead, that closed the eyes, had no conviction of Heaven? Long before the Jesuits discovered Pessoa's aptitude for law, long before the Holy Office claimed him, the gift of comfort formed his contract with the Church. *I will deceive, and give this thing,* he had promised, arms outspread on the flag-stones. *And in return, you will feed me.* Never had he asked for aught else, except for some harrowing nights when blackness squatted over the hills and wolves bayed on the road and the prayers he uttered dissipated like incense.

Pessoa gave obedience and never expected faith. Tonight he learned how much he longed for it—enough longing to seek purpose from the un-expected, to look for pattern in chaos. Enough longing to send him, weep-ing, to his knees.

He rushed down the penultimate hill, skirting the next. The wind shifted, flinging pungent grass smoke into his face. Wrapped in lantern glow, Cândido's eldest stood, holding the reins of two horses, the grassy incline around him sparkling like mica-laden earth. Beside him, children.

Pessoa cupped his hands to his mouth. "Mario Torres!"

The boy held up his lamp, looking wildly into the dark. "Who calls?"

"Father Pessoa!" Head down, stumbling on stones, Pessoa hurried. "How many?"

The boy had still not sighted him. He stared at a place to Pessoa's right. "What?"

"How many felled?"

"One, I think," came the answer.

Another child? Or their mother? Around Mario the pair of children milled. Whose children were they? Pessoa thought of his own inert seed and felt such a rush of protectiveness that it made his eyes swim. And then he was closer, and while his mind was still saying "children," his eyes were telling him no.

He might have fled then, but it was too late, for one of the child-shaped things turned to look. Pessoa stumbled to a halt, adrift in those eyes, at peace.

It mattered not that the face was a smooth mask, nor that the eyes seemed carved from polished jet. It mattered not that the hands were not hands at all, nor that the whole of the creature was so whimsically improbable. The only importance was, for that instant, the night was neither dark nor lonely.

Then Mario said, "Beware their eyes, father. They tell stories."

Pessoa tore his gaze away, his heart thundering. "*Miserere nobis!* What manner of creatures are they?"

From the pall of smoke Cândido came, bearing an inert bundle. When he reached the glow of his son's lantern, he set his burden down. "Heard the clamor, father? I've sent for constables. There's a silver acorn over the lip of the hill that birthed these things. Imps, you suppose?"

Two living creatures were wandering about, their silver garb as tight as skin. The third lay where Cândido had put him, fanciful eyes open to the heavens. Pessoa came closer, despite dread of questions and more fear of answers.

"Watch your step, father. There's comet litter about."

Confetti. Gold leaf. Pieces of pewter. Pessoa picked his way through the clutter and knelt beside the fallen child. "Mario," he said. "Quickly. Get me water. And oil, if you can."

"But . . ."

"Quickly! Is there no stream nearby?"

Mario dropped his argument and ran off through the dark.

Cândido said, "Don't think water will do much good, father. Unless you believe he's asleep, not dead."

"I mean to baptize him. And grant extreme unction."

"Why?"

"I must." Because it was all that he knew to do. Besides, any child of God deserved that much welcome to life, that much eulogy leaving it.

The two other creatures still roamed the hill. One picked up a bit of shiny metal, acquisitive and curious as a magpie. But watching them was too much a strain of logic, and Pessoa looked away.

"So. Demons? Faeries? Where do you think they come from, father? Heaven or Hell?"

Two legs, two arms, one head. Nearly human in the shadows, but disorienting in the light. "Borneo," he said.

"Um?"

The day had held far too many embarrassing misconceptions. Pessoa would not allow circumstance to make a fool of him again. "Really, Cândido. Let us not give in to superstition. They are odd, yes, but still flesh and blood." Flesh slick as oiled paper, strange and cool to the touch. An open wound, and blood like milk. Pessoa wiped his fingers on his cassock and put his trembling hands in his lap. "Obviously from Borneo or Brazil. Or Africa. Yes. Perhaps Africa. I've read stories of giants in the African highland, with black hair all over their bodies and silver stripes down their backs. And men no taller than my waist who kill by blowing through their mouths. And men tall as trees who can converse with cattle. Why, these creatures may look curious, but for God's sake, Cândido, can you not see they live and breathe?" His voice had risen to an indignant bellow.

Cândido shrugged. "Imp looks dead to me. Might be hard to tell, though."

Then Mario came, bearing water in his cap. With whispers, Pessoa blessed the soaked wool. He wrung the cap over the Borneo man's head, and watched drops slide the smooth gray slope. *"In nomine Patris."*

Behind him came a clamor of raised voices and Cândido's angry, "Jorge! I told you to bring Marcio and João. Half the damned village is here!"

The boy whimpered, "I couldn't help it. They all followed."

Pessoa did not look up. Undaunted, he stroked the cross with his thumb, forcing his hand to be steady, compelling his lips through the benediction: *". . . et Filii et Spiritus Sancti . . ."*

Then a woman screamed, "Kill them!"

Pessoa shot to his feet, holy water blessing his cassock, the ground.

In the light of the torches, Dona Inez had started for the nearest imp, lung-
ing like a fearsome demon, moles abristle, hair wild, garden hoe raised like
a pike. "Lustful, lustful angels! I saw! God threw you out of Heaven!"

Cândido wrested the hoe away from her. "Not fallen angels, you idiot
woman. Can't you see they're just men from Borneo?" He waved the hoe at
the crowd. "Go home. Nothing more to see here. Go on home. These are my
prisoners now, under arrest for destruction of private property and trespass."

I T WAS LATE in the evening when Afonso and his company came upon the
place the star had fallen. He expected wonders, but found only the aro-
matic remains of a grass fire and two boys huddled in the glow of a lantern.

The captain kicked his mount forward, his armor clanking, and asked
of news.

A boy called back, "Something fell from the sky. That acorn there just
over the hill." The one Afonso's age pointed upslope, toward a meadow of
scorched and sparkling ground. His voice trembled like Afonso's did when
he was very cold or very afraid. "It birthed imps from Borneo. Who are
you? And why do you come armed?"

The two boys snuggled against one another. The elder was so like
Pedro that it made Afonso ache.

"I ride with the king." And then the captain said, a chuckle in his
voice, "Who might you fierce soldiers be?"

The two peered curiously into the darkness where Afonso sat astride
Doçura. "I am Mario Torres, and this is my brother Jorge. The king? You
won't take the acorn? I warn you—I have a dagger. Father said we must guard
it with our lives. And he says not to let anyone go inside, because he has been
in there, and he says it is full of mysteries and impish Borneo things."

"I want to see!" Afonso said, and felt Jandira's tug at his sleeve. "But
I want to *see!*"

The two boys shielded their eyes against the torchlight.

"I am the king," Afonso told them. "And God has called me. You
must show me the mysteries and the imps."

"Imps are in the village," Jorge, the younger, said. "You can't see them. Father put them under arrest for the Inquisition. He's the inquisitor's bravest familiar, and he wears a sword, and pledges himself to the Church and Holy Office."

Mario elbowed his brother.

"Well, he *does*."

Afonso climbed off his horse and walked to them. Mario scrambled to his feet and pulled his brother up beside him.

"I wish to see the acorn and talk to the imps," Afonso said.

Jorge said, "They don't talk. And you can't go in, because father went in there, and he is a soldier, and he said it scared him near to weeping."

"I say I want to see."

"I'll take you." Mario picked up his lantern and started up the incline, Afonso at his heels.

From behind him came the jingle of a snaffle and the captain's querulous, "Sire?"

Afonso waved him back.

"Sire!" Jandira called. "Stay awhile. We will see it later."

"God wants me!" His voice was so big that it caused the captain to start. Afonso stood straighter than he ever had stood before, and he ordered them all to stay—the captain, the company, Father de Melo, even Jandira. To his surprise, they did. Then he and Mario, shoulder to shoulder, mounted the crest of the hill.

"How many imps?" Afonso asked.

Mario looked up, his brow knotted, his eyes anxious. "Highness?"

"The imps. How many?" Ahead was strewn a rose-petal scattering of silver.

"O. Three, if you count the dead one. Father Inquisitor baptized it, and it didn't vanish in a puff of smoke, so I guess it wasn't a demon. Don't you have imps in Lisbon?"

Before them stood a scorched boulder; beside it, a scar in the earth. "Not good imps," Afonso said.

Then they were over the rise. The acorn below was huge. From a rent in its side poured light so strange that it made the hair on Afonso's arms and neck stand. He came forward, anyway, and peered into the acorn's gashed side. Silver walls. Silver floor. An icy-white light came from nowhere, illuminating a hallway that beckoned to wonders, that led to terrible deaths.

"Father found them just inside." Mario spoke with quiet awe. "He said what he saw there would have aged another man twenty years. Here."

Mario was holding the hilt of a dagger toward him.

Timid, he said, "Take it. Please take it, Your Highness. And if you cannot return it, well, that's all right."

Afonso shielded his eyes against the cold illumination. It felt as if his soul was coming loose from his body.

Doubt in his voice, Mario suggested, "Maybe it's better by day."

Afonso swallowed hard. He wanted to see more. The little he sighted was so tempting: curved walls, shadowless spaces, a groundhog tunnel of a hall.

"Day, you could maybe see better. Maybe that ugly light would burn out by morning."

Afonso listened, the buzzing silence drawing him. A whisper teased down the curved hall, just out of range of hearing. God calling? Or Death?

"I'd go with Your Highness, but I have to guard the thing. Besides, father made me take an oath not to go in. He says he wants his sons brave, not stupid. O, sorry. I didn't mean . . ."

Mario was as broad as Pedro in the shoulder, as slim as Pedro in the hip. Like Pedro, he stood as if already commissioned a soldier: legs apart, chest out. But Mario's chin was trembling.

The whispers from the corridor hushed. Whatever called Afonso was waiting. Truly, morning might be better. "I'd like to see the imps now."

Mario whistled his relief. He wiped his brow with a sleeve. "Yes, yes. Let's go."

THE STRAIN ON Pessoa's credulity was intolerable. They simply could not be. Faces like smooth gray pears, expressionless but for brief, probably imagined suggestions of wisdom. Legs too spindly to bear weight, heads too huge to lift, the living imps stood by their brother in the jail cell's sweet straw.

"Look comfortable enough," Cândido said. "I'd bury the one, but you can't tell about imps. Might be up and around by the morrow."

Comfortable prisoners in a cozy jail. The basement of the old inn was high-ceilinged; its floors and walls dry. It smelled of straw and dust and the faint ghosts of soured wine.

A commotion started up at the door. Cândido drew his sword and called up to the constables at guard. "Ho, João! See you keep them out!"

It was only Soares. The old Franciscan came stumbling down the stone steps, his eyes scanning the brick arches, the inset iron bars, the vast rooms where kegs twice the height of a man had once been stored. Then his gaze fell to the creatures, and he crossed himself.

Cândido said, "Good-looking imps, aren't they, father. Well, but for the one. Come see."

Soares came, his expression dazed, his hair in just-awakened disarray, his mouth moving. When he was closer, Pessoa could hear the hushed three-word litany: *"O magnum mysterium."*

The old priest's cheeks were so pale that Pessoa feared for his health. "Luis," he cautioned softly, and tried to hold him back.

Soares shouldered past. One of the imps raised its huge head, and to Pessoa's flustered embarrassment, Soares dropped to his knees. The old priest held on, white-knuckled, to the iron bars. *"Sanctus, sanctus."*

"Luis, please."

His voice was a hoarse whisper. "Look! O look what is there, Manoel. God in their eyes."

What wonders did Luis think he saw? After the peace that came with the shock of seeing them, Pessoa had felt naught else. Now he searched those black eyes for miracles, stared until his own eyes watered, until his head ached.

Cândido was nodding, satisfied. "Pair of good-looking imps."

"Not imps." Soares slumped. He rested his forehead against the rusting iron. "Cherubim."

Malefica. Why couldn't the damned Franciscan be more circumspect? "Very interesting theory, Luis," Pessoa said. "However, I don't know if we should . . ."

Soares's expression was pinched. His voice was firm. "Cherubim."

"Whatever." Cândido cleared his throat. "Still, don't think we should bury that one. Can't ever tell about cherubs."

Shouts rose outside. Metal clattered against metal. The door flew open and Mario Torres came running down the steps, another boy in tow.

"Mario! Damn you for a coward!" Cândido shouted. "Where is your brother? And what makes you leave your post?"

Mario halted. Under the lash of his father's voice, the roses in his cheeks turned to ash. The other boy, stout and slope-shouldered and awkward-limbed, stopped beside him. The stranger wore a rich tunic of plum velvet. His face was as bland and sweet as pudding.

"The king," Mario said.

"May the king be fucked!" Cândido's profanity brought a murmured admonition from Soares. "Sorry, father. But, damn it all, Mario. Where did you leave Jorge?"

"No, *pai.* Please." Mario wrung his hands. "You're supposed to bow. I brought the king."

Somewhere outside a horse whinnied. From its perch on a nearby wall, a lantern sputtered and hissed. Pessoa heard the crackle of straw as a creature moved, heard the meaty thud as Cândido's knee hit stone.

The king scrutinized the imps; the pair of creatures scrutinized him. Suddenly the moon face went alight. "O!" the king cried. "O, how clever! There are great haunted reaches between the stars; and the earth goes round and round and round the sun!"

Day 5

THEY CAME UPON BERNARDO IN THE CHAPEL, PRAYING BARE-KNEED ON the stone.

"Urgent message," Friar Costa whispered.

Bernardo had no strength in his legs to rise. When Costa helped him to his feet, he left blood puddled between a sharp flagstone and the grout.

"King's seal," Friar Costa told him. "And Monsignor is in his rooms. Not appeared for matins nor Mass nor breakfast."

Bernardo's knees ached. Later, when they warmed, they would sting. "Ill. I will take it." He slipped the envelope into his habit pocket and left.

Beyond the row of windows a gray dawn was breaking. Light silvered the dark walls of the corridor, cast shadows of blue. Saints slumbered in their niches.

He opened the ornate door to find Monsignor moaning on his chamber pot. The room reeked. "Message," Bernardo said.

Squatted, frowning, Monsignor raised a hand. Bernardo put the envelope between the waiting fingers. He went to fill the censers with incense. He opened the curtains, let morning and air fill the room.

"Freezing," Monsignor said.

Bernardo pulled the curtains to.

"Damn, damn, damn, and damn."

Bernardo turned. Monsignor was pounding the wadded message against his hairy thigh, his expression terrible. Thunder exploded in the chamber pot. With a groan, the message dropped, forgotten. Monsignor's face suffused with a longing that approached adoration. "Damn," Monsignor said.

"Shall I draft a reply?"

Monsignor grunted, ejecting a muddy patter into the bowl, one that held the Hellish stench of loose bowels and sulfur and half-digested chestnuts. "Burn it."

Bernardo picked up the message and took it to the candelabra.

"Wait."

He paused, flame crisping the edge of the page.

"Read it to me. I barely credit what was said."

Bernardo put the page on the tabletop and flattened it with the heel of his hand. When he saw the words, they robbed him of breath and reason.

" 'A fall of angels in Quintas.' " *Angels*. The paper trembled. " 'And the scepter voices the heresy of the apostate Galileo Galilei.' "

"Damn," Monsignor said.

A fall of angels. Bernardo's eyes flooded. The candle became a lake of fire. "Reply?"

Memento me, he prayed.

Another grunt birthed a sodden, malodorous avalanche that ended on a sustained flute note. "No reply. Pack my bags. Send a message to the Marquis de Paredes. I need at least ten men—two of his inquisitorial-trained lawyers, three state-sanctioned executioners, the rest in trained armed guards—and I need them by noon. Inform him they are to carry their own food and clothes. I won't deplete the coffers for this idiocy."

Bernardo set the letter aflame and put it in the pewter dish. A word blazed in dying glory: Angels.

Memento me. "Where do I tell the marquis that his men ride?"

"Bernardo, you misbegotten *imbecillus*. We ride to Quintas. And make certain that you bring enough paper and quills."

Joy shot him through. Angels. And Bernardo would see. Angels. Falling from Heaven bright hot, yet gentle as feathers.

TWENTY-SECOND SUNDAY, Ordinary. No feasting, no fasts. Pessoa co-celebrated, heard Soares read from Jeremiah the anguished and betrayed cry: You seduce me, O Lord. I would speak Your name no more, but my flesh pines. . . .

Marta Castanheda, small and ardent, among the crowd.

Then a breath of sanity: St. Paul's letter to the Romans. Next, Jesus spoke to his disciples saying He must to Jerusalem and suffer greatly there.

They all had come: Castanheda, Teixeira, the soldiers of the moon-faced king. At Communion, Soares offered the host, Pessoa the wine.

Marta Castanheda came to the railing, mouth open like a baby bird.

Flee.

Pessoa thought escape to her as he offered the chalice, then wiped its edge. When her father knelt, Pessoa fixed him with a blistering stare. *Damn you. Make your daughter flee.*

Castanheda misunderstood. His eyes sought the sanctuary of the floor and he opened his mouth for Soares.

"Corpus Christi."

The wine. *"Sanguis Christi."* Pessoa's voice held so much rancor that it caught Soares's attention.

Castanheda left the railing. Soldiers came, the ones who would receive those to be strangled, those to be burnt.

to suffer greatly at the hands of the elders

Then Teixeira and his wife and, to Pessoa's astonishment, their daughter. Soares gave the sacrament—so Maria Elena was confessed and absolved, but for which sin? Pessoa gently lifted the chalice to the girl's split and swollen lip. It took an effort to hold his hand steady. *Dear God, flee.* She drank, and her mother helped her to her feet. He wiped her imprint from the cup and leaned toward the next communicant.

The line to the altar dwindled. Finally came the prayer and, none too soon, the *Dominus vobiscum, et con tuum* and *Ite, Missa est.*

Pessoa watched the church empty. He did not follow Soares outside for the glad hands and the lovely-day-isn't-it-fathers. Instead, he sent the altar boys home. In the sacristy he folded his vestments and put them away in a drawer of extra candles and incense, a gesture of permanence that dismayed him. Should he send word to the next town that he was delayed? For his own safety, should he inform the provincial tribunal at Mafra? Dizzy with worry, Pessoa braced himself against the cold marble top of the chest.

suffer, and then be put to death

He grabbed his coin purse and his hat and walked out through the small rear door, past the remains of the old rectory, and up the next hill.

On the way to her house he hoped to spy her, but the road was empty. When he arrived, he found her house unoccupied, her hearth fire cold, her burro gone.

Gone.

He sat at her abandoned table, hands clasped on its worn top. She had fled quickly and left everything: pots, plates, herbs, the cheap cross he had given her. Gone without a word.

Grief overcame him. He lowered his head and cried—not enough tears to breed weakness or humiliation, not enough to bother wiping. And when he was finished, he searched for her, anyway, down a path worn like a hair's parting in the hillside grass, through a sun-freckled glade. His pace quickened. She had gone, and well considered, but still . . .

Ahead he spied the silvered leaves of an olive tree, the dark of a laurel. Smells of wild carrot and red clover pursued him past a forested copse, then through an expanse of grass and past a fallen stone wall and a climbing rosebush, long overgrown and riotous with petals.

His pulse jumped. For she was there, her back turned to him, her burro grazing nearby. She carried a basket on her arm, and she was gleaning herbs.

Lifting his hem, he hurried, jumping thistles, his boots crushing lavender. He was at her as she turned, the basket falling, spilling foxglove and rose hips, calfsfoot and yarrow and nettles. He cupped her small face in his hands.

"The king . . . It has all gone badly. The Holy Office will know."

"Manoel. You speak nonsense."

"Listen!" At the shout, those flawless cheeks paled in shock, that all too fragile neck reddened in anger. "The king is come, and there are strange creatures fallen." How could Soares find wonder in the black orbs of those creatures, and not in these perfect eyes?

"The king? I don't . . ."

"Go! Word will out. There is no way to stop it. Take your burro and flee. I brought you all my money." He tried to give her his purse. She tried to push his hand away. Their gestures were too reckless, the ground uneven. They fell to their knees in the late-summer grass, holding each other like children.

"Go, Berenice. Please go. I can save no one."

B ERNARDO WAS OVERSEEING the packing of Monsignor's feather bed when the gates to the monastery opened and Castelo Melhor and his men galloped through.

The count jerked his white stallion to a halt by Bernardo. "Where is he?"

Bernardo peered up through his lashes. The count was ill-shaven and slovenly dressed. His mustaches were shedding their fraudulent indulgence of hair. *"Pax tecum,"* he said.

"Damn your *pax tecums* and shit-filled *gloria tibis*!" Horrified, the monks halted their packing. "Tell me that I do not spy the Marquis de Paredes's men there lounging on the steps. Tell me!" The count's voice rose to a hoarse scream. "The Marquis de Paredes! What betrayal is this? Tell your master to stop skulking and come out to answer!"

The oak door flew open with a crash. Monsignor stood, scowling and fearsome, at the top of the steps, a gaggle of wide-eyed monks behind him.

His voice rang through the courtyard. "Kneel when you come before this office. You rule only by the consent of God."

Bernardo shifted his gaze. The marquis's two lawyers sat quietly at one end of the steps. The rest of his men, snickering and elbowing one another, sat at the other.

The count flung himself from the saddle and dropped, as if momentarily tripped, to one knee. Monsignor hurled a *benedicto.* "What right have you to question my choice of familiar? The marquis is pledged to the Holy Office. Since he cannot wield a sword himself, he sends his men."

The count clasped hand to sword hilt and stalked closer. The monks behind Monsignor retreated. "You ride to Quintas. Tell me you do not."

An eloquent lift of the Monsignor's eyebrow. "Of course I ride to Quintas. There is heresy there."

The count's confusion broke surface and was as quickly drowned. "Heresy? No. I meant that the king was to ride to the Alentejo, yet he arrived in Quintas."

"Circuitous route."

Bernardo dipped his head farther to conceal a smile, but not so far that he failed to see the count blink.

"And so . . ." the count began. "And so . . . as I come directly to inform you of what I have learned, I see you about to leave the city, surrounded by the armed men of my sworn enemy."

"The marquis always speaks well of *you.*" Monsignor strolled past the count and down the steps. He paused to inspect the wagons and their lashings.

The count whirled and trotted down the stairs after him. "What heresy?"

Monsignor pulled at a strap, turned to a nearby monk. "Make this tighter."

"What heresy?"

The monk came forward and bent to repair his work.

"The heresy that the earth moves about the sun."

The count bobbed his head to peer into Monsignor's face. He flapped his arms. The intense frustration made him look like a goose. "And?"

Monsignor studied the strap, pronounced it fit.

"And?"

"And the king's soul is in deadly peril."

Monsignor walked to the next wagon, the count at his heels. "I don't understand," the count said.

"The king agrees with the apostate Galileo Galilei."

"But the king is an idiot."

"An idiot, certainly. But heretic."

The count's cheeks went pasty. "You would not."

Monsignor whirled. "Well, we cannot have that, can we? A belief that all natural order is out of place. And especially not in a king. It would be the same as Hobbes saying that the Church must bow to the state." He put his hand to the count's shoulder and firmly, if politely, moved him aside.

"You know of a plot!"

Monks scattered, robes aflutter, like chickens from a yard. Monsignor turned, his hand on the wagon.

To Bernardo's surprise, the count's tone thickened with grief. "Dear God, please. Do not do this. Twenty years of war. Do not force us to take up arms against each other. Portugal will be a graveyard and all her women widows. For the love of Christ, man, consider. Pedro would align himself with Protestant England. Whatever you think of me, I cleave to Catholic France. I am the only hope you have."

Monsignor fixed him with a glare. "God is our hope."

THE FEARSOME LIGHT had not burned itself out, but Afonso could not wait. Despite its cruel glow, the acorn summoned.

"Were they honorable," Jandira said, "they would come out and greet their king."

Before him stretched a promise of wonders better than spyglasses, more grand than etched swords. Afonso raised his foot, put heel to the silver floor, and heard such a contented sigh from within that it made him go chilblained.

"Sire." The captain's voice was thinned by worry. "Let me come with you."

Afonso shook his head. Marvels waited. Things so important that only a king deserved to see.

His other foot. The floor was neither hard nor soft; the air not warm or cold. The acorn was a place of eerie in-betweens. He turned. It seemed that Jandira and the captain stood behind a gossamer wall.

"Come out, sire," Jandira said.

He heard her well enough. But he heard, too, at his back, a breathed welcome.

"Please, my sweetling. As you love me, do not go."

The corridor bid him come, and so he went where the honeycomb walls leaked light. He went, and was not as afraid as he expected.

He looked back, but could no longer see Jandira, no longer see the warm yellow of day. What if there were demons at the end of his quest? What if Death was waiting?

Yet that inviting whisper summoned. Ahead stood banks of jeweled lights: topaz and amethyst and ruby. A sapphire diadem gleamed in the wall.

The whisper in his head birthed pictures clear enough to be words: *Ready.*

One step. Another. He clutched Mario's dagger so hard that the hilt nearly sprang from his sweated palm. His heart beat, fast as a sparrow's. Another step and the walls fell away to vastness.

The great silver room welcomed him with a pageantry of ideas. They came and went in his head—so many ideas that Afonso could not follow their flight, ideas so quick that he could never hope to catch them. He fell to his knees, overcome and trembling.

Colors flared behind Afonso's lids: pink happiness and orange expectancy. Speaking in colors, God asked, *What is your command?*

He dared not command, and he had aught to request. It was enough to kneel in this place that smelled and felt of nothing, where colors were words—this spot of God that was like the soul itself: caged and finite from without; limitless within.

God asked again, in patient blue, *Your command?*

Afonso cradled his dagger to his breast, holding it as the likeness of his father held the sword that adorned his tomb. "Please," Afonso said. "If it is all right, Lord, I would like to see Heaven."

And from one beat of his heart to the next it was there—a starry void, velvet and wide and deep. He clutched the dagger and cried out, for the walls were gone, and the floor, and nothing was left but a fall into dark Heaven.

At his wail, God returned the world. Afonso said a Pater Noster and an Ave Maria, the way he had been taught. Still, he could not stop shaking. He got to his feet in the huge room and bowed. "I need to go now, Lord, but thank you for showing me Heaven. And I'm sorry that it made me so afraid. Maybe I can see some of it again. Maybe one day I can even go there."

I would take you, but there is damage.

Ah. Afonso's soul. Of course he could not yet see Heaven. He nodded, resolute. "It cost many, many pages for even Don Quixote to became a hero. I promise I will try to do better."

The colors went dark, and Afonso became afraid. "Lord? I'll try very hard, really. And every day I'll come to see you," he said, for it seemed to him that God sounded lonely, as he himself often was. Rulers understood such things.

Afonso bowed one last time and then took his leave, letting the tunnel swallow him.

From the room behind came sad violet, and a jumble of images so curious that Afonso knew he had misunderstood: *Can you mend me? There is damage.*

"**D**ID YOU SEE him, Bernardo? Our wicked and decadent boy?" Monsignor swayed with the wagon, his shoulder bumping his

satin pillow, his expression that of a cat with cream. "Ha. Thinking to im-
press me because he discovers the king gone to Quintas. Even now he must
wonder how much I have paid for my spies, and if he is getting value for
his coin. Close that curtain."

Bernardo leaned forward and pulled the wagon's curtain to, protecting Monsignor from an unwelcome invasion of sun. The confines of the
carriage were bothersomely close. Outside, the clop of hooves was as
steady and slow as a heartbeat. Wagons groaned, wheels squeaked. A narrow strip of radiance fell across Bernardo's lap, turning the sooty wool of
his habit to gold. He moved his fingers through the sunlight, feeling in his
pulse the warmth of glory.

A belch came from the opposite seat, and with it, "Take a letter."

Bernardo took up the writing plank and balanced it on his knees. He
plucked a quill from the box and set the ink pot in its hole. He opened the
red ledger. The carriage wheel struck a rut, jarring the ink pot, causing the
ledger to slide. Bernardo caught it before it could fall and quickly opened
to a loose page of foolscap.

" 'To my esteemed, illustrious Count Castelo Melhor.' Are you keeping up, Bernardo?"

"Yes." The carriage swayed around a corner. "Yes, thank you, Monsignor."

"So. 'Illustrious, et cetera, as you have been anxious for the fate of
our mutual friend, I may now write with glad'—wait, Bernardo. Let us say
hopeful. Yes. 'Glad and hopeful heart that, as I have now reached Quintas,
I find the heresy perhaps not so grievous as feared. Yet ever in the command of God, I remain to shoulder the burden. Look for me not in Lisbon
for at least a fortnight' . . . *Maledictus*. Strike that. 'Look for me not until
my task is done.' If I am granted a vacation, let it be without limits. Good
God, Bernardo. Don't take that part down."

"No, Monsignor." A rough patch of road made the ink pot dance in its
holder.

"So. 'Look for me not until my task is done.' I should add a small 'to
God's pleasure,' I think. 'Pray for us all' . . . No no no. Far too much melo-
drama. 'May God be with you and' . . . Wait. That could be misconstrued,

should—*salva me*—the note fall into the marquis's hands. And we must not get our boy's hopes sc high that he again turns headstrong. Better an insipid 'Yours in Christ.' Blah, blah, blah. Affix my signature. Tonight, Odivelas. Tomorrow, Quintas. As soon as we arrive there, charge one of the king's men with the delivery. Do not allow the marquis's soldiers, please, to see."

"Yes, Monsignor." He scrawled Monsignor's name, pressed the letters with a lamb's-wool blotter. The carriage squeaked and rocked.

"Is God not perfection, Bernardo?"

Bernardo's hand paused. He dared not look up. "Yes. Yes, Monsignor. He is." Actions slow and deliberate, he folded the thick paper thrice.

With a fingertip, Monsignor pulled the curtain back. In rushed a fanfare of sunlight, a smell of horses and dust. One soldier called to another, words overwhelmed by the ringing of harness and the low complaint of wood. "I tell you, this intervention is divine. What better to call us away at such a time than a little heresy."

From Monsignor's direction there sounded a meditative fart: brief noise, and lingering brimstone. "Graveyards and widows apart, Bernardo, let the nobles squabble among themselves. I will not have them running hither and thither, pulling at the Holy Office like a brat at his mother's skirts. The Church's place should be over the state, not part of it."

Bernardo put the letter in the box. He repacked the ink and the blotter and the writing plank. When he looked up, Monsignor was still staring out the window, his ruddy face cheerful with sun.

Bernardo asked, "Who will win, you think?"

"Um?"

"The rule of the country, Monsignor. Who will win?"

"Who always wins." Monsignor loosed the curtain and, disinterested, let it fall. "The Inquisition."

A MISERABLE "NO no no no no no." Black-frocked Father de Melo sat forward, plucking at Afonso's sleeve like a fat crow at a corpse.

"Now, please. Think carefully, sire. We cannot have the Galileo heresy followed by something like this. I beg you to consider what you say. I doubt that you mean—"

"God lives in the acorn." Beside him pressed, with a rustle of silk and the smell of vanilla, the warmth and heft of a body. Jandira put a hand on his arm. Afonso said, "Well, He might live elsewhere, too. I didn't ask Him."

Father held his head as if his brains threatened to leak from his ears. He whispered, *"Misericordia,"* then: "Please, Your Majesty. Let us not be swayed by the oddity of the moment. If you will stop to consider, you will realize that the earth remains forever stationary, and it is the sun which moves."

"But the cherubs told me not. Well, at least they showed me pretty pictures."

"If you will forgive me, I think perhaps not cherubs, sire."

"The soldiers gossip that the other priest said cherubs. I don't understand, father. When you saw the star before, you fell to your knees. If it was holy then, why can't it be holy now?"

Westering sun transmuted a side of the tent into stripes of fire and brass. Wind sang in the rope supports. Pollen drifted past the open door as if Heaven were misting gold.

"The star *fell,* Your Majesty. Do you not see? And—remember your lessons, now—what are the fallen angels?"

"But God was in the acorn, and He spoke to me in colors."

Father de Melo covered his eyes. His plump body wrung itself into a knot. *"Culpa Satanas est."* He peered out through spread fingers. "Sire. There are rules: no meetings with God without a proper intercessor, a saint preferably, an archangel, a pope, a priest, perhaps even Christ Himself— not to say that it is impossible, not at all. For Moses did, although one might consider the burning bush a sort of—"

Jandira said, "Who are you, Father de Melo, to naysay a king?"

"Goodness! Not particularly *naysay . . .*"

"I want the wine," Afonso said. "You must give me the wine now. It is Sunday, and past midday. You always read me from the Bible and then give me the bread and the wine."

"Yes, well, we've had our little reading, haven't we? And our homily, but I do not see how I can—"

Afonso slapped his thigh, not so hard that it would hurt, but hard enough to get father's attention. "It is important to receive the *Corpus Christi* every week. You taught me that. Every week without fail, for otherwise I cannot be a good and blessed king."

Father de Melo scratched his jaw until he raised a pink welt. "Ah. You recall that on Fridays before the midday meal we have the king's confession?"

"This time greed and gluttony." Afonso bounced in his chair, proud to remember. "I hoarded toys and ate too much chocolate. I lied to Castelo Melhor—"

"Exactly so! Venial sins. And had you died with a venial sin on your soul, you would go to . . . ?"

"I know! Purgatory!"

"Yes!" Father de Melo went limp with relief. "O, yes! Wonderful, Your Majesty! Purgatory! But now, what if you died in mortal sin?"

Afonso furrowed his brow and thought. "I would go to Hell?"

"Very, very good, sire! Yes, absolutely! You would go to Hell. Fire and brimstone and gnashing of teeth and wailing and no one to save you: Hell. And so, and so . . ." Father de Melo's amiable face became, by fits and starts, utterly woeful. "I feel there may be a grievous sin here, Your Majesty. I'm a bit unsure what it is as yet. Perhaps hubris. Do you know 'hubris,' sire? No? The sin of Lucifer? Very like the sin of pride, only much, much greater. And then, too, we have the Galileo heresy, although we shall not speak of heresy, as that is not my field of expertise. A simple parish priest, really, going about my duties best I can. But definitely, sire, without any doubt, the two taken together form some sort of dreadful mortal sin."

From the storehouse of his mind, Afonso brought out the memory of those colors and ran them through his fingers like jewels. "It's all right, father. Don't be afraid for me. God is too nice to send me to Hell. We understood each other because He sounded lonely, the way I get—and indeed all kings get—sometimes."

Father de Melo flung his gaze aloft. "Let us pray. . . ."

"But I want the *Corpus Christi*."

"Let us pray and then we shall see. Another confession, perhaps. An Act of Contrit—"

"You must give me the *Corpus Christi*." Afonso had never gone a Sunday without. How could he sleep tonight? How could he rule on the morrow?

Father de Melo's hands fluttered like startled birds. "Would you pray with me, sire? Please? O please? Clasp your hands, yes, clasp them thus. Say after me: *Veni, sanctificator, omnipotens, aeterne Deus . . .*"

Afonso bolted up, overturning his chair. His heart pounded as if it would escape his chest. If he could not have the *Corpus Christi,* he would be no king.

Father de Melo recoiled, flailing and gasping. He caught himself before his chair toppled, and scrambled to his feet.

"Say *Corpus Christi!*"

At Afonso's shout, three guards rushed in, swords drawn. They cast about for danger, found none.

"I order you!" Afonso said.

Father de Melo clutched the beads he wore at his side. His voice shook so, it was difficult to understand him. "O God help me, sire. For I cannot."

I T WAS A difficult subject to broach. Pessoa waited until day was done and they both had sat down to dinner and the blessing said. He watched Soares spear a slice of roast pork.

"Priests are not safe from the Inquisition, Luis."

Soares looked over the dancing candle at him.

"Even high-ranking clerics have been jailed, and worse. Yet here I am, faced with the arrival of the king, and you on your knees weeping and talking of cherubs. There were probably ten or more witnesses to your self-indulgent heresy."

The old Franciscan clapped his spoon to the table. "Then will you arrest me?"

"No, damn you. And how could you ask me such a question? You know that I care not whether you see God in those imps' eyes, or Vasco da Gama, or João de Avis, or even Lucifer himself, just please, please—can you not be more circumspect about it? You have a responsibility to your flock."

Soares shoveled food into his mouth and spoke furiously around it. "Quite right."

"What do you mean by that?"

"I meant that you are absolutely right, Manoel: you do not care, neither for your mission nor for faith. If you seek sin, look to the mote in thine own eye."

"*Maledictus!*" Pessoa shoved his plate away. Gravy slopped, fava beans spilled. "Who are you to judge me? You, who gave the Teixeira girl the sacrament? I warrant, if she confessed to murder, you should encourage her to go to the constables with it. If she did not—"

"Maria Elena is of my flock, and her confessions are none of your affair." He gestured with his spoon. Flecks of potato flew. "Besides, who are you to judge anyone? For I assume you beg forgiveness for your fornication, but I do not see how you can sincerely vow to sin with her no more."

Pessoa's cheeks went hot. "I need not justify myself to you. And all heresy *is* my affair. I tell you, Luis, it is difficult enough to contain this outbreak of lunacy. I need help, not maudlin superstition!"

A flurry of knocking at the door interrupted the argument. Soares threw his knife down with a clatter, then rose and went to answer.

A priest, plump and mild-expressioned as a pigeon, stood in the twilight. He was Augustinian by dress, and by manner, overwrought. He wrung his pale hands. "Father Inquisitor?" he asked Soares.

Soares pointed to the table. Pessoa said, "I am inquisitor for this district."

"O, dear! And here I bother you at dinner. . . ."

Soares murmured politely, "Not at all."

"Well, then. *Dominus tecum.*" The little Augustinian shifted his weight, scratched his ear, cleared his throat. "My name is Joachim de Melo, and for the past four years . . . No! Five! Yes, five years last autumn—O, forgive me. I digress. What I am trying to say is that I am the king's confessor."

"Yes?"

"Manoel, where are your manners?" Soares said. "Come in, Father de Melo. *Et con spiritus tuum.* Sit yourself. Have some dinner. I am Luis Soares. This is Manoel Pessoa."

The Augustinian came in timidly, head bobbing, eyes darting as if looking for assassins in the corners. "Bless you, but I've already eaten. Attached to the king's service, and the royal cooks feed me until I groan for mercy."

"Wine, then?" Soares asked.

A haunted flicker in his eyes. After a panicked hesitation, he said, "O! O, I see! O yes, thank you. I'll have a drop." The Augustinian clapped palm to breast and collapsed onto the bench next to Pessoa. Straightaway he drank the cup Soares offered and began downing another.

"Is this concerning the Galileo heresy?" Pessoa asked.

De Melo bobbled his cup. Wine sloshed, ran the joints of the table like royal purple blood.

Pessoa cast a forgiving, if condescending smile toward Soares. He would demonstrate what compassion was. "Have no fear, Father de Melo. If you tell me that the king recanted, that is enough. He need not recant personally to me. The king is certainly young, and thus outspoken—and, if you will permit me—seems to be of a somewhat simple mind. No. The inquiry will end in this room, and I will be glad to consider that the ill-conceived statement was never made."

Hand trembling, de Melo filled another cup. He drank, and searched Soares's face. "It was gossiped that . . . and I do hate to ask you so directly, but—cherubim?"

After a glare in Pessoa's direction, Soares shot to his feet and, with a furious busywork clatter, gathered his empty plate, Pessoa's full one.

"O, dear," de Melo murmured. "I am being too forward. I would not ask at all, Father Soares, but believe me the answer is very . . . well, I should say, vital."

Crimson fury climbed Soares's neck. Keeping his head lowered, he turned and took the plates to the soaking tub.

"Please." De Melo stared beseechingly at the old priest's back. "Are these creatures messengers from God?"

"No," Pessoa said.

With thumb and forefinger, de Melo massaged his eyes. "I find myself in a muddle, then. But there is no other remedy. I must pass the responsibility of the king's soul to you, Father Inquisitor. There is more heresy than what at first it seemed, for His Majesty has entered the fallen acorn and it seems—well, at least he seems to believe—that God spoke to him there."

AFONSO LAY CURLED in his bed, gloomy with fear. When the sun set, Jandira came and bathed his hands and face with rosewater. She sang a song that had no words. With her fingertips she brushed the hair from his forehead. She told him, as his mother often had, that he was a good boy.

"Please, Jandira. I don't want to go to Hell."

She shushed him and stroked his face. "No, my liege."

"God is in the acorn, and He spoke to me."

"I know."

"And I cannot help it if the cherubs told me things. I don't understand how Father de Melo can know that they didn't, if he was not there talking to the cherubs, too. Tell me truly, Jandira. Will I go to Hell for making Father de Melo so angry?"

"No, sire. For kings are never wrong."

But Afonso was no king. Kings were splendid and sat astride their horses like warriors. Kings were always certain of things. They busied themselves with grave decisions and affairs of state. Afonso had not known his father well, yet he was sure that his father was a real king. He remembered him clearly, and in all acorn colors: proud purple, gold, and regal blue.

"You shiver. Let me hold you as I used to do."

He made a place for her. She wrapped her arms about him, and they lay in the smell of roses, her heat against his back.

He put his palm to her. Strange, but just as he had thought: under the extravagance of robes her belly was swollen. He laughed. "Jandira! You get fat."

She kissed the nape of his neck. "No, sire. I ate a melon seed with milk, and now it grows inside me."

Fear cut him like a knife, a fear sharper than Hell's bludgeon. "You will not die?"

"Shhh. No. I bear a child."

"O."

He drowsed and thought of nursing babes with round melon heads and black seeds for eyes—eyes that told him stories. And when Jandira's body made him think of things that he should not, he told her to get down. When she went, she left his back sweated, his *pau* a little achy. He slipped his hand under the covers, and until he fell asleep, he held himself the way a girl would hold a favored doll.

PESSOA SAW THE gap of light around her door, so had time to prepare for dismay. He put his hand to the rusting lock, lost his courage, and knocked instead.

Footsteps inside. So she was not gone yet. Not safe. Berenice opened to him, pleasure and surprise lighting her face, then dread shadowing it.

"No," he said, offended. "I have not come to arrest you, no."

She stepped aside to let him in. The room was as it always was: nothing disturbed, nothing packed. A poor dinner sat on the table, his full purse beside it.

He breathed in the strawflower scent of her hair, the house's smells of thyme and rosemary. His concern for her was as potent as lust.

He turned away from her sight, her smell, so that words could come. "Listen to me carefully, Berenice. Just tonight I am told that the king is embroiled in a grievous heresy. Soon I will be caught between the crown and the Holy Office. I haven't the luxury of worrying for anyone else's sake. Go." And then Castanheda's words: "Take the money."

"No use."

He seized her slender arm hard enough to bruise. "Take the money! There is nothing for you here! Nothing but me, and I can offer you naught but a blessing. Get out. Go to Palestine. Be among your own people—"

"Jews?" She pulled free. "I am no Jew!"

At the sound of her rage, her burro became unsettled and trampled his straw.

"I don't know how to be Jew." She rubbed her arm where he had grasped her. "How do Jews act? How do they talk? What are their holy days, the prayers?"

"Surely you remember a little some—"

"I remember a book that was not the Bible. I remember that my father sometimes wore a tasseled stole. I remember that we hid things when visitors came." She gave a dry laugh. "Do you think that enough?"

She left him for the solitary place she had set at her table, and pushed her plate away.

He said to her back, "You could learn."

Facing the hearth flames, she said, "Find a Jew in all the kingdom, then. Have them teach me."

The fire smoked, pine-fragrant. Burning resin sizzled.

"I know all about Palestine, Manoel," she said, her tone as indifferent as a draft. "For when I was six, my parents went there. They left, and apprenticed me to a woman who spoke not a word but to tutor or chide. A woman who did not smile. And now that she is dead, I wonder if she mourned her Jewishness and grieved for being made Christian—if it was your church that turned her spirit wormwood. My Jewishness meant nothing to me, except that it took my parents away—that being Jew was more important to them than I was. I spent my whole childhood waiting for them to come back."

He came up behind her, near enough to touch that dark silken fall of hair. His fingers ached for it. "Anyplace, then. Another town, another name. Lose yourself in the kingdom. Come back in a few years when it is safe."

"Too many burnt," she said. "Portugal will never be safe."

Her hopelessness sparked in him a tinderbox of rage. "You think to control me, Berenice. But you will not. I tell you I will let myself be arrested before—"

"Manoel. You don't know me."

"Know you? I see through you like water. You are lonely. You feel you have no one, and here am I to grasp at, perhaps. And yet, sadly, I am forsworn. Now you think to revenge yourself—"

She lunged up from the bench. Prudent, he stepped back.

"So I am lonely? What but that useless meat between your legs ever told you that I needed you?"

"Well?" His rage foundered. "Well? Why else would you stay except to punish me by having me jail you? Else you cling to me, and cannot let go. You must learn to live for yourself, Berenice, not me."

She snatched up the purse and shoved it into his cassock pocket. Her touch was a dizzy surprise, like the taste of brandy. He caught her in his arms. She pushed him away.

Her words cut. "I do not stay for your sake. I would not risk myself for you." Then more words, ones that gouged to the bone. "My man of light bids me stay."

"Well." A log in the hearth charred through and fell in an avalanche of burnished cinders. "So. You would stay and die for a fantasy. Well. How excellent."

She walked away and poked at the flames. Although the room was warm, she took her shawl from a peg and wrapped herself in it, an embrace more reliable than his.

He sighed. "Berenice, don't give yourself up to delusion. I love you, you know that. I am sure that your parents loved you, too. They must have fled in mortal fear. And I'm sure they would have come back, had they been able. They most probably died."

Her shoulders heaved. He went to comfort her, but before he could get there, she turned, expression merry. "God bless, Manoel!" She laughed. "If I fall ill, do me the favor of not offering consolation."

With an angry wave of his arms, he retreated. "And . . . what? Better to heed a fantasy than sense? Why not drink wine and hyssop, then? Be all besotted by vision. Sainted Mary! Are you blind? Can you not see that we attract the notice of the Holy Office? The wrath of the Inquisition will soon strike here, and careful as I try to be, innocents will fall. And *you*. You do not dare to be brought before a tribunal. If you are asked, you do not know your catechism. You know nothing of sacraments or blessings. Why, I doubt your mouth has ever tasted the Host."

She snickered and held her sides.

"Stop laughing! I have seen such Inquisitions before. When it starts, Berenice, all of Quintas will accuse each other. They tolerate you, and only because of your healings. But I warrant that, as soon as it begins, you will be brought to answer accusations, and me sitting in judgment at the bench."

Watery-eyed from hilarity, she slapped his chest. "I absolve you."

"Stop!" He pulled her to him, and despite her struggles, he would not let her go. "You cannot do this to me." His fury changed, and he was kissing her, and she was no longer struggling. Then their mouths met, and her fingers were on his cassock buttons, and his hands were lifting her blouse.

She led him to her pallet. She put a blanket around them, and they lay together on her sweet woodruff-scented straw.

"Berenice," he whispered. "Berenice. Do not do this to me."

She put her fingers to his lips.

"Please," he said. "I fear that you will die, and I will not know what to do."

Her hand slid down face and chest, down stomach, down belly. The world shrank to the size of the room, shrank further until it was so small that she held it in her arms, then between her legs. And when they were coupled, and he had long ceased caring about resolutions, he heard her say, "Don't be afraid for my sake, Manoel. Dying was the best tenderness I've known."

Day 6

I T WAS NOT A THING WHICH COULD BE MADE EASIER BY ACCUSTOMATION; NOR a thing any officiousness could assuage. The armed guards made Pessoa no braver, lent him no company, made him no more secure. During his life, on how many stoops had he waited? On how many doors had he knocked?

Three magisterial raps of his knuckles and the door flew open. Senhora Teixeira stood there, the scowling cook behind.

Pessoa stared at a spot on Senhora Teixeira's forehead. "I come for Maria Elena." He knew without looking that her eyes would be fixed on the guards. He knew what expression her face would wear.

A chill breeze, herald of autumn, trumpeted through a dying jasmine's lattice. From a geranium, ruby petals dropped like spatters of blood.

She said, "You are a coward, Manoel Pessoa. Five armed guards and a priest to take a small wounded girl."

The wind blew, flapping the hem of his cassock. It harried a lock of gray hair free from her bun.

She craned her neck to look past him. "Cândido Torres! I see you there! Don't turn your face away. Are you so afraid of my daughter that you need four field-workers with swords to arrest her? Will you clap her in chains? For I warn you, she may turn and slay you all."

Pessoa heard a restless shuffling of feet behind him, and a nervous cough.

"Call out Maria Elena," Pessoa said.

Senhora Teixeira came at him so impetuously that only shock caused Pessoa to stand rooted, his nervous sweat turned to ice.

"Why my daughter, Manoel Inquisitor? Why not all of us? You know the names of those who have seen the signs, who have talked to the Virgin, who have slept with angels. Why, I myself saw them."

Cook clamped a warning hand on her arm.

"I would speak with Duarte," Pessoa said. "Go fetch me Duarte."

Eye to eye now, and Pessoa dared not waver. As she spoke she misted him with spittle. "Fetch him yourself, priest. See if you can wake him, befuddled as he is by drink. You will find him snoring hard by the hearth. If God is sweet, he will blow an ember onto his clothing. That would cure one affliction. I must be patient, I suppose, to see what God will make of you."

Pessoa looked to the cook. Her face was set; she held a wooden spoon like a club.

"Angels," Senhora Teixeira said. They were so close now that he could smell the juniper she wore in her pockets to banish the *gripe*. He could smell the sharp, rank scent of her; the fennel and onion on her breath. "Angels came into the house. And bright and terrible they were."

What deadly game did she play? "Dona Teixeira. I ask you: where is Maria Elena, your daughter?"

She leaned forward as if she meant to kiss him. "Maria Elena is within." Hot breath stirred the hair near his ear. "For men are like the angels. When the angels had their way with her, they left her downcast and ruined."

Cheek to dank cheek, her sweat-smell ascending like a vapor. He bent to her and whispered, "You have other children. Think what you do."

She stepped back. Her voice was loud. "I think more of my daughter than any man ever thought of woman. I vow before you and God and these witnesses that hers was a virgin conception, her womb quickened by angels. Will you not take me, too?"

A nod. A weary "Yes." He stood aside and ordered Cândido to treat her considerately. Then he said, "Will you not call out your daughter? Else the guards must go inside and bring her out. I think you do not want the other children to see."

Senhora Teixeira bade the cook fetch her. Maria Elena came, bruised face lowered. The maid begged them to wait. "Please! O, just a moment, father. A blanket!" The maid's hair was wild, her face hectic. She took a pile of folded blankets from the entranceway and put them in Maria Elena's trembling arms. "And cook packed food! A feast! Roast chicken and honey bread and potatoes and an apple torte. She put in a store of mint for digestion, and a supply of fennel for the breath. All manner of things, didn't you, cook?" The cook was sobbing too bitterly to answer, so the maid took the basket from the entry and placed it in Senhora Teixeira's hands.

"See that Ana does not kick her covers off at night," Senhora Teixeira told the maid. "And do not let that lout of a husband hit my Cláudio."

Cook and maid nodded, daubing at their faces with aprons. Safe in their houses, hidden by shadows and lace curtains, neighbors watched. Cândido's attention was fastened on a thrush singing in a persimmon tree. His four hired men stood in a fit of embarrassment, their gazes meeting, then bounding away.

She said, "And see that my Cláudio does not climb the fig tree nor throw stones at the geese. And before Ana goes to bed, always tell her the story of the man in the black hat. She likes that story."

Pessoa gently took Senhora Teixeira's arm. She looked at him, perplexed. He told her, "We must go now," for there was one more stoop to visit. One more door to knock.

She started down the road with him, but he soon felt a pull on his arm. She had stopped to look back. "See they do not forget me."

Pessoa let Cândido take her. One step. Another. The first few always the hardest. Then the weeping of the household became hushed by distance, and the gray cobbles began to look alike, and all the stoops the same. Pessoa walked, head down, hands clasping his breviary.

The two women were whispering. Prayers? The clank of swords and the muttering of men nearly drowned them out. The small processional rounded the next corner and the next.

Pessoa stopped at a white wall with a blue tile frieze which bore letters entwined like ivy: CASTANHEDA. He took a breath and clutched his breviary tight, then mounted the stairs. Before he could knock, the door flew open. Senhor Castanheda came out.

"Leave my sight."

Pessoa blundered back, holding the shield of his missal between them.

Castanheda was ill-shaven. His tunic was begrimed, his cheeks flushed. "You! Cândido Torres! You come as this devil's familiar?"

From the street came an apologetic "He just wants to talk to her. And she was the one who said the Virgin. Seems logical to me. Besides, jail's warm enough, and I put in clean straw. Chased the rats out. Imps seem to like it. Just a few questions, Guilherme, and then she can go home."

Castanheda's desperate, questioning eyes sought Pessoa's. Pessoa's bolted to the refuge of the man's forehead. "Bring Marta out, for she has questions to answer."

"But she is just a little girl."

At the base of Pessoa's throat throbbed the lunatic beat of his pulse. "Bring her out, Guilherme."

"Please." The man reached for Cândido, then put an empty beggar's hand toward Pessoa. "Have mercy, can't you? Please, can you not show mercy? She's only a little girl."

Acknowledged by silence, Castanheda let his arm drop.

Marta came to the door. She held a rosary in one hand, in the other she clutched a basket. She walked out, her father trying to stay her, and she eluding his embrace. Head up, she descended the stairs to the street, bid a good day to Maria Elena and her mother. She told Cândido that he looked well.

When Pessoa went to join them, Marta said, "I will be asked to abjure."

"We only seek the truth."

"I warn you, I will not forswear Our Lady. And I know she will not forsake me." Her words finished on a hesitant flutter, and she clutched her rosary tight.

It always ended thus: the same mounting of the stoop, the same knock, sometimes debate, but in the end the jurisdiction of fear. Pessoa might have consoled her, but lies had become moot. "Best you bring a change of clothes," he said, not without kindness. "And food, too—although the Holy Office will certainly feed you potatoes and turnips enough. Marta Teresa da Penha Castanheda, are you prepared?"

She nodded. They continued down the cobbled road, Castanheda bellowing her name and begging for Pessoa's mercy long after he was gone from sight.

"**B**EDBUGS."

Monsignor's voice roused a blear-eyed Bernardo from his nap. He blinked, confused by the mid-morning sleep, puzzled to find himself riding in a carriage. What was it that Monsignor had asked for?

"Lice." Monsignor looked out the window. "They might have been lice." He scratched one arm, then another.

The air in the carriage was hot; it stank of horse dung and sweat and dust. Bernardo squinted and tried to capture the magic of angels; but he was too tired, the sunlight through the window too bright, and the rhythm of the carriage too tedious.

"Fleas possibly," Monsignor said, scratching. "Some sort of vermin."

Bernardo wiped a palm over one eye, then the other. His mouth was stale; his skin greasy; his mind torpid.

"Cayenne in the bedclothes, the only remedy for rural travel, Bernardo. See to it before I retire tonight." Monsignor pulled open the curtain and called in a voice to wake the dead, "Ho! I need a man to ride to Quintas straightaway!"

In the window appeared a dun horse's side, a pantalooned thigh, a sword. "Sir?"

Monsignor scratched his chest through his robes. "Have you your letters, my son? For you must possess either a sharp mind, or you must be able to read."

"I read well enough."

"Good. Bernardo, take this down so he does not forget."

Shaking off the dregs of slumber, Bernardo reached for the writing plank. He fumbled for the ink pot and a trimmed quill.

"Not all day, Bernardo."

"No, Monsignor." From the stack of journal pages, he plucked a single piece of foolscap. "Yes, thank you, Monsignor. I'm ready."

"Cayenne. Plenty of it. Are you both listening?" Monsignor called through the window, "Hallo out there! Are you listening, my son? What's your name?"

"Alfredo Pires."

"Alfredo! Ride ahead and secure me lodgings. Better than the accommodations of last night." Monsignor clawed furiously at a shoulder. "Understand that I do not sleep in tents as the king chooses to do. And I have no love for infested inns. Perhaps the rectory, although I have little faith in country churches. So if the rectory is ill-appointed—do you understand 'ill-appointed,' my son? Ill-appointed, for example, would be the inn that you found us last night. Best a house. And, please, let us not accept the hospitality of a parishioner, unless of course, our host is substantially wealthy. Rent a house, and let the landlord know it is for the Church, then tweak either guilt or fear of God—I refuse to pay more than a pittance. But arrange for a decent house, mind; one with space enough for a rather large feather bed." Monsignor rubbed his neck raw. "Bernardo! Have you all that?"

"Yes, Monsignor."

"Hallo! You there outside! Hallo! I want you to inform the king's company of my arrival. . . . Ha, Bernardo! Would it not be fine to see the surprise on their faces? A little mystery. Yes, yes. Make them wonder how I knew their destination. You there! What was your name again?"

"Alfredo."

"Yes. Just so. You will inform the parish priest of my expected arrival.

Tell him he needn't overtire himself preparing some rustic welcome with pathetic choirs and flower-bearing children. And tell him, no, I do not need to celebrate a special Mass. A purely judicial trip—that's what brings me to Quintas. He is free to attend his parish business, and can simply pretend I am not there. And further, ah . . ."

Bernardo whispered, "Alfredo."

"Further," Monsignor called. "Tell the king's cook that he will be preparing meals for me. No doting parishioner's tiresome suppers, please. Let the parish priest dine on white beans and tripe. And God save me from the devout's frightening experiments with salted cod." Monsignor scratched the inside of a thigh, then reached for the paper. "Note."

A flourish of Bernardo's quill. Monsignor snatched the note, held it out the window. A gloved hand lowered to accept.

Monsignor tossed a *benedicto* out with it, and a "God speed, my son."

"Alfredo," the man said.

MARIA ELENA CAME to her prison cell with lowered head, holding her blankets tight. Marta walked the steps, her knuckles paling on her rosary. Pessoa watched Senhora Teixeira's eyes dart here and there, from the sunlit squares of the high windows to the lamplit reaches beyond. Then her gaze fastened on the creatures, and she halted.

"They will not hurt you," he said.

Stuporous, Maria Elena lifted her head. Blankets fell, rash fluttering suicides, to the floor below. She dashed headlong down the steps—heedless of Pessoa's staying hand, ignoring Cândido's shout and her mother's sharp warning.

She halted at the cell, clasping tight the bars. "Where is my baby?"

One creature turned to regard her. Then the other. Their eyes glinted like basins of dark water. They stood in a shaft of sunlight, in a square inferno of straw.

Maria Elena, her cheek swollen and purple, her lip torn, rested her forehead on the iron. One of the creatures came near her and put its skeletal fingers to her face. She leaned into the touch. "May I see my baby?"

"Those are nothing," Marta said.

The intense dark-eyed regard gave Pessoa pause. He studied the gentle dance of those thin fingers against Maria Elena's battered cheek.

"Maria, those are not angels," Marta said.

"They are the angels that I saw." Senhora Teixeira had discovered the limits of her courage. She guarded her daughter scrupulously, but only from her post at the bottom of the steps.

Tears glazed Maria Elena's face. Pessoa went to her, relieved beyond words that the creature retreated. He took out his handkerchief and dabbed at her eyes. "Come away, child."

"The angels that I saw were beautiful," Marta said. "All tall and white with wings. They had hair of gold and silver, and faces so perfect that it was hard to look. These things are not angels."

"Please, child." Pessoa bent to Maria Elena. "Come away."

From Marta, a snort of exasperation. "O, come away, Maria. Don't be a goose. And leave those things alone. Demons, most likely. They're certainly ugly enough."

With a great clank of iron, Cândido unlocked the cell opposite the creatures. He guided Senhora Teixeira inside. He motioned for Marta, and she came, sour-faced.

Pessoa gathered Maria Elena up with one arm, cradling her head on his shoulder. "Come."

A miracle: her ruined lip lifted into a radiant smile. "Father Pessoa? The angels told me my baby lives in Heaven."

He patted her cheek, but had not the light touch of the creatures. To his chagrin, she winced. "Forgive me." As the words emerged he knew that it was not present pain, but the future's, which wanted absolution.

AFONSO LEFT THE protests of the captain and Jandira's chidings to go inside the acorn. He walked to the silver room alone and bareheaded, hat in hand. There he begged forgiveness and asked to be saved from Hell, but God greeted him with such glad colors that forgiveness was pointless. This was grace—this sunlit yellow, this shimmer of tender green and grateful sapphire.

He sank to his knees and let the colors hold him the way his nanny had done. The colors smelled of her: the sour yellow and salt white of her skin, the orange of the cloves she chewed, the blue of her apron's lye soap.

From a flare of eager crimson, the question issued: *Can you mend me?*

Afonso was not worthy.

You can mend me.

And Afonso said, "Show me how."

Ropes of pink, threads of vermilion and ocher, a woven skein so complex that no eye could follow, that no hand could grasp. The colors became a road, and the road led to a city, and there he saw where God was torn. A rent in His side bled indigo and emerald, pouring out the cold hues of pain. Afonso wept for God then, for he felt His infinite agony, His vast and uncharted fear of Death. Afonso wept because he knew he had not the wit to mend Him.

The colors bore Afonso up in unrelenting tapestries, saying, "Here is this; this is such; that is my nature," things Afonso could not understand. And still God spoke, spoke until the colors were gone, and only the pain remained.

"I will stay with You always," Afonso promised. "I will come visit You every day until the rivers run dry, and the stars fall, for surely those things will happen if You die."

Afonso lay down on the silver floor and put his head on his folded hands. He closed his eyes and, since he was drowsy, asked if God would be kind enough to tell him a story.

And so God did—He told a tale of how stars are born in burning fogs, and how they die in coals. He told of stars birthed in violence, and stars which die in flashes that leave hungry things at their cores. God took him to a gray cool place where dark-eyed angels came and went. He showed him everything: the roundness of worlds, the attraction of moons.

God showed him all there was of Heaven, and Afonso was not afraid.

F ATHER DE MELO came to the door of the old inn. He arrived smiling, Pessoa's note conspicuously in hand. "You sent for me?"

Pessoa took hold of de Melo's sleeve and drew him inside, closing the door behind him, shutting out the cool breeze and the sun. De Melo let himself be led to the ornate dining table which Cândido, for a fee, had lent the Holy Office.

Pessoa avoided Soares's questioning look. Instead, he contemplated the table and pictured what they were about to hold there: a feast of judgment. His tone was overly curt when he ordered the Augustinian to sit.

"O, my!" De Melo's head bobbed up and down, quick as a chicken's. "Are we . . ."

Soares tapped a warning finger against his lip.

"We must keep our voices down." Pessoa paced the area where the accused would face their judgment. His scuffing raised airy wraiths of dust. "Father de Melo? You seem to be anxious for the king's sake."

With a chest-expanding breath and an "Ah," de Melo's eyes darted to Soares, then to the shuttered windows. The room was haunted by the smells of spilled wine and burned oak. "I am hoping, of course, that things—or perhaps I should say heresies, although I pray that His Majesty may be dissuaded. The good Lord knows I sadly lack the skill—which is why I came to you—and he truly is a sweet boy, Father Inquisitor, if you will permit me. He works very, very diligently, and takes to heart my lectures. . . ."

De Melo paused for breath, and Pessoa took advantage of the momentary quiet to tell him, "I swear to you on my soul that everything spoken here will stay inside these walls."

De Melo's hand arrested itself on his cheek, mid-scratch. "O. Well. That's . . . Well."

"So, promise made, how far would you be willing to go to save the king from the Inquisition?"

De Melo's hand hit the table with a thump.

Pessoa asked softly, "Would you lie?"

"Lie? I don't—not quite . . ."

"Bend the truth?"

A circular sort of nod. "Speaking hypothetically, of course, Father Inquisitor, and only in the most dire of . . . but given certain circumstances . . ."

"Then no more discussion, Luis. He can be trusted, I think. At least we have no choice. This will be my *consulta*. Right in this room."

"A *consulta*?" De Melo sat straighter. "*Da fé?* O, not for the king!"

From Soares there came a negligent wave and a "No."

Pessoa studied the charcoaled pegs in the wall where shelves had once stood. His eyes traced the sooted strokes of the planks' remains. "There are three women in the prison downstairs, Father de Melo. Because of your inopportune arrival, we must dispense judgment on them without delay. I warn you: this *consulta* is illicit, but I bear responsibility. The most punishment you can expect from the Holy Office is a sharp reprimand."

"Punishment? O, well, much as I would like . . . bless me! A *consulta*? A great deal of study required, as I understand. A law degree, have you?" he asked Pessoa, his spaniel eyes watery.

Soares sniffed, derisive. "Two."

"Well, then. Two law degrees, and—"

"We will interrogate the women," Pessoa said. "Luis will take notes. All I require of you is that you remain in your seat and stay awake. Afterward, I will talk to the king. In fact I will, Father de Melo, put the fear of God into His Highness—a picture lesson of Hell he shall never forget."

Pessoa fell silent. Singing. One of the women below was singing, and the clear sound was bright, and as keen as grief. He whispered, "Then it will be over." The notion of "over" was unblemished, too, and so powerful that, like alum, it constricted his throat. "And then I will continue my rounds. You will go back to Lisbon. Luis can care for the women. This place is spacious and clean enough. They can remain jailed a year or two. . . ." His voice trailed off, he imagining songbirds in stone cages. "Just a while— until all talk of angels and virgin births has ceased." When he was certain his expression was under control, Pessoa turned. "Two of them are young girls, Father de Melo. The third a doting mother. Prison is penance enough. And we shall entice those creatures into leaving. Let some other town receive them." He offered a wry, if forced, smile. "Some town not, I pray, in my district."

Soares trimmed the lantern. In its expanded glow, Pessoa could clearly see de Melo's pallor.

"Virgin births?" he asked.

"I call the girl's claim not heresy but insanity. Neither infant nor corpse has been found, so I will vow that she was never with child at all. She is the easiest case, really. For insane, she cannot be judged, and will be released from jail tonight."

"Ah. So. An inquisitional court, is it? I'm sure this is all very . . . O, I was going to say 'important,' but perhaps that falls a bit short. I'm not a man of words." He leaned to Soares. "Enough for the king's purposes. Every Sunday a simple—very simple—homily. But as to questions of doctrine . . ."

"*Salva me.*" Pessoa dug his fingers into his scalp and ran them roughshod through his hair. Who sang so enchantingly in the jail below? Marta? Maria Elena? Certainly not her mother, for living coarsened voice and soul. "I cannot do this alone. You both must help. No matter what you think of the Holy Office. No matter what you think personally of me. I have two young girls and a matron languishing in an ecclesiastical jail—"

Soares snorted. "Not my fault, Manoel, that you went so far."

"Had you stopped these angel stories in the first place, Luis, this would have never happened. I would choose my sins of commission over yours of apathy."

"Go ahead, Manoel. Decide what judgment God should lay down, then pray inform Him of your decision."

De Melo rose, hesitant. "Ah. Well, I see you have matters to discuss. I'll just—"

"Sit!" Pessoa snapped.

"Pôrra!" Soares threw a cup across the room, and it hit the wall with a crash, clattering to the tiles in pieces. He crossed himself, muttered a tight-lipped *"Mea culpa."*

De Melo sank as far as he was able into his straight-backed chair. The singer hushed, the thread of melody broken. Pessoa had been so suspended by it, he felt a jolt as time resumed.

"If you ask me heresy, Manoel," Soares said, "I would let them all go. For I don't see heresy, I see angels. I have looked into those creatures' eyes and seen God there."

Would she not sing again? "You and your flights of fancy. You have no discernment. Given free rein, Luis, you would see Christ in cats and the Virgin in puppies. You would find God in everything."

"We are priests. Should we not?"

"But a murder? And all the town's gossip? That potato field? What did you expect of me?"

De Melo clapped hand to cheek. "Murder?"

From Soares: *"You* say murder, Manoel."

The girl needed to sing, for silence would forever after seem barren. "Now I say insanity."

"Well, I say miracle."

"Fine! May you choke on magic." Pessoa strode the floor. "Let us say miracle, then, even though only logic can save the child. But take all the miracles, Luis. Say that angels lie with girls and beget children. Say that dragons stalk the land and cows fly. Now. The hour grows so late that even our mock interrogation will last well into the early morning. Let us call the first accused, shall we? And let us pretend to be civilized, and feign that we are stalwart warriors of the Church."

Soares sat, chin in hand, expression miserable. "Those creatures are angels, and you jail them. What will God think? They come to us helpless, and this is the way we take them in? Manoel, I see no heresy here. I see salvation. I see mercy. We have known each other six years, and I've never spoken so freely to anyone. But now I admit that, as God is infinitely forgiving, I have always been troubled by this entire concept."

"Heresy, Luis. Heresy is simple. Take the crown of thorns from off the crucified Christ, put a fool's cap atop Him. Peek under the Blessed Mother's skirts. . . ."

That jarred a scandalized titter from de Melo.

Then Pessoa noticed a golden stripe of sunlight down the wall. He whirled. The door of the inn was open, and an armed man was standing there, smirking.

"What would you see, father?" the man asked.

"Get out."

The man tucked a gloved thumb into his sword belt and propped a hip against the doorframe.

"I told you: get out," Pessoa said between clenched teeth. "Best be wary of me, my son. For I am an inquisitor for this district."

"You?" The man laughed. "An ass-lick Jesuit?" Catching sight of Soares and de Melo, he ducked his head in shame. "O. Sorry, fathers. And a good day to you both. Well, so. You have a heresy in Quintas, do you? And three women jailed?"

Pessoa said, "None of your affair."

"No. Not *my* affair. But I am sent by Monsignor Gomes, Inquisitor-General of Lisbon."

Pessoa heard a mutter from Soares—a prayer? Light-headed, he braced a hand on the table.

"The monsignor sends his regards. He bids you not disrupt your schedules for his sake. And he says he needs no ceremonies upon his arrival."

A mad humming pressured Pessoa's ears, and through that din he heard de Melo's querulous "Arrival?"

"Indeed, father," the man said. "I expect him sometime near dinner.

He was quite anxious to speak to the king concerning the theories of Galileo, and to see those fallen angels of yours."

THEY WERE WAITING outside the acorn just as he had left them, as if Time had caught the soldiers up in a breath and, when Afonso emerged, had gently let them out. Jandira came and put her arm through his. "You seem weary, sire."

He rubbed his eyes. "God made me sleep. He told me a story, and he showed me Heaven." He slipped his arm from hers. Alone, he walked down the hill, through the camp, and into his crimson-and-yellow tent. He sat down on the edge of his bed.

Her shadow fell across the tent's carpet. "Are you hungry, sire? The midday meal is long past, and you sequestered in the acorn."

He nodded, and her shadow went away.

She brought back a meal of rabbit and rice. With a golden spoon, he chased a broad leaf of basil through sauce.

Jandira's warm hand dropped to his knee. "What is it, my good liege?"

His chin quivered and would not stop. A tear escaped and rolled down his cheek. "We will all die."

"No, no, sweetling."

Suffering in violet, dread in amber. "We all die."

"No, love. Not for a long, long time."

When his grip loosened on the plate, Jandira gently took it from him and set it aside.

"I went on a quest, Jandira, but I was so stupid that I could not even find my brother, not even with a whole company of soldiers. I found God, and that was stupid, too. For the sun and moon are going to fall, and the seas turn to dust, and what good is that, when I had gone to save all Portugal and instead ruin the world?"

Jandira's voice, when he closed his eyes, was all hues of brown and saffron. "God does not punish you, sire. Despite what Father de Melo says."

"God talks to me in the acorn, Jandira."

"I know, sire. He talks to me, too. He whispers through the grass. He sings in streams. Priests are tone-deaf. They can't hear quiet voices like that."

She put her arms about his neck. He leaned his head on her breast, and let her rock him. "God is dying," he said. "And then the earth will die."

"Shhh. The God of the acorn becomes one with the earth, sire. Do you not see? He merely fell from Heaven where the priests put Him, to the place where He belongs."

"But He bruised himself when he fell, Jandira. And He hurts."

"Of course He does. Every seed cries when it bursts to seedling. The worm aches itself into butterfly. To make child turn adult, they cut my face. These are the truths that my mother's people taught me—it always hurts to become."

He hurt, too, all through his chest. He hurt as if he was supposed to be holding something, and yet found his arms empty. "God misses Heaven. I don't know how to make Him better."

"Let Him have His memories, sire. Don't think to cure Him of that." Her fingers traced his face. "It is like when you travel to some beautiful place; and when you come home, you are glad, but you think of the other place sometimes. I will tell you how things are, sweetling: true people walk upon the earth unshod." Jandira leaned him back into the pillows, and they lay curled together like a pair of cats. "True people are fed God through the soles of their feet. Monkeys cannot be as smart, because trees take in God at their roots, but forget him by their branches. So how can priests see God when they look to the sky? And here is the best kindness: since priests could not see Him, He came down, that's all. God came down to teach you of His nature, all you who wear shoes."

A FTERNOON ROCKED AND jolted into evening. Out the carriage window all was darkness but for solitary lamps in isolated farmhouses. While Monsignor ate a traveler's meal of cold roast lamb and pears, Bernardo looked into the glittering sky and counted a rosary of stars.

The carriage bumped to a stop. Monsignor poked his head out. "What?"

The driver called, "King's camp."

Bernardo looked out the other window to see a hillside of tents, their lamps lit, and each glowing like a deep-wicked candle. Around campfires, soldiers laughed and ate and scratched themselves. That confounded Bernardo—for them to see all that they had seen, and yet sense no lingering grandeur.

Monsignor rapped his walking stick on the wall by Bernardo's head. "Go on, driver!" The carriage lurched into motion. "I tell you, Bernardo, I'm far too travel-weary for obsequious bendings of knee and smiles— *salva me*. The smiles. Good to see you, Your Majesty. I pray Your Majesty has been well. And all the time that idiot boy looking past you, or up into the rafters, or into his own pants."

Bernardo sat up straighter. Down the road clustered warmly lit houses. The evening air smelled of moss and cookfires. He dug his fingernails into his palm to quell his excitement. Yet . . .

The coach's matched pair of bays walked at too slow a gait. He caught glimpses of town lights between turns of the dark hills. Quintas. The sky here should be different, the very earth should be changed.

Another jarring halt, and a voice called from out the night ahead. "Ho!" Bernardo looked out the other window and saw a rider with a lantern.

"Ho! Driver! Do you bear Monsignor Gomes?"

Monsignor leaned out the window. "Here!"

A snaffle jingled. Bernardo heard the leisurely clop of approaching hooves. "Alfredo Pires of the Marquis de Paredes's service come to greet you, and to say that all the tasks you gave me have been done."

"Yes, yes! As to lodgings?"

"Arranged, Monsignor. But more interesting news than that: as I arrive in Quintas, I discover a local inquisitor already there, finding heresy and jailing accused."

"And the cayenne, my son? You did remember the cayenne?"

Too long a hesitation; too curt of an "Arranged." Somewhere in Quintas a shopkeeper was bound to be roused. "Do you know the inquisitors from this district, Monsignor? This one, Pessoa, had already gathered a *consulta,* a strange one."

"Um." Monsignor raised an eyebrow at Bernardo.

Bernardo had already taken out the white ledger. He trimmed the carriage's lamp and flipped pages. "Father Manoel Pessoa . . ." The next notation stopped him: S.J. No. If Monsignor did not remember, the end of a long and tiring trip was not the time to tell him. "Degree in ecclesiastical law, University of Coimbra; degree in civil law, University of Evora. In service to God these"—Bernardo hastily subtracted dates—"eighteen years. Called to the Holy Office from his post as instructor of law at Evora, ah, nine years ago, and attached to the provincial inquisitorial tribunal at Mafra. Interesting. There is a notation here that he has chosen as his mission to ride circuit."

"Circuit?" Monsignor snorted. "Good God, is Mafra deranged? A circuit ride is money down a rabbit hole."

A note scribbled on the margin caught Bernardo by surprise. "And he travels year-round, it says. Even during harvest and planting and in winter."

Alfredo had ridden closer. He bent down to the window. "You neglected to say that he is Jesuit."

The only sign of displeasure was Monsignor's grunt.

"Would Monsignor care to see the strange creatures that were fallen?" Alfredo asked. "I can take you. They are just ahead here, in the jail."

"Imprisoned?" The word burst from Bernardo so abruptly and with such heartfelt dread that Monsignor blinked. "But Monsignor . . ." Bernardo clutched his rosary so tightly that the apex of the cross cut him. "No. They cannot have."

Monsignor waved his hand, shooing the protest away. "Really, Bernardo." Then he leaned out the window again. "And the lodgings?"

"In the jail, as I said."

"No, no, my son. *My* lodgings. You have obtained my lodgings, and they will be comfortable enough? You are certain?"

"Very adequate, Monsignor."

"Adequate."

Bernardo could scarcely restrain his panic. "Monsignor? Perhaps we should ride by the jail and examine the creatures, for if they are angels—"

That won him a lifted eyebrow and an admonishing series of *tsks*.

Alfredo was speaking again. "Your Honor, I know not if this is important, but I found them all together, meeting in secret, The Jesuit and the parish priest and the king's confessor. I heard some of what they planned, but not all. And they would not tell me the rest. Thinks himself above everybody, that Jesuit."

Monsignor sighed. "A house?"

"What?"

"My son, did you rent us a house?"

"O well, there was no house, sir. Only the inn. But it is quite warm and spacious and—"

Monsignor closed his eyes and muttered darkly, "Inn."

"I'll take you. It's really very nice." Alfredo, more subdued, called to the driver. The carriage lurched ahead.

Monsignor flipped open the basket and selected a sausage, a bite of cheese. "I tell you, Bernardo. It is a mark of the Holy Office's desperation that they would take a Jesuit. And, I must point out, he was given his post the year before I received mine. Not my fault they made a Jesuit into inquisitor. Suspect, the lot of them. On the verge of apostasy themselves. No wonder the provincial tribunal sent him off on a circuit-riding mission— undoubtedly praying that he would lose his way. Look where Jesuits have led us! Rome furious at their meddling; Portugal independent, yes, but with an idiot for a king. And a dearth of bishops in all of Portugal, that they die and Rome refuses to replace them."

Hunched in his robes, Bernardo shivered. Imprisoned angels. O fools. *Father, forgive them.*

All the time they rode, and even when they reached the inn and Bernardo was left alone with Monsignor's majestic dismay at the surroundings, he could think of naught else but bright winged beings, mild-tempered, and caged like doves. When Bernardo had lit the room's hearth fire, he said, "If you will permit me a speculation, Monsignor: perhaps it is because this inquisitor is Jesuit that he fails to understand."

Monsignor meditated upon the room's cheap pottery lamp. "Um?"

"For Jesuits are more bound by logic than others, and thus cannot imagine miracle. If I may be so forward, Monsignor, it is my opinion that if the mind is forever clamoring questions, it cannot hear the quiet whispers of the soul."

"Um." Monsignor pondered the straw bed. "Will he bring the cayenne soon, do you think?"

At the knock on the door, Monsignor said, "Good, good. I long for bed, but will not lie down with fleas."

Bernardo went to answer. A woman stood without—tall and haughty, almond-eyed and dusky-skinned. She reeked of vanilla, of exotic tropics and lust. "Monsignor," she said.

He gave her a glance through his lashes, and a shrewd smile. "A moment," he told her, and closed the door.

Monsignor's curiosity had been piqued. "Who?"

"That ginger-skinned slave who belongs to the king."

"*Misericordia.*" Those ruddy cheeks paled. "Have her in. Quickly, Bernardo! Quickly."

Bernardo opened the door. She entered, gaze too brazen, chin too high, stride too free. She gathered her silken robes and knelt at Monsignor's feet, kissing his hem.

"You should not have come." He pulled himself away and took a chair.

She sat, attentive as a hound, on the floor beside him. "No one saw me, Your Honor."

Bernardo discreetly looked away. "More news?" he heard Monsignor ask.

The husky answer: "Always news. Many messages. All scribed by my hand and fixed with the king's seal. Are you not pleased?"

"Bernardo, bring my purse."

Head lowered, he brought it, put it into Monsignor's hand. He watched the blunt fingers extract one gold coin, then hesitate and take out another.

She said, "But it is absolution, not money, that I require, Your Honor; for I have taken what you said to heart. It is hard for me to understand the catechism, seeing as I am only small part Portuguese and the greater part savage. But I have learned my prayers, and I say them every night."

The coins went back into the bag; the purse strings were tugged tight. Bernardo reached down, retrieved the bag, and took it away. At his back, he heard her say, "And I say the prayers with the king as well, but he talks of the movement of planets and of speaking with God. Still, you needn't worry for Portugal's sake, Your Honor, for I have him tell all to me, and no one else. I keep the king's secrets."

Monsignor sounded skeptical. "Um. And you wish nothing else?"

"Hear my confession," she said.

In the shadows of the corner, Bernardo could not help but turn. The two were looking at each other, her scrutiny far too intimate. He would have left then, but Monsignor sat forward in his chair, put his elbow on the rest and his head into his hand. She said, "Bless me, father, for I have sinned. It has been six months since my last confession."

Bernardo knew he should turn away. Amazement held him.

Monsignor's quiet, "A long time, my child."

A cold thrill ran Bernardo's spine when she touched Monsignor's arm. "But as I am informer for a great and noble cause, I cannot tell my sins to any other, even protected by the seal of the confessional. And, since my duty is to lie, and I cannot promise to end the lying, no one else could shrive me."

Monsignor gave a surprised grunt. "Well considered. Go ahead, child."

She rested her forehead against the arm of the chair and whispered, "Father, forgive me the sin of fornication, for I have lain with a man, although I was not willing."

Bernardo, himself sinning, looked to where the two were gathered in a lamp-fall of light, in the intimacy of confidences. He heard a muffled question from Monsignor, and then he heard her reply: "I bear the king's bastard."

PESSOA FOUND SOARES where he supposed he would find him. The old priest was kneeling in prayer by the jail's iron bars, before the silent creatures. His eyes were closed. His deft fingers ran the well-traveled road of his rosary.

"Luis?" he called softly.

From the dark beyond the stairs, Pessoa heard the women stir.

Soares raised his head and, blinking, looked around.

"It's late, Luis." He lifted his lamp. "See? I've come to take you to the rectory." Straw rustled. Marta Castanheda came forward into the circle of lamp glow by the bars. She was yawning.

Pessoa smiled at her. "Are you comfortable enough?"

"Um-hum." Her face was sleep-swollen.

"For you must tell me if you are not. Or if the others have any complaint. It is my duty to see that you are comfortable." And then he whispered, "Go back to sleep."

He sensed Soares standing at his shoulder. The Franciscan marked his prayer book and put it in his pocket.

Marta rubbed her eyes with her knuckles. "Those aren't pretty enough to be angels, father. Come bless me." She put her hand through the bars.

Soares knelt with her and took her hand in his own. "But, child, how can we judge Heaven's beauty, when Heaven to us is so foreign?"

"Pray with me," she said.

"*Ave Maria, gratia plena . . .*" Then her clear soprano joined in. "*Dominus tecum . . .*"

Pessoa looked up the stairs and saw Cândido's man staring down. He lifted the hem of his cassock and walked up to join the guard.

The man dipped his head. "Father. That monsignor sent two soldiers."

"Keep your voice down. I don't wish to frighten the women. Where?"
The man jerked his thumb. "Up there. In the inn—well, upstairs,
what's left of it. They just come, and them drinking and all. Don't know
that I like that."

Pessoa whispered, "What is your name?"

"José Domingo Rios, sir, ah, father."

"I will not have the women disturbed, if you understand my meaning. . . ."

José Domingo's eyes grew round. He crossed himself. "O no, father.
Never. I mean, if anything happened to the women, Senhor Torres would
flay me, ears first. O no, never you fret, sir—"

"Good. And whatever the creatures need, you are to get."

His head bobbed like a fish-struck cork. "The imps got plenty of blankets. And they took some water, sir, about half a jar full. And they liked
their bread well enough. They left the meat and wine, but I didn't touch it.
I won't touch no one's food or belongings, not me. But those soldiers up
there, sir? They're ruffian looking."

Pessoa walked around him and made his way to the head of the stairs.
The two brawny strangers, one mustachioed, the other bearded, had
cleared themselves a place near the ruined hearth. By the light of their
lamp, they were drinking and pitching coins.

"Why were you sent?" Pessoa asked.

The two smirked at each other. With a flick of the wrist, one man
tossed a *maravedis*. The coin hit the wall with a clink. Two gruff voices
raised: blistering curses from the loser; the winner's laugh.

"If you bother those women or my own guard, I will see you handed
over to the crown for hanging."

They looked at him then. The bearded one said, "Will you? Well, I
was soldier ten years, then jailer for Lisbon's Holy Office, in service to the
Marquis de Paredes and the Inquisition. I've been commissioned by the
crown. I have strangled seventy, and set over forty heretics afire. I know
the *potro,* and how to best put feet to the coals. There's nothing any fancy-
boy Jesuit can teach me about prisoners."

Pessoa imagined throwing the lantern in his face, and the desire was so keen, the vision so clear, that for an instant he was convinced that he had done it. Then he took a deep breath and mastered his fury. "Leave the women alone."

The man got to his feet.

An arm slipped through Pessoa's. He turned. Soares.

"Such a long day, Manoel! Goodness. I am made so weary that I stumble." A smile for the soldiers and a pleasant "Good evening to you, my sons."

The mustachioed man scrabbled to his feet. With two cheery "good evening, fathers," the pair bowed, all the time grinning like a pair of simpletons.

Soares blessed them, and they lowered their heads. "My. Such a responsibility—three frightened women in your care."

Before the "O, yes, fathers" were fully ended, Soares nudged Pessoa out the door. Once in the street, he dropped his arm.

The night smelled of coming autumn, coming rain. In the dark canyon of the street they walked, Soares's sandals flapping a lackluster rhythm. They went past a doorway scented by the astringent smell of geraniums.

Pessoa asked, "Why did they not flee?"

The flapping rhythm slowed.

Pessoa slowed with him. Soares was but a dimmer smudge among the shadows.

"I went beyond what was safe, Luis. Before they were yet arrested, I warned them to search their hearts. I told Castanheda the exact day and time that Marta was to be arrested. I warned Maria Elena's mother of what was to come. They had time to send their children to safety. No one would have pursued them. Why didn't they just go?"

From the gloom ahead came a kitten's questioning meow. Soares, either answering the need or out of habit, bent and clucked to it.

"So many years of the Spanish, Manoel. And they came but rarely." Kittenless, Soares stood and dusted his hands. "We had no Judiazers— none but yours, anyway, and she is survival-clever. O, there were stories of burnings in Lisbon and Evora and Braga, and you sent tailor Magalhães to Mafra for a trial and a *sanbenito*. But all in all, there was never an Inquisition here."

Stars blazed, a glorious ceiling, above the close corridor of the houses. Pessoa put his hands into his pockets. His fingertips touched his missal.

"And then you," Soares said. "Likable enough, and never pushing. Smiling and reading the Edicts as if they did not matter. Smiling at the congregation of a Sunday. You had too many smiles, Manoel."

Pessoa's heart lurched. Somewhere in a nearby alley the kitten mewed for its mother in a voice as poignant as song. Three women—none frightened enough to escape. Three women doomed because he had neglected his duty.

Day 7

B ERNARDO WOKE IN A PANICKED SWEAT, HIS COCK SPURTING, HIS TESTIcles still making their pleasure.

He thrashed out of the covers, bringing the dregs of impure dream with him, part of him wanting yet to linger, to touch, to impale. He hit the floor with both knees, the pain of his impact stunning, and was surprised to find that the floor was not stone but planks. The window was out of place, too, and the room too large. Then he remembered the inn and Quintas, and what he and Monsignor were to do there.

Quintas. So in the presence of angels, he had yielded to lechery. The succubus arrived smelling of vanilla, mouth ripe as a plum.

He rose and, hands shaking, searched the darkness for steel and flint. He lit a candle. He snatched his robe over his head, picked up the nightstand bowl, and poured its water down himself. The cold plundered his breath and left him gasping. His muscles knotted, his flesh chilblained. Judas cock shrank to a pale nub.

Hidden in his travel bag was a small carpet woven of stinging nettles and a handful of nails. Not for his knees; this time he must punish the offender. Bernardo put the carpet on the floor and lay belly-down, legs spread, grinding himself into it.

The nettles stung his groin in an ant-bite frenzy. He held a nail in each hand, the sharp point in the center of his palm, his middle finger pressing.

He thought of Psalms, but recoiled from its impassioned poetry. He thought of Judges and Ecclesiastes and quailed. Wisdom 3:1—yes, that one—God's promise to the righteous: *"Justorum animae in manu Dei sunt."*

In God's hands. God's hands. That mad stinging and the icy predawn air. He shivered so hard that bones threatened to wrench from joints. He felt exquisite pain at the center of each palm, and on the tender skin of his testicles was such an unbearable blistering agony that his lungs quaked and his eyes coursed tears.

In God's hands.

Between his legs, flesh charred and blackened skin peeled away to expose a body pink and renewed. God's grace covered him like a blanket. Bernardo lay, numbed by mercy, half drowsing, listening to the slow patter of his palms' blood against the floor.

Into the silence of the inn, he whispered the rest: *"Et non tanget illos tormentum malitiae."*

In God's hands. And a promise to the souls of the righteous, that no torment would ever touch them.

THE KNOCK CAME at breakfast. Pessoa looked up, alarmed, from his plate. Soares went to answer.

At the door stood nightmare. The Dominican was young and whippet-thin. Head lowered, he mumbled, *"Dominus tecum."*

"Et con spiritus tuum." Soares opened the door wider.

He ignored the welcome. "I bear a message from Monsignor Gomes, Inquisitor-General of Lisbon, who early this morning has gone to see the king and bids—"

"Where are your manners, Luis?" Pessoa bolted to his feet so quickly and with such desperation that the Dominican flinched. "Come in, my boy! We don't have much to offer, but a little something to fill the belly. And coffee, although I must warn you that Luis always burns it." As he approached, the young man's gaze fled his.

Doggedly chasing his attention, Pessoa bent. "I am Manoel Pessoa, one of the inquisitors for this district. And you are . . . ?"

From those tight lips came a faint whisper. "Bernardo Andrade, Monsignor's secretary."

"Bernardo! Well! Young for so important a mission. Twenty? Twenty-one?"

Such a low, moody "Twenty-three" issued from the boy that Pessoa despaired of even desultory talk, much less a harvest of information.

"Young indeed, and yet I am reminded that you are but three years younger than our beloved Count Castelo Melhor, whose burdens are so weighty. Well. And I imagine that you have not eaten. Such a long trip, and so much to do." He grabbed the boy's sleeve before he could shuffle a retreat. "You must have coffee. Sugar? Honey? Milk?"

The boy gave a quick suspicious glance, a shake of his head.

"Plain, then. Luis!"

Soares was standing spellbound. At the sound of his name, he turned to hearth and kettle.

Pessoa clapped the boy on the back, ushering him across the room and into a chair. "So. Imagine this. All in one week Quintas receives a king and an inquisitor-general. Will you be staying long?"

Bernardo sat and contemplated his folded hands. "Monsignor Gomes bids you meet with him at the seventeenth hour today, in the place the prisoners are jailed."

He was a boy of few words and less humor. A sad boy, one of a steep-walled and moated nature.

"Your coffee." Soares put the cup on the table.

With a spare restrained motion, Bernardo reached for it. Pessoa caught sight of the boy's palm, and his pulse leapt. "Bread!" Pessoa's cry startled both priests. He went to the sideboard for the loaf. "A rough sort of bread, to be sure, Bernardo, but an honest one."

Smiling, he held out the remains of the loaf, saw the boy look warily through his lashes. Then the left hand opened to accept, and Pessoa caught glimpse of a second raw wound. Not accident, then; but key to a stronghold.

Bernardo gathered his food and drink and sat hunched.

Pessoa sat down opposite. "It is my belief that too much soft bread softens the soul. One should work for things, even bread, as one works for salvation."

From the left, Soares's frank bewilderment; but from the boy an instant in which their eyes met, a moment of clear blue orbs and breath-catching candor.

"I remember when I was your age, and every day seemed filled to bursting with God. Does it you? Each sunrise was a miracle, each leaf a blessing. How I do envy you that."

Through that brief azure gaze wafted a question. *Ask it. Damn you, ask it.* The boy was distracted as Soares went to refill his cup, but then Pessoa saw a second flicker of interest, and, "What made you change?"

"The Jesuits."

He had the boy's attention now. Fingers moved along the cup as if counting beads.

"They gave me so much, my son, and yet their training robbed me of wonder."

An earnest little nod. "Yes. It is difficult to capture, and easy to lose."

It was just the two of them now: that zealous regard, and Soares faded into background. Pessoa leaned close. "Yet I remember when I was younger, and that grace would come over me—"

"Like a great sea of light," Bernardo said in his timid voice.

"Yes, just so. Yes. Like a sea. And I was blinded by it and felled by it and swept away, like a current. It drew me."

"You drown."

Pessoa was struck by the intensity of the boy's stillness, muscles and tendons taut as harp strings—a small body that could never be at rest.

"O yes, my son. Indeed. Drowned in splendor. Transformed by holy pain. My lungs exploded with light. They turned my skin outward, soul first, so that I became a new creature. And when the thing was over I was left shaking and wearied, fearful of God, yet aching for Him again. I know not quite how to describe it. . . ."

"O, but you do. You take wonder and put it into words."

Pessoa seized him by the wrist. "Let no one steal God from you. Let no one leave you jaded with reason."

A quick shake of the head. Who had taught the boy such frugal gestures? Such punishing joys?

Pessoa let go the boy's wrist and stumbled up hastily, wiping his eyes. On his back he could feel the heat of Bernardo's curiosity and the quiet cool of Soares's. Pessoa put another log on the hearth, poked at the fire, and wiped his eyes again.

Say it.

He could hear breathing: Soares's was measured, the boy's quick.

Then: "We have had news of a happening here."

Pessoa filled his lungs with the smell of burning hardwood, the stench of Luis's scalded coffee.

"Is it not true?"

Pessoa said, irate, "I will not gossip about the king, my son, or any other man. That is not my—"

"No, father. I meant what fell from the sky."

One more stab at the fire drew sparks from a log and opened in it a flaming wound.

A small shy voice came from behind him. "Are they not angels?"

Pessoa turned. The boy's eyes were wide and wet with yearning. "Yes," he told him. "Angels."

OVER BREAKFAST, FATHER de Melo made a great to-do. "Remember to bend your knee to Monsignor so that you may have his blessing," he reminded Afonso. "A little humility, particularly toward important clerics, is a handsome trait in a king—besides, you will need every jot of Monsignor's goodwill. Mind you, it's best that you do not speak until asked. We want no unpleasant topics raised. And heed closely what he tells you. Even if you do not understand, nod and nod and nod and I will explain later."

Even though he did not understand, Afonso nodded. He looked into the basket, chose a roll filled with jam.

"And please, please, sire. Be polite, and let us always remember that even if you are made anxious, or even if you must use the chamber pot—do not, I pray you, touch yourself in the shameful place."

Jandira wiped jam from Afonso's mouth.

At the noise of an arriving carriage, Father de Melo leapt to his feet. "Here already! O, O dear, he is come. Now, think on what I told you, sire. Do you remember at least some of it?"

Afonso did not, and so he nodded.

"Up! Up! We must go to greet him, mustn't we. And if you would be so kind as to put your roll down, Your Majesty? Good. And smile, yes, just so. Excellent, sire."

Afonso walked outside. He saw the fat priest with the small pig eyes, and remembered that he did not like him. Still, when the priest approached, Afonso went to one knee and let him say the *Patrii* and *Spiritus Sancti*.

Then he got up and dusted his knee. "Would you like breakfast?" he asked.

At the priest's, "Why yes. Thank you, sire," Father de Melo called for the royal cook, who asked for the fat priest's pleasure. From those pink lips came such a list that cook sent for quill and ink.

When the list of food was finished, Afonso said, "I cannot remember your name."

The fat priest tipped his head. His jowls shook so amazingly that Afonso barely heeded when he said, "Monsignor Gomes, Your Majesty."

Afonso turned back to his tent. "I want my roll," he said.

Priests and soldiers followed. Afonso sat down on his inlaid mother-of-pearl chair and, mindful of his manners, did not eat until the monsignor had sat down, too.

"You are well, I hope?" He plucked a sweet roll from Afonso's basket and spread onto it a great golden nugget of butter.

Afonso said, "Yes."

"Um." A nod was soon followed by two more. Had he said something that the monsignor did not understand? "Very good, sire."

"The rolls are very good," Afonso said.

The monsignor looked at him from under his brows. He stuffed so much bread into his mouth that Afonso thought he might choke. Afonso could not hold himself the way he wanted to, yet he was too anxious to sit. And so he tugged at the hem of his tunic. He fidgeted in his chair. He watched the monsignor swallow another bread whole.

"The miracle of the loaves," Afonso said.

The monsignor halted mid-chew. Behind the monsignor, Father de Melo covered his eyes. His mouth moved silently and fast.

"Beg pardon, sire?"

"You. How you eat, in one huge bite. Is that not a miracle?"

The monsignor sat back and did not answer. Cook brought him sausages and cheese, and still he did not answer. He ate. Afonso waited.

Then the monsignor said, "Do you agree, sire, that the sword should not brandish the soldier?"

It was such a funny notion that Afonso laughed.

"No, sire? Then should the butter churn the milkmaid, or the hammer swing the carpenter?"

Afonso laughed until his sides ached, and was confused as to why the fat monsignor did not join him.

"Then, as all tools serve their masters, so the sun goes round the earth."

Afonso, overcome by laughter, looked up into the heights of the tent.

"Even Galileo Galilei himself, Your Highness, saw the error of his logic in time to save his soul."

Sun climbed the pole supports. Through the painted canvas came filtered a scattering of brilliance. "Fog has weight," he said, for that was what the acorn had taught him.

"Sire?"

"I don't know how, but it comes together in Heaven, the fog, and is set aflame." He tugged at his tunic. He looked at the sun with one eye, then the other. "That is what the sun is—just burning fog."

There came a great rumble of throat clearing, then: "Interesting theory, Your Majesty, but—"

"And I do not know why the earth and the moon and the other planets did not join the sun's fog, but God tells me that they were spread too far out, and were not large enough—although one of them came near. Anyway, instead of becoming hot and fiery, they became thick and cold. That's all."

"Sire?"

"That's all there is to sun and earth."

"Your Majesty, God created Heaven and earth in six days. The Bible does not teach of fog."

Afonso rocked and blinked. The sun dazzled him. "The fog spun, and so the sun spins, too, although we don't see it. That's what makes things go round—the planets remember being fog."

After a while he lowered his eyes and rubbed them. When he was no longer sun-blinded, he saw that everyone was staring.

Father de Melo emitted a lunatic squeal. "O! His Highness makes a joke! Very good, Your Majesty. Amusing stories of fogs and spinnings."

Cook and soldiers laughed, then fell silent. Everyone waited.

The monsignor belched. He brushed crumbs from his robes and stood. Afonso, mindful of his manners, stood up with him.

"By the time I return tomorrow, I would suggest that His Majesty achieve a more solemn turn of mind. The Inquisition is not fond of jests, if Your Majesty gets my meaning."

Afonso did not. He nodded.

FATHER MANOEL ASKED Bernardo to pray with him before they went to see the angels. They left Father Soares and walked together to the church, heads lowered, hands clasped on their missals. The company was fitting, just the two of them; for at the seventeenth hour there would be noise and bureaucratic mandates. Father Manoel told Bernardo that if he waited to see the angels, wonder would be broken. And Father Manoel, more than any other priest Bernardo had known, cherished wonder. They trod the narrow streets, and unlike Monsignor, the Jesuit did not taint the silence with words.

At the church they lit candles. They knelt before the altar. Father Manoel unobtrusively left his side. When Bernardo's prayer was ended, he searched for the Jesuit and found him prostrated on a niche's stone floor.

He waited until the father's prayer was done, then they walked past the confessional to the nave. At the door, Father Manoel put out a hand to stay him.

"Do not be disappointed, my son. They are not what you imagine."

Bernardo felt the Jesuit's gaze on him. "I dare to imagine nothing, father."

"They are not beautiful, nor do they speak."

He lifted his head and in the dim light of the nave saw beauty in Father Manoel's face—the sort of beauty which could only be bought with sorrow.

"Bernardo, I must confess to you—they speak only to those of pure heart, and so they do not speak to me."

"O, but—"

"Luis speaks with them. I know that from their own lips came the command to put them in prison, for they wished to share the arrested women's pain. And they will not be freed until the women, too, are let go."

"We must free them all!"

"Shhh. I can't, for the women speak of angels, and you understand, Bernardo—that we have odd beings, surely, but no proof of miracle."

"But—"

"The angels will not help themselves. They will not converse, except through their eyes, and few can interpret. I know prison hurts them. Their fall to us nearly outdid them. It seems that one has died from his pain. This may sound overly ardent, but so few understand that glorious sort of anguish—not a destructiveness, you see? But such a fearless transforming agony that it flings open the windows of spirit."

"Yes! I know of it!"

"Do you? Excellent. For I know of it, too. And that, Bernardo, is the pain in which these angels live. Their souls still blaze from Heaven."

"Yes. Yes. I've never dared speak of it before—but, father, I myself have felt such pain."

Father Manoel seized his wrist, and Bernardo could feel faith surge through him. The shock nearly sent him to his knees. "The Inquisition's guards stand just inside. It is best that we not appear friendly. We must pretend that I have merely come to show you the prisoners. No one must know what was said between us. I put my life in your hands. Swear you will tell no one, Bernardo." He hissed, "Swear."

Bernardo crossed himself. "I swear."

"Then come." Father Manoel pulled him through the door. Once outside, he dropped his arm. Together they walked to the place where the tribulation was to be held.

The Marquis de Paredes's men eyed them as they entered. Bernardo dipped his head in greeting as they passed.

He and Father Manoel arrived at the stairs which led to jail—which led to miracle—and on the first step, Bernardo lost courage. He became light-headed and faint. *O Jesu dulcis.* So long a trip—an entire lifetime— but at the end of it, a wise man and angels.

His eyes filled with gratitude. The air below seemed glazed with light. But just this morning he had been guilty of terrible sin. It was too soon. He could not yet be cleansed. Bernardo groped for the wall, and encountered Father Manoel's hand.

"Come," the Jesuit whispered. "Come see the wonder. Angels below . . . *beata Seraphim . . .*"

Bernardo quoted the rest. "*. . . exsultatione concelebrant.*"

Father Manoel led him, blinded by awe, down one step, then another, saying, *"Osanna in excelsis."*

Bernardo shivered and could not stop. He felt Father Manoel's arm about his shoulders. His feet fumbled for treads. *"Osanna,"* he breathed.

"Look!" The Jesuit's voice was as commanding as God's.

Bernardo wiped his eyes. First he saw only a smear of sunlight; then he blinked and the room below resolved into form and shape, brilliance and shadow. In the straw beneath, a pair of cherubs stood beside their fallen brother. They looked up, those two ancient children, and their black flat gazes acquired depth. There, inside those eyes, he found it. Peace washed him—the profound comfort of "Fear nots."

He did not know that his legs had failed until Father Manoel caught him. Bernardo sat on the steps, able to go no farther, able to see naught else. When the quiver in his belly began, he thought it was a quake of weeping; but it climbed his throat as mirth.

He heard a guard's query from above. "Anything amiss?"

And Father Manoel's answer. "He slipped, but I believe he is not hurt."

Bernardo held his sides and laughed as he had not since childhood, laughed until his lungs were empty and his insides trembled and his eyes ran tears. Divine merriment rang in his head. And in the end, it purged him.

Pessoa returned to the rectory just past midday to find Soares seated at table. On its top sat an open missal, a Bible, and a bowl of figs above which circled an indolent quartet of flies. Soares shooed them just as indolently. His focus was inward, his brow grooved by thought. The fingers of his right hand and the places he had touched on his right cheek, were ink-stained.

Checking to see that he did not shut out Soares's light, Pessoa closed the rectory door. "Wrestling with the Sunday sermon?"

Soares put his quill down, plucked a fig from the bowl, and peeled it. "Twenty-third Sunday, Ordinary. The homily of the Watchman."

"Um." Pessoa poured himself a mug of wine, then sat at the table with his head in his hands, wearied by the morning's passions.

Around him flies buzzed. He heard the dry scrape of quill against page and Soares's "If you love your brother, you will correct him."

"Um." Pessoa was uncommonly weary, so exhausted that his eyes refused focus, that his mind resisted thought.

Pessoa sat back, thinking of the young Dominican's wounds. He noticed the wrinkled skin at his own thumb, the knotted blue veins of his hands. When had old age come on him? He thought he remembered that only the year before his hands had looked strong, his skin sun-browned. He recognized what browned him now, for he knew a liver spot by sight. It was simply difficult to recognize the speckle on himself.

" 'I have appointed you Watchman for the house of Israel.' " Soares had stopped writing, and was watching him. " 'I have appointed *you*.' "

Pessoa wasn't sure what was meant. "Ezekiel?"

"First reading, twenty-third Sunday, Year A. 'If you do not speak out to dissuade the wicked from his way, he shall die for his guilt. And I will hold you responsible.' "

"Well, Luis, I am trying to dissuade him. Did you see the stigmata that poor boy had made on himself? He hid it very cunningly, but . . ."

"I saw. I also saw how he is wrapped up in himself."

"Good God. The boy's a damnable mystic. Forgive him, please, his self-absorption. I imagine even your beloved Teresa d'Avila bore little interest in the world. And did you note how suspicious the boy was? Comes of working with Gomes, I warrant. For I have heard stories, I tell you. Hah. Just think on it. What an odd pairing. A burgeoning mystic with a blustering political fool."

"Ai, but you are thickheaded!" Soares clapped his missal closed. "I meant that I must dissuade you."

Pessoa stared at the old Franciscan's gnarled fingers, the smattering of dun spots. How long did he have before his hands were like that? "You can't dissuade me. I have finally gained his trust."

"And that is the sin of it, Manoel: that he has come to admire you. When you began your game this morning, I kept silent. But don't you see? I must try to stop you now, or I imperil my own soul."

Pessoa stiffened. "No. Listen to me. I can pry the boy's loyalty away from Gomes. I know I can. We have been given a weapon with which to defend those women and your beloved creatures. You're a compassionate man—God knows you are far more compassionate than I. You want no one to suffer."

Soares crossed his arms and studied the table. The rectory smelled of the cats' spilt milk and Soares's figs. But for the drowsy hum of the flies, it was quiet. A sparrow alit on the windowsill, pecking for crumbs. Pessoa met its darting glance.

Soares crossed himself, startling the sparrow into flight. "You tempt me." He shook his head and heaved a sigh. "All right. But understand that I cannot join in your lies."

"I alone will bear the responsibility."

"O Manoel." Soares was grim-faced. "God will not let you."

"**N**OW, WHAT ARE we to say, Your Majesty?" Father de Melo's brow was so salted with sweat that in the late-morning sun, he sparkled. Afonso turned his head this way and that to catch his rainbows.

"Tomorrow . . . ?" Father de Melo sat forward. The rainbows extinguished as he exited the light and entered the tent's shade. "Sire. Please pay attention. When Monsignor Gomes returns tomorrow, what are we to say?"

"That we are sorry."

"Very good, Your Highness. And?"

Afonso twisted in his chair. He looked to the pole supports. The sun was higher now. "What o'clock is it?" he asked.

"Sire? Please? What else are we to say? The matter of the earth and the sun?"

Afonso kicked the table again and again, kicked it until the crystal butter dish danced on its golden base.

Jandira touched his arm. "Tell the father, sire."

He stuck his lip out. He kicked the table.

"Remember what we spoke of?" Father de Melo grabbed Afonso's knee and stilled it. "Sire? Remember that? You were shown a vision—and I firmly believe that you believe you saw it, sire—but perhaps you misinterpreted. That could be. After all, you are not a saint—O, a very, very good boy to be sure, Your Highness, although not mentally strong for—"

"He is fat," Afonso said.

Father de Melo sucked in a quick breath. His eyes were wide and still. "Sire, perhaps it's best not to confront Monsignor Gomes again with such—"

"I want to go back in the acorn now. I promised God that I would visit each and every day. He is waiting for me."

"Hell, Your Majesty. May we talk about Hell?"

"No. And I don't know why I should tell that fat priest that I am sorry. He has a face like a pig. He brings me no presents. He eats all my food."

Father de Melo squeezed Afonso's knee so hard that it hurt. "Think of Hell, sire! Eternal damnation? Pain? Lakes of fire and never-ending sorrow, and—remember?—in Hell there will be no cooling plantain to wrap your wounds. May we just take a quiet moment here, sire, to imagine everlasting agony?"

"I want to talk about something else." Distressed, Afonso held himself between his legs.

"Sire? If you just tell the monsignor that you are sorry and that you were mistaken, you can have the *Corpus Christi*. Wouldn't that be nice?"

"I don't need the *Corpus Christi* anymore."

Father de Melo closed his eyes and clapped his hands to his cheeks. He rocked back and forth until he nearly made Afonso reel. "Say after me, sire: *Misereatur tui omnipotens Deus, et dismissis peccatis—*"

"No," Afonso said.

"Not no!" Father de Melo's cheeks mottled with color. "Never no, sire! I will accept your willfulness, but God will not. I know of no other way to say this, Your Majesty, but time has come. You must recant now lest your soul be lost forever. The whole kingdom would be lost, too, don't you see? Dire events. God turning his face away. Plagues—you know of plagues, Your Highness? Corpses rotting in the streets, ravens feasting on eyes? Or, or other calamities, ah . . . great tempests! Yes! Rains of frogs and snakes and such. Many, many bad things. So. You have a duty to your people, Your Highness. Besides, even if God does not send disaster, your people may follow your lead. They would, like you, reject God's word. Think of it! A whole kingdom damned to Hell, just like the English and the Saxony Germans."

"I can tell them." Afonso held himself and rocked. He wanted to go back into the acorn. He wanted to ask God how He was, and if He still hurt, and if He knew that it was not Death that was about to greet Him, but change. God would like to know that. "I will tell them that they needn't worry. That God is sweet. That there isn't any Hell or flames or the like."

Father de Melo seemed unable to catch his breath.

Then Jandira said, "A temporary lunacy, father. That is all." She tugged Afonso's hand loose from its moorings. He struggled and whimpered, but she would not let go. "Listen to me, sire. Listen! You must tell no one of what you learned in the acorn. See how stricken poor father looks? Pay attention! Don't look at the wall. Now listen close and I will tell you a great truth: these things God tells you are meant to be secrets. For you are a king, and worthy of God's instruction. The common people cannot receive God so directly. It would send them into the streets screaming and maddened."

He looked at the carpet: the green wool trees and red velvet apples and white satin birds.

"It is a great responsibility that God has given you, sire, to keep His secrets."

Afonso nodded. "I will go into the acorn now. God and I have much to talk about."

From beside him came Father de Melo's persecuted sigh.

Jandira said, "Shall I walk you part of the way, then?"

He nodded, and she took him by the hand. They went over the hill together. "Tomorrow you will apologize to the fat priest, sire."

He didn't want to.

She tugged on his fingers. "And you will tell him lies, all about the sun turning about the earth, and the world in six days."

Just over the lip of the hill, just within the sight of God, he halted. "But it is wrong to lie."

"Is it, sweetling? Who tells you that?"

"Father de Melo."

"And when Father de Melo says that the sun goes around the earth, is he right?"

Afonso rolled his head back and forth on his shoulders until his neck pinched. "No."

"Always beware of priests, sire. When the Jesuits came to my mother's people, they promised happiness, but gave the pox. And when I was orphaned and my mother's people dead, the Jesuits stole me from the forest. They put shoes on me, and took God away. They taught me that knowledge is good, but when I did not learn their lessons fast enough, they beat me. They preached of peace, yet made Brazil pay gold for Portugal's revolution. So I ask you—who is lying, then?"

M ONSIGNOR WAS ALREADY at the inn when Bernardo returned. "Where were you?" he demanded.

Bernardo dropped his eyes. From the other side of the room came a magnificent basso profundo belch, and at the end of it, a "Well?"

"I had to deliver your message, Monsignor."

"Three hours? Did you crawl to the rectory on your hands and knees? Ah. Thinking on it, Bernardo, I would not put that excess of enthusiasm past you."

Three hours? Had he been so long? It seemed that he had looked upon angels for a heartbeat. And what could he say that was neither outright lie nor dangerous truth? Bernardo sweated so, he was afraid it would cause Monsignor to wonder. "I went to the prison." His admission was met by grim silence. He floundered on. "It seems clean enough, Monsignor, and the prisoners well cared for."

"The women?"

Women? Bernardo did not understand. His throat tightened. His heart flew into a commotion. "I'm sorry?"

Another thunderous belch and a bird-tweet of a fart. "Damn the king's sausages! He likes them with an excess of garlic and a sprinkle of—if you will believe it, Bernardo—cardamom. He speaks of the sun as a burning fog, and will not abjure the Galileo heresy. I can choose to ignore it, of course, depending on outcomes. But the women, Bernardo? I've heard today of the women and their lunacy of Mary visions and angels."

"Sorry, Monsignor. Yes." His words came breathy, and rapid as the ninth repetition of a novena. "Yes, the women are well. Did you wish to hear news of the angels?"

"Good God, why? In the highly unlikely event that they are angels, our stupidities cannot harm them. And if not angels, they would do me the favor to disappear. I tell you, Bernardo, I asked the king three times to abjure. The idiot boy finds his spine at last, and for the most hazardous of causes. And how do you find the Jesuit?"

The question was bland, completely without guile, yet it robbed Bernardo's knees so of their stiffness that he had to sit down. "The Jesuit?"

"*The* Jesuit, Bernardo! The Jesuit! *Salva me!* We are not overrun with Jesuits. The district's eternally traveling inquisitor, who else? You live in a fog. Ha, ha! Watch that your brain does not spin together suddenly, and a fire break out."

Bernardo felt his cheeks drain of blood. He looked up, nearly speechless with confusion. "Monsignor? I don't . . ."

Monsignor had so amused himself that he had fallen into a fit of laughter and farting. "You should have seen the boy, pulling at his own limp little sausage and nodding like a fool—well, no 'like' about it. Fool he undoubtedly is. The fog burns, I know not how, he says." Monsignor spread his arms and, in dramatic excess, contemplated the ceiling. "*Misericordia,* Bernardo! Look at the mold on those beams!"

The knock on the door startled them both. Bernardo rose to answer, and found a small balding man on the threshold. Pale eyes searched Bernardo's lowered face. "Inquisitor-General?"

"What business have you?"

"Inquisitor-General?" The man cupped an ear.

Bernardo raised his head. In a bellow that approached Monsignor's conversational tones, he asked, "What bus-i-ness?"

The man wore a rash of pinpricks on his fingertips. A sewing needle, trailing cream-colored thread, was stuck in his tunic's lapel. "O, could be that I have an information."

"Name?"

"Eh?"

"Your *name*!"

The man looked right and left, then whispered loudly enough for all the street to hear, "José Filipe Magalhães."

"A moment."

"Eh?"

Bernardo shut the door. "Someone with information, Monsignor."

"Station?"

"Tradesman. Tailor, most probably."

Monsignor contemplated the rafters. "Does the room not stink of mildew?"

Bernardo took a deep breath. In the air was a lingering of sulfur and sausage. "Not to my mind, Monsignor. Should I let him in?"

A wave. When Bernardo opened to him, the little man entered, hat in hand. He peered about, squinting as if purblind. He evidently caught sight of the huge dark mass that was Monsignor, for he headed directly to him.

A meter away, he knelt. "Care for your blessing, Your Honor."

Monsignor tossed a *benedicto* in the man's general direction and then sat down. Bernardo backed until he was at his own chair. Quietly he took out the writing plank and the red journal.

Still on his knees, the tailor said, "Talk of angels in town, Your Honor."

Monsignor picked at a nail.

"And visions of the Virgin Mary."

Monsignor sucked a tooth.

Bernardo dipped his quill, and waited.

"There's a Judiazer, too, that herbalist witch, the one of the evil eye. And the girl who sees the Virgin, Your Honor? That Castanheda girl?

Moor, without doubt. Heard her singing songs in a curious language sometimes. They make much to-do over Saturdays, seems to me. And he has a
painting of El Cid, brazen as can be, right in his hall for all to gawk at."

"What is your sin, my son?"

"Eh?"

"Your *sin!*"

The tailor convulsed. He dropped his hat, and fumbled picking it up.
"Sir?"

"You come to me with accusations of others. I ask if there is any blot
on your soul."

"O, well . . ." A shrug. The tailor looked ceilingward. Bernardo wondered if he could see angels there or if, like Monsignor, he spied only
mold. "Years ago, sir. A little disagreement with the wife, and I abjured
myself straightaway in an *auto da graça,* and Father Pessoa gave me a *sanbenito,* and that was the end of it. Never had any trouble again."

Bernardo wrote in the journal: *José Filipe Magalhães, abjuration de
vehementi.* He pictured Father Manoel's judgment, in his wrath as glorious
and terrible as Gabriel.

"I realize you have given the Church no more trouble, my son, as you
are alive here to tell the story."

"O, Your Honor!" The tailor crossed himself. "Nothing to do with it!
I've never seen aught but a little light in the sky that could have been a star.
I'm a humble man, and God doesn't feel the need to talk to me. But that
Castanheda, now—a haughty family. And wealthy, I've heard. Come back
from that war, his saddlebags bulging. And he trades in things, all on paper.
Loans money on expeditions, just like a Jew. And that Teixeira. Not one of
the New Christians, but rich—a trader with the cunning of a Moor. Buys
gold, Your Honor, and trades spices; buys spices and trades slaves. To my
mind, you can't trust a man like that. Never know how much he owns nor
what he stands for."

"Do you owe them money?"

A wild, "What, Your Honor?"

"Do you owe them money, man? The truth now, for an inquiry will
find out if you are lying."

"No money, no sir. Not a copper. Not a *maravidis*." He thumped his chest so energetically that he nearly felled himself. "Just come to you out of love of God, sir, and Christian virtue. And . . . and, too? I'm reminded, sir. That Castanheda? He once told me there was no God in Spain, sir. I heard him myself, as did the wife and Dona Inez. And he has a hooked nose, sir, if you take the pains to look at it right." He leaned and squinted, demonstrating.

Bernardo scribbled: *Castanheda: No God in Spain, witnesses Sra. Magalhães, Sra. Inez. To question: Sat. Sabbath?*

"And that Teixeira girl? That Maria Elena? Got herself with child and said it was angels, Your Honor. And everyone gossiping how she's virgin. Then from one day to the next, she loses that bulge in her belly, and no baby to show for it. Now the girl's all downcast, and the house in an uproar."

Bernardo's hand trembled, quill tip drumming the page and leaving a spray of ink. *O Jesu Fili Mariae.* Foretold that He would come again. Now in Quintas, a gathering of angels and a virgin named Maria.

"Yes, yes, yes. Very interesting. Have you all that, Bernardo?"

Pulse hammering, he wrote: *Maria Elena Teixeira, virgin birth.* His hand was unsteady. The last word was a scrawl. "Noted, Monsignor."

"Well. So. If we have need, Senhor . . . ?"

"Magalhães, Your Honor."

"You're quite right: Magalhães. So, having a need, we shall certainly call for you." Monsignor dismissed the tailor with a flutter of his hand.

The little man glanced at Bernardo as he left. When the door closed, Monsignor lifted a hip, let go a trumpeting fart.

"And *that*, Bernardo, is my frank opinion of the day."

I T WAS LIKE being swallowed whole by color. The tunnels were happy in pink and apricot because God was glad to see him. But they were sad in indigo and violet, too; for part of God was dead.

Afonso walked the narrow honeycomb tunnel, passing his hand over dark cold spaces where color no longer sparked. "You're becoming something else," Afonso told him. "That's all."

Is it? Fear was marbled with orange panic.

"Don't be afraid." Afonso rested his forehead against God's soft metal flesh and felt the vibration of His colors. "I promise You're not going to die. You fell to earth because You wanted to teach us things. Father de Melo taught me all about sacrifice, and he said that sacrifice means giving up something you like very much, something it hurts you to give. On Lent I sacrifice chocolate. So I think that's what happened with You."

I forget so much now, God told him. *I forget why I fell, and how, and if I killed those who traveled with Me.*

"Let's see. . . ." Afonso watched colors come and go. "There were one—two—three angels. Only one of them doesn't move anymore, so I suppose he might be dead."

God wept in bitter yellow. *I don't remember.*

Afonso tried to explain sacrifice again, but God was not listening. After a while he went to the big silver room and lay down on the floor, drifting in and out of God's sorrow.

"Tell me a story," Afonso said.

This time God told him of duty, which Afonso knew well. He told of toil, which Afonso knew little. The colors became too delicate to distinguish. Then God repeated that long story of responsibility.

Afonso told Him, "My chancellors and Father de Melo already told me this story, and I didn't like it. Tell me about heaven again."

God showed him veils of blue and red where swaddled stars napped. He showed him comets opening like luminous buds in their race toward the sun. God told of frigid black reaches where nothing moved but Him.

He took Afonso into the void. And there in that great barren waste they rested together, Afonso cupped in God's colors. He realized that God loved that place, that He breathed of its emptiness and basked in its chill. Afonso wondered if the cold dark spots he felt in God were places where He remembered—a part of Him which would forever be Heaven.

Afonso understood such things, for he loved his quest, but he loved home, too. Even if he left it for good, part of him would always reside in the castle. That's what hauntings were.

I remember the darkness, God told him.

"So you probably haunt it," Afonso said. He thought of his rooms, his tall postered bed, the tapestry of his parents' wedding on the wall (father tall, mother beautiful). He took a deep breath and smelled the damp of the castle, the tickle of dust, his pomade of cinnamon and cloves and orange peel. He saw everything so clearly that he wondered if the guard at his chamber door felt the chill as Afonso passed; if he saw a flicker out of the corner of his eye.

But still . . . God's sad azure sigh. *I don't remember falling.*

ÂNDIDO'S SON MARIO arrived at the rectory winded and blowing, his cheeks crimson from his run. "Fathers! Fathers!"

Soares came out of his chair, round-eyed.

"Come quick! *Pai* says for you to bring all your holy water and oil and things. There's a trouble at the jail."

Fire. O, a fire in the jail. It was an inevitable tragedy, was it not? The deep dry straw, the lamps. Those brutal iron bars. Pessoa bolted out the door. Half a block later he realized that he'd forgotten the oil. He whirled, saw Soares coming out of the rectory carrying his black leather satchel. Pessoa raced on.

Clouds had rolled in, shrouding the afternoon. Pessoa searched their huge underbellies for tattletale smudges. Dear God. What had he done? Lost in the immensity of fate, that insignificance of self. *Ne me perdas. Neither, Lord, I beg you, lose sight of me.* Straw flaming up with tinderbox speed and helpless women in that bright enormity, shrieking.

The next block his feet went out from under him. His shoulder crashed into an iron gate. His toe caught on a cobble and nearly sent him sprawling. A milk seller and his swaybacked dray stared.

He sped on, leaving even Mario's quick footsteps behind. Then the jail was in sight. No smoke, but Cândido was standing in the street with his men. Two of Monsignor's henchmen there as well. A fight? Someone wounded? Cândido caught sight of him and waved.

"Relics!" he shouted. "Come see!" And he ducked inside the inn.

A hot stitch knitted Pessoa's side. Whooping for air, holding his ribs, he followed. Inside, he found the limit of his strength. Pessoa's steps slowed to a bewildered and exhausted stumble. His bruised shoulder pained him, his toe throbbed. The place smelled of old smoke—nothing of new peril. "Cândido? Where—"

"Here!" A call from below. "Look!"

Steadying himself against the wall, Pessoa descended.

"Look!" Cândido stood in the cell with the creatures. Pessoa surveyed the dark eyes, the gaunt bodies. Nothing about them had changed. He was down the steps and into the cell himself before he realized where Cândido was pointing.

"Not corrupted! Two days, father. But even better: look here." Cândido brushed straw away from the fallen creature. A puddle of water leaked from its side.

"Smells of honey and peach flowers. So my guess is angels, all right." Cândido dipped his fingertips and held them up for Pessoa to sniff.

Flowers. Before Pessoa could stop him, the man stuck his finger into his mouth. Cândido's face contorted. He shivered hard. "Like green persimmon." He grimaced, dismayed, at his finger. "Still, smells good enough."

Then Soares was there, panting from his haste. He held missal in one hand, satchel in the other, and he was scanning the room for the dying.

"Got proof of angels, father." Cândido ran his fingers through the puddle again. He held up his hand. "Come smell. All blossoms and sweets. Should take it up in a vial or something, would be my guess. Good relic, angel water. Church could keep some. Could sell the rest off."

Soares knelt beside Cândido, snatching his hand.

"Ai! Wait!" Cândido pulled away. "Don't go licking on it now. Smells a lot better than it tastes."

"Flowers." Soares's voice was faint from either the sprint or his exhilaration. "A liquor like honeyed flowers. *Domine, mundum reple dulcedine.* The body desolves itself into sweetness. And no corruption of the flesh? You're certain?"

"Certain as can be, father. O, they're cherubs for sure."

OUTSIDE THE INN'S windows, day darkened. Trees and hills cast shadows of blue. At the seventeenth hour, by Monsignor's porcelain clock, Bernardo asked if they should not leave for the inn. Monsignor trimmed the lamp and kept reading.

Bernardo lit candles. He watched one quarter hour pass, then a second. He put his hands into his pockets, entwined his fingers in the cloth, and twisted them nervously this way and that. He said, "Monsignor?"

A furious slap as Monsignor threw the book to the floor. Bernardo, startled, withdrew.

Monsignor was glaring out the window into the dusk. "If we are to believe that English idiot Locke, I would not know that my feet smelled, or that the king is a dullard, or horses give out great flat turds. I could not be certain of anything." He grasped the chair arms and, with a grunt, hauled himself to his feet. "What o'clock?"

"Half-past five, Monsignor."

"Um. I believe that the damned king's infernal sausages have long since turned to noise and vapor. Bind me tight." He lifted his habit.

Bernardo took the linen from its box and hurriedly began wrapping, all the time thinking of Father Manoel in the jail and, waiting below, the cherubs.

"Tighter, Bernardo. I would look my best. Never let a Jesuit see weakness, for they'll take the advantage."

Reckless haste compelled Bernardo to have to undo a length of linen and rewrap it. It bought him a rebuking grunt from Monsignor.

"Um. I see it approaches six. Well. One must always remember that these rural folk have little concept of time. All 'later' or 'sometime soon,'

especially if there is work to be done. They tell the o'clock by the passage
of the sun, and crawl into their flea-infected beds at sunset."

"Yes, Monsignor. Done, Monsignor. And thank you." Bernardo
stepped away.

Monsignor dropped his skirts and perused himself in the glass. Then
picking up his ivory-bound missal, he walked downstairs and out into the
street, Bernardo at his heels.

The evening was blustery and indistinct, all lashing wind and mist.
He and Monsignor walked the blue-hazed streets beneath a darkening roof
of clouds. Ahead, in a circle of lamplight by the jail, waited the three state
executioners and two of Father Manoel's armed field hands. They bowed
when Bernardo and Monsignor entered the inn. And in the place the inquisition was to be held, Father Manoel stood alone: one spot of warmth
in the room's cold indigo sea.

Monsignor halted in the glow of Pessoa's small lamp. Lips pursed, he
studied the Jesuit from boot to pate and back. Bernardo cast Father Manoel
an apologetic look from underneath his lashes, but, head high, Father Manoel had met Monsignor's gaze and seemed not about to let it go.

Monsignor's hand shot forward. "Your notes."

Without protest or flourish, Father Manoel gave him a cream-colored
journal.

Monsignor flipped open the marked page and read. Then he clapped
the journal closed. "Where is the rest?"

A quiet. "That is all."

Monsignor's reply was deafening and incredulous. "*All?* Where are the
corroborating witnesses? The other accusations? Damn you for a fool!" Monsignor's voice boomed through the room, startling even the shadows. " 'That
is all,' you say, as if you are blessed with wit enough to find your way through
a door. O, well and fine. You jail three women on one man's deposition? We
have no legality. With no more witnesses, the women must be let go. You realize that, do you not?" Monsignor jutted his face forward: an onslaught before which a weaker man would have retreated. "Well? Answer me! Do you?"

"I stand witness," Father Manoel said.

"You?"

"Yes. I stand as witness to a declaration of virgin birth and a statement as to the intercession of angels. So either we have a lunacy here, Monsignor, which cannot be punished, or we have heresy, and the jailing is lawful. Or the story is true."

In a terrifyingly still voice, Monsignor said, "True."

"Since we may possess some proof, I believe it worthy of inquiry."

Wind rattled down the ruined chimney, whipped an invasive tendril of ivy against the windowsill. It crept into the room, tickled the hair at Bernardo's cheek, and whispered in his ear the magic incantation: *Proof.*

"Come. I'll show you." Father Manoel walked toward the stairs. Halfway there, he stopped and turned back. Monsignor had not moved; and so Bernardo, even though his feet begged to follow, had not moved either. The monsignor's face was a study in scorn. Never had Bernardo felt so constrained. Never had he felt so forceful a temptation for disobedience. *Miserere mei,* he prayed, uncertain what God would want him to do.

Then Monsignor, as if contemplating an evening stroll, moved toward the stairs, down to where a virgin stood swollen with child and cherubim proclaimed the news. Bernardo clutched his rosary as they began the descent into adoration. *O beata Virgo.* Why had he not noticed her earlier?— all his attention on the heralds.

But the veneration below was in the cell opposite the women, where straw had been cleared to form a bed of stone. And there lay the fallen cherub, his arms crossed over his chest, his head on a lace pillow. Around him burned a serene conflagration: two tall funeral candles at his head, two at his feet. In the oily scent of beeswax, Father Soares knelt, missal open, rosary in hand, at prayer.

Bernardo did not realize that Monsignor had stopped until he nearly stumbled into that broad meaty back. Father Manoel waited for them at the cell door, his hand on the iron bars, looking up to where Monsignor stood, rigid.

"The body shrinks inside the clothing," Father Manoel said. "So there is death, but no corruption." He whispered the invitation: "Come see. For from the body drips a liquor which smells of sugared flowers."

Monsignor took another step and Bernardo noticed that he was not peering at the fallen cherub at all, but at the living ones. The cherubs were staring back.

Father Manoel said, "My own familiar tasted of it. Then he took some outside and anointed one of his men with it. The man claims that he felt he was coming down with a *gripe,* and that the liquor cured him. Not enough proof of miracle, but—"

"Satanas," Monsignor hissed. He held his missal aloft, and the pallor of his cheeks mimicked the ivory in which the book was clad. *"Videsne, Bernardo?"* He cried, pointing down to the angels. *"Videsne hoc?"*

"Yes," Bernardo answered. "I see it."

"O here. O here. *Adsum mallus!"* Monsignor crossed himself furiously.

Father Manoel's cheeks paled as well. "No, Monsignor. Please come see, I beg you. No corruption. No blood. Yet the body disintegrates into a sweetness. Such a miracle cannot be evil."

Monsignor whirled and, still crossing himself, beat a swift retreat.

Day 8

A N EERIE HOWL THROUGH THE DARKNESS JOLTED BERNARDO AWAKE. IT made his hair bristle. It banished reason and all promise of mercy. That sound was followed by a second shriek—the discordant music of a soul in torment.

He sat up in bed, digging his fingernails into the flesh of his arm. He peered at the solid black wall of the night—making the world concrete not with vision, but with his own cruel touch.

He was not dead, was not with the damned. He was in the inn, and someone was screaming. Fear was so preposterous, so unknown for that voice, that Bernardo first thought the weeper to be a stranger. Then he knew.

Astonished, he stumbled from his bed, groped for the door, and felt his way to the neighboring room. Another piercing cry came, one that ended in a terrified babble, half-Latin, half-Portuguese. Entering the room, Bernardo called, "Here. I'm here, Monsignor."

A thin cry for "Light!"

Bernardo found the tinderbox and sparked a candle. When he turned he saw Monsignor sitting up in bed, his eyes wide and sightless.

It was so unearthly a scene that Bernardo's veins ran ice. He whispered, "Monsignor?"

He received only a blind gaze in answer, then an eerie hiss, Monsignor pointing at the blank wall. "I see it. See it, there? *Videsene, Bernardo?* The Church fallen to nothing. Nothing. Seminaries emptied, rectories abandoned. Clear as day."

Bernardo lit another candle, then a lamp. The room sprang to life and color: the blue of the rumpled coverlet, the crimson where Monsignor had, in his distress, scratched himself awake.

Gently: "Monsignor?" Bernardo came forward, placed the lamp on the nightstand.

Monsignor seized his wrist and his eyes gained focus. "I saw it: nuns and archbishops murdered, priests subjected to scorn."

"You dream."

He gave a vicious shake of his head. "No. Armies marching. An invasion of ideas. The elevation of the rabble. In all of Europe, kings overthrown."

"Let me fetch you a tincture of valerian, some catnip tea. It's not yet three o'clock. You can sleep."

Such horror crossed Monsignor's face that Bernardo was made terrorized. "Not sleep!" Monsignor cried. "No! Keep the lamp lit! The world ends! Changes of rule like will-o'-the-wisps. They care not for the Church. On the wall! See? O, I see their eyes yet, Bernardo—black and demonic. Look, and you view Hell."

"The angels?"

"Demons." He said in an oddly plaintive tone, "Will you not stay with me, Bernardo? The shadows come too close."

Bernardo sat down at the edge of the bed. "Tell me about your vision."

The air was heavy and hushed with night. Over Bernardo's head, mice stirred in the attic.

Monsignor's eyes fluttered. "Armies of commoners," he said. "The kingdom of the devil. A dominion of men with unruly ideas." His eyes closed. "God save us from men with ideas." The face, at long last, found peace.

THE QUINTAS FAIR was a tumult of smell and noise and color. Geese and hens stuck heads from cages to squawk. A human squawking rose among the vendors, too, cries of "Fat pullets!" and "Eels! Fresh ribbon eels!" and "Apples! See no worms. Apples!" Even the Gypsies had come, bringing wagons of cracked iron pots and herds of spavined horses.

Pessoa walked past lowing milk cows, cages of rabbits, carts piled with turnips and white beans. The meadow smelled of decaying cabbages and dung.

When Soares stopped to buy some cheese, Pessoa stopped with him. "Buy an extra," he said.

Soares laughed. "Manoel, I promise not to eat it all."

"Buy an extra. I will pay you." Pessoa leaned toward the Franciscan. "For the Pinheiro woman. I promised her. Just some cheese, a little fruit. A hen, perhaps."

He expected an objection, but Soares bought the cheese and walked on, stopping at an apple stall and lifting an eyebrow.

"None for me. Three for her."

There followed a clinking exchange of coins. From fair goers came passing nods and smiles and "Good morning, fathers." Ahead, a pair of royal soldiers had stopped to flirt with a milkmaid. Royal cooks strolled the stalls, shaking their heads in dismay and arguing loudly.

The fair held so much zest and life that Pessoa found himself smiling; then the geese in their cages reminded him of the women, and the soldiers reminded him of trials.

"Are you ready to go?" he asked Soares.

"Just another stall or two."

They passed bushel baskets of brown eggs packed in straw and a selection of fine fruitwood casks. Soares paused to buy rabbits. Pessoa watched as the fragile necks were broken under the vendor's practiced hands: a quick and silent death. Pessoa turned away as they were skinned.

The stench of their blood and the smell of their guts reminded him of

a garroting in Evora, and the state executioner's swiftness, the accused's
brief struggle. Unlike those burned, the strangled died mute on their stakes,
as mild as rabbits.

Fair day. Wednesday. Only the week before—had so little time
passed?—he remembered the expectation that had so illuminated Marta
Castanheda's small face.

They walked on. Soares bid a potato seller good day and stopped for
a visit amid the crush of the shoppers, the cries of the hucksters, and the
stench of offal and blood. Uneasy, Pessoa looked around. Across the way,
a group of king's soldiers stood surrounded by gawking country folk. Pessoa put the basket down and, interest piqued, walked closer.

A soldier saw him coming, displayed first consternation; then guilt.
A hand was shoved too quickly into a leather sack. A warning was muttered.

Pessoa quickened his pace. There was panic now, of soldiers turning.
Among a pallid sea of faces he could see the questioning looks from the
farmers.

Then Pessoa was among them, demanding "What? What are you hiding here?" and reaching for hands. Prying open one soldier's trembling
fist, he found a piece of scorched silver. A farmer drawled, "Is it not pieces
from Heaven, then, father?"

Behind the crowd was a blanket piled with melted pewter. He heard
the country people's "Came down from Heaven, didn't it? That's what the
soldiers told us. That's what we're paying for."

Pessoa snatched up a corner of the blanket. Pieces of star whirled into
the air and came down in a glittering shower. A soldier put out a hand to
stop him, but with a cry, Pessoa knocked him to the ground. Before his
wordless howling rage, farmers scattered. Soldiers backed, white-faced,
hands on their swords.

He felt a tug on his arm. Pessoa whirled and nearly met the tug fist
first.

It was only Soares. "Come, Manoel," he whispered, pulling him
away. "They will do as you said, I think. And I think the fair is over."

Pessoa let himself be led. By the time they had gone a half league down the road, his anger had cooled. He took the heavy basket from Soares's hand and said curtly, "Remind me to pay you for the Pinheiro woman's food."

They passed a farmhouse, then through a spot of road where the stench of pigs lay thick as a cloud. Beyond a nearby wattle fence came snorts and grunts and the movement of heavy bodies.

"No matter. I should do more, I think. Bless you, Manoel, for reminding me. She is not Christian, to be sure, but that does not excuse my lack of mercy."

"And excuse me for my anger. I embarrassed you. I'm sorry."

"Don't give it a second thought."

"No excuse for what I did." The road unraveled like rope, curling over one hill and circling the next. He hungered for travel; he loathed it. So many years, thinking he had escaped the dolorous climate in Mafra— only to find that the Inquisition had followed.

"I have been far too haughty, Luis," Pessoa said. "You are absolutely right."

"Um."

"Thinking I could contain all this. Deciding matters on the spur of the moment without consulting you."

Shoulder to shoulder, they passed under the spreading branches of a cork tree, its shade as viscous as night.

"All other avenues are gone now. I find myself forced to prove angels, and I don't know that I will be able. My own fault. I should have clapped the women in jail early, if only to keep them from talking. Now the whole town has heard of virgin births. And if I am to prove *that* . . . Dear God. Only Duarte Teixeira and Berenice Pinheiro as witness to the girl's virginity? Bring Berenice forward, and I doom her. What an inquisitor I make! I am an incompetent. A buffoon. Scorned by Gomes's men and all of Quintas. No one fears me."

To his surprise, Soares burst into hearty laughter. "Soldiers flee from you in terror. Single-handed, you put an entire fair in disarray. I swear, Manoel, you alarmed even the Gypsies." He patted his arm. "No, no, my boy. Christ among the money changers. That's what you were."

MONSIGNOR HAD AWAKENED rested. There was a sly sparkle in his eye. And when the king's courier arrived with a cinnamon-fragrant basket, he breakfasted with abandon.

"I meet with the royal idiot this morning, Bernardo," he said, pointing with a butter knife. "I want you to remain in town. Collect the two secular lawyers that the marquis sent us. Let us add a little something to that Jesuit's account—O, a bit of testimony, shall we say. The troublemaker seems overly fond of the blank page. What was the name of that witness again?"

Bernardo, who had sat the night in vigil by Monsignor's bedside, squinted blear-eyed at the journal. "Dona Magalhães. Dona Inez."

"That one precisely! Dona Inez!" An overly exuberant gesture with a loaded fork sent morsels of sausage flying. "So, to repeat: gather the lawyers. Talk to this Dona Inez. And go to the jail and speak with the women. Make certain that all dictates have been followed. See that the accused have been told to search their hearts, to confess the truth, to trust in God, blah, blah, blah. Make certain they have been offered counsel, and if so, who their lawyers are. See what rebuttal, if any, they have to offer. See if the Jesuit's story has any correlation to fact."

"Yes, Monsignor." Bernardo made a note. Did the man not remember his nightmare? Bernardo dared not look up lest Monsignor see hope in his eye.

"Well, go! Go!"

Bernardo set a spare inkwell into his box of quills. He tucked the box under one arm and the red journal under the other. He walked out, closing the door quietly behind; then he strode through a sunlit corridor and down the narrow backstairs. At a chipped door, he stopped and knocked. A duet of jovial voices bid him welcome. On a bed inside, two men contemplated a backgammon board. The pair looked up so optimistically that Bernardo presumed the game's attraction had paled.

The man with the goatee lifted his hand and said, "Emílio."

"Tadeo," said the rumple-haired scarecrow. "I remember you. Father Andrade, correct? I've seen you in the company of the monsignor before."

"You the notary?" the other asked.

Hugging his journal and quills to his chest, Bernardo inclined his head.

"The rooms are terrible. And breakfast was worse. And some idiot screamed all night."

Bernardo looked at them through his lashes. Which was Emílio and which Tadeo? He was so dulled by lack of sleep that he could not keep them straight.

Goatee snorted. "Have you not yet learned that Gomes pays for nothing? Best take your complaints to the marquis."

Scarecrow laughed. "No. *You* complain to the marquis."

"Two days on the road, and now stuck here. Listen, father. I do not mind aiding the Holy Office—after all, they trained me. But I have other clients besides the marquis, and my business languishes."

"Ha!" A thigh-slapping guffaw. "Emílio hires out to the Holy Office, then hires out to the accused. Slap them in jail; bail them out."

Emílio. Goatee was Emílio. But the next instant Bernardo had forgotten.

"So you finally have a duty for us, father?"

"And what is all this secrecy? Gossip about something fallen from the sky, and—"

"I heard of a stone falling from the sky once. Hah! The stupidity of peasants! As if a stone could fling itself into the air and come down when it wills."

"Are we not to bring the accused to Mafra, father? That is the district, is it not?"

"Quite right, Emílio: provincial district of Mafra."

"Probably better lodgings there."

Comments and questions flew like arrows, too fast for Bernardo to follow. The tempo nearly took his breath away.

From Scarecrow: "So what is the heresy?"

"No! Don't tell him, father! Asking the notary is highly irregular."

"Really, Tadeo! You are so constipated by the law that I'm surprised any decision is expelled."

Suddenly they popped to their feet. "Shall we go?"

Hugging his quill box, Bernardo led them into the courtyard and past a leaf-choked fountain. At the stables, he asked a boy for directions. Then it was up an alley of garbage and cats, both lawyers complaining of the route, then down a street no cleaner and not much wider. Scarecrow suggested they return to the inn for a carriage.

Bernardo kept the pace steady. They crossed a bridge spanning a rocky stream. Scarecrow asked if it was much farther. Goatee asked what o'clock, and said that he was getting hungry.

He chose a shortcut through a meadow, where Scarecrow orated upon the price of new shoes and the damp of muck and cow dung.

Bernardo called over his shoulder, "The third house after the cistern, the boy said. See it there ahead?"

The pair stripped themselves of their coats, even though the breeze was chill. The brisk walk left them huffing. But when they arrived and Bernardo had knocked and no one had appeared at the door, the two suddenly regained their wind.

"Well, not home. See, father? You should have sent a runner ahead to make certain they would be here."

"O, come now, Tadeo. The accused and the witnesses should be called before the tribunal, not the contrary. The boy has it all turned about. Were Monsignor here—"

The door flew open. In the doorway stood such a gargoyle that Bernardo's first impulse was retreat.

"What?" she barked. "What are you on my threshold? And what priest are you?"

An eye-wetting stench of old urine and sweat and rotting fish came either from her or from her cottage. Bernardo heard a shuffle as the lawyers withdrew a pace.

"I said"—her voice was the screech of saw against nail—"what priest are you?"

Her face was adorned by three huge moles. Bernardo found himself staring and quickly lowered his eyes. "Father Andrade, notary of the Holy Office, come with two Inquisition lawyers to take your deposition."

"O?" Just that.

Bernardo longed to gauge her expression, but given the grotesquery of those moles, he did not dare.

"Well, well, well. My deposition, is it? I was wondering when the Inquisition would smell what this town had stepped in. Come inside! I have barley water for what ails you."

Before Bernardo could think of a gracious way to decline:

"What a lovely day! Don't you find it lovely, Tadeo?"

"Just smell of that air!"

"Ah! And a sky clear as a crystal! Don't see that in the city."

"No, no. Absolutely. And—you know?—I spied a spot, just in the shade of that elm."

The voices receded. "O! Lovely spot."

Bernardo held his breath as the woman emerged. He followed her and sat downwind. He took out a quill, uncorked the ink, and opened his journal. Beneath the tree, she made a great show of straightening her skirts, and looked so flirtatiously at Scarecrow that his gaze sought refuge in the branches.

"Randy angels," she said. "That's what it's all about. Had congress with that Castanheda girl, and she giving them potions. Lifted up that Teixeira girl's skirts, too. Wasn't any virgin birth about it. Was those angels, who should have known better. Lifted even my skirts and poked it right up inside me, big as you please. That's why God threw them out of Heaven."

Bernardo paused his scribbling and peered through his lashes. The lawyers sat, blank-faced models of the perfect inquisitor.

Then: "Would there be anything else you care to tell us?"

She pulled on her lower lip. "Well, not as I liked it, myself. But those girls all agiggle. If angels decide to put it in you, I figure you have no way to stop it. But you don't have to enjoy it, all the same."

Bernardo had culled the interrogatory wheat from its chaff. He looked at his most recent finished product: *Sra Inez: did not enjoy the congress. Question women.*

Scarecrow: "Were there any corroborating witnesses?"

"Eh?"

Goatee: "Was anyone else with you at the time of the . . ."

"Lying with," Scarecrow suggested.

Bernardo put down his quill. He watched an ant bumble its way down the side of the box and over a white feather.

"Quite right." Goatee nodded. "The lying with the angels."

She sniffed. "Not as I would gather a crowd."

The two lawyers observed a moment of silence. Then Goatee asked, "Anyone else you wish to accuse?"

"Just that Jesuit priest who can't keep his pants buttoned, either."

Bernardo's quill halted mid-stroke.

"And him with those angels, all plotting together, I warrant."

His fingers cramped. The muscles of his hand twitched, and he lifted his arm so as not to ruin the page. He heard Scarecrow say, "We are talking of fornication?"

"Hah! And a master of dipping his *pau,* he is."

"Please use his name. Let us be exact."

"That Father Manoel High-and-Mighty Pessoa."

"And you accuse Father Manoel Pessoa of fornication with whom?"

"That Jew witch."

"A name please."

"Berenice Jew Witch Pinheiro. Her of the evil eye. O, pretty enough, like Lucifer is pretty. And he must think so, too, for putting it in her is the first thing he does when he arrives in town and the last thing he does before leaving."

Father Manoel's stern mouth sampling strawberry-ripe lips. Father Manoel's keen eyes, that sad gaze, feasting upon rose-tipped nakedness. Those hands wantonly fondling places swollen and moist.

Bernardo could see Scarecrow watching him, watching his hand. He could not bring the quill tip down to the paper, could not make his hand move. Such outrage swept him that it was all he could do not to knock the lying hag down. He lifted his head. She met his indignant glare.

"My notes," Bernardo said. "In my notes it states that we are to question this witness concerning a heresy which was spoken by one Guilherme Castanheda, and what he said about Spain."

"Spain?" she said. "I know as how he didn't like it."

They waited.

"Wife died as he came back."

Scarecrow slapped his knees. "Well. The Holy Office thanks you for your cooperation, Dona . . ."

"Inez Rodrigues," she said.

Bernardo corked his ink. He packed his quills.

She nodded, satisfied. "Ask me anything. Anything at all. I'll tell you."

The lawyers clambered to their feet and dusted their pants. Bernardo collected his box and tucked it under his arm.

"You go ahead and have me before that tribunal," she told them. "I'll look those wanton angels right in their black evil eyes, and tell everyone how they can't keep their trousers buttoned."

She was still prattling when the lawyers started down the road, Bernardo at their heels.

Beyond the first turning, just out of sight of the cottage, Goatee halted in his tracks and stooped over double, as if he would vomit. He grabbed frantically, blindly, for Scarecrow. In a strangled voice he said, " 'They stuck it in me, big as you please.' "

Scarecrow held on, helpless as a drowning man, to Goatee's sleeve. He lifted his face to the sky and howled, " 'Not as I enjoyed it, myself.' "

They laughed so heartily that they were forced to sit down in the road.

"LET US CLARIFY, Your Majesty. The earth what?" In the quiet of the tent, the fat priest leaned forward, his bulk pressing against the sweet-burdened table. His mouth fascinated Afonso. It reminded him of the backside part on a dog which is tight and pink and puckered.

"Sire? Are you listening? The earth what?"

"I forget your name," Afonso said.

Those lips constricted even more, so much so that Afonso thought neither turds nor words could pass. But then the fat priest slipped a chocolate almond between them, smooth as the royal physician with a suppository.

"Once more: I am Monsignor Gomes," he said. "The Inquisitor-General of Lisbon, Your Majesty. Given charge over banishing heresy from your kingdom, and given that mission by the Holy Father in Rome himself." The pudgy fingers plucked up another almond, inserted it. "Do you understand what 'heresy' is, sire?" Suddenly the fat priest turned to a waiting cook. "I'll have half a bushel of these made up to be sent back with me, please."

The cook bowed and left.

The fat priest ate another almond. "So. Heresy. Do you know what heresy is, Your Majesty?"

Behind where the fat priest sat at table, Father de Melo was making hand motions. There was something he wanted Afonso to remember. Afonso nodded.

"What, then?" the fat priest asked. "Tell me. Please define heresy for me, sire."

Father de Melo was beside himself. Afonso nodded again.

"No? Heresy, sire, may be said to be all those statements which go against Holy Mother Church and the word of God. Statements such that there is no Hell, for example. That God may be whatever the whimsies of each and every individual decide Him to be. That the earth revolves about the sun. This is heresy."

Afonso waited for an almond to slide out of those lips like a tiny brown turd. When it did not, Afonso lost interest. He got to his feet. "Thank you for coming." It was important to thank petitioners. His father and his advisers had taught him that.

The fat priest looked up in surprise. Would he not stand? That is what petitioners were supposed to do. Yet not one of them stood: not the fat priest nor the guard who had come with him nor Father de Melo.

Another almond disappeared. Three of the fat priest's chins quivered. "Sit down, Your Majesty. It is essential that we end this here."

"God is waiting. I need to go into the acorn now."

Father de Melo was making snatching motions at the air as if he would, by force of will, pull Afonso into his seat.

"No, sire," the fat priest said. "I do not think His Highness will quit an audience with the inquisitor-general unless the Pope himself gives him leave."

Afonso looked around the tent. The footmen had been caught between rising and sitting, and seemed unable to decide. The king's guards stood at attention, but looked ill at ease.

"Sit down," the fat priest said.

"No. I will go into the acorn and talk to God now."

Father de Melo began, "O please, Your Majesty, if you would be so kind, I think perhaps—"

"Sit *down!*" The fat priest's voice was harsh with rage.

"No!" Afonso was angry now, too. "You stand up! You are fat, and you have a mouth like an asshole, and you will stand when I stand, and you will sit when I tell you to."

Father de Melo seemed to be near a faint.

"My father, King João, said . . ." Afonso pointed his finger into the center of the fat priest's scowl. Ideas and words tumbled so fast that he could scarcely sort them. "My father said I am firstborn Bragança. That means king. And all must obey me. So you will stand now. You will even kneel if I want, or I have soldiers who will make you."

The fat priest came to his feet so fast that he jarred the table. The platter of almonds flew. "You rule only by the grace of God, sire, and by the consent of Castelo Melhor. I warn you. I have the count's ear."

"Well . . ." Sentences fell apart. Words spun away so fast that Afonso could barely catch them. "Well . . . but I have God's ear. And He tells me of Earth around sun and no Hell and such. And I would believe Him over Castelo Melhor, who thinks he is clever and speaks in riddles and sometimes even lies. Why don't you believe me when I say God is in the acorn?

I never lie, and when I do I always confess it. Why don't you come see for yourself? God probably wouldn't mind. I can introduce you."

Three stray almonds rolled off the table and dropped, hitting the silver platter and striking brief music.

The priest said, "I believe that God and I have been introduced."

"Well, then! He would be glad of seeing you. For God is lonely and forgetful. And He is scared sometimes. I feel sorry for Him, mostly." Afonso walked out of the tent and toward the acorn. At the camp's perimeter, he stopped and looked back. The fat priest stood frowning in the sunlight, Father de Melo and the Church's guard behind.

"Don't be afraid," Afonso said. "God's really very nice."

The priest called loudly for a large crucifix and for his vial of holy water and he said that, with Holy Mother Church at his side, he was willing to confront Satan himself.

Afonso walked on, hearing the fat priest trample the grass behind. At the door to the acorn, Afonso stopped and waited. The fat priest came huffing and puffing, and at the acorn, he drew himself up. He held the crucifix high.

"*Moneantur, diaboli! Dominus Deus Sabaoth!* I put myself into Thy hands."

Just below the lip of the hill the captain of the guard and Father de Melo and all the servants had gathered to watch. Afonso remembered that he had once been frightened of the acorn, too. And he felt badly for the fat priest.

He remembered the dagger that Mario had loaned him, the one which he had not yet given back. He took it from his belt and held it out. "If you're scared, you can borrow this. It's a good dagger. I got it from a boy who was given it by his father. And his father was a soldier who killed many Spaniards. I bet there is Spanish blood on it yet. That's what Mario told me."

The fat priest muttered under his breath, "Spawn of a mutinous, murderous traitor. Yes. Exactly like your father."

Afonso was not sure what the priest meant. He nodded. "All right, then. Stay right behind me. God talks in lots and lots of colors, and when He gets excited, He talks fast and He makes you dizzy."

He tucked Mario's dagger into his belt and led the way. At his heels he could hear the fat priest wheezing. Amid the confines of the narrowing corridor, Afonso could smell the priest, too: a mix of onions and old incense and red pepper.

One turn and then another, the road now so familiar. Afonso felt the first touch of blue comfort coil about him, then a brush of welcoming flaxen.

And then he heard the scream.

Afonso whirled. Drops of holy water splattered his cheek. The fat priest was flinging the vial madly.

"It's all right," Afonso said. "God is just saying hello."

With a cry of horror, the priest bolted down the corridor, crucifix hoisted. Afonso apologized to God and followed.

Outside in the meadow, the fat priest was shouting at the soldiers, "Bury it! Hide this blasphemy from God's face. Put it in the earth with the other demons, where it belongs." He flailed the vial. Holy water splashed the air, the grass, the acorn, Afonso's tunic.

The soldiers looked to where Afonso stood. The captain of the guard shrugged his shoulders in unspoken question.

"Bury it!" the fat priest shrieked. "Lest all of you be brought before the Holy Office. Lest you join this insurgent Bragança excuse for a king when Satan drags him down to Hell."

The meadow became very still and quiet. The fat priest looked around at the soldiers. He looked at Jandira and at Father de Melo. He turned to Afonso.

"Thank you for coming," Afonso said.

P ESSOA OPENED THE door to find her kneeling at her cold hearth, tying bundles of marigolds. The wash of sunlight from the doorway struck gilt from the flowers, copper from her hair. As she turned, light glowed in her face. His eyes held her, and for one flawless instant that was embrace enough.

"Since your own foolishness has enticed you to stay, I thought I should bring you food." He put the basket down on the table. "Burn you must for your own stupidity, but while I have breath I will not see you starve."

He picked up the rabbit by its still-oozing haunches and laid it on the tabletop. "Skinned and gutted. And there are apples and honey and salt."

She rose and went to the door. He grabbed her wrist to stay her. "From now on, we must leave it open."

She twisted her arm free. They were so close that he could see the reflection of the window in her eyes. So close that he was made a drunkard by her smell. He looked away. "And cheese, too. And this." He took the crucifix from his pocket. The chain twisted, a rich slick eel, on the tabletop. "From now on, you must wear it."

"But that is the one your brother gave you the year you took your vows."

"I doubt he will ask where it is. I have seen him but half a dozen times since. You would not take my money. Is this not good enough for you, either?"

She took up an iron pot and put the carcass of the rabbit in it. She knelt, piled up kindling in the hearth, and sparked it alight.

"The cross is yours. I will not take it back. Do what you will with it."

She added water to the pot, bunches of wild onion, and a pinch of salt from the bag.

"People are going to talk about the virgin conception, Berenice, and I imagine that Dona Teixeira has told people what you found during your examination. Were Maria Elena my daughter and so gravid, I imagine that I would tell the world. And if your name is mentioned, there is no way I can stop you from being called before a tribunal. For the Inquisitor-General of Lisbon himself has come to Quintas."

She looked up, and the dread he saw rocked him.

"Berenice," he whispered.

She ducked her head. Her hands flew so fast, like the vendor and the rabbit, like the executioner and the accused. The snap of a wild carrot from off its lacy green stalk came as sudden as the breaking of a neck.

"Berenice. I brought my purse. Take it and leave. Go to England or Saxony. Go to some place the Inquisition is not. And take the crucifix, for it is solid gold, and fine work. Even melted, it will buy you a journey."

Another snap, but this time her hand trembled. "I can't."

"Because some fantasy tells you not?"

"Because he told me it matters not whether I go or stay. That I will die here or there. I know it is true, for he could hardly bring himself to say the words." A cracking separation of root from stem, her hands so practiced. "When he speaks, I hear him in the draft down the chimney, in the breeze through the window. I ask him questions, and he answers, so close, and his breath so warm. And when he has a bad news to tell me, his voice is even softer. He speaks in words that would not stir a candle. He loves me in whispers."

"Stop this," he said.

Her furious hands moved, breaking a stem. "He loves me more than you do, you who must leave the door open, you who comes but once a season and always leaves before daybreak—"

"Stop!"

"You, who only visits me betimes. Who dares not laugh out loud for fear the neighbors will hear."

He grabbed a handful of shawl and blouse. Wild carrots spilled from her fingers. She tried to pull away, but he held fistfuls of her. He shook her so hard that her hair flew free of her pins.

"Witch! You seduce me—all kisses and loose thighs—then you tear my heart out!"

He shook her and shook her, and only when he realized she was sobbing did he let her go. He stood back, helpless and ashamed. Then he remembered the open door and he looked to see if anyone had overheard.

Berenice noticed. When their eyes met again, hers were cool.

He said lamely, "Well. I shall leave the money. If you flee, Godspeed. For I will not be back."

Kindling flamed. Worms of fire crawled the skin of a log. She gazed into the pot as if she would scry into its green-specked water. Pessoa caught glimpse of a pink body floating beneath the surface.

"If you are brought before the tribunal, I will do my best to save you."

"You cannot save me."

He said, "Not if you are determined to die." And he left, not daring to look back, even though he might never see her again.

BERNARDO SEARCHED THE lawyers' faces, but the cherubs merited only a slowing of the pair's descent. Upon reaching the foot of the stairs, however, the lawyers turned not toward the women's cell where they were due to go, but instead toward the angels'. When they reached the iron bars—Scarecrow all the time blowing through pursed lips and shaking his head; Goatee toying with the point of his beard—Goatee said, "*This* is very interesting."

Before Scarecrow could put his hand to the unlocked chain and the open latch, one of Father Manoel's armed field hands barred their way.

"I remember as I saw you." The man jerked an ill-shaven chin toward Bernardo. "But I doubt as I've seen these others."

The lawyers nodded affably. "We're with the Inquisition, and come to take preliminary statements."

The man bowed with the proper respect. "Good luck to you, then. This pair don't talk much."

Bernardo met the angels' black eyes and the floor dropped from underneath him. The heartbeat of vertigo passed and the gaze left, the floor firmed. Bernardo realized that he was hearing prattle about funeral candles and silver basins.

"Ah, that," the guard was saying. "Put there to collect the honey. A hole in his side, here." He lifted an arm, letting out a noxious cloud of body odor. "Just here. Didn't see it before, seeing as how it was small. But that's where the honey comes from. Look." He proudly displayed his hand. "Burned myself with the lamp, and I picked up a drop of that honey on my finger and spread it on. Ended the hurt, O"—he tugged on an ear to underscore the efficacy—"just like that!"

"Um." Goatee chewed at his lip. "Dead, yet no corruption? The water from him causing some small evidence of miracle? Mark that, please, Father Notary. Not direct proof of sainthood, but I suppose—"

"Yes," Bernardo said. "I will make note."

Scarecrow: "Frankly, I do not care for this at all. I know nothing about evidencing miracle. I am not trained in that."

Goatee: "Might mean truck with the Holy See in Braga."

From Scarecrow a gloomy, "Or Rome."

Goatee lifted his eyes to Heaven.

Scarecrow pointed to the cherubs. "And they don't speak at all, man? They just stand about like that?"

"Pretty much," the guard said.

Scarecrow asked Goatee, "Do you have a need to go inside there?"

Goatee said, "No. You?"

Scarecrow gripped the bars. "Ho!" he called out.

How could he not quail before those wise and immortal gazes? It was all Bernardo could do not to fall to his knees.

"You! Ho! We are with the Inquisition, sent to gather statements. Will you speak?"

Goatee: "At least tell us if you have hired counsel."

Scarecrow: "You have a right to counsel."

Bernardo felt himself drawn into that blackness, like Jonah, swallowed whole. Below, a glint of something opulent afloat in the depths. He swam toward it, lost all memory he had of Earth. His lungs filled with the weight of dark water. He sank.

"Well!" Goatee exclaimed.

Bernardo popped to the surface like a cork.

The lawyers threw up their hands and, muttering among themselves, walked to the women's cell.

Bernardo said, "The parish priest talks to them."

They turned.

Part of Bernardo still drifted. His body felt dense and strange, his hands clumsy. The lawyers were staring at him. *O Jesu. Miserere mei.* He had just implicated Father Soares.

The guard chirped up. "Right, father! He does. Says they talk to each other through their eyes. The women, too—at least the Teixeira girl. Seen her looking out her cell into the other, and the cherubs all staring back. Kneels there for hours at the bars, and sometimes she cries."

Scarecrow said, "The parish priest and the girl talk to them. Father Notary? Mark that."

They put hand to the lock, and the guard sprang forward to open the cell. A solitary young woman looked up from her nest of blankets. In the corner, a matron held a bruised girl in her lap.

The lawyers bowed and swept off their hats. "Tadeo Vargas and Emílio Cabral, assigned as inquisitors to the Holy Office. Are you being treated well?"

The girl in the blankets was a pretty thing, and saucy. "Well enough for being in a jail, I suppose. I've never before been in one."

"And you have food?"

She opened a large basket next to her. From it came the enticing scents of summer savory and garlic. "My father visits every day, and brings enough for the Teixeiras, too." She inclined her head toward the other two women. "And he brings sweets for the guards."

Scarecrow inclined his head to the matron. "And you, *dona*? No complaints?"

"None."

Bernardo peered through his lashes at the girl the woman cuddled in her lap. The girl was hollow-eyed, as if the beating she took had pounded emotion from her.

"Good. Good," Goatee said. "And do you any of you have counsel?"

The matron snorted. "As if that lout of a husband would buy us one."

Murmurs of commiseration from the lawyers, pitying shrugs for the burden of husbands. The pair asked, quite genially, if the women had any statements to make.

There was a yes from the solitary girl.

"Just a moment, please." Bernardo perched himself on a sill near the bars. He took out his writing devices and set them in order. He dipped his quill. "Continue."

"I was called to come before the Blessed Mother," the girl said. "Would the Inquisition wish me to ignore that summons? If you do not find miracle here, then you are blind."

When he finished with that note, Bernardo stopped writing. No. She was far too haughty to be a messenger of the Blessed Mother. Mary had been female perfection itself: mild of voice and meek of act. The two lawyers waited courteously.

Her cheeks flushed. "And . . . and if I were you, I think I would not make Heaven so angry."

Scarecrow nodded. "Thank you. Is that all? Yes? You're certain? And you, *dona?*"

"Must I make a statement?"

Bernardo wrote at the top of a new page: *TEIXEIRA*. It confused him to see impudence in the matron, too. How could God choose these: two bitter women and a battered child?

"Not unless you wish," Goatee said. "But it is customary to ask the prisoners if they have searched their hearts, and if they have, if God has pressed them to make a statement."

"Once I thought I understood God," she said. "Then my daughter was ravished by angels. They got her with child against her will. What's worse . . ." She shot the cherubs a look of such venom that it made Bernardo lose the flow of the script. The word *child* came out deformed. "They took the baby away, and would not give it back. And they took her maidenhood with it, for she was intact until the birth. Now no man will marry her."

Bernardo stopped writing. *Beata virgo*. The look in that girl's face. No. He was wrong. It was not blankness at all, but so calm a serenity that other emotion was laid waste.

"She was intact?" Scarecrow asked. "Until when?"

"Seven months heavy with child, and virgin."

Goatee drew in a quiet, but interminable breath. "Are there any witnesses you would like us to call?"

The mother stroked her daughter's hair as if, through the touch, she bestowed what she knew of love. "Her own father felt of her. Bring him before you, and even though he doesn't believe angels, he will tell you maidenhood certain enough."

From Scarecrow, a disappointed "Her father. Well. Would there be anyone else?"

She said, "That herbalist, and she is better at midwifery than any, and knows more medicine than any bearded doctor."

"Um. And her name?"

Bernardo heard her say it, and he wrote it down. The name she spoke was all lush hungry mouths and moaning sweated bodies. He looked down at his journal, and it surprised him that the letters he had scripted had not trembled.

Call Berenice Pinheiro.

AFONSO CLOSED HIS eyes. Tent and bed drifted like God did through the void. Sailing that emptiness, he felt Jandira tuck the coverlet about him.

He heard the captain's hushed voice. "Asleep?"

And hers. "I think so."

Today after the fat priest left, Afonso had visited God. And once inside, he saw that His colors had stanched their bleeding, and that, although God still did not remember, He was no longer afraid.

"You needn't trouble yourself with what happened today, my lady. We remember when the monsignor plotted with Spain against the Bragança throne. We don't fear Gomes. And it matters little to my soldiers whether sun moves or earth or moon. As far as I am concerned, I know not what the acorn is, but I think it goes beyond the Inquisition's authority to decide. And my men don't believe it demonic, either. They saw how holy water struck the acorn, and yet did not make it vanish in flame and smoke."

Afonso heard a rustle of clothing and smelled vanilla. An edge of the bed sank, spilling Afonso into night. He fell far, and he fell gladly, tumbling past the blue-white ball of earth.

Through the abyss, he heard Jandira's low "And Castelo Melhor?"

An even quieter answer. "He is no Bragança." Then: "But you will be safe enough here, my lady, even if war rages about us. It was a luck, in fact, that we are not in Lisbon. The count would be pulling him one way, his brother another. Bless him for the sweet-natured soul that he is. Love and duty would rend him in two."

She said, "Yet if the count sends a message, you will tell me?"

A sad "Ah. It depends on what is said. For I warrant, Pedro and his sister will usurp the throne. Yet if the count sends word for me to join him in battle, I cannot obey. I made an oath to King João that I would not fight any of the house of Bragança; not Afonso, not Pedro."

Pedro rose up in the darkness, gleaming. Afonso put his hand out and felt the warm grip of his brother's fingers.

I have brought you a present. See?

In Afonso's hands rested a statue of Don Quixote, holding a little velvet banner and a tiny silver sword.

Tell me all about the windmills, Pedro said.

The captain's voice trembled. "But I swear before God, I will let no one harm him."

Mᴏɴsɪɢɴᴏʀ ꜰʟᴀᴘᴘᴇᴅ Cᴀsᴛᴇʟᴏ Melhor's message so energetically that it seemed it might take flight. "As you love God, the fool says!" His voice boomed through the inn. "As you love God! Were I to do my best by God, I would hand over that drooling Bragança to be burnt. And—I promise you, Bernardo—if Pedro is successful in his endeavors, I shall write the relaxation order myself!"

Bernardo prudently shut the door.

"You should have been there! Face-to-face with evil, and yet I did not shrink. Entered where none else but the idiot—who obviously knows no better—dared go. Like a warrior I went inside, only Holy Mother Church as my cross and shield. O, the horrors I saw! All anarchies of form and color, so that I could tell not what. His soldiers, mind you—his soldiers ordered to bury the thing. Yet they stand all agape, obtuse as that king himself. I tell you, it breeds a foul-smelling wickedness."

"Yes, Monsignor." Bernardo pulled back the coverlet to dust the sheets with cayenne. The cotton was already speckled with red, both crimson fresh blood and rusty old—a certain sign of fleas. He shook the bottle harder. Cayenne rose up in a cloud, and he sneezed. The bed stank of a long and varied succession of unwashed bodies.

Monsignor hoisted the message up in his fist. "Give me your blessing, Castelo Melhor says! Frightened, is he? All the nobles in arms against him? Give me your blessing, indeed! Ha, ha! May he fall down and kiss my feet. I promise you, Bernardo! I will see him do so before this thing is ended. Well? Don't just stand there! Call the marquis's two lawyers. Now! I want them here and now, Bernardo! Be quick!"

Bernardo put down the cayenne and hurried to their room. He found the pair seated on their bed, cards in their hands, a pile of silver coins between them. Breathless from his run, he told them that Monsignor was calling. The lawyers let drop their cards; they abandoned their coins. All together, they hurried up the stairs and down the corridor, turning right to Monsignor's room.

They found him sitting glum and motionless in the shadows, watching the sunset. His anger had vanished, and some quietness in the room had possessed him. "Rain coming soon," Monsignor said.

The lawyers, chests heaving, stood by the door.

A dreamy "You can smell it, can't you? The rain?"

Castelo Melhor's message had been dropped forgotten to the planks. Bernardo came forward, picked it up, slipped into his pocket. He lay his hand on Monsignor's shoulder. "Monsignor? The lawyers have come."

Ah. The uncanny emptiness in those eyes. "Lawyers?"

"The Inquisition-trained lawyers, Monsignor. The ones who were sent by the marquis."

A nod. A whispered "Then get your quill and ink, boy, for we have much to do."

Bernardo gathered both journal and foolscap. He uncorked the ink, dipped his quill, and waited.

Staring fixedly into the twilight, Monsignor motioned the lawyers to his side. "Come look," he said. "This is order. Do you not see? Each day the sun rises and sets over the selfsame hills."

Bernardo sat, quill poised, above the blank page. Scarecrow and Goatee exchanged troubled frowns.

"Tomorrow," Monsignor said, "we will begin an inquisition. I have gone over all the notes and familiarized myself with the case. I would have the Teixeira family first—all of them. Have one of the marquis's guards see to that. Then the herbalist. Then the Castanhedas. From their testimony, we will see if there are any others."

Bernardo's quill scratched across the page. He hurried to keep pace.

"We will end it quickly," Monsignor said. "Whatever happens outside this place, whether war or revolution or invasion, we will not move until our work is finished. Further . . ." Monsignor met Goatee's eye. "What happens remains a secret among us. Notation will be made, of course. But I will decide later whether the pages are to be burnt together with the heretics."

Scarecrow rocked back and forth, toe to heel, toe to heel. He shook his head. "This is highly irregular."

Monsignor came out of the chair so quickly that Goatee stepped back.

"I think we should take this up with the provincial seat in Mafra," Scarecrow said. "There is a process to a tribunal, and it must be followed."

"Indeed, sir." Goatee nodded. "One can't simply take the bit in one's teeth, go off, have an inquisition, and ignore the law."

Monsignor's eyes had narrowed, his cheeks were mottled. Bernardo knew storm was coming, and put down his quill.

An earsplitting "Law?" Another shout of "Law?" One that shook the walls. "You dare talk to me of law? I have gone eye to eye with evil. I fought Satan armed only with the word of God."

"With all due respect, Monsignor," Scarecrow said, "the law is law.

You cannot change that. It is as eternal as those hills there. You yourself hold a degree, and more than twenty years in court. That I must point illegality out to you is quite—"

"God Himself speaks to me!"

The lawyers again exchanged glances.

"And God has shown me my mission: to restore order in this place. For from this very spot comes such an anarchy that it will end the world."

Goatee nodded. "Ah."

Scarecrow said, "Compelling argument." Then a meek "Perhaps Monsignor might care to give us a note absolving us for any consequent suits brought? Otherwise, I don't see how . . ."

"O, indeed. Such an honor, sir. But I don't see how we can afford to serve."

"Yes. If it was found that we conducted so illegal a tribunal, well . . . Damage my reputation with the Holy Office, no doubt. For I travel, as you must understand. Evora, Braga. All the Holy Sees use me. Without some written guarantee, I must—although with a heavy heart, I assure you— plead to step down from the case."

"Also, this might cost more than was originally settled on," Goatee said.

"Um. Yes. Expensive, this sort of thing."

To Bernardo's intense surprise, Monsignor clasped his hands behind him, and walked to the window. "Write up whatever document they wish, Bernardo. I will sign."

Day 9

I N THOSE BLUE-BLACK HOURS WHEN BATS WHISK THROUGH THE SKY LIKE leaves—that time when owls navigate the landward wind—Pessoa awakened. Lying swaddled by night and the warmth of his bedclothes, his first thought was of the jailed women. And he believed that worry had pulled him from sleep until he heard the sound.

Pessoa sat bolt upright, letting blankets fall. The room was cold. The hearth fire had gone out. He peered about, sightless. "Luis?"

His own heart beat as loud as the stirring, and yet . . .

"Luis?"

A rustle of straw came as answer, then a creak of wood and leather, then breathing that was too unsteady, too akin to pain. Pessoa got up so fast that he upset his cot. His flailing toppled something and sent it skittering through the dark. He fumbled for flint, for candle. When he struck light, he saw the old priest hunched over the edge of his cot, his face pale and strained, his hand pressed to his chest. He was laboring for breath.

Pessoa's own heart felt as if it would stop. *O Mater Dei.* No. The chill of the room was nothing to the deathly cold between his ribs. Berenice. He would get Berenice. She would know what to do. He took a step and halted, picturing the old man alone, dying, calling for extreme unction. He pictured himself alone, watching a friend slip from life. At the door, Pessoa danced a jig of indecision.

Soares's hand reached out, grappled for air. "What?" Pessoa came to his side. "What is it you need?"

Soares coughed, his lungs phlegmy, his chest rattling. "Water."

"Yes. Certainly. Right away." Pessoa trembled so hard that he spilled half the jug. He brought the cup and knelt beside him and helped him drink. "I will send for Berenice."

"No." Soares's cheeks were drawn, his voice weak. "A dream." He drank, then set the empty cup down. He patted Pessoa's arm. "Go back to sleep."

On impulse, Pessoa put his palm to Soares's forehead. Warm, but not fevered. Or was it? Soares regarded him curiously and with mild amusement.

"Go back to sleep. I'm sorry I awakened you."

"More water." Pessoa filled the jar from the bucket, drenching the hem of his nightshirt, his feet. When he came back, Soares had pulled his blankets around him.

"Cover yourself, Manoel. You'll catch your death."

"Yes, yes. Just a moment." Shivering, teeth chattering, he knelt and filled Soares's cup.

"Not to be critical, Manoel, but you wet yourself more than you do the cup. And to be quite frank, your legs are not so handsome that you should go about in your nightshirt."

Pessoa looked up. Soares was smiling.

"I'm not dying, Manoel. *Gratia Deus.* And thank you for your efforts. Now get back into bed before you get a *gripe* and find that I make as clumsy a nurse as you."

Pessoa went to his cot and set it aright. He took a blanket and wrapped himself in it. He rekindled the hearth fire. He found the three-legged stool that he had kicked across the room, took it to Soares's bedside, and sat down.

"You will ogle me like a crow until morning." Soares sipped his water.

Inside his shelter of blanket, Pessoa slowly warmed. He yawned.

"Well then, if you must sit my death vigil," Soares told him, "we should at least have some brandy."

The suggestion brought Pessoa alert. "Brandy? I've never known you to have brandy."

"Hidden behind that top shelf of books. O, don't peer at me so indignantly. I don't hide it from you. One of my housekeepers has a taste for it. I never discovered which, and I have never complained. After all, their duty is given to the Church freely and with a generous heart. Mean-spirited of me to hide it from her, since she asks otherwise so little."

Pessoa went to the bookcase and stood tiptoe, moving aside clean-spined tomes, stirring nose-tickling dust on the shelves behind. Concealed there was a straw-clad glass bottle. Not just brandy. French brandy. And the bottle nearly full.

He brought the bottle and two clean cups. He and Soares sat drinking in a companionable gathering of shadows.

"I dreamed I was in the inn." Soares stared into the warm pulsing heart of the candle. "On the second floor. In the front room. You know the one."

"I believe that Gomes sleeps there now."

"Yes." Soares nodded slowly. "Yes. I believe he does. And I was just standing there, Manoel, looking out the window into the street. Only the building beyond was not the greengrocers, but the old inn—Cândido's new jail."

Pessoa looked at the shuttered windows. Behind them, he could feel the steadfast press of night.

"It was dark outside," Soares said. "And they were burning bodies. Carts lined the street, like from a plague. It was so dark that I thought the carts filled with logs until I saw the children."

Pessoa tipped the bottle, pouring Soares and then himself another finger of brandy. He watched the candle flicker. The liquor's fruity perfume was underlain with the wood cask in which it was aged. It tasted like honeyed fire.

"There were priests there, Manoel. They were the ones doing the burning. And the wind whipped bright flames and dark robes this way and that. It scattered sparks and sent embers flying." He took a breath. "It was so beautiful."

Soares's thin cottony hair was mussed. His face was sad and rumpled. "Then I realized what a great sin it was to find loveliness in it."

He sighed and put down his cup. He lay back on his cot and stared at the ceiling. "Go to bed, Manoel. They will call you to the inquisition just past matins."

Pessoa nodded.

"Promise me you will not sit up all night."

"Yes."

Soares's eyes closed. In a while his breathing deepened. Pessoa sipped brandy and guarded Soares as the old priest journeyed into sleep. Then he rose and snuffed the candle. In the light of the hearth fire, he fumbled his way to the window and opened it a crack. The air smelled of pine. When the wind changed hours later, it smelled of the sea. Pessoa stood sentry, guarding night as it crept to its hiding place in the valley, and protecting what he could of silver morning on its climb up the hills.

MARIA Elena Teixeira, a girl of fourteen years, was brought before the tribunal to be interrogated concerning a statement of a virgin birth. When it was seen that she did not answer the tribunal's questions, one of the two secular inquisitors present inquired concerning certain wounds on her face so as to ascertain whether she had been made senseless by state torture. Upon being assured this was not the case, the provincial inquisitor, Fr. Pessoa, then questioned whether the girl was fit to stand trial, as she appeared to be dazed. Comment was made by Msgr. Gomes that since the accused was the focus of the town's heresy, the tribunal had no choice but to make her answer.

The interrogation continued, the prisoner continuing to peer about the room until she was asked as to the whereabouts of her infant; and at that she began to weep and say the angels had taken it, for she had committed some sin, that she knew not what. And then she asked the gathered inquisitors, since they were learned men, if they knew her failing. Fr. Pessoa suggested that perhaps it was not the accused who was unworthy, but the world itself, that the angels gave a baby and then took it back. Msgr. Gomes asked the accused if she had murdered her infant and she wept loudly, pointing to the air and saying, "They are coming. Can you not stop them? O stop them. They come marching through the wall," at which time Msgr. Gomes asked if she had sighted demons. The accused did not answer but continued to wail and tear her cheeks until she bled, and it was ordered that a jailer come forward and return her to her cell.

Maria Elena howled her way down the stair, so that even when she was gone and the room quiet, Pessoa thought he could hear the stones resound.

What o'clock was it? Still early. The day too long. The strongest light on the tabletop yet came from the lamps. He studied the nervous, tapping fingers of Tadeo Vargas, the secular inquisitor, who sat next to him.

Tadeo said, "To be quite frank, Monsignor, we cannot discuss demons. Superstition is a matter for the state to deal with, not us."

Pessoa heard Gomes suck in a breath. Time hung, waiting for the exhale. Tadeo drummed his fingers.

"I am of the opinion, Inquisitor Vargas, that what we witness here is an infernal twisting of the story of Christ's birth. The star does not light the way. It falls. Angels act not as heralds, but as randy-natured Pans. We have a supposed virgin mother who scarce knows her own name, and who can much less keep her skirts down. The product of that birth lies not in a manger, but has disappeared no one knows where. And who arrives to witness this nonbirth? Not a wise man, but a drooling idiot of a king. No, Inquisitor Vargas. This is not superstition. This is Antichrist."

Tadeo's fingers halted. No. Surely Gomes did not believe . . . Pessoa's mouth went dry, his tongue ran aground.

Gomes called for the next prisoner and Pessoa dared not look up.

What o'clock was it? The morning must be over—it must—and time for lunch arrived. They would stop the absurdity, if only for two short hours.

He heard Gomes ask, "Name?"

He heard Senhora Teixeira's voice. "You have it writ there."

Louder. "Name?"

"Amalia Teixeira."

"Mother of Maria Elena Teixeira, who makes claims of a virgin birth?"

"Yes."

"And do you, too, make such a claim for your daughter?"

Pessoa jerked his head up and met her hurtful stare.

"Yes."

Gomes said, "Make your statement, please, so that the notary may write it down, and so there is no question as to what is confessed."

"Angels came into the house." Pink dawn poured through the eastern windows, invading the room with ethereal light. "They took my daughter away, screaming. They took her even as I slept in her room. They tore her from my arms. It was as it always is when men want a thing—women cannot stop them."

Gomes said, "Is that all?"

"No." Delicate morning glowed across her cheek, putting color where color had long faded. "The angels forced themselves in her, and her all the while pleading for mercy. And, as men sit here in judgment, you will find my daughter and not the angels guilty. You will burn her because you cannot manage the fire between your own legs."

Pessoa heard one of the two secular inquisitors clear his throat.

Gomes said, "Is that all?"

She looked toward the window, to the sun. "I have had much time to think on it, and I wonder if Mary herself was forced, and if God hurt her, too. But one blessing: at least this time He did not wait thirty years to steal the baby."

Pessoa heard the scratch of the notary's quill against paper. Scratch. Scratch. Then nothing.

And Gomes said, "That is enough."

A jailer came and led her away.

BROUGHT before the tribunal Duarte Teixeira, age forty-nine, man of commerce, husband to prisoner Amalia Teixeira and father to the accused Maria Elena Teixeira. He stated that he had no belief in either woman seeing angels. He credited their claim to female fantasy, and Maria Elena's swollen belly to her having lain with a boy.

He was asked by Fr. Pessoa the name of said boy, which Sr. Teixeira did not know. Sr. Teixeira was then asked by one of the secular inquisitors if he made claim as to his daughter's virginity, and Sr. Teixeira said that he did, that he himself had felt inside and found her intact sometime after he was made aware of her shame. He was of the opinion, however, that waywardness and female deception being what it was, Maria Elena had found a way.

Then Msgr. Gomes asked where the infant was, and Sr. Teixeira said that not only had he no idea, but that he cared not, except that it was gone from his sight. For he would have sent the baby to a wet nurse in another province, and sent the girl to a nunnery.

He was asked if that was the end of the testimony he wished to give, and he said that it was not, that he denounced both the women and their story, and that he was glad of the Inquisition setting things aright. He stated that business had sent him to the port at Cascais as the stories began, and that he returned too late. He apologized to the tribunal, and said that he no longer considered Amalia his wife nor Maria Elena his daughter.

Fr. Pessoa sharply admonished the witness for trying to sunder a tie that God and Holy Mother Church had made. He asked the witness if he believed himself a pope, with the power to dissolve a union.

The witness paled and crossed himself and begged the tribunal's forgiveness, that he had spoken out of turn, and what he said was meant only as a form of jest; and Fr. Pessoa said he was of the opinion that jests should not be so near to a heresy, and then he called the next witness.

THE MAID of the Teixeira household was brought forward, Maria Madalena Antunes, age thirteen. She was asked as to the claims of virgin birth and of the disappearance of the infant, and she replied that, as she was assigned to sleep in the youngest girl's room, she had seen nothing. Nor, upon being questioned, had she ever heard either of the accused speak of virgin births or angels.

THEN THE COOK of the Teixeira household was brought forward, one Clara Sales, widow, age thirty-one. She was asked as to the claims, and after being asked twice, once by a secular inquisitor and once by Msgr. Gomes, she said that she knew nothing. She was asked for detail, and she replied, to the amusement of the two secular inquisitors, that details of nothing are still nothing. She was dismissed.

CLÁUDIO TEIXEIRA, age ten, was called. He was asked about the claims, and he stated that one night he had seen a ball of light float through his room. When asked by Fr. Pessoa if it might have been a dream, he said that it could have been, but that he had pinched himself when he saw it, and it did seem that he was awake. He was asked about angels, and he said that he had never seen them, but that he had heard his sister cry out in the night, and could not get out of his bed to go save her, and that it very much distressed him to lie abed and hear his sister weep. On being asked why he did not go to his sister's aid, he said that he was unable to move, although he tried, and that all he remembered was looking across the hall and seeing a light under his sister's door.

Fr. Pessoa said that the experience sounded very much like

a dream, in that the boy was helpless to awaken and frightened by something that, upon reflection, made no sense at all. The secular inquisitors agreed, and so the boy was dismissed.

THE TRIBUNAL called Ana Teixeira, age four. When queried about the claims, she said that she liked angels. Asked when she had seen angels, she said she had seen them in pictures. She said that when she died she wanted God to make her an angel so that she could fly. She was again queried as to her sister's claims, and she said that she missed her mother. She was told to answer the question, and she said that she had forgotten what the question was. She was again asked about the birth of her sister's infant, and she told the tribunal that she had a baby doll which her sister had given her. She asked to see her mother, and was told to relate all that she knew about the night her sister gave birth. She said that she was thirsty, and a jailer was ordered to bring her water. She said that she wanted her mother, and was told to answer the tribunal's questions. She said that she had to use the chamber pot, and since no answers seemed to be forthcoming, she was excused.

BROUGHT before the tribunal, the herbalist Berenice Pinheiro, an unmarried woman twenty-seven years of age . . .

Her voice was soft and sweet, barely audible. Bernardo stopped his scribbling to look. Berenice Pinheiro had the dark exotic beauty of a Moor or a Judiazer; and she sat meekly, head lowered, peering at the tribunal through her lashes. She was poorly clothed, but neat enough, with one lone extravagance—and not one of vanity: the gold crucifix she wore round her neck.

This was the portrait of Mary—not the demented girl, not the saucy child. At the end of the table Father Manoel sat, his gaze so longing that

Bernardo was struck by the possibility that the stories about them might be true.

> . . . asked by a secular inquisitor if she had indeed examined the girl, and she said that she had, three times: once when the accused, Maria Elena, had announced to her father of the pregnancy, once when she was quite heavy with child, and the third time after the infant was ripped from the womb. A secular inquisitor inquired after who she thought had taken the infant, and why the witness would use such a word to describe a birth, and she said she did not know who might have taken it, and that she used the word because of the violence done to the girl, that although all blood had been stanched, the maidenhead was torn apart. She verified that the girl had been intact some three weeks before the baby disappeared from her belly; and when asked how she could be certain there was an infant, she said that she had midwifed over fifty, and that she herself had felt the child move. The witness further stated that she fretted for the delivery, for the girl's maidenhead was such that it would need the help of a knife to open it, and therefore the witness had cautioned both girl and mother to call her straightaway as the pains began.
>
> The witness was questioned by Msgr. Gomes if such a maidenhead would resist ordinary congress, and the witness said that neither mere congress nor birth would be sufficient to tear it. He then asked if it was not possible that some sort of congress had taken place. She said that she could not judge, not being a man. She demonstrated, by marking the second joint on her finger, how deep the maidenhead lay.
>
> At this, the two priests inquired of the secular inquisitors, who were married, if they thought such a congress possible, and one then asked the witness if the maidenhead was supple. She said that it was not, and that further, the girl suffered great pain when probed. The two secular inquisitors then conferred among

themselves, reaching the opinion that, not being a satisfying nor well-joined length, the man would in his urgency either spill his seed elsewhere, or would not spill his seed at all.

Msgr. Gomes asked if anything could pass through the maidenhead, and the witness said that monthly blood passed. He then asked if seed could not pass as well. A secular inquisitor said that it was not customary for a man to hold a woman's legs up in the air and pour his seed down in her, at which point a guard began to laugh so loudly that Msgr. Gomes banished him from the room and then cautioned the others that he had seen them smirking, and that he would not have it. Then Msgr. Gomes told the witness that she had been accused of being a Judiazer, and she said that she was not, that although she was daughter of new Christians, she believed with her whole heart that Jesus Christ was the Son of God and that He had died upon the cross for all our sins. She said that, as the town believed her possessed of the evil eye, she could not show herself at Mass lest she cause a commotion; but that she confessed herself to Fr. Pessoa, who as inquisitor and Jesuit, was not superstitious, and would bless her and give her the Eucharist.

Msgr. Gomes then inquired of Fr. Pessoa if that was true, and he said that it was, that the first thing he did upon arriving in town was to see what care was needed for her soul. At that point, a secular inquisitor fell into such a fit of coughing that he excused himself from the room, and interrogation was halted for lunch.

Pessoa dared not address her, and so he passed by where Berenice sat, head lowered, waiting again to be called. He sneaked down the steps to the jail. A surprise. Soares was not in the cell with his angels, but with the women. And he was not kneeling in prayer, but playing cards.

Pessoa watched at the bars until Senhora Teixeira spied him and stiffened.

Soares put down his cards. "Ah! Manoel! I am caught. No devotions this afternoon. Even so, games are a comfort."

Near her mother's feet Maria Elena lay, arms and legs drawn up as if all about were flames.

"Who wins?" Pessoa asked.

Soares threw up his hands. "Who can tell? Who can tell? We wager with lengths of straw, and I think that Marta plucks more from the piles about her and cheats." Chuckling, he got up and dusted himself. "What o'clock?"

"Past one. And the tribunal is halted for lunch. Is there anything left at the rectory?"

He gave an apologetic shrug. "But there is fried rabbit in Marta's basket, and cod cakes and three kinds of bread and cheese. Her father spoils us. Marta? Could Father Pessoa not have some of your rabbit?"

Pouting, Marta snatched up Soares's cards, then took Dona Teixeira's hand, and shuffled the deck.

"Bless you." And before Pessoa could stop him—for Marta's temper had stolen his appetite—Soares had gathered into a napkin a haunch, three cod cakes, and a loaf.

The guard opened the door. Soares brought the food out and led Pessoa across the hall, hissing, "Let her give it, Manoel. For she is a spoiled and miserly little thing. The more frightened she becomes, the worse she acts, so that Dona Teixeira and I come near to pummeling her. How goes the tribunal?"

Pessoa took the rabbit haunch, and feeling the grease on his fingers, smelling the garlic and thyme, his appetite came roaring back. "Badly," he said between chews. "Gomes believes we have birthed the Antichrist."

Soares's eyes flew heavenward. He crossed himself, kissed his fingertips.

The rabbit haunch was quickly dispatched. Pessoa plucked a cod cake from the napkin. "The seculars are appalled, but what can we do?" The cod was expensive and well prepared—the cake tasted more of potato and onion than of salted fish. Pessoa ate it in three bites and took out another. "He looks ill to me, Gomes does, as if he is not sleeping. And his voice has an edge to it that is entirely lunatic. I tell you, Luis, he frightens me. If I would have held an illegal tribunal, this one is insane. Today, hearing Berenice's testimony as to Maria Elena's maidenhood, his voice went shrill, and he would not leave the question alone, no matter how many times she answered. I expect to look up at any time and see the man barking like a dog, frothing at the—"

There. Like an apparition. Gomes's young secretary stood at the foot of the stairs. Pessoa stepped away from Soares so hastily that he nearly dropped his half-eaten lunch.

The secretary, hands clutching his beads, came shuffling forward. "I have spoken with the seculars," he whispered, "and they do not yet dismiss the claims of miracle. What leaves them doubtful is the reported violence of the angels and the whereabouts of the child."

Pessoa grabbed his arm and spun him toward the cherubs' cell. "Look there!" he commanded. "Do you see evil?"

He saw the instant when the boy's timid gaze was captured. "No," he breathed. "O no. *Angelicis virtutibus*. O, never evil."

"And yet a strength that is so powerful that—"

"Yes! I see what you mean. A holy power so fierce that it terrifies, that it causes pain. Yes. I will point this out to the seculars. Your suggestion today that the world may not yet be worthy for such a miracle affected them greatly. As it did me."

"Is it enough?" Pessoa asked.

Bernardo shook his head. "They still question. And their necks are yet under Monsignor's boot. But, father? I would speak with you concerning something else." Through those pale lashes, Pessoa could see pale blue eyes dart. "Not here. Some spot that is private."

A S ARRANGED, BERNARDO came upon him as if by accident. Father Manoel was sitting at the fountain, his elbows braced on his knees, his hands entwined. Bernardo thought of those hands pulling open the Pinheiro woman's thin shawl, lifting up that ill-made blouse; those fingers sliding over passion-fevered skin, tweaking nipples to firm pink arousal.

He tried to chase the thoughts, yet they returned, sweated and inflamed. No wonder the cherubs had taken back the child.

"*Pax tecum,*" Bernardo said.

Father Manoel looked up. His gaze was harsh, as if he had read Bernardo's thoughts. "Sit down."

Bernardo dug his fingernails into his palms until his mind was clean. He took a place beside Father Manoel on the ledge, in the music of the trickling water, in the smells of damp and moss.

"What is it?"

No. The story could not be true. Not Father Manoel. Not lechery in such a man as this. Bernardo lost courage. He took out his rosary. *Jesu pie.* He had not expected irritation.

The question came quick as a thrust, and knife-sharp. "What?"

"Concerning the vow of chastity . . ."

Out of the corner of his eye, Bernardo saw Father Manoel's head snap around, saw his hands clench.

"Me," Bernardo whispered.

Those strong hands relaxed.

"I come to beg your help, for by age fourteen I had lain with girls thrice, and then began study for my vows, and have never since been tempted—at least not greatly. And yet after arriving here, I think of it all the time."

Father Manoel leaned toward him. Their shoulders touched and Bernardo thought he could feel, under habits, skin spark to skin. He whispered, "No one said that you could not think upon it. Has no one ever talked about this to you, boy?"

He held his beads so tightly that his fingers cramped. He shook his head.

"To not think about it—especially at your age—would be an impossibility. Christ doesn't ask the impossible, He merely asks the difficult. Chastity becomes easier with age. In the meantime, pray. Go for walks. Visit the sick. Busy yourself into an exhaustion. I remember that I would run the rear stairs of the seminary at night, up and down, until I could barely stand." He chuckled. "Sometimes I would quite literally run into other novices."

"They say you lie with Berenice Pinheiro."

Father Manoel sat back, his warmth going away, leaving Bernardo's shoulder cold. Behind them the fountain splashed. A thrush lit, warbling, on a pomegranate branch.

"Who says?"

"Two doubtful witnesses: a tailor, Magalhães; an implausible woman named Inez."

The thrush trilled again.

"Did I not tell you," Father Manoel said, "that the angels will not converse except with the pure of heart? And thus they will not speak with me?"

Bernardo ducked his face into his hands and could feel the pressure of his beads against his cheek. *O immaculata castitas.* All purity gone.

"But I will tell you of another thing."

Father Manoel was quiet for so long that Bernardo raised his head. The Jesuit was sitting, staring across the plaza, hands braced on his knees. His toe tapped a fast and troubled rhythm. "My sin . . ." He cleared his throat. "My sin which has been confessed and absolved—was not one of lust, but of affection." The Jesuit looked to Heaven. "I love her, Bernardo." And Bernardo heard a jarring of ardor his voice. "She is a thorn in my heart."

Bernardo looked up as well, to blue sky and a curdling of buttermilk clouds. He could sit thus forever in the lyric of the fountain, in the scent of damp stone.

Father Manoel asked, "Can you forgive me?"

"No! I mean—please. I am not one to . . . I thought I was of a virtuous nature, but no more. You are so much better than I, for it is not affection I feel, father, but base lust, and not even lust toward a woman of sweet voice and sweeter nature, but everything. Anything. If the world has been judged by the cherubs and found guilty, why, I am most guilty of all. And seeing the woman herbalist's timid looks, well, I can fully understand how you could come to . . ."

"It is her sweetness I crave," he said. "For it is sweetness I lack."

"O, but—"

"It is true. And I tell you what I have never told anyone else. It is a revelation, in fact, to speak to you of things which have never yet crossed my lips. It is a great freedom."

"Yes! Yes, father. I feel the same!"

"And so I tell you this, trusting that you will understand. I once scourged myself to banish lust. And then when I arrived at an age when passion should dampen, this great affection came upon me. I confessed it and was shriven and swore a sacred promise to give her up—O, what a hardship! Then I understood that God Himself had sent her to me, wishing to reveal my stern sins by her very gentleness, for from lack of her, I became harsh with others, and that was not an answer, either. Can you see that?"

"Yes. Yes, indeed."

"And so to test my faith, I at times lie with her in my arms, but do not otherwise touch her. Desire stings worse than lash ever did; but as we lie, nakedness to nakedness, lust becomes a white-hot purifying pain. It sweeps me away more wildly and more freely than scourging, for scourging was merely of the body, and this is a pain of the heart."

Suddenly Father Manoel reached out and seized Bernardo's wrist. Bernardo would feel underneath his skin a divine inferno.

"This must be our secret," he said.

Bernardo nodded.

Then came a startling request, humble and contrite: "Bless me, father. *Mea culpa, mea culpa . . .*"

Bernardo gently caught the Jesuit's fist before it could again strike chest. *"Indulgentiam, absoluntionem, et remissionem peccatorum nostrum . . ."*

Thus they prayed together in the trill of the thrush, in the trickle of the fountain.

CALLED before the Inquisition, Marta Teresa da Penha Castanheda, age fifteen, to be asked concerning her claim of conversations with the Blessed Virgin Mary. She said that the Holy

Mother had charged her never to divulge these secrets to men, and therefore she was obliged to silence. She was then forcefully admonished by Msgr. Gomes and cautioned that she would be compelled to loosen her tongue. When she still refused to speak, he called for a state executioner to take her to a place of punishment, and for coals to be prepared for her feet, at which time Fr. Pessoa said that such a strict enticement could be used only after all other avenues had been tried, and that he was of the opinion that the accused had not yet been thoroughly questioned. The seculars agreed, but also pressed her to answer, at which time she replied that she would rather obey the dictates of the Mother of God than she would the orders of sour men.

A secular pointed out that arrogance was unseemly, since the accused appeared to imagine herself a saint; an indictment to which the accused had no reply. She was asked by Msgr. Gomes if, since Christ was a man, He would not be privy to the words of His own Mother. The prisoner had no reply.

Fr. Pessoa sternly warned the prisoner to search her heart once more, and to trust in the wisdom of the Inquisition, since they were given this charge by God. He warned her that if she refused to give a full statement, the tribunal would have no choice but to lay her feet to the coals until she confessed. He ordered her to be taken forth and clapped once more in jail and he admonished her further that she should recite her prayers and ask for guidance. He said that the Blessed Mother was not only wise, but good, and that she would not allow her daughter to languish or to be put to torture by forcing her to keep such an improper silence. The seculars agreed with Fr. Pessoa's decision, and she was taken away.

GUILHERME Castanheda, age thirty-eight, father of Marta, and man of commerce, was brought before the tribunal. He was asked concerning his daughter's claims, and he replied that she

was a good girl and not given to lying. He was asked if he had
direct knowledge of her dealings with the Virgin Mother, and he
said that he did not, but that his daughter had explained to him
that he was not deserving of the Blessed Mother's words. He
said that this was understandable to him, since he considered
himself a rough man, although now retired to a life of quiet commerce. Once he had been a soldier, however, and had killed
many, and was probably not worthy of any consideration by God
at all.

He was questioned by Mgsr. Gomes concerning a statement made that God did not reside in Spain. The witness then
spoke at length, stating that in his opinion war was fashioned by
the devil. He said that battle was a thing of noise, of shouts for
mercy and the explosions of cannon, and of horses' screams. He
said that even after conflict had ended, the terrible shrieking
continued, so that the survivors, no matter how wearied, could
not find sleep. He said that sometimes soldiers stole onto the
field or into the surgeons' tents. And there, despite the danger
and despite the darkness and despite the sin, they slew their
comrades who lay slowly and too loudly dying. He said that he
himself had been driven thus, and that no amount of confession
or shriving could ever cleanse him. He said that he had seen
men with skulls cloven in two who were fortunate, and men
who had had arms and legs blown away, who were not; for the
latter were compelled to lie, their bodies pumping out life,
while all about them battle continued. He said that in Spain, no
one took heed of the dying. No priest came to offer extreme
unction or comfort. The witness said that to die surrounded by
battle was to die alone; and that even six years after, he often
awakens in the night, clutching at his blankets as he would at
the soil, for he dreams that, in full sight of a crowd, he is being
buried alive.

The witness spoke eloquently, saying that war soaked
Spain's earth with the stink of gore and vomit, that it looted its

towns and left its trees blasted by curses. He said that God had no place there.

When the witness was finished speaking, the tribunal sat for a while in silence. And then Mgsr. Gomes asked how the witness could say that God had no place in Spain since God resided everywhere, to which the witness had no answer. At that time Mgsr. Gomes told a jailer to come forward, and imprison the witness in a cell.

Afonso had just sat down to luncheon in his tent when outside sprang up a bedlam of running and shrill commands and screams. Jandira jerked him up from table. In a nook between the bed and the travel dresser, she made Afonso sit. She wrapped him in her arms and told him to be very, very quiet.

Afonso didn't know why he should when all around him was noise. Three guards with muskets rushed into the tent shouting for Afonso to stay hidden.

"A game, isn't it, Jandira?" he said.

She must have been cold, for she was shaking. She held him so tight that he could scarcely breathe. "Yes, sweetling. Just a game."

Cries of "to horse, to horse," and "Hold them you ass-lick cowards, or fall where you stand" and "bring up the muskets." Then a tumult of hoofbeats and a bellow from the captain to hold! Hold fast!

A familiar voice said, "Will you shoot me and end this?"

In a blink, Jandira had pounced to her feet and run from the tent. Freed, Afonso crept from his cubbyhole and, under the watchful eye of his guards, peeked through the flap.

Before the tent was a bristling line of standing pikesmen, one of kneeling musketrymen. And facing them all was Castelo Melhor, with a band of soldiers and packhorses. The count sat astride his white Andalusian stallion; and the captain of the royal guard stood beside.

"Did you think I would harm him?" Castelo Melhor looked tired. "I have done my best to save the boy." His mustaches drooped, and his tunic was dirty. The white stallion was lathered and blowing. "Bishop Días says in doing so, I safeguard my soul." He laughed. "It is enough, I suppose, that Pedro lets me save my money."

He sat up in his saddle and peered over the heads of the pikesmen. He waved to Afonso, and Afonso waved back. "You remain king, sire!" he called. "For that is the peace I made—that your brother agreed to." He spoke to the men with the muskets. "Can you not point those away? Do you not see that I and my men are unarmed?"

The captain ordered his men to stand down. The pikesmen sat on the grass.

Castelo Melhor said, "I have heard some confusing news from this place."

The captain came closer. He put his hand to the white stallion's neck. "There have been some confusing happenings."

"So, angels or demons?"

The captain laughed so that the stallion shied and tossed his head. "I wouldn't know. I'm a plain man, and a soldier; and there are four degreed lawyers in Quintas who cannot decide."

"Well, captain, you may tell that obese, flatulent excuse for an inquisitor-general that Pedro leaves the title with his brother. Pedro might rule, but he orders Afonso to be treated with the deference due a monarch." He snatched his hat off and threw it down. "*Pôrra!* I still cannot believe it! Me, who has killed scores of Spaniards, who has gone face-to-face with Death itself—I turn my back for an instant only to have a boy stick it in me."

Afonso spied Jandira standing beside the lounging musketrymen. He waved to her, but she wasn't looking. Her hands were folded over her belly, so that anyone could see the melon child that grew inside. She cried out to Castelo Melhor, "My lord! My lord!"

He nodded to her. "My lady." Then he said to the captain: "Pedro sends you a request: to keep Afonso here until his leadership is fully settled and the ministers changed. He bids you guard the king with your life, as he knows you will. And he thanks you for your devoted service."

Jandira smoothed her robes over her belly and cried, "My lord! Will you not heed me? I cannot remain here!"

Castelo Melhor's eyes swept over her to the flapping banners, to the encampment of tents. "I will miss it," he said, and Afonso was not sure if he would miss tents and soldiers or royal banners and bright flags.

"Where do you go, then?" the captain asked.

"Um. First to Oporto where my ship awaits, then to England, if you will credit that."

Jandira started across the clearing, but one of Castelo Melhor's men kicked his horse forward and barred her way. "My lord!" she called out. "Can you not see? I bear a royal burden, as you commanded. You cannot leave me here!"

Afonso would have gone to her, but one of the guards held him back.

"Well." The count nodded in Jandira's direction, but Afonso could tell that he had not truly heard. Then he looked dismally about the camp. To cheer him, Afonso waved again. The count sighed and waved back. "Well, so. I will have gold enough, God knows. And the English are not so dour now as they were under Cromwell. There is a queen there who may not care for me overmuch, but who at least speaks my language. Best, there is no Inquisition."

"Will you stay and dine with us? Your horse and your men seem weary."

"Ha! I think not! Pedro gave me little time to quit the kingdom, and he proves himself neither fool nor someone to be thwarted. To his credit, though, he is kind enough. I warrant—somewhat against my will, mind— that he will rule well."

Then Castelo Melhor cried out, "Grant me Godspeed!" He wheeled the stallion and spurred him down the road, his soldiers and packhorses galloping behind.

Jandira's scream startled Afonso. It made the captain whirl in surprise. She ran headlong and barefoot down the road after the horses, her hair loose and streaming, her robes flying. Afonso left the tent and watched as the horses drew farther and father away, as their dust shrouded her. Then she was lost from sight as she went over the lip of the next hill; and he grew frantic with wondering if she would come back, if she would run so far that she would lose her way.

So he held himself and wept. Father de Melo told him not to fear, that the news was good, that Afonso would remain king with Pedro to help him. He patted Afonso's arm and asked if that wouldn't be nice.

Afonso looked at the place where Jandira had vanished: a lonely spot that would never again look complete. The captain came and bent his knee and said that Pedro would be honorable—a thing which Afonso already knew.

Afonso reached out and tried to grab that place on the road which had swallowed Jandira and left only haze as reminder.

"He weeps for the bitch," the captain said as he got to his feet.

Father de Melo dipped his head to the captain and whispered, "I doubt he even knows it is his get, but one brown bastard more or less will not threaten Pedro."

Then the captain stood close and peered directly into Afonso's eyes. "Sire? Sire, calm yourself. She'll be back soon enough."

And indeed, Afonso soon saw through the dust on the road a colorful dot, a dot all the hues of God. Then the dot was closer and he could see that it was she, and he could see how she walked: head down and too slowly, her hands clutching her swollen belly.

He stood there while the guards dispersed to their duties, while the captain ordered the cavalry to unsaddle their mounts.

Afonso waited a long, long time. And when she finally reached his side, she did not speak. She went into the tent and lay down on her pallet and turned her face to the wall. When he asked her to tell him a story, she said she had no more stories to tell.

REQUESTING an audience before the tribunal, Cândido Torres, age forty-two, vintner, and familiar to inquisitor Fr. Pessoa. The witness defended the jailed Guilherme Castanheda, saying that

Sr. Castanheda was a good enough man for any, and braver than most. Sr. Torres said that he himself had been busied by battle for a few years, but that, all in all, Sr. Castanheda had fought in the bloodiest; battles such that a dog should not see. He said that war changed Sr. Castanheda, that he had left one man and come back another. Worse, he came home to the bosom of family only to find his wife dying. Sr. Torres stated that grief for his wife had so crazed Sr. Castanheda that afterward the man could see no wrong in his children. Sr. Torres was of the opinion that Marta was pretty enough not to hide under the covers, but that the girl was far too sharp of tongue to ever wed—lest she find herself a man who was deaf. He said that Sr. Castanheda let her grow up untamed, for he had not the heart to chastise her. The witness begged that clemency be shown, since Sr. Castanheda's mistake was one of maudlin fondness, and he asked that the prisoner be set free from prison in order to care for his son.

Msgr. Gomes thanked the witness for his testimony, and said that there were more heresies charged against Guilherme Castanheda, and that the prisoner could not be set free until all the accusations could be satisfied. He excused the witness.

CALLED before the tribunal, Rodrigo Castanheda, age eight, son of Guilherme Castanheda . . .

Bernardo saw the boy and his script halted on the page, words failing. Soft of eye and face—*Plena Dei pulchritido*—the boy was so startlingly beautiful that Bernardo, lest he find himself blinded, looked away.

He heard Monsignor's grating voice. "Do you know the heresy of which your sister is accused?"

And the boy's melodious "I know that she talks all the time of the Virgin."

"And what does she say?"

"She won't tell me what the Blessed Mother says, as if I would care to hear girl-talk. I can't see the Virgin saying anything important to Marta."

There followed a weighty quiet. Bernardo noted how the afternoon light caressed the brass ink pot and the blinding white barbs of the quill. And then he heard Monsignor say, "Notary? Asleep already? Or have you broken your hand?"

"Sorry, Monsignor." A dip of the quill. He made a few quick scribbles, his hand unsteady. "Just thinking, Monsignor."

"Dear God, Bernardo. Notaries don't *think*! Boy! You—what is your name again?"

"Rodrigo Castanheda."

"Rodrigo. Yes. And do you know why your father is jailed?"

He said, "Because you are wicked."

Bernardo looked up. A mistake. He was so enraptured by the boy that his hand forgot again to move. His head swam. Bernardo was put in mind of a dove, and he imagined how it might be to cradle such a small soft thing; to feel against his own chest the throb of such a chaste heart.

Father Manoel said kindly, "Rodrigo, I do not think—"

"It is all a wickedness, the Inquisition." The boy sat in judgment like the cherubs in their cell—small in stature, an immensity in his eyes.

Monsignor snorted. "No doubt that is what your father tells you. Make a note, Bernardo."

"No! Father doesn't tell me! He doesn't have to. I'm old enough. You think you'll scare me into crying like you did the tailor Magalhães, like Gregorio Neves. I'm not afraid of you."

Monsignor's palm slapped the table so hard that he rattled the ink pot. "You had best! God Himself has charged me to protect Holy Mother Church."

The boy said, "I don't believe the Blessed Mother talks to Marta; and I don't think God talks to you."

"Jail him," Monsignor ordered. "Excuse the remainder of the witnesses. The inquiry is finished for the day." Then he leaned over, whispering into Bernardo's ear: "Have the marquis's men seize the Castanheda house without delay. See they take care with my feather bed."

PESSOA WATCHED BERENICE rise and leave. He heard the seculars walk away, embroiled in an argument not of wonders, but some obscure point of law. He watched Monsignor stride from the room, and Bernardo stand to set his journals in order. Outside the windows, the sun began to set.

"He cannot hold the boy," Bernardo whispered to his quills. Precise little movements, an ink pot set just so. "For it is no heresy to doubt someone speaks with God." A quill was nudged in order. "But just the opposite."

How dull could his mind be not to realize? Or had Monsignor's behest caught him unawares? Pessoa brushed past Bernardo, giving him a cautious and mumbled "Thank you." He walked from the room, leaving the young priest alone with the twilight.

On the way to the inn, Pessoa saw soldiers in the streets; and when he sat down in the smell of roast pork and potatoes and wine, he heard the gossip. Castelo Melhor had fled. Afonso was deposed by his brother. Pedro would kill Afonso. Pedro would not. Words flew over his head like arrows—no smile or friendly greeting struck. He ate alone while history roared about him. A shoving match started, one man championing Castelo Melhor, the other defending Pedro and the rebellious nobles.

Castelo Melhor was despot; he kept the country in order. The count would ride to France and return leading a victorious army; he would lay Portugal waste. One man laughed and said that he would easier believe the count arriving on a Bethlehem star, leading hosts of angels. At that, the inn grew quiet and all eyes flew to Pessoa.

Pessoa sopped the last of the gravy with the last of his loaf. He finished his wine. He left two brass coins for the serving girl and walked out into the night. When he reached the street, babble and laughter erupted behind him.

He shoved his hands into his pockets against the wind. He walked, dodging the foul hail of that evening's tossed garbage. Eggshells and potato skins splattered the cobbles. Rats came swarming. Cats emerged from alleys.

He walked through the stench of boiled salted cod and cabbage. From an upstairs window came a cacophony of baby's screams. Where was Maria Elena's infant? What would become of the kingdom, what would become of them all?

He rounded a black corner, taking a shortcut through a garden until he was in sight of the rectory. Soares was in the open doorway, clucking to his cats.

Pessoa stopped on the other side of a wattle fence to watch. The Franciscan's long gaunt shadow eclipsed the hanging lantern: one side of him bright, the other mystery. Pessoa thought to tell him the news—a change of kings—but it was not so important after all. He was torpid of mind, bone-achingly exhausted. Instead of joining Soares in companionable light, Pessoa returned to darkness.

He passed the fountain, the square, the Teixeira house, shuttered as if already in mourning; then by the Castanhedas', where armed guards stood outside, and wagons.

He went to Marta Castanheda's blighted tree. Under a quarter moon, he walked the meadow. He sat down in the center of that barren circle and waited for vision to come. He wrapped his arms about himself, and when the moon did not descend, when he heard no angel voices and saw no blue-clad Queens of Heaven, when he could no longer stand his own helpless shivering, he got up and left.

Where was Maria Elena's baby? What was the nature of the strange beings?

He stepped on a pebble, collected a stone bruise, and walked on, limping. What—other than reason—was to say that miracle had not happened?

No. She had birthed it, and smothered it, and her mother had dug the small grave. They would never find the body, for the women would rather burn than have the town know their shame.

And the creatures? Perhaps more like animals, perhaps not even conscious. But from where? Easier to believe that they were fashioned of the women's dreams, a nightmare turned flesh. And when the tribunal had run its course, and the women were dead, the beings would vanish.

And afterward, Pessoa would make himself forget, for it was fruitless to wonder and ever be denied answer. Inquiry should lead to conclusion, that's what his order taught. If asked, he would say that he imagined that he had seen something like a star fall. That he thought he had spied something once in a cell, but that it was a trick of the eye, the mind, the light.

Pessoa found himself at the jail. Just inside the door a group of Monsignor's men were gaming dice. One man noticed him enter, and that one noticed him but barely. Pessoa stood in the gloom beyond the lamps and listened. They laughed about Castelo Melhor's hurried escape and of how Monsignor would bring Afonso to heel—that is, unless his brother slew him. They talked of new laws. And over and under their talk, Pessoa could hear from the downstairs jail a music so fine that even conversation of kings became chatter.

A well-played lute, with two voices in harmony weaving the same soprano range. Quietly, Pessoa made his way to the stairs. Halfway down, in the wash of the voices, the monsignor's secretary sat, back to the wall, face uplifted, his closed eyes leaking tears. Pessoa's footsteps must have startled him, for he hurriedly wiped his face with his sleeve.

"O, it is you," the boy said.

Pessoa sat beside him. The music rose and fell, the voices cutting the silence like a sharp prow would the sea. Marta Castanheda played her lute at the women's cell bars. Across the way Rodrigo sat in the straw of the men's cell, flanked by two attentive cherubs.

"Palestrina," Bernardo whispered. " 'Sicut cervus disderat ad fontes aquarum.' "

Pessoa nodded. He closed his eyes and let the music take him. "Psalms. 'So as the hart yearns for springs of water.' " Stunned, he felt Bernardo's hand clasp his own. He dared not flinch. The determined squeeze of those fingers that would never pluck magic from a lute, never bring a woman groaning to pleasure. Meticulous little ink-stained fingers that would know aught but quill. Was it love the boy felt, and not simple admiration? The song ended. The fingers slipped from his.

Pessoa put his hands in his pockets. A chord from the lute, and Rodrigo's sweet piercing soprano. *Regina caeli.*

"Who brought them the lute?" Pessoa asked.

Bernardo said, "I did. For the monsignor has seized the house, and he and the seculars and the state executioners already moved in. I wanted to save what personal belongings I could before inventory was made."

"Um." Pessoa's eyes felt grainy, his lids weighted. "I will perform my legal magic and see if I can save the boy tomorrow." He caught sight of Guilherme Castanheda sitting by himself in a corner. He shook his head. "At least," he whispered, "save the boy."

The two strange beings had gathered about Rodrigo to listen. Their large heads were tilted, their expressions blank yet attentive. And—was he imagining it?—devoted. Pessoa turned to remark upon it, but words forsook him when he saw in Bernardo the selfsame ecstasy.

Day 10

J ANDIRA WOULD NOT GET UP FROM HER PALLET, NO MATTER HOW LOUDLY Afonso called, no matter how roughly he pulled on her arm. She would not speak, she would not bring him breakfast.

Father de Melo came in from the rain, his cassock dripping. "What is it, sire?"

"She is lazy! She is drunk!"

Father de Melo went to her. Then he rose up and called loudly for the captain.

"I need to use the chamber pot," Afonso said. "She needs to dress me."

A damp breeze blew through the tent. It rattled the supports and made the lanterns flicker. It blustered under the tent skirts and moaned louder than Jandira, who did not moan loudly at all.

A guard came and helped Afonso to piss. He gathered the royal garments and dressed him. "She is lazy. She makes no sense whatsoever. Make her talk to me."

The captain hiked his cloak over his head. He dashed out into the rain and came back with the company surgeon. The surgeon arrived, shaking the wet from his tunic. He knelt beside Jandira, putting his palm first to her face and then to her swollen belly. He threw up his hands. "I know nothing of women." And he withdrew.

Afonso held himself and rocked from foot to foot. "Make her talk to me," he ordered.

The captain opened the flap of the tent and called for a soldier to gather the midwife. "And be quick! We've a dying woman here!"

Not dying. Afonso stamped the carpet. "Not. Not."

"Sire," Father de Melo said.

"Not! Not!" He pressed his hands to his ears and spoke loud enough to drown out all other words. He looked to where Jandira lay, her robes bright, her eyes glazed, her face hectic.

Father de Melo tried to make him sit, but Afonso lunged up and ran to the flap of the tent. He opened it wide and let the rain pepper in. He shrieked, and his word billowed clouds into the cold, "Not!"

Under the shelter of their cloaks, soldiers whirled to stare. In the dining tent, cooks stood, spoons poised.

"Not!" Afonso howled. Rain pounded the ground. It drenched his tunic. Water poured from his eyes. Not Jandira. Not dying like his father, his wet nurse, his nanny.

Father de Melo gathered him up in a cloak and led him from the rain. Afonso sat, wrenching his body back and forth in his chair. He shivered. He looked to where the captain sat on the floor beside the pallet. "Jandira is playing a game."

Father de Melo knelt by Afonso's side and held his hand. "Say after me, sire: *Munda cor meum ac labia mea, omipotens Deus. . . .*"

"Make her get up."

"Shhh. Bless you, sire. Will you not go with me, and kneel before the altar?"

"You tell me that she will get up now! You tell me!"

Father's white-faced pity frightened him. "Shhh. *Gloria Patri . . .*" His fingers were cold against Afonso's forehead. "*. . . et Filio et Spiritui Sancto . . .*" A touch, one shoulder to the other. *"Amen."* He brushed his thumb against Afonso's lips and said, "All things that live must die."

Not Jandira. He got up and went to her. "Don't play. I don't want to play. Tell me a story."

He rang the golden bell that Salvador de Sá had given him. He rang it and he rang it and he held himself and wailed. After a while a dark-haired woman ducked in from the rain. She sat down by Jandira. She put her hand under the blankets. She called for the cook to make an infusion of white willow and barley. She ordered onions to be peeled and cut and blanched until they were soft. She ordered all the men to stand outside. Afonso said that he would not, that it was his tent, and that he would not leave Jandira with strangers. He asked who she was to order him out. Father de Melo took Afonso's arm and led him into the gray morning. Behind him, Afonso heard Jandira scream. Afonso did not want to hear that, did not want to hear; and then the screaming stopped and Father de Melo stood staring at the tent, wiping rain from his face. The captain stood, too, letting the cold wet roll down.

A cook's boy, carrying a fragrant pot of onion, went to the tent to inquire, and was ordered in. Suddenly the morning was frantic with cooks running and servants calling. When Afonso said that he wanted to go to Jandira, Father de Melo said he could.

Inside the tent, by the pallet where she lay, sat a brass basin and tiny bloodied sticks. The dark-haired woman was washing Jandira's face.

"Will she recover, then?" the captain asked.

"I know not." The woman shrugged toward the basin. "She thought to abort herself, and the reeds she shoved into her womb have caused a poisoning of the blood," the woman said. "I packed her with onion to draw the infection."

Jandira's eyes were closing. She would go away. She would fall to sleep without him. "I want her to tell me a story. Make her talk to me."

"Your servant is too tired now, sire," the captain said. "Let her sleep for a bit, and she will talk to you later." Then he spoke to the woman. "Do what you can, midwife. As you can see, he is attached to the bitch, and the child she carries is royal."

"No matter the parentage." She dipped rag into water basin, wrung it out. "It no longer lives."

CALLED before the tribunal an unnamed creature of unknown age. The being was put into a chair, but immediately rose and began to wander the room. It was ordered to sit, but did not obey, and so a guard seized it by the shoulder and sat it down again.

The creature was asked its name and origin, to which it did not reply. Msgr. Gomes warned the creature against silence, lest it be taken into the other room and its feet be put to the coals. Fr. Pessoa was of the opinion that the creature might not speak the language of the tribunal, at which time Msgr. Gomes addressed the creature first in Spanish and then in French. A secular addressed it in English, another in German. Fr. Pessoa asked of the tribunal if any of them spoke the language of Heaven.

At that, Msgr. Gomes became agitated and swore unlike a priest and warned Fr. Pessoa against more jesting tricks. A secular spoke up and said he had heard that the parish priest might act as the creatures' translator.

The parish priest, one Luis Soares, a Franciscan, was called. The dilemma was put to him, and the Franciscan explained that he was not sure if he could help, since the creatures spoke not in words, but in passionate emotion.

Msgr. Gomes ordered the Franciscan to fervently tell the creature, then, that it was charged with a heresy. He ordered the Franciscan to advise the prisoner to abjure that heresy, using sorrow or dread if he could not use words. He said to tell it to repent, lest it and the fellow it had arrived with be relaxed to the state for burning, at which time the Franciscan asked what heresy, and Msgr. Gomes said the heresy of pretending to be angel.

The Franciscan said that he imagined the creature to be angelic, that he heard no speech when he looked at the creature, but did hear the whisper of God. He said that the body of the dead creature had proved saintly, for it leaked a honeyed fluid that the guards had stolen betimes to use in healing their wounds. Msgr. Gomes replied that true angels do not die.

Fr. Pessoa said that he himself was not so acquainted with Heaven that he knew the true nature of angels. Msgr. Gomes swore again, and asked if Fr. Pessoa would care to become so acquainted, for Msgr. Gomes could make certain that he was. Fr. Pessoa said that he was glad Msgr. Gomes could be so sure of his salvation. Fr. Pessoa said that, although faith had promised him deliverance, he was not one to take Heaven for granted.

Then Msgr. Gomes made a great shout and got to his feet and rushed from the room. The questioning was halted, and the remaining members of the tribunal decided among themselves to partake of an hour's rest.

The day was too gray for God to move in it. It smelled of mildew and damp and wet earth. Rain made a noise against the tent roof like muffled drums. Afonso ordered that the banners flown, but the merry flags hung on their poles, sodden and dark.

He wrapped himself in his cloak and went though the wet grass and mud to the acorn. There he begged God to heal Jandira. He promised that he would be good, and said that he would apologize to the fat priest if that had caused her sickness. He said that he would do anything, for he could not stand to lose her the way he had lost his nanny, who had fallen down the stairs and broken her neck. He said that he could bear losing Jandira far less than he stood the death of his father, who never played games. He told God that it had taken his father many priests to die, and that Jandira was of little means, and had no retinue for death.

Afonso told God how his favorite hunting dog had died in his arms, struck by his own wayward arrow. He told God that he had never gone hunting after that, never owned another living thing, even though courtiers brought him hounds, and ambassadors brought him parrots.

Afonso told God that he himself liked happily-ever-afters and did not understand why God created such cruel endings.

God was quiet for a long time. Then in bleak lilac He said, *I cannot remember.*

So Afonso went back through the cold and the rain. His tent was close and much too warm. It stank. The smell stung Afonso's eyes, it made him feel sick. Not even Father de Melo's incense could banish it. The basin was full of blood and onions. A guard was holding Jandira's arms, and the midwife was calling for poppy.

"Jandira is angry," Afonso told the guard. "You should not hold her down so, for she has a temper."

Father de Melo wrapped his arm around Afonso's shoulder and tried to entice him to leave.

"She is angry," Afonso said. And indeed, her cheeks were bright red, her scars white. Her hair was matted. "You must let her up."

"Are you all deaf?" The midwife was in a temper. "Do you not have tincture of poppy?"

The company surgeon was sent for, and he came running in from the rain, asking, "What?" When the midwife asked for poppy, he dismissed her with a wave of his hand. "For this one? She is a barbarian and a black-assed slave, and an ungrateful whore at that, who would kill the royal baby inside her."

The surgeon would have left, but the captain seized his arm. "You will give the poppy, sir, or else the blood from out your neck."

Jandira's lips were drawn back, her teeth bared like an angry dog. Her eyes were wide and wet and shiny, and even though she stared very hard, it seemed that she saw nothing. Her skin was as thin as brown paper; the bones of her skull showed under her face. She was panting. Under the blankets her legs went up and down, up and down.

"Look. She pretends that she is running," Afonso told the father.

Father de Melo patted Afonso's hand and asked if he would not care to leave.

Afonso sat in his chair and watched Jandira's legs. She ran, she ran so hard and yet went noplace, like she had run after Castelo Melhor's horses.

"Will she live?" the captain asked.

The midwife wiped Jandira's face with chamomile water. She wet her mouth with white willow. "The baby needs to come, but she lacks the strength to expel it."

Father de Melo asked if he should give extreme unction, and she said to stand ready with the oil, for oftentimes with the dying there comes a moment of lucidity, and then she would want comfort.

"What she needs now is the poppy," she said.

The poppy was brought. The midwife dipped her finger in it, and put drop after slow drop on Jandira's tongue, until her breathing slowed and her eyes rolled back and, exhausted, she stopped running.

B ERNARDO STOOD AT the top of the stairs. Below, in a wash of silvered light in the men's cell, Father Manoel was talking to Guilherme Castanheda. The Jesuit's back was straight as a warrior's, his gaze so fierce that the sight made Bernardo's heart flutter in his throat. And behind them, in the same cage as his father, was the dark-eyed, milk-skinned dove who sang so sweetly.

Today. As God was just, Bernardo would see the boy freed today.

Castanheda caught sight of Bernardo, and pointed him out to Father Manoel. "We are summoned back to the judgment," Bernardo called.

Father Manoel took his leave and mounted the stair; as he passed Bernardo, Bernardo whispered, "Tread lightly."

As if no words had been spoken, Father Manoel walked on, pausing to nod and bid good day to one of his own guards. Bernardo followed, saying a silent *gratia Dei* when he saw the almonds he had ordered being put by Monsignor's right hand.

Monsignor looked ill—not just from the king's chocolate, but from dream. He had awakened in the dark of early morning, calling for light and again more light, and Bernardo could not tell which pained him more, the agony in his stomach, or the one in his mind.

Bernardo sat down, gathered his journal to him, dipped his quill. Monsignor's hand plunged into the bowl, brought up a handful of chocolate-dipped almonds, and shoved them wholesale into his mouth.

"Who next?" Monsignor asked, chewing.

Bernardo consulted his list.

BROUGHT before the tribunal, Marta Castanheda, who had been asked to search her heart. She was asked again concerning the apparition of the Virgin Mary, and she said that the Virgin appeared to her because she no longer spoke to men. She said that the Blessed Mother tired of men never listening, as men were wont to do.

Msgr. Gomes then exhorted the prisoner to answer the question lest she be put to torture. The prisoner lifted her eyes to Heaven and said that if they wrapped her with rope, the Blessed Mother would loosen her; that if they hanged her by her wrists backward, Mary would bear her up. She said that if she was brought to the fire, the Mother of God would douse the flames.

Fr. Pessoa entreated the prisoner not to be foolish, that no one wished to hurt her, but only to find the truth. The prisoner said that the truth of blessed chastity could not be seen by Fr. Pessoa since he was a fornicator, to which Fr. Pessoa replied very sharply, asking if she was still of the opinion that the creatures in the cell were not angels, and if so, why the Teixeira women and a pious cleric such as Fr. Soares thought they were. The prisoner had no answer. Fr. Pessoa then asked if it was not likely that the angels in the cell below were true, while her tall, winged, and beautiful beings were a pubescent fiction spawned by a childish mind. She said Mary told her that it was men who were wrongheaded, and at that Msgr. Gomes said he was weary of her stubbornness and ordered a state executioner to take her away.

Fr. Pessoa told the executioner to wait, and begged Marta to answer, that he could not stay the hand of the tribunal, and did she wish to injure her father and brother so, since the place of torment was in the jail itself, and they would bear witness to her suffering. She said that she would not suffer, and at that, the executioner took her from the room.

She lay quietly while the coals were prepared, a promising sign. Bernardo would watch her face as he did all of the tortured. He must bear witness when fire was put to her feet. If God was kind, he might share in her transformation.

From the jail windows beyond came the ceaseless drumming of the rain. In the room of torment, the blind stone was damp and moisture-beaded. He peeked around the corner and saw the dove peeking back. Bernardo smiled at him and wriggled his fingers in greeting.

Then he heard the executioner say, "Hold her ankles."

Bernardo left the corner and walked deeper into the lamplit windowless room. He sat down at the small table they had set for him, and took his quill in hand.

The executioner asked him if he was ready, and Bernardo said that he was. He dipped his quill, watching the play of the iron tongs among the coals. Disturbed, the fire flared red, spat sparks. Then the tongs plucked up an ember. The executioner brought the coal to her with practiced slowness so that she could watch its approach.

The first scream was a pure sound, sharp and startled. Bernardo saw Father Manoel flinch, saw that Monsignor did not. He saw the two seculars look away.

THE PRISONER WAS asked to confess, and she said that she had done no wrong, and to let her up lest evil befall us. The ember was applied a second time, and the prisoner cried out, "O Mother Mary, save me. O sirs, as you are merciful, let me go."

She was asked to confess, and she asked if loving God was a sin. The ember was applied, and the prisoner cried, "Help me. O Mother of God, can you not see how they hurt me? O God, she abandons me. Sirs, let me up." She was asked to confess, and she said that Mary had visited her and said that she would show the world a sign. The prisoner was asked as to what sign, and the prisoner said that she did not know. The ember was applied, and the prisoner said, "I do not know. If I knew it I would tell you. Please, can you not take the coals away?" The ember was again applied and the prisoner said, "O please. I forgot what Mary said. She told me as in a dream. And when I awoke, all I can remember of it is Mary warning me: 'Never tell. Never tell.' " The prisoner was asked to confess, and she said, "O but sirs, you see I do confess it. I pretended to remember what Mary told me, and made the rest up. God gave Maria Elena the baby, and her such a whining brat, and not nearly so devoted. It was only fair that I have something special, too. O please, sirs, this is now the truth." She asked for water, and the questioning was halted.

Bernardo put his quill down. The girl was too tired to put voice to her weeping, but instead let tears roll unchecked. He studied her sweated face, how she fought for breath. Pain had made her beautiful. *Exultate in Domino.* He wanted to seize her hands in his, to pray and rejoice along with her, for he had seen the moment that God had taken pride. He had witnessed when God took self. He watched her soul become naked. Now the room rested in the aftermath of that hard-fought battle—a battle which she, in losing, had won. It smelled of hardwood fire, burned flesh, and rain.

He looked up and, to his surprise, saw that Father Manoel had covered his face.

Pessoa vomited in the chamber pot, this time bringing up only a deluge of stringy water. Weary and sickened he knelt, resting his forehead on his cot. He crossed himself once, twice—and upon further reflection—thrice. He muttered, *"Et nuc, redemptor Domine, ad te solum confugio . . ."*

Behind him came Soares's laconic, " 'And now I take refuge in Thee,' Manoel? Is that not a little late?"

Pessoa turned to see Soares standing in the rectory doorway. He thought of Marta's cracked and blackened feet and his stomach heaved. He reached for the chamber pot just as bile stormed his gullet. It burned up his throat, stung the tender lining of his nose, and hit the pot with a force that sent ropy liquid spattering.

He felt a nudge at his shoulder. Soares was offering him a dampened towel. "I suppose it would be futile to suggest lunch."

Pessoa blew his nose with an edge. With the rest, he wiped his sweated face. Under the warmth of his cassock, he was shivering. Soares brought him a blanket, and wrapped it around his shoulders.

"Lie down for a while," Soares said.

Pessoa buried his head in the towel. The cloth muffled the distress in his voice. "I cannot."

"I'll call you when they are ready."

"I cannot go back."

He would pack his bags. He would steal away. He would hide himself in England, in France. He would strip off his cassock, discard rosary and missal; he would learn Protestant prayers.

Soares cleared his throat. Footsteps left, footsteps returned. A finger prodded his shoulder. The Franciscan had brought him a cup of brandy. Pessoa drank. Outside the rectory, rain fell. It pattered against the sill. It conjured from the damp hearth the memories of old fires.

"I have some fennel for your breath," Soares said. "Nothing is more unpleasant than a mouth that tastes of vomit."

Pessoa's teeth chattered, and he pulled the blanket tight. The afternoon ran gray torrents. He took the fennel when it was handed him. He chewed the seeds and sipped the brandy. France. He would go to France.

"You have seen this before, Manoel."

In the quiet between raindrops he thought he could hear a scream, faint and far away. "Always someone else's sheep." He leaned back against the cot's wooden frame and watched the day weep, the world dissolve. "Never mine."

I N THE AFTERNOON, Jandira roused herself and asked for water. Afonso went to her side and said that, as she was feeling better, she should entertain him a little, since he had entertained her all day.

The midwife helped Jandira drink, but Jandira drank so much and so fast that water spilled from her lips and wet all her blankets. Father de Melo asked if it was time for the extreme unction, and the midwife said that it was. He went out into the rain.

Afonso took hold of Jandira's fingers. Her hand was scalding. Her eyes closed, and he tugged on her. "No, don't go to sleep. You have to talk to me, Jandira. You've been asleep, and I have been bored all the morning."

Of a sudden she sat up, rigid. "Take off my shoes!" Her eyes were like polished amber. "Quick. Take off my shoes."

The midwife took off Jandira's sandals and rubbed her feet.

"No. Not that way," Afonso said. "She wants to feel the dirt on her feet. She takes God that way. Don't you, Jandira?"

The midwife peeled the carpet up, and let the grass poke through. "Like this, sire?"

"Yes! Just that! She likes that." Afonso bent Jandira's knee and put her bare foot to the earth. "I told God, Jandira. I told Him that He was not dying. You hurt so badly and you are so hot that I think that you are becoming, too. Your scars will heal. Your skin will blanch milk white, and your hair will burn to gold. Then I will wed you—would you like that?—and everyone will bow to their queen."

Father de Melo came back. He took off his cloak, shook it, and knelt by Jandira's head. He lifted his stole and kissed it. He asked if she cared to confess.

Jandira took hold of the stole as if she would strangle him. Her lungs wheezed like cracked bellows. "Send word . . ."

Father de Melo tried to pry her hand away, but she held on.

"Castelo Melhor . . ." She struggled up, up. She labored at rising. Her grimace was like a ogre's. She nearly pulled father off his knees. "With my own hands. You tell him. I killed his black-assed bastard." She loosed her grip, fell back to the pillows. She closed her eyes. Father de Melo asked if she would like to confess herself. He said she should not die with such a terrible sin on her soul. After a while he got up, sat in a chair, and waited, missal in hand.

With his sleeve, Afonso wiped spittle from Jandira's open mouth. The midwife asked quietly if Jandira was awake, and Afonso said that he thought she was, but that she did not want to talk, and that she was stubborn like that sometimes. The midwife bathed Jandira's cheeks and said that she herself had died once, and that Death was nothing to fear.

Afonso saw Jandira's eyes open to slits. He saw the pupils move underneath the lids. He thought she watched him, but saw that she watched the rain.

"It is a blessing, really," the midwife said. "For I remember that I hurt so, and I was angry at those who did not come to my aid when for years I had come to theirs. I hated God and all the town, because they had abandoned me. Is her foot planted well, sire? Are you certain? For, either with poppy or with prayer, we want to give her every comfort."

He pressed cool grass blades between Jandira's fevered toes. The midwife put cushions under Jandira's knees.

"O! How clever! God can come to both her feet now," Afonso said.

The midwife smiled. "God comes to us, anyway." She bent over Jandira and took her hand. "Listen. Can you hear me? We are taken in a dark humming rush. Are you listening, my lady? Don't fear the journey. There is a kindly company at the end."

Jandira whimpered and stirred under her blankets. The midwife stroked her forehead and shushed her. Rain beat itself against the tent. Sweet incense rose in wraith-white ribbons, collected in ghostly throngs under the roof. Afonso saw the captain by the door to the tent, regarding them. He saw Father de Melo watching.

"My lady," the midwife said. "You are not alone. Feel my hand? Do you? Yes, good. Hold on tight as you will, for you do not hurt me. I will tell you of final secrets, for I have seen many die. Children hold out arms to the air. Men and women smile into corners. Someone is come for you, too. They are here in the tent, in this very moment—do you hear me, my lady? Look about. Do you see them?"

Jandira's lids fluttered. She licked her lips.

"Press my hand tight," the midwife said. "Good. Good. Don't be afraid, for I will not leave you until they take you by the hand and lead you from me."

ORDERED before the tribunal one Gregorio Neves, charged with the heresy of having said that God had visited his potato field. An officer of the Inquisition came forward to attest that he and two of his men had that day gone to collect Sr. Neves, and found him fled along with all his family. It was then mandated that Sr. Neves's goods and lands be seized and inventoried and sold immediately for what they could bring, and the monies given to the Holy Office to defray the costs of the tribunal.

BROUGHT before the tribunal, one Rodrigo Castanheda, age eight. Fr. Pessoa asked the prisoner if he recalled saying that he did not believe his sister's story of angels. The prisoner said that he did remember making such a statement. He said that he also remembered having told Fr. Pessoa that he prayed that the angels would throw his sister into the pit. The prisoner said that he was very sorry for praying that, and he wanted to take it back. Fr. Pessoa said that the affliction his sister had gone through had nothing to do with his prayer, but had everything to do with his

sister's own stubbornness. Fr. Pessoa said that he believed God
sorted the good wishes of children from the bad, for, as He Himself had made them, He knew that children had little discernment. Fr. Pessoa admonished the boy not to feel guilty, then
conferred with the rest of the tribunal and said that he was of the
opinion that the boy had committed no heresy. The seculars
agreed, and Fr. Pessoa then excused the boy, and said that he was
free to go. The accused asked if his sister and his father could go
with him, and Fr. Pessoa said that they would see on the morrow.
He said again that the boy should leave, at which time a guard
came forward and led him away.

BROUGHT before the tribunal Guilherme Castanheda, accused
of saying that God did not reside in Spain. Msgr. Gomes asked
him again about the statement, and asked if he had searched his
heart. The prisoner came of a sudden to his feet, knocking over
his chair. A jailer restrained him, and Msgr. Gomes and Fr. Pessoa both asked the prisoner to sit. In a loud and distressed voice,
the prisoner said that he had heard what the tribunal had done to
his daughter. He had seen and smelled the burning flesh, and saw
how she now huddled weeping in her cell. He bellowed, "May
God strike all of you dead where you sit, for only this will be a
justice." And when he was finished shouting and shoving at his
guards, Msgr. Gomes asked if that was all the statement the prisoner wished to make; at which the prisoner fought his way free
of his restraints, picked up the fallen chair, and flinging it at the
tribunal, cried, "See there. I have prayed a just prayer, and yet
He does not answer. I knew He was not in Spain, and now I find
that God is not in Portugal, either."

T he gray day darkened. A soldier came and lit the lamps. Jandira
stared glassy-eyed at the wall. Her breath came so hard that it
jolted her, head to toe. It did not sound like breath at all, but more like the
snick of an iron key in a lock.

The captain asked the midwife if a grave should be dug. The midwife
said to dig it. Father de Melo said that Jandira's grave should be dug apart,
and Afonso knew that was because Jandira's death would be special.

Afonso looked across at the midwife, where she held Jandira's hand.
"Jandira is going to become something beautiful."

"Yes, sire. I am glad that you can see that."

Afonso understood that becoming hurt, yet he wished that Jandira's
breathing would calm. He thought how weary it must make her to work at
breathing that way. He tried it himself, and felt the midwife's eye on him.
"How can you tell the melon baby is dead?"

She said, "By the colors."

"O! God talks in colors!"

"Shhh. I know, sire."

"Well, have you gone into the acorn, then? No? But how can you see
the colors if you have never gone into the acorn?"

She laid a finger across her lips. "Shhh. We must be quiet, and not disturb her now. Agreed? Anyway, it was when I died, as I told you. And
when I came back, I saw rainbows around each and every thing. The pink
around you tells me that you are kind, but of a certain nervous energy. The
yellow tells me that you are happy, and of good health."

"Jandira has a lot of colors."

"Indeed she does, sire."

"And she wears robes that are like a chatter from God. She laughs
quick, and she makes jokes. I cannot keep up sometimes with Jandira's
colors."

The midwife stroked Jandira's forehead. "She is like I was: an angry
little thing."

"She will come back from Death, like you." He bent down to
Jandira's gaze, but her eyes did not meet his. "It is time to get up now," he

told her. She took a rib-cracking breath. "I am tired of watching you become."

She would not talk to him, so he took out his book of *Don Quixote*. He looked at the illustrations. He admired the windmills. He drew his finger along the page and pretended he could read. He turned the book upside down to see if the words made better sense. Bored, he put up his book and got the little golden bell. He rang it. Jandira convulsed. He rang the bell, and Jandira made a noise like wind through dry leaves. He rang the bell, but she didn't move. The midwife loosed Jandira's hand. She crossed Jandira's arms over her chest. Since Jandira would not close her eyes, the midwife shut them for her.

The captain left and came back with two servants. Father de Melo asked Afonso if he would like to leave; Afonso said that he would not. Father then asked if Afonso would sit in the chair, for the servants had preparations. Afonso took his bell with him.

He watched the midwife pull the pillows from under Jandira's knees and head. He saw her straighten her legs and put her feet neatly together. Servants brought a length of fresh white linen, and Afonso watched them wrap Jandira, head to toe, like a present.

"She is becoming, now," Afonso said.

Soldiers came to say that all was ready. Afonso watched the servants lift Jandira, one by her shoulders, and the other by her knees. They carried her away, and Afonso thought of how she would burst from the linen, all the hues of a butterfly. He thought of how she would surprise the soldiers when she came running to him through the gray rain. He rang his bell so that she could hear it, and know that he was waiting.

The midwife packed up her herbs and asked if he was well, or if she could prepare him a valerian tea. There was blood pooled, a boisterous happy red, on the blankets. Afonso said that he was fine. He rang his bell.

Night darkened at the window. The rain softened to mist. Servants came and took away Jandira's pallet. They cleared the dirty basins. They scrubbed the red spots on the carpet until they lost their joy. They asked if Afonso wanted dinner, and he said that he did not.

They left. Afonso sat in the glow of the lanterns, in the emptiness of his tent. He wondered where Pedro was, and if he wouldn't visit. He wanted to lie in Jandira's arms. He wanted her to tell him a story. He rang his bell.

THE CASTANHEDA DINING room was too lavish for honest digestion, being all crystal and china and silver. Especially for a Friday, the food was far too rich. Bernardo plucked a clam from its shell and ran it listlessly through the wine sauce.

At the head of the long table, the seculars were arguing. "Not demons, surely, Tadeo," Goatee said.

Scarecrow broke a loaf and called for a waiting servant to bring him more polenta and cheese. "No, no, no. But neither angels. Good God, they're blank-gazed and dull-witted, seems to me. Ho!" he said, peering down the length of linen and lace to where Bernardo sat. "Notary! You've said you've seen something. An emotion? A fright? A what?"

"Holiness," Bernardo mumbled. The table was too long. He raised his voice. "A holiness!"

"Ah." Scarecrow knit his brows, turned to Goatee. "But you see nothing?"

"No. You?"

The servant bustled in with a platter. Scarecrow watched his plate being filled. He shrugged. "So it cannot be proven."

"It puts me in mind of basins of water." Goatee pushed his dinner plate away and pulled his dessert plate to him. He chose an apple from an alabaster bowl and, with knife and fork, began to peel it. "You know how when you peer intently into a basin—when there is only faint light?—and the basin seems to cloud over, and then it appears that you see visions?"

Scarecrow paused, fork in mouth. He frowned across the expanse of silver and china. "No."

"Well, scryers do it." Goatee had denuded his apple. There was now a curl of red on one side of the plate, and white moist pulp on the other. "They think they see things, if there is shine and dimness. Of course they don't." He sliced off an edge of pulp, speared it with his fork, and popped it into his mouth.

The house carried memory; the sight and smell of the boy. Bernardo looked into a wall mirror and thought he saw the dove's reflection. The dove would be sitting where Goatee sat, at his father's right hand. Bernardo thought he caught sight of a dark-haired milk-fair boy lost amid icy glitter. A mutter drew his attention. Castanheda's servant was standing by with the platter of fried polenta. Bernardo shook his head and the servant went away.

"Their eyes are dark and featureless, therefore . . ."

"Yes, yes." Scarecrow said. "I get your meaning. The viewers imagine something in their own reflections. Precisely."

Goatee, fork in one hand, knife in the other, stared down at the sacrificial apple. "But then, if not supernatural, what?"

"Animals. Lord knows there are enough strange animals in Africa, in Brazil, in the Spanish New World."

"Ah!" Goatee hoisted his knife. "Of course! Brilliant, Tadeo! A Spanish plot! They find the strange animals in some New World colony, see that they are very like human, and they drop them where? Precisely where they know the king to be. They planned this all along, the *disgraçados*!"

Scarecrow sawed into his polenta. "How?"

Goateee leaned forward, cupped his ear.

"How did they drop them here?"

Goatee sat back.

Bernardo pushed his plate away, half-eaten. He put an orange on his dessert tray, impaled the thick skin with his fork, and cut it into tidy, fragrant segments. The dove would have a taste for oranges, for other sweets. He would have sat thus. If Bernardo looked up quickly, he could see him in the mirror.

Goatee slapped the table. "Catapulted!"

"Ah, good! Yes! Well, then. All decided. A Spanish plot."

Bernardo said, "What about the women?"

Goatee leaned over, cupped an ear.

"The women's story." Bernardo put down his silverware. "What about that? And although Gregorio Neves is not here to testify, he told Senhor Magalhães that he saw the selfsame star hang in the air above his fields before darting away the same direction it had come. Is such a thing possible with a catapult?"

Goatee and Scarecrow looked at each other. Goatee sucked a tooth. "Ah! The catapulted acorn came over the field, thus." He demonstrated a slow arc with his hand. "And when it reached its apex, from the perspective seen below . . ."

"Of course." Scarecrow nodded. "It seemed to hang. A trick of the eye."

Goatee's hand came down, fingers meeting the table. "And so it fell, a long ways away, thus was never discovered. Who knows how many acorns they shot? Apparently the aim is not exact."

Scarecrow crossed himself. *"Lauda Dei."*

"Praise God, indeed. And the women?—well, perhaps they lie."

Scarecrow poured himself more wine. "Amalia Teixeira strikes me as sincere. Heretic, certainly, and bound to be burnt—but altogether most painfully sincere. So much so that I sat down after her testimony and wrote a most loving letter to my wife."

Goatee sighed.

From the stairs came a bellow of "Bernardo! Where is the boy? Bernardo!"

Neither secular looked up. Goatee said, "Dreaming."

Bernardo wiped his mouth with a lace-trimmed napkin. He heard Scarecrow say, "It seems to me to be a great difference between dreaming that one's daughter has been ripped from one's arms, and actually experiencing it."

From the floor above: "Bernardo!"

Bernardo got to his feet. He dusted his robes, he set his chair neatly to the table. As he left the dining hall he heard: "True, Tadeo, despite what the notary says about God's terrible and hurtful glory, this still sounds more like Spaniards."

"Bernardo!" The shout came blustering down the hall and sought out Bernardo where he stood, regarding himself blankly in a gilt hall mirror. A passing guard laughed. "He's in a fit with his belly, Father Andrade, and has been all night. Mind you don't strike a candle too near him."

Bernardo could not remember stopping in the corridor. Could not remember—but for an ache of loneliness—what he had been looking for. Then the bellow: "Bernardo!" He lifted the skirt of his habit and hurried up the stair.

So many almonds, and yet no odor of them. Monsignor's room stank of sulfur. The bed curtains had been pulled to. The moan behind the drapes carried in it all the afflictions of Hell. On an ivory inlaid table, a candelabra burned. The window was flung open, and a wet breeze stirred velvet, brought inside the sweetness and sound of the rain.

"Some senna tea, Monsignor?"

"Bend over and let me shove your senna tea hot and in you backward." Another groan, and a creak from overburdened wood, and with that, the noises of a heavy body floundering on the mattress. "Once you rubbed my back," he said piteously. "Once you would hardly leave my side. So damned overtaken by your angels, are you?"

"No, Monsignor."

"Deluded, boy. You are deluded by the devil." Monsignor discharged a tight little squeak of a fart.

"Shall I bring you some dinner now?"

There came another creak of wood, and a groan. "Bring me that herbalist."

Bernardo remembered the wink of crystal. The heady scent of citrus. A doe-eyed boy. He remembered seeing his own face in a glass, and it frightened him that he could not recall when it had happened, or which image was reflection and which was flesh. "Herbalist."

"The herbalist! The one that Jesuit finds tasty! Did you see his eyes upon her? I warrant he knows her as well as a shepherd knows his favorite ewe. Send her up to me."

Bernardo lost feeling in his hands, and realized that he was clasping his fingers so tightly that they had turned milk white and unblemished; the nails had turned blue. It came to him that he was picturing Monsignor's neck there. He shoved his hands into his pockets. "What should I tell her that you want of her, Monsignor?"

"God, boy! I don't seek entertainment! Not in this distress. Tell her you need some herbals for digestion."

Bernardo left, and in the downstairs hall found a jailer. "Have you seen the herbalist Berenice Pinheiro?"

The man looked surprised. "I thought we had not evidence to jail her."

"Monsignor calls for her, as he is in distress."

His quick smirk was even more quickly hidden. "Ah, well. May God look more benevolently, then, on the monsignor's digestion. And would that I knew medicine, for that herbalist obtained a goodly amount of gold today from the king, and now attends that girl prisoner's feet. Take the wind from out Monsignor, and she will have earned herself a few dinners."

Bernardo thanked him and, collecting his cloak, went into the rain. Puddles soaked his boots. He hurried and, in his haste, drenched his hem.

By the time he reached the jail, he was shivering, and his mind had cleared. He rushed inside, ducking, shaking water from his cloak. The guards had built a fire in a round of gathered stones, and they huddled there, warming their hands.

There was no singing from below; no sounds but whimpers. Bernardo descended the stair, his eyes drawn first to the funeral candles, to the angels. Guilherme Castanheda sat hard by the bars, watching over his daughter.

Marta lay in the cell opposite, her head on Senhora Teixeira's lap. Berenice Pinheiro sat at the girl's right foot, applying a poltice. Bernardo put his hand to the bars and looked down at her. "Monsignor Gomes suffers an indigestion."

Senhora Teixeira snorted. "Have him hike his skirt. I'll put coals to it."

"Hold her," the Pinheiro woman said. She touched the knife to the edge of the charred left foot. The girl kicked savagely, and twisted out of Senhora Teixeira's grasp.

The Pinheiro woman's shy eyes met Bernardo's. "Please, sir. Can you not help us?"

Bernardo went upstairs and asked for a jailer to let him in the women's cell. A guard took the ring of keys, and Bernardo followed him down, hearing from the guards behind mutters and lewd little chuckles.

"Should I stay, then?" the guard asked.

"I will call." Bernardo heard the door clang shut at his back, heard the key click in its lock.

"Hold her ankles," the herbalist said.

Bernardo knelt. The girl's feet were swollen to twice their size. Where the soles were blistered, they leaked a clear fluid. He took one ankle and held it gingerly. The skin was as pearly as her brother's. He imagined his hand moving up, up, exploring the forbidden. His hand—all independent of him—himself all blameless—only his hand, and out of Bernardo's control. Only his hand, moving into the damp heat.

"Both, please," the herbalist said. "You must hold both, sir, and hold them well, or she will kick. She is wild with pain and brandy."

Bernardo seized both ankles and squeezed. The girl gave such a shout and fought so hard that he nearly let her go.

"Hold!" the herbalist cried. "You hold her!"

Senhora Teixeira pressed the girl's arms to her sides. She cooed nonsense in her ear. The girl smelled of apricot brandy and raw potato. Her gaze was vague, but for the anguish. Her mouth was slack.

"Done."

Bernardo looked around. Blackened flesh and blood rested in a bowl, and the herbalist was dousing her gore-covered knife into a basin of water. She rubbed the blade with horseradish root, then wrapped it in thyme.

"Less brandy, more water," the herbalist told Senhora Teixeira. "All the water she will take. And in a while unwrap the bindings from her feet, throw away the old potato and plantain and give her fresh. If the seepage from her feet turns yellow or green, send for me."

She packed her things. Bernardo called for the jailer. He led the way up the steps, her presence behind him like a kiss to his nape. In the street, he forgot to lift his cowl, and she reminded him. He noticed that she had naught against the rain but her thin shawl.

"You must take my cloak." And when he took it back from her afterward, her smell would wrap him. He would sleep in it.

She ran, splashing water, and took shelter under an overhang. Since she would not take the cloak, he let her have the refuge of the balconies while he walked the pelting rain. They passed through the warm light from a window, then another.

"What is the nature of his indigestion? A vomiting? Does he pass watery or bloody stools?"

Bernardo leaned close to whisper. O such danger. She was small, not much taller than the dove. So delicate that in his clumsiness he might crush her. To have something that Father Manoel so treasured; to share of his vigor, to possess that very thing which the tall Jesuit enjoyed. Bernardo caught from her a clean perfume of herbs, a whiff of sweat, the musk of passion.

She turned, her lips suddenly too close. "What?"

He backed, laughing, drunk from the glimpse of wet blouse clinging to breast, from wanting to see the nub of nipple, to thinking about the chaste little nub of the dove. He started to shake.

"What?" she asked.

He strode ahead and looked back over his shoulder. "Farts," he said, and his voice shook with laughter. "An entire opera of farts, from coloratura to basso."

The rain fell harder. Ahead the windows were closed, the street dark. She who had been temptation, became a black nothing.

Bernardo crossed himself. *"Pro innumerabilibus peccatis et offensionibus, et negligentiis meis . . ."*

She hurried to catch up to him. "What are you saying?"

"Praying."

"Is he so ill as all that?"

"O! No, I pray for forgiveness. I should not have made light of his affliction."

They walked on. He heard her stumble and put out his hand to steady her. She recoiled from his touch, a gesture so timid that it nearly felled him.

"I ask, for I have lost one patient today and would not care to lose another."

Bernardo slowed. "The guard said that you were called to the king, I . . ."

"The king's dark-skinned slave."

"What . . . How can that be? I saw her not two days ago and she seemed well. What killed her?"

"When all the rest is taken away, I would call the death a suicide."

He crossed himself, offered up a prayer for her lost soul. He pictured those lush lips caked by grave dirt, those wanton eyes sunken, a playing ground for worms. He pictured a horned devil running his hands . . .

"Here." The Pinheiro woman's voice came from the dark distance behind him.

He turned, and caught a faceful of rain.

She was standing by flagstone steps and an ornate railing. "This is the Castanheda house, sir. Here."

They went up the stairs together. A servant came and took his cloak, her shawl. She opened her basket, and gave over a handful of strawflowers, sprigs, and mint. "Boil this, please," she told the servant. "Make a strong hot tea. Strong and hot as you can make it. Bring it to the monsignor's room. And please be quick."

It was like a graceful dance, how the servant and the herbalist never joined gazes.

"Where?" she asked.

"O. Yes. Up here." Bernardo led her up the stair.

In his room, behind his bed curtains, Monsignor was moaning. She stopped by a table to put down the basket. She called for a basin, and washed her hands. "Are you dressed, sir?"

The curtains parted. An eye peered out. "Nightclothes."

"That is enough." She called for Bernardo to bring a lamp. He stood next to her as she parted the curtains. Monsignor lay sweating under a mound of blankets. She tugged them down, exposing the enormous lace- and linen-covered belly. Hands busy, she probed his right side. Under her touch, Monsignor fretted and twitched.

"You hurt me," he complained.

She pulled the blankets over him again and walked to her basket.

"What?" Monsignor asked of her back.

"I have called for a hot tea of chamomile and anise and spearmint. Add to it tinctures of bogbean and valerian. You must drink the mixture without sugar or honey. More, it will not work unless you drink it scald- ing."

Bernardo said, "I always used senna tea. And poppy for his distress."

She nodded without looking up—a flawless guardianship of the eyes. "The poppy constipates. Do not use it unless he cannot bear the pain. And the senna tea loosens his bowels, yes. But the bowel is not his weakness. It is an excess of gall."

Monsignor grunted and sat up. "Hah! That Italian doctor—remember him, Bernardo? He told me once gall. And there is a three-day fast for a remedy, and then the drinking of a liter of olive oil all at once—do you re- member him saying? And something of an enema, too. He said I would shit out cups of stones, all green black. Remember? Not that I was prepared at the time for—"

Her soft, "No." Head lowered, she went to the bed, took down the covers again, and prodded him in the side. He winced. "You must never. For you have one stone too large to pass. I suggest a diet of lentils for him, sir." She turned to Bernardo. "And grains. No butter. No meats—"

"No meats?" Monsignor sat up, throwing the covers off. "No meats?" When he tried to rise, a cramp nearly toppled him.

"Potatoes and greens, as much as he will eat. Vinegar on them. Noth- ing with a sauce. Dry bread, or sopped in turnip water."

"Good God!" Monsignor bellowed so, he passed gas at either end. He reached for the nightstand and pulled himself to his feet. There he stood, bent by pain, railing at his own toes. "Dry bread? No sauces? And you say I must eat lentils? I would fart to bring the house down."

"Sir, beans and cabbage are not at fault, but rich foods such as nuts and meats and butter sauces. Do you not find that when the indigestion comes upon you, it comes always an hour or so after eating? So, gall, sir. And if you do not eat more plainly, one day the body will try to expel the larger stone." She touched Bernardo's folded hands, and he felt all through himself the shock of that contact. "You will know if it happens, father. It is unmistakable, for there is no suffering so great. Use as much poppy as he needs then, for it will take him days to die."

"God! *Malefica!*" Doubled over, Monsignor shuffled to her. "You are a liar and an incompetent! See you, Bernardo? She means to frighten me. That is her game."

She picked up her basket. Monsignor seized her wrist, leering up into her averted face. "Where did such a pretty wench get such a pretty gold cross, I wonder."

Bernardo could see a swift pulse beat in the hollow of that fine neck. "A gift, sir. I did not steal it."

"Ah. A fine cross. An expensive gift. I noticed it at the tribunal. Yet when I asked, the townsfolk told me that it was the first time they had seen such."

She whispered, "Sir, they do not look."

"You lie, my girl. I know what you do. And I know your partner in fornication. I know that he cannot shrive you for it. You will burn in Hell for this, my child. Come, kneel down at my feet and beg God to grant you forgiveness. For the debauching of a priest is no small transgression."

She tore free and ran, leaving a trail of daisies and marigold behind.

Bernardo ran after.

"Bernardo!"

"The tinctures, Monsignor. She took them." And then he was gone. He saw the track of leaves dropped from out her basket. He heard her footfalls on the stair. "Wait!" he cried.

He rushed around the corner. She was below, by the door, tying her shawl. "Wait," he said.

She looked up, frightened, poised to flee. He came down the steps slowly.

"I am a friend."

From the dining room he could hear the voices of the seculars as they dawdled over their evening brandy: ". . . advanced catapult, Emílio. Think of it."

In the shadows of the entry, her eyes were as luminous as a hare's. He reached her, stood within an arm's length. "You forgot to leave the tinctures."

She rummaged in the basket and brought out two corked bottles. "Three or four drops of each in his tea. Too much bogbean will cause him distress. And give the valerian not to settle his stomach, but to relax him. The gas passes easier if he is relaxed."

Their fingers met on the glass. He looked down at her, saw that her damp hair strayed from its bun. He studied the dusky lashes against her cheek. She was shivering.

"Wait here." He took the tiny bottles, and squeezed her fingers. "I'll bring you something against the wind. Please. Will you not wait a moment?"

A quick nod. Bernardo crept back up the stairs to the room where Scarecrow slept. In the ornate dresser he found a cloak. His heart twisted when he returned to see her still in the entry, and knew that she had trusted him enough to wait.

He heard Goatee's voice. ". . . Spanish could as easy turn the weapon to France."

And Scarecrow's "How far do you imagine it can throw things?"

"Kilometers! God help us. And throw acorns the size of a house."

The cloak was of thick Alentejan wool, embroidered with silken leaves. She passed a hand over its folds, then gave it back. "Sir, I do not steal."

"It is not stealing."

"It is Marta's."

"Take it, or the Holy Office will. She is to be burnt." He put it into her hands. After a hesitation, she wrapped herself in it, pulled up the cowl, and walked out in the rain.

Bernardo went to the stoop and stood in the wash of light from the tall dining-room windows, watching her go. She was not two meters down the road when he heard a hiss of "Marta!"

She halted. Bernardo peered down the steep side of the steps. In a cubbyhole among the planter boxes crouched a small figure. Such melody resonated in that voice that not even whisper could mask it. "Marta!"

Bernardo's heart leapt. There. Below, the dove was coming out of the shadows, cautious as a deer from out the forest. Any moment he would run.

"Hold him!" Bernardo cried.

The boy was quick, the herbalist quicker. She gathered him up. "Rodrigo! Easy, easy. It's only me, Berenice Pinheiro. I have borrowed your sister's cloak. Please, my sweet, don't fight. You remember me, don't you? The herbalist? You're cold as Death and shivering. Have you been out here all evening?"

When Bernardo descended, he saw the two shadows joined, both quiet now. He approached, bending to the dove's height. "Rodrigo? It is me, Father Andrade. I'm the father who brought you the lute. Have you eaten?"

The dove shoved away the herbalist's restraining arms. Rain soaked his dark hair, and rolled down that fresh, unblemished face. "You hurt my sister."

"No." Bernardo crouched lower. He put his hand out. The boy's cheek was as cold and smooth as that of a churchyard angel. "O, no," he whispered. "I merely took down the words she said. It is my job. Have you not seen me write what is said at the tribunal? Well, then. Come inside. There is cod in clam sauce. And polenta fried in butter. There is warmth and oranges."

The boy hung back. Gently, the herbalist pushed him forward. "You have nowhere to sleep, Rodrigo. And it's cold. He is all right, truly. And it is your house, besides. Go ahead."

Bernardo took his hand. Such a tiny hand. Such little fingers. He rubbed the blood back into them. "We must be quiet, and not let anyone know you are here. I'll get you food and dry clothes. You'll have a warm bed to sleep in."

The herbalist bent and whispered, "Go with father."

The dove went. Bernardo pressed him against the folds of his robe. They walked together into the house, past the upraised voices of the seculars as they argued wars and weapons. Bernardo took him into the back, and there, in the room that had been assigned him, he lit a lantern. He sparked a fire in the hearth.

"This is the *mordomo*'s room," the dove said.

"Yes." Bernardo took a blanket from the bed and wrapped the boy in it. "You must take your wet clothes off. I will get you a nightshirt and dry clothes for the morrow. Are you hungry?"

"No." The boy stepped out of his breeches so quickly, so without thought of shame, that the sight left Bernardo staring. Those legs—man shape underneath soft childhood—pale skin mottled from the cold. The bashful nub between his thighs.

Bernardo dug his fingernails into his palms and left the room. The chill of a stray draft reminded him that he was wet. He stood for a while, shivering, letting cold douse his cravings.

The room where Goatee slept was dark. Leaving the door ajar, Bernardo searched dressers, and found a heavy nightshirt, some leggings, breeches and a tunic and cloak. Footsteps in the hall brought him bolt upright. The steps passed, stopping at Monsignor's room. Bernardo put his hand into his pocket and fingered the tincture bottles. He would not bring the nostrums now, but later, after the dove was safe and tucked and warm.

When the footsteps receded, Bernardo stole downstairs. There, hidden like a gift, he found the dove waiting. The boy was by the fire, wrapped in the blanket, his clothes a wet pile in the corner.

"You could have gotten a better room," the dove said.

"Monsignor told me this one."

"He cheated you. This room belonged to a servant."

Bernardo smiled. "No doubt." He handed the boy the nightshirt, and his head swam when the blanket dropped. That clean-limbed, heat-blushed body was as beautiful as cherubs in paintings, as ingenuous as statues of Mary's boy child. Then the nightshirt was in place, and Bernardo's eyes could move elsewhere. "Take the bed," he said. "Wrap yourself up well."

"Aren't you going to sleep?"

"Later."

Bernardo knew himself possessed by a demon which would rip innocence asunder and force hot appetite in. It was such a demon that could not be outrun. A plunge in cold water would not drown it. He was being tested, for God would have Bernardo bring lust to heel.

Bernardo crawled to the corner, away from the warmth of the fire. He shivered. Tonight he would seek permissive remedies. He was tired, and would be stronger on the morrow. He took out his rosary and counted beads: the Apostles' Creed, the Pater Nosters, the Ave Marias, the Glorias, the Ave, Regina Sanctus, and then the Oremus. Again and again, Bernardo pushed the demon back with litany and winter. He counted the hours through, kneeling on the hard chill of the flagstones, guarding the dove's rest.

Day 11

BERNARDO AWOKE DULL-HEADED AND SHIVERING. THE FIRE HAD BURNED to embers and someone was knocking on the door. "A moment!" he called.

He scrubbed his face with his hands. The dove was sitting up in bed, watching him.

From beyond: "Father! Monsignor wants you!"

"Yes! A moment!" Bernardo got up from his corner, whispering, "Rodrigo, let no one know you are here. I will be back to bring you breakfast, if I can."

Such a sweet sleep-muddled expression. Dark hair that stuck up in sheaves. Plump milk-white cheeks that wore the rosy imprint of bedclothes. Bernardo gave in to temptation and ran a fingertip down the dove's face.

The cry was desperate. "Father Andrade! You must! No one else can deal with him!"

"Right away!" Bernardo opened the door a crack and slipped into the hall.

The guard was pacing and anxious. He brightened when Bernardo emerged. "You'd best hurry. He's in a mood."

Bernardo walked to the stair, shoving his hands into his pockets against the cold. His fingers touched the tincture bottles. *Miserere mei.* How could he have forgotten? Monsignor would not have slept the night. Now he would rail against everyone and everything. He would cuff Bernardo's ears.

But Bernardo found Monsignor bright-eyed and dressed. The room's windows were open to a pearly morning fog. "Good God, Bernardo. What has happened to your hair? You look like a racehorse that has been stabled all a-sweat."

"They called. I came straightaway."

"Well, do something to yourself before the day progresses further." He peered intently into Bernardo's face. "Not an excess of drink, I hope."

"O no, Monsignor, I simply—"

"Gird your loins, boy, for what is to come. Great events. Momentous battles. And for God's sake, splash your face. You look stuporous."

"Straightaway, Mon—"

"I go to visit our former idiot monarch, for it is time for him to put away his toys. It is time for all in this place to come to God kneeling and contrite." Monsignor picked up his ivory-clad missal and studied himself in Guilherme Castanheda's glass, first this way, then that.

Bernardo caught glimpse of himself in the selfsame mirror: a pale wisp in dark robes—a vision as mournful as forecasted Death.

A rap on the door sent Bernardo to answer. A servant had arrived with Monsignor's breakfast. Bernardo took the silver tray and laid it down on a fruitwood table. "Sausages, Monsignor? Fried pastry?"

He turned frowning. "Perhaps . . . O, perhaps just that plain loaf there. It happens that I am not so ravenous this morning."

"And did the tea settle your stomach?" The air from the window was damp and smelled of salt marshes. Bernardo cut the loaf into thick slices, and brought the plate near to Monsignor's hand.

Monsignor plucked up a slice, frowning at it. "Well enough, I suppose, seeing that it was ordered up by a liar and a whore. It took three cups, but then I farted so that I near brought the walls down. Mind you remember the recipe, Bernardo. It makes a sweeter medicine than your senna tea, which merely sends a tempest out my ass." He took in a great draft of air, puffing out his chest. "Ah! I feel utterly robust."

Bernardo poured coffee from a silver pot whose handle was of carved malachite. How much gold would this inventory harvest? Should he remind him that Castanheda left an heir? No. Monsignor knew full well, and any complaint might endanger the dove.

"A completely wonderful morning! Sugar, cream, Bernardo. Plenty of it." Monsignor snatched up a sausage, laid it between slices of bread. "I want you to have the seculars review the cases this morning, for I shall return midmorning, no later than ten o'clock, I should think. At that time we shall decide judgment. Tell that Jesuit. He must be present. I must strike now while Pedro's thoughts are elsewhere and the country is in an uproar. Tomorrow is Sunday, Bernardo. The *auto* is to be held Monday. That will give the condemned time to make peace with their fates. O, yes! And stop by the tailor shop to order up *sanbenitos,* nine of them, without matching caps. Order the *sanbenitos* black, with simple flames at the hem. No cavorting demons, for I will not pay for frills. Tell him we will need a pair of straw effigies. . . . *Salva me!* Do not peer about like an idiot, Bernardo. Effigies for Neves and his wife, who will surely be found guilty *in absentia.* Tell him to keep it secret, since the judgment has not been announced. . . . Ha! Ha! Not even to the rest of the tribunal! Bernardo, I tell you—to be selected as God's warrior, to know that I alone deliver the world from anarchy—it fair humbles me."

Bernardo looked up through his lashes. Monsignor, chins high, glared at the fog as if posing for a coin. "Will you not take some sausages with you?"

Monsignor fingered his missal. He contemplated the platter.

Bernardo shrugged. "Pork and sage. They seem not so rich to me."

"I know not what idiocy the woman was speaking." With his nimble, fat fingers, Monsignor gathered sausages and fried pastry into a linen napkin. "Stones rattling around in the belly. Hah! And she thinks I will go faint from what she says, and miss the devilment that her lecherous Jesuit plans." He sucked his fingertips. "Just a dusting of sugar, Bernardo, on those pastries. Very elegant."

"Yes. And not so rich, I think."

Monsignor started for the door, tossing over his shoulder a "Comb your hair."

FONSO WOKE, CONFUSED. No one had put his nightshirt on him. No one had turned down his bed. He had fallen asleep alone atop the covers, wrapped in his fur-lined cloak. Where was Jandira? Outside, all the hills were fog. The standing guard asked if he wanted something, and Afonso said that he did not know. He went back into his tent and waited. Suggestions should be made: Would His Highness not care for some breakfast? Was it not time to change His Majesty's clothes? Would the king care for cakes this morning, or a chop? There should be simple choices: yes-no, now-later, cakes-chop. To be asked what he wanted— well, the whole bewildering world stood as answer.

He wanted Jandira. He wanted Pedro. He wanted to go back to bed and hide under the covers, even though he was not sleepy. He knew that if he cried out, they would come—father and the captain and the guards and the cooks—and none of them would know what to do, either. He wanted to feel Pedro's hand on his cheek. He wanted to ask Pedro a question and hear something definite in response. O, and something had happened only two days ago—hadn't it?—something about Pedro. Two days. Afonso must mark that, lest he reach the end of his numbers and the news of Pedro be lost.

A cook's boy came with breakfast. Afonso said that he had to use the chamber pot, and the boy, all left hands and thumbs, tried to help him. Then he stood there, a boy no older than Afonso, who probably did not know the decisions to make, either.

"I should be dressed," Afonso said.

"Yes, sire."

"I think the dark blue tunic and the black breeches."

The cook's boy brought them.

"But underclothes first," Afonso said.

The boy rummaged among the cedar chests. "O, they are silk. Look! Silk and lace. How fine."

"You may have a pair," Afonso said, and the boy stuffed them into his pocket. "You must kneel here at my feet so that I may put my hand on your shoulder. And then you hold the underpants out, and then the breeches, so that I can step into them."

They managed together, but by the time Afonso was dressed and the battle of the ill-fitting boot won, his head was weary from giving instructions. He looked at the platter of meats and cheeses and pastries and fruit and breads, and walked out, not having the temper to decide.

The camp was quiet. Through the fog came noises, most muffled, some sharp, giving no hint of distance or direction. If he called Jandira, if he rang her bell—how would she find him?

"Did you wish for something, sire?" the standing guard asked.

"I want to go to Jandira, for I do not think that she can find me."

The guard bowed and ran off, coming back in the company of the captain. "Sire?"

"I would go to Jandira now, for I think that I have had enough of decisions and giving instructions, and of people who do not know what to do."

"Sire . . ." The captain lifted his arms, then let them fall with a great sigh. "Perhaps I can send word to your brother that he buy you a new slave to replace the one."

"O?" Afonso wondered if Brazil held rooms and rooms of Jandiras. "But this one knew me. I would rather have her back."

"Sire, I know. And if I were able . . ."

"Where did they put her?"

"Let me call Father de Melo."

"No. I don't want Father de Melo. I would go to Jandira and ring my bell for her and see if she has been changed—for I think she has had time enough."

The captain did not look happy, but he nodded. "Call the pair who dug

the grave," he said to the guard. The guard left and came back with two
soldiers. "Escort the king to the grave site," the captain said.

One soldier scratched his beard. "But we did not mark it, sir."

The other said, "Sir? Father instructed us not to mark it."

"You have some glimmer of an idea, do you not? Good God, men.
Did you walk south? East? Did you go uphill? Down?"

The two soldiers looked at each other. "Downhill," one said.

"I think more westerly," said the other.

And then they politely, and very correctly, asked if His Highness
would not care to accompany them. Afonso followed through the fog, past
the campfires and the cookfires and the tents. Afonso slid in the mud and
they caught him up between them, their gloved hands strong. All together
thus, they walked downhill until they reached a rivulet. There the soldiers
stopped and argued.

"There was no stream," one said.

"It has been raining."

"It was raining last night like God's piss, don't you remember? And
us bringing up clumps of mud."

They peered about. Halfway up the hill, fog swaddled the grass.
Afonso rang his bell, and sheep baaed in reply.

"This way." One soldier walked back the way they had come.

They searched that hill, then the next. They found a muddy place
where one soldier thought that she was. The other said that the slope was
too steep for a grave and asked if any barren spot looked good enough to
him. The first soldier said that he would be buggered before he lied to the
king. The second asked if he was sure of the site, and the first looked down
and shook his head and said that he did not know.

They went on, searching through mud and dung, Afonso ringing his
bell. They blundered through jagged outcroppings and slid in grass.
Afonso watched sheep, all dirty white, move like small ghosts through the
dingy mist.

Father de Melo called through the fog: "Ho! Your Highness, ho!"
Then suddenly he was there, stark and black. "Monsignor Gomes has
come to see you, sire. He awaits you in the camp."

"Where did you put Jandira?" Afonso asked. "We cannot find her."

He sighed. "Sire. Will you not come?"

Afonso turned around and around, ringing his bell. Dew collected on the wool of his cloak, on the breastplates of the guards.

"Sire?"

"Tell him to come here."

"Sire," Father de Melo said, "I think it more politic that you go to him."

They went, Afonso ringing his bell so that Jandira could follow. In the camp, amid the dripping tents and the smoking fires, the fat priest waited with a rough-looking guard. The captain stood beside, scowling at the ground.

"I will not kneel this time," Afonso told the fat priest. "For there is mud all around. Besides, I don't need your *Paters* and your *Filii Sanctis* anymore."

"You may not, sire," the priest said. "What you need is my goodwill, but you shall not have that, either. For I come not to ask but to command. I command, for instance, that your captain dig a hole large enough for the acorn. I command that the acorn be put in it and be buried. I command—"

Afonso's heart went into a tumult. "No!" he cried.

The captain brought his head up fast.

"You!" Afonso said. "You tell the fat priest no!"

The fat priest raised his voice. "I command that this blasphemy be buried straightaway, and grass planted atop it, and no sign left to show its grave, buried as nameless as your black-skinned slave who slew her own infant, and whom God saw fit to slay as well."

"Jandira is not dead! She will rise up, you will see! I know that it can happen, because the midwife told me. And you are an asshole mouth to think God killed her!"

The fat priest bent forward. "The midwife told you what, sire?"

"That she died, and when she came back, she saw the colors. She sees God in the colors, so she knows God better than you, who are a liar. So you had better leave, hadn't you? You had best get in your carriage and go away, or I will have my soldiers send you."

"Will you." The fat priest took out a piece of paper. "Well, I have a note, Your Highness, writ in your brother's own hand, and received this morning. If Father de Melo would be so kind as to read it?"

"You are a fat pig's belly and an asshole mouth!"

Father de Melo touched Afonso's arm. "It is from your brother, sire. Do you not care to hear it? Listen! Listen, sire. 'To his most excellent Inquisitor-General Monsignor Gomes: I regret that I cannot quit Lisbon, being otherwise occupied.' O, what a shame. But this part is sweet: 'However, I beg to remind Your Excellency that as Christ showed forbearance, you should show forbearance to the king. He often says things which he does not himself understand; and oftentimes finds great significance in baubles. He means no evil by it.' Ah. Now I understand the importance. It further reads, 'If you feel this acorn has attracted him in ways it should not, then you, as arbiter of what is proper, must take it. I beg you to take it gently.' And it is signed, 'Pedro de Bragança, Regent.' Well, sire. I am sure that were he able, he would come."

Afonso did not understand the note, except that Pedro was not coming and the captain looked angry. He said to the fat priest, "You are an asshole mouth and you shit my chocolates. They are my chocolates, and you cannot have any."

The fat priest turned to the captain. "Dig day and night if you must, until the grave is made. In the meantime I will take twenty of your men to help prepare the podium for the *auto-da-fé*, and the pyres."

"They are my chocolates," Afonso said. "You will give them back."

The fat priest said to Father de Melo, "The *auto* is to be held on Monday. See to it that the king is present and properly dressed and that he does not make a spectacle of himself. He will attend the Mass, but is to be prevented from partaking of the Eucharist. Then he will stand by and witness the burnings."

"Burnings?" Father de Melo said. "O, Monsignor, I know you will forgive me for pointing out, well . . . There exists the possibility that it may not be proper for the king to attend the executions. It certainly is not customary."

"Customary or not, he will stand witness." Afonso felt the weight of the fat priest's gaze. "This *auto* is no exhibition for idle townsfolk.

The *sanbenitos* will be plain, the ceremony short, the podium un-
adorned. There will be no Inquisitorial banners. No processions. This
auto is an act of purging. And so I would have the king look upon the
flames in Quintas. I would have him hear the screaming of the condemned. And then I would have him consider carefully the torment of
his own soul."

Q UINTAS WAS WREATHED in dripping enchantment. Ghosts floated
at the level of the tile roofs. Bernardo found the sign shaped like
a shirt which read ALFAIATE, and walked the four steps to the door. As he
opened, a bell rang. The two daughters and the wife and the tailor looked
up, and the wife gave a sharp cry.

"No." Bernardo put his hand out to her. "Not come for that."

The tailor had already retreated to the mouth of the hall. The younger
girl stood, scissors at the ready.

Bernardo told them, "Monsignor has asked for *sanbenitos* to be made.
Nine *sanbenitos*. And two effigies. And they must be ready by this Monday."

The wife was nodding. The tailor came forward, his ear cupped.
"Eh?"

"*Sanbenitos!*" the wife shouted.

The tailor shook his head. "Had one," he said. "Never done aught
since to merit another."

"Sew them!" the wife bellowed. "Nine!" She held up both hands, fingers spread, one thumb folded. "By Monday!"

The tailor's eyes went wide. Then they went sly. "O, father. That
might cost, you see? Hurried job such as this." He came close, peering into
Bernardo's lowered face. "And the particulars?"

"Painted black."

"Eh?"

"Black!" the wife shouted.

"And with flames."

The tailor heard that part right enough. "A bad business, talk of virgin births and such. A bad heresy of impostor angels."

"No demons."

"Eh?"

The wife looked perplexed. Bernardo raised his voice. "Monsignor does not want demons!"

The tailor shook his head. "O sir, like as not no one wants demons."

"On the *sanbenitos*! No painted cavorting demons. He will not pay for demons."

"Ah."

"But he wants pitchforks, surely," the wife said. "Pitchforks are cheap. And nine? Well, we could make a special price."

Bernardo waved his hand, "No, no. No pitchforks or demons. Only flames, and just at the hem."

The tailor rummaged through the clutter on the cutting table, found a quill and an ink pot. He looked about for paper, found a scrap. Then he discovered that the ink pot was dry. "Catarina!" he cried. "Ink!"

The girl fetched it. He scratched behind his ear. "So." He dipped the quill. "Nine *sanbenitos,* black and with flames at the hem. What sizes?"

The question laid Bernardo's thoughts waste. Large for Senhor Castanheda, broad at the shoulder, long at the leg. Small for his daughter. Yet even smaller for the virgin. The mother, certainly—a medium size. That was four. Two more for the effigies, so six. Still three left.

No. Never. The angels would be transported to Heaven, taken up in a shaft of light, their flesh too much air and vapor to burn.

"What sizes, father?" the tailor asked loudly.

"Two to fit the effigies," he said. "One for a large man. One for a grown woman. Two for young women. Three for children."

The tailor peered up at him. "Children?"

Bernardo's chin quivered. He rubbed his jaw to still it. Monsignor might dare try, but God would not let him. "Three children," he said.

Instead of growing brighter, the day grew more foreboding. Pessoa arrived at the jail to find the seculars already gathered. The two, dressed in fur-lined cloaks, were huddled to an iron brazier, warming their hands.

"Yet colder, father," Tadeo said, wiping his nose.

Pessoa looked around. Lamps smoked on wall brackets. All but for one, the windows had been shuttered; and that admitted more damp than light. He pulled his cloak closer about his shoulders. His neck and feet were chilled. "We should see that the prisoners are comfortable."

Emílio said, "Already done. Tadeo and I ordered more blankets brought, and saw that everyone had something hot to drink. I warrant they're more comfortable than we." He coughed and ducked his head into his fur collar.

"When is Monsignor due?" Pessoa asked.

Emílio laughed. "He takes his own time. Probably closeted somewhere with a coffee and brandy."

"And enough food for an army," Tadeo said.

"But God help *us* if we left to find someplace warm."

Tadeo echoed bitterly, "God help us."

Emílio paced back and forth before the brazier, flapping his arms. "When that notary comes back, we should take a statement from the girl— what is her name? Marta? The one whose feet were burned."

Fog barricaded the window. "Yes," Pessoa said, faint-voiced. "Marta."

"Always arduous to watch the tortures," Tadeo said quietly. "Let us hope she does not retract her statement, so we need no repetition of it." Then he said, "Emílio. Tell him."

"Yes, yes. We should." Emílio halted in front of Pessoa. "Father, we feel it best to warn you how we lean, for your arguments as to the creatures' divinity have been compelling."

"Even brilliant," Tadeo said.

Pessoa felt ache come on him. He would have sat down had there been a chair near; would have held on to something had there been support.

"We see no sign of angels."

"O but, sirs." The angel debate was a froth of sugar and egg white. As he had always known it would, it crumbled to dust in his hands. "Have you not considered the virgin conception?"

Tadeo shrugged. "I have heard of cases where women bloat, and pregnancy is suspected, and yet no infant is found inside. A rare instance, but to be frank, virgin births have proven rarer. One pop"—he clapped his hand together—"and the pregnancy is gone, either in tumor or liquid or, I suspect in this case, air. Such an outspilling of air that it ripped the maidenhood apart. Women." He threw up his hands. "A mystery."

Pessoa turned to Emílio. "And yet the creatures below in the cell. How do you explain them? Even I, as a Jesuit, cannot. You do not think demons, do you? Not with the leaking of the honey . . ."

"O no, no, no, father. We agree: no demons. We suspect the creatures of being New World animals which the Spaniards catapulted to us in order to cause a consternation."

"Indeed," Tadeo said. "Think of the timing. And the presence of the king. That cannot be coincidence."

"Absolutely correct. Very suspect, the timing. And obviously, father, the catapult, or perhaps even cannon—"

"Ai, Emílio! Do not speak of such nightmare! I had not thought of huge Spanish cannon!"

"Perhaps . . ." Pessoa's mind whirled. His heart sank. "Perhaps we should not dismiss the possibility of—"

"No, no!" Emílio said. "We don't dismiss your theory altogether."

Tadeo shook his head. "It would not be prudent. We must proceed very carefully, lest we ourselves commit a heresy."

"Yes! I see a deadly danger." Despite the cold, Pessoa was sweating. "And the girl, Maria Elena. She looks to me ill, and not fully possessed of her faculties. And Guilherme Castanheda, I think some acknowledgment should be made as to his suffering. It is not heresy he speaks, but anger."

"O, I quite agree." Tadeo and Emílio exchanged nods. "Yes, quite right. Those two should be released without delay, and Guilherme Castanheda's goods restored to him. The Teixeira woman, though, and the Castanheda girl, well, heresy without doubt, and such a heresy which calls for relaxing to the state."

Pessoa said, "Still, even their cases merit close consideration. Monsignor must give us more time."

"Ah, time?" Tadeo looked doubtful. "More charitable for the condemned that it be over quickly. And I admit frankly, father, that I will be glad to return to Lisbon. My practice languishes, and I piss money."

"The Holy Office does not pay well as a rule," Emílio said, "and the monsignor pays even less."

A glum moment of reflection. Into that silent pool, Pessoa dropped three pebbles. "There is gold."

Pessoa watched the words sink. Tadeo blew on his hands. Emílio wiped his nose.

"A great deal of gold," Pessoa said. "It lies in a Lisbon bank, but is easy for Guilherme to access."

"Well," Tadeo said.

Emílio bent and added more kindling to the fire. They watched it blaze cheerful yellow. Pessoa caught the clean scent of pine.

"Not that a little money is not welcome," Emílio said, "but in this case . . ."

"Yes, father. I would say that in this case . . ."

The seculars' eyes met, rebounded. Emílio cleared his throat. "To live to spend it . . ."

"Um. Yes. True. One must live to spend it, otherwise where is the good?"

"And Monsignor seems so taken up with this case."

"Obsessed, no doubt."

"We have discussed it, Tadeo and I. And we have come to the conclusion that he may be dangerously insane."

Tadeo swept his hand to the side, a gentle and restrained gesture, like a nun's. "Nothing we do here must be in question. Let him receive the brunt of the Holy Office's displeasure. You and I and Emílio are out of harm, you see."

Day had been misplaced. Not yet noon, and Pessoa sensed night assemble. The stone walls wept. "Not the Antichrist."

He felt Tadeo's icy hand on his own. "No. But neither can we bring ourselves to believe your story. To us, the earth is rounded not by wonders, father, but by sameness. O, one day Christ will certainly come again, but we do not believe that He has visited here."

P ALE GHOSTS HAD flown away, and demons were come. They gamboled in the mouths of the dark alleys; they prated among the eaves. Bernardo hid himself in his cowl until his view was circumscribed to that part of the world which lay before his feet. Quill box under his arm, he hurried toward the jail. He thought of the dove secreted in his rooms—waiting just for him—and the idea flared warm in his chest as a candle.

He hurried down a mud-slick road, past a trellised rose whose flowers were dropping their petals. The last of morning failed. He could barely see the cobbles. Bernardo felt a vertigo, as if he had been flung into an uncharted sea where day was not day, where sin had been turned upside down. He trembled, remembering Christ, the death, the darkening.

He hurried faster. Father Manoel would be at the jail amid the happy patter of the seculars. No. It could not happen now, not happen yet. *Tuba mirum spargens sonum.* Wind blared its trumpet, and thunder rolled like Apocalypse at his heels. Ah, God. *Per sepulcra regionum coget omnes ante thronum.* Bernardo did not want to be alone when graves disgorged their dead.

And then he was within sight of the jail. Borne on a bluster of wind, fiends plucked at him, demons caught at his hem. He rushed, splashing through puddles, his breath coming fast.

He burst inside the building, swept past curious guards, and hurried to the room where the trial was held. Father Manoel and the seculars looked up suddenly. They stepped apart. Something in their faces . . .

"Good morning, father," Scarecrow said, bowing.

Goatee inclined his head. "We were just discussing you, that we should verify the statement of the accused Marta Castanheda, now she is no longer under burden of torture."

O, how dark the day was, as if light would never come again. Could they not see it? *Jesu, Jesu, confutatis maledictis.* Monsignor had set all Hell into motion, and nothing could be done to stop it.

Father Manoel asked gently, "Bernardo? Are you well?"

"Monsignor has ordered nine *sanbenitos,* black, with flames at the hem." Truth was out before he could stop it, but it did not matter now. Nothing mattered. "The End Time has come. He means to burn the angels."

AFONSO WAILED TO see the soldiers take up shovels and begin the hole. "God is sad! He is taking the colors away." He lifted his head and watched morning darken.

A few soldiers put their shovels down. The captain called to pick them up.

"Whose orders do we obey?" came the response. "Yours? Or God's?"

Father de Melo held up his lantern. Thunder muttered through the hills. "Do not be afraid, my sons," he told them. "A storm is coming, that's all. You've seen storms before, haven't you? It is by the orders of the Holy Office that you labor here. And the Holy Office is the protector of the Church. Dig! Dig for what is right! God gives strength to your backs."

Afonso wanted to warn God what was happening, for he thought how frightening it would be to suddenly find dark earthen weight all around. Father de Melo held him back.

When Afonso pulled loose, it was the captain this time who stayed him. "O sire, please. You must not protest. Pedro reigns now, and you have become aught but a useless bother to the Inquisition."

"I want Pedro," Afonso cried. "I want Jandira."

The captain fell to his knees and caught Afonso's arms. He shook him hard, which startled Afonso very much. "Listen to me, sire. Listen! Your position is all of a danger now. I will keep you from that acorn if I must imprison you myself. For you to hold to this heresy will mean that Pedro is forced down with you. The Inquisition has never been friend to the Braganças or to Portugal. Let the acorn go, Your Majesty, and save your kingdom."

Afonso raised his face to the mist. He knew then that Jandira was not coming back, for the earth in Portugal was not the earth of Brazil. That soil was rich and warm and tasted of coffee; the soil of Portugal was all cabbage and cod. And he knew that God was not becoming; He was dead. Dew collected on Afonso's open eyes and slid down his face. He watched clouds mass, watched the sun disappear.

"Come, sire," the captain said gently.

Afonso would not leave. He would stay by the grave his soldiers opened, and then watch God be put in it. Afonso would stand until the rain stopped, and the seas dried, and stars fell all around.

OMES CAME IN from the gloom of Bernardo's End Time. As if a single muscle, Pessoa felt the entire room tense.

Tadeo prodded the fire in the brazier. "Past midday, Monsignor Gomes."

Gomes whipped off his hat. "Yes. It was dark out."

Pessoa saw Bernardo lift his head and look Gomes full in the face. How could the man not shrink before that naked contempt?

"Notary? Are you ready? We will to the tribunal now. Marta Castanheda's verification next, I think."

Emílio looked away, muttering, "Already done."

And Bernardo, shy once more, was needlessly consulting his journal. "She repeats her confession of yesterday."

"Good, good." Monsignor rubbed his hands briskly and looked about the sparsely furnished room, never catching sight of resentment.

"If we are to decide judgment," Tadeo said, "we might find someplace warmer."

Gomes grunted. "One more accused."

Pessoa looked about. "But who?"

"If you will take your seats." Gomes waved toward the tribunal table. "Grievous heresy. A deadly one. Should not take long, I think."

Pessoa watched the two seculars and Bernardo trudge listlessly to the table. He caught the sidelong glance Gomes threw him as he passed.

"Whom do you call?" Pessoa knew the name before it was said, knew it from Gomes's smile, had known it forever, really. Certain stories, however pleasing, were destined for bad endings.

"A liar and a fornicator and a heretic," Gomes said. "Do you stand to be judged along with her?"

And there she was, coming through the door, so small between the huge terror of her guards. The room shrank. Mist darkened the edges of his vision. Through that new gray world resounded the deafening and labored pounding of a heart that seemed about to stop. Pessoa sensed someone standing at his left shoulder.

Tadeo. "Come. Sit at the bench. You do her no good standing here."

BROUGHT before the tribunal, Berenice Pinheiro, herbalist, accused of the heresy of saying that she had died and come back from the grave, an accusation that the prisoner denied. Msgr. Gomes then asked the prisoner to search her soul, for accusation was made by none other than the king himself, and did the prisoner dare to call the king a liar. The prisoner said that the king, being distraught at the death of his slave, had mistook her meaning. Msgr. Gomes asked if the king's confessor had mistook as well, for Msgr. Gomes had interviewed him, and the confessor attested to the king's accusation.

The witness stated that she had never been buried, nor any rites read over her. She related a story of having lain deathly fevered in her twenty-first year, without water or the means to get it, or any neighbor to fetch. She told of noticing suddenly that she stood in the middle of her room, yet could not recall rising from her cot. She told of being flung through a dark cave and of seeing a light at the other end which resolved itself into the figure of a man. She said that the man of light greeted her and told her that he knew her life had been lonely. The man then told her that he loved her, and asked if his love would not be enough. He asked, knowing that, could she not now go back and learn the lessons of charity? The witness began to weep and, upon being asked why she was weeping, said, "Because he was so kind to me. No one had ever been so kind. And that's why I know he was sent of God, for he had no expectations nor demands, and would have loved me just the same if I had told him no."

A secular admitted that he was very much moved by the story, and he asked how she came to live again. She said that she came back to the cot with a great jolt, and that she awoke thirsty and sweated, for her fever had broken. She said that she crawled out of bed, since she could not walk, and made her way to a nearby puddle, where she lapped up water like a hound. She said that, as it rained that day and the next, she was able to set a pot outside and gather the rain, and that some days later she was strong enough to rise and make her way about.

Msgr. Gomes then asked the prisoner if she believed she was a Christ, since only the Savior had the power to be raised from the dead; to which the prisoner replied that Lazarus had been raised also. Msgr. Gomes asked if Christ was present in the room to raise her, and the prisoner replied that it was her belief that He had been; that indeed, Christ was forever present, for did He not promise that He would be with us always? Then the accused looked out the window at the day, which was unusually dark, and said, "Even unto the end of the world?" at which the guards became very agitated and began crossing themselves and loudly uttering prayers, and Msgr. Gomes was forced to order them into silence.

As it was seen that the day had darkened even more, more lamps were ordered to be lit, and one of the jailers under the command of Fr. Pessoa's familiar began to weep and ask if he could go home to his family before the graves vomited up their dead, at which time Msgr. Gomes harshly admonished the man to silence, lest he be charged with a heresy himself. Fr. Pessoa told the man that he might go to his family if he feared the approaching storm and thought his wife and children might have need of him, at which time the jailer bent his knee, thanked the tribunal, and left.

Msgr. Gomes chastised the prisoner, charging her to witness what superstitious rebellion she had started up, to which a secular replied that quotation of scripture was to him no superstition, and the tribunal should accept as valid her assertion as to death and resurrection, for the prisoner's answer had been not only humble but elegant, and pointed to no heresy at all.

Msgr. Gomes asked if the prisoner believed that death enabled her to see colors in things and tell illness from those colors; and the prisoner said that it was so, that the dark red and purple over Monsignor's right side told her of his excess of gall; that a yellow on one of the secular's wrists told her that he had begun a rheumatism in it, and that he should drink parsley and juniper tea each day upon arising. The secular was very surprised at this, and said that he indeed of late had had a pain and swelling there, but that it was not so much that he would complain. The prisoner assured him the pain would only worsen should he ignore it, at which time the secular requested that the notary take down the tea's recipe. Msgr. Gomes spoke very sharply to the secular, and said that an Inquisitorial tribunal was not the place for a medical consultation, and then he asked the prisoner if she remembered telling the king's slave that ghosts lead the dying away. She said that she had, that often the dying see in the room those who had died before. She said that the dying would often call the names of the dead, and it seemed to give them a great comfort. Msgr. Gomes asked if the prisoner was saying that the Angel of Death was not sent to harvest souls; and she said that the Angel was perhaps not what we had thought, and not to be feared. She said that the Angel was husband or wife, father or mother, beloved sister or brother, and that the harvest of souls was a thing of joy. Msgr. Gomes then asked if she had been present at a death when a priest was not yet come, and she replied that she had had patients slip away of a sudden, before Fr. Soares could reach them. Msgr. Gomes asked if any of those had imagined seeing spirits in the room and thus had died happily, and she said that many of them had. She was asked if she often told the dying to look for a spirit and she said, if the dying were awake, she told them to search the room, for seeing the loved one calmed their fears. At that, Msgr. Gomes sat back and in a loud indicting voice asked the prisoner if she believed that those who died in sin received the same welcome as those who died shriven, and she replied that she was not one to tell sinner from saved, but that she saw joy on most faces. She was asked by Msgr. Gomes once more if she instructed the dying to look for ghosts, and a secular warned that she consider her answer. The prisoner replied that she saw no harm in it, and where was the harm? She was asked by the other secular to please answer, at which time Fr. Pessoa spoke up and said that he was of the opinion that the prisoner was not fully rational, that her illness had so damaged her eyes that she saw colors and so damaged her brain that she had fallen into delusion. A secular said that in his opinion the prisoner was lucid. Then the secular again charged her to reply to the question: did she instruct the dying to

look for ghosts who would lead them into death? The prisoner
said that she did, and asked once more where was the harm?

Fr. Pessoa said that the prisoner did not understand what
she had said. He stated that she was lonely, having been shunned
because of the villagers' superstition. He said that the prisoner's
loneliness had caused a morbid yearning for company in her,
which was why she had created in her mind the man of light. He
said that, as her confessor, he had noticed that she clung to any
sort of attention given, and that she was more pathetic and needy
than heretic, and begged the tribunal to show mercy, for her life
had been dreary and sad. He admitted that her sin had been
partly his; and he promised, now that he had been made aware
of it, he would teach her how to patiently wait for a priest. He
said that he would exhort her, if she needed to speak any words
of comfort to the dying at all, to tell them to trust in Christ.

Msgr. Gomes said that in his opinion such precautions came
too late. That the prisoner had talked many into apostasy and
thus into Hell. He said that because of her heresy there were
souls, even now, suffering unbearable torment, and that she
should be severely punished for it. Then he ordered that the prisoner be taken away to a cell, thus to await with the others the decision of the tribunal. A jailer came forward and led her away.

MSGR. GOMES declared that guilt or innocence of the prisoners should be decided without delay, at which point a secular objected strenuously, saying that Msgr. Gomes ordered them to be
ready at mid-morning, when Msgr. Gomes was not come until
midday. The secular said that he, like the other members of the
tribunal, was hungry and cold. He said that even though Msgr.
Gomes had most probably dined, he saw no reason not to delay
decisions until after the rest of the tribunal had eaten. The other
secular spoke up and said that he was further of the opinion that
deliberations as to judgment should be held in a place that was
warm, that he and the other secular and the notary and Fr. Pes-

soa had had plenty enough of the chill of the day, and that he himself was so frigid that his brain was sluggish, and he could stand a brandy to warm it.

Thus it was declared that the tribunal would take leave for a midday meal, then meet at the fifteenth hour in the house of the prisoner, Guilherme Castanheda, and there rule on the prisoners' fates.

Pessoa rushed downstairs in a wild flurry. His feet tripped over themselves. His cloak flapped.

Below, the jailers were gathered close about a conflagration of lanterns. Three steps from the bottom, Pessoa looked to the women's cell and spotted what he had feared: Marta's warm cloak folded neatly and returned, Berenice in a corner all alone and shivering.

"Blankets! Damn you! I want blankets here! And open the door!"

A clang of keys. Averted gazes. Mutters of, "Yes, father. Right away, father."

And then one man at the back said in a trembling voice, "Dark, isn't it, father?"

Dona Teixeira called out merrily, "Black as your souls!" She sat in the shadows, her daughter curled to her one side, Marta Castanheda curled tight to the other.

Pessoa said to the guards, "Quit the room."

"But . . ." They exchanged glances.

"Fear to go up top, don't they," Dona Teixeira cackled. "Fear God might see them and pinch their heads off."

Pessoa told her, "Shut your mouth."

Thunder rumbled through the jail and set the walls to vibrating. Lightning blinked madly at the windows. Wind struck the westerly wall, sending candles guttering and stray paper into sudden flight.

"Believe you now that they are angels?" Dona Teixeira asked. "Watch! For soon my daughter's baby will come, sword in hand, through the clouds."

They backed away from the women's cell, their faces turned from the windows. When one man brought the blankets, Pessoa tore them from out his grasp. "Leave us," he said.

They looked at him, fearful.

"Good God, men. It is but a storm. You've seen a storm such as this."

"But the women . . ." said one.

Another: "The cell door is open. Should we leave the door open, then?"

And yet another. "What if Monsignor finds out?"

"Wait at the top," Pessoa told them. "Draw your swords. If any of these women come raging up the stair, you have my permission to run them through."

When they left, Pessoa went into the women's cell. The smell of her—strawflowers and spices—blessed the corner. Longing nearly toppled him. She could not be here, not so small and so imprisoned. The Holy Office would send word that mistake had been made.

He threw the blankets down like in a stoning, but she did not stir. He took in breath to shout, and aborted it in a sigh. "Are you hungry?"

Movement stirred the shadows; clothing rustled.

"Damn you, Berenice. Are you hungry?"

She whispered, "No."

He whirled to Dona Teixeira. "Look at her! Look! Has she not cared for you when you were sick? Has she not comforted your dying? And you make her sit here all alone? God! God! May you be struck down for it!"

He stalked over and opened up Dona Teixeira's basket. He took out a loaf, a pear, tore a piece of roasted lamb from off the shank. He wrapped it all up in a linen cloth and brought it to her.

"Take it!" He threw the food into her lap. The napkin opened, spilling the meat. The pear rolled onto the straw.

Was she frightened? Was she weeping? Her face was turned away and he could not tell. He felt damp heat prickle his eyes. Before he could lose control, he stalked out the door.

RAIN CAME DOWN, drenching Afonso's cloak. It wet his tunic and his undershirt. His clothes became all of a cold weight and felt so strange about his body that he wondered if this was how it was to be dead.

The captain shouted in his ear, "Sire! Come away!"

Below him, the soldiers had put down their shovels. They had covered their heads from the fierce glare of the lightning and the crash of the thunder.

The captain pulled on his arm. "Sire!"

Lightning danced. A bolt struck nearby and shook the hill to its stony roots. Soldiers broke and fled for their tents, and the drays of a nearby wagon whinnied in terror. The captain's frantic jerk on Afonso's arm sent them both to their knees.

And then the stars fell. Fell all around and with a great clamor. They fell cold and round and white, clattering against rock, pelting the grass. They rang against the captain's helmet, his breastplate; they dealt hammer blows to Afonso's shoulders.

"The stars!" Afonso cried.

"What, sire?"

"The stars are falling!"

"Yes, yes." The captain pulled him to his feet, nestled his head against his shoulder, and star-pounded, they ran to camp.

BERNARDO TOOK SCRAPS from the kitchen and tucked them into his pockets. He went to his room. Pure as moon in a midnight sky, the dove's face shone from the shadows. Each time thunder cracked, the boy cowered.

"It's all right." Bernardo went to him, kneeling to lay a hand on his knee.

"I know. I know it's all right. I'm not afraid." But his eyes searched the dark for monsters.

Bernardo brushed hair back from that alabaster brow. "No, of course you aren't." Outside the diamond-paned windows a tempest whipped through the Gates of Hell, chasing winged and fluttering demons.

"I have food." Bernardo brought his hands from out his pockets. The boy snatched the loaf, the cheese. He put a chunk of sausage whole into his mouth.

Wind trumpeted down the street. "Do you hear it?" Bernardo cocked his head and smiled. "The tribulation? Today Monsignor will condemn to death your father and sister and her heralds. Day after tomorrow he will send them to the stake. But—*de morte transire ad vitam*—before the flames can touch one hair, God will bear them up."

"I want *pai*," the dove said.

He took the boy's hands in his. "You know your rosary, do you not?"

The solemn nod stole Bernardo's heart. He kissed the boy's cold fingers. He lowered his forehead to the dove's knuckles and closed his eyes. Brother of Marta, sister of Lazarus, sent by God to shore up that part in Bernardo which was weak.

"Then say your rosary, Rodrigo, and stay quiet and hidden." He tucked the blankets about him more securely, put another log on the fire, and left the room.

Father Manoel was waiting in the dining hall, looking dejectedly out the windowpanes to the black day. Bernardo tugged on the Jesuit's sleeve and bent his head to whisper, "He will not win."

"He always wins, Bernardo. I see it in his eye. And he will yet force the seculars to agree with him, for they rightly value their skins."

"No." Bernardo tugged at his sleeve once more. "It matters not that Monsignor sends the condemned to the stake. There are no flames which will burn them. Do you not see? Heaven is coming."

A stirring in the hallway carried with it the sound of voices and Goatee's merry laughter. The tribunal had arrived.

Father Manoel moved away to his chair, shaking his head and muttering, "God have mercy."

THE CASE of Marta Castanheda, age fifteen, was brought before the tribunal for a decision as to her fate, and it was ordered that, as she had confessed to lies concerning her visitations by the Virgin Mary, she should be found guilty of grave heresy and be relaxed to the state for execution.

Msgr. Gomes declared, and the tribunal unanimously agreed, that Marta Teresa da Penha Castanheda, having confessed to her lie and having sincerely abjured, should be put upon a pyre of wood and pitch and tied to a stake, whereupon the state executioner, after having allowed her to say her prayers, might come forward and dispatch her mercifully and quickly with a garrote so that she should not suffer the flames. And when her soul had fled her body, her pyre should be set alight, and her body burnt, and to this all that were present agreed.

AS TO the matter of Guilherme Castanheda, man of commerce and father of Marta, the seculars and Fr. Pessoa agreed that, since war had embittered him, Sr. Castanheda should be shown compassion. It was suggested by the three that Sr. Castanheda be cautioned against more heretical statements and freed from prison and be given a *sanbenito,* white with a red cross upon it, which he should wear each and every feast day in penance for his wrongdoings. Msgr. Gomes disagreed, suggesting that the prisoner's heresy was too grave to ignore, and that relaxing to the state was called for. Since neither compromise nor unanimity could be reached by the tribunal, the matter was set aside.

CONSIDERING the case of Amalia Teixeira, wife to Duarte, the tribunal was in unanimous agreement that she be relaxed to the state for burning, and the statements read as follows: the seculars condemning her for fostering heresy in others after having been warned to silence by clerics; Fr. Pessoa condemning her for statements made before the tribunal itself as to the Blessed Mother's being forced by God; and Msgr. Gomes for her avowed belief in her daughter's virgin conception and angels.

As the tribunal was unanimous, although for diverse reasons, it was ordered that Amalia Analinda Teixeira, on the day the *auto-da-fé* was to be held, would be given over to a state executioner who would then bind her to a pyre of wood and pitch; that the pyre was to be set alight and that she be burnt to death in front of her judges and other witnesses, and her ashes scattered.

AS TO the case of Maria Elena Teixeira, daughter to Amalia, Msgr. Gomes elected that she be relaxed to the state for burning. The seculars and Fr. Pessoa were of the opinion that the girl was insane and thus must be set free. As the tribunal was not unanimous and consensus could not be reached, the judgment was set aside.

AS TO the case of three unnamed beings, two apparently living and one apparently dead, Msgr. Gomes was of the opinion that they were fallen angels who had taught the king the heresy of Galileo Galilei, and thus were wicked liars. It was his opinion that they should be relaxed to the state and burned straightaway. The seculars made objection, saying they believed the creatures to be dumb beasts, and thus not deserving of punishment. Fr. Pessoa objected to punishment also, he being of the opinion that the creatures were angels of God, and sanctified. He said that he had additional proofs as to their divinity, having been told by the guards that the creatures partook of water and of bread, yet had not been seen to relieve themselves of it. He said further that the guards had searched the cell, looking for dung which they meant to use as a curative, but that they had found no trace. Fr. Pessoa questioned the other members of the tribunal as to how the creatures could eat and drink and yet yield nothing. A secular related that monkeys, if sufficiently distressed, were known to consume their own spoor, and perhaps that was why the guards had not found any. Fr. Pessoa asked if such habit did not make them ill, and the secular said that he had been told that monkeys often choked and died, as the feces caught in their throats. The other secular spoke up, asking if the discussion on offal was ended, as he had just eaten and contemplated enjoying dinner; and the matter of the creatures' fate was set aside.

ON THE matter of Berenice Pinheiro, herbalist, Msgr. Gomes and the two seculars agreed that leading the dying into such apostasy was a grave heresy deserving of burning; and Fr. Pessoa was of the opinion that the woman was insane and should be set free. He said that he had further proof, and that he would bring it that evening or on the morrow, and so the decision on the herbalist's fate was set aside.

THUS the cases of Marta Castanheda and Amalia Teixeira were judged completed, and note made to instruct the two women straightaway concerning the decision of the tribunal, so that they be given time to make peace with their souls.

AS THE DAY was damp and cold, it was suggested that the tribunal order up brandy and take an hour's leisure before returning to arguments. Msgr. Gomes spoke up and said that God had set him to a great task: that of banishing heresy altogether. He stated that he had prayed and God had sent him answer in the form of terrible dreams, thus it did not matter that brandy was brought and leisure taken, for he himself assumed the burden to decide the fates of the prisoners, and that he felt obligated to reverse the decisions of mercy.

A secular spoke up, saying that Msgr. Gomes had not the authority to do so; to which Msgr. Gomes replied that God had given him the authority. Fr. Pessoa said that neither he nor the seculars had sign of that, and if they believed Msgr. Gomes, why should they not also believe the women's story of angels. He said that there was more proof of the women's story than Msgr. Gomes's, being that the women had witnesses and Msgr. Gomes did not. Msgr. Gomes swore and said that the women had not been charged by the Holy Office to protect and defend the Church, and that if Fr. Pessoa saw no difference between the angel story and his, then perhaps Fr. Pessoa should join his lover on the fire.

A secular said that such personal reprimands were highly inappropriate. He said that he himself had long ago wearied of Msgr. Gomes's remarks. In fact, he was of the opinion that the tribunal should be halted immediately and word sent to the Holy See to bring another inquisitor-general. He said that he was paid as expert in inquisitorial matters and that to reverse his decision was to make him out a liar, and he would not have it.

Msgr. Gomes replied that God had told him to burn all the prisoners and have done with it. That if he did not act, the world would fall into a tumult, and compared to that, one three-penny lawyer's reputation did not matter a mouse fart.

The secular got to his feet and pounded the table with his fist and said that he would see Msgr. Gomes stripped of his position. He said that it mattered not about the animals, but that Maria Elena Teixeira was obviously not in possession of her faculties and that to penalize her for it was highly illegal and immoral and flew in the face of the reformed Holy Office. He asked if Msgr. Gomes fancied himself a cleric more of the French or German ilk, who would burn poor women believed to be witches. He asked if Msgr. Gomes believed the herbalist Berenice Pinheiro, for example, possessed of the evil eye, and went about in the air astride a broom? And if Msgr. Gomes believed that, then perhaps he should set fire to the entire town and rid himself of all the heresy, to which Msgr. Gomes replied that he had mind to do that, and that if the town was burnt at least he might sleep at night; to which Fr. Pessoa said that it appeared Msgr. Gomes wished to gain his own sleep at the cost of the rest of the tribunal, and exhorted the seculars to imagine the screamings of Maria Elena, who knew not what she did, and the cries of Guilherme Castanheda, whose only crime was a sentimentality for his daughter.

The other secular stated as how the entire affair was ridiculous, that Msgr. Gomes looked about Quintas and saw superstition, when he himself looked about Quintas and could see lurking a dangerous Spanish plot. He said less attention should be paid to lighting pyres and more paid to informing the king's regent of a terrible sedition.

Msgr. Gomes suggested that the three ride out to the Holy See and ask for a replacement straightaway, and could he have horses sent up, the statement intended in the form of an irony, for a violent storm was then raging, and word had arrived of floods and uprooted trees and hail.

Msgr. Gomes said that the jailers and guards and executioners had been given unto his command and that he would make use of them.

THUS he ordered Maria Elena Teixeira, age fourteen, Guilherme Castanheda, man of commerce, and Berenice Pinheiro, herbalist, and the unnamed creatures of unknown origin, even the creature who appeared dead, to be all lashed to pyres and burnt unless they asked to be forgiven their sins, at which time they might be shown compassion and be strangled before the fires were lit. Then in a loud voice he called an inquisitorial guard to him, and instructed that the guard take three jailers and go to the rectory and there gather the parish priest, Fr. Luis Soares, for the priest had much to confess concerning the nature of the creatures, and so the guard went out into the rain.

Pessoa leaped to his feet. "Have you not ordered murders enough? God!"

Monsignor Gomes said, "Sit down!"

How could Pessoa sit through this? This usurpation of reason? The room was quiet suddenly, the storm outside holding its breath, the fire lessening from roar to crackle. Castanheda's great room smelled of burning wood and the cinnamon and cloves of the sweet cakes the seculars and Monsignor were eating.

But rage would avail nothing. And so, as his teacher of dialectics had instructed, Pessoa pictured himself putting a bull back into its stable, and imagined locking it up. He said more calmly, "It is most natural that Luis sees divinity in the creatures, for Luis sees God in everything. I know him well, and I will attest to his sweet nature. As I have traveled, sir, I have never seen a better pastor, or one more dedicated to his sheep. But Luis is like a child sometimes, perhaps even the sort of child Christ would have us be."

Gomes's face quickened to an unhealthy red. "That is just the problem with this town: maudlin gullibility. Perhaps Soares is the chief culprit here, as it was he who had charge over the village's spiritual well-being. Hah! I bend your own reason back upon you. Well? Is that not a logical deduction? Do you not see that yourself? Or have you given your Jesuit logic up to mysticism?"

Breathing hard, Pessoa paced the length of the marble hearth. "Loyola teaches that questions should lay an inescapable path toward understanding. This is pure bickering, sir, and it gains us nothing."

"Admit it: Satan found here a weak parish in which to put his sword."

Pessoa halted. Rage came charging out of its stable, Pessoa helpless to stop it.

But before he could give voice to his shout, Tadeo spoke up. "I feel no need to question Father Soares. Really, Monsignor. An elderly parish priest? His only sin is kindliness. As far as I can see, Father Soares has done nothing. Bringing him before the Inquisition is unthinkable."

"Unthinkable? Believe you so? Well, this kindly old man has stated in front of witnesses and has also claimed before this very tribunal that the creatures are divine. He has fostered deviltry. So, sirs, I warn you: I will thus call Father Soares, and ask him again, and I shall decide heresy on his answer." Those small eyes moved from Tadeo's now blushing face to Pessoa's. "And you? Have you changed your mind?"

Pessoa shoved his hands into his pockets before Gomes could see them clench.

A curt "Well? Have you? Or say you angels still?"

"We will all know the truth before the Throne, will we not, Monsignor?"

"I don't take your meaning."

"Of course you do. You could not be so dense as to not. There is such unearthly marvel here, and such diverse opinions among the inquisitors themselves, that we cannot be certain of anything. In any case, I would prefer to err on the side of mercy. If we vote to execute these creatures, and they are indeed sent of God, I would think such a murder worthy of God's full ire, and I would not join you in Hell."

"Ah . . ." Emílio held up a hand. "I myself have never suggested the creatures' punishment."

Tadeo said, "Notary? Will you take that down, please? Emílio and I voted against their punishment."

"I will cut that crooked lying Jesuit tongue from out you!" Monsignor said. "Do you forget your vow of obedience? Can you not answer a question straight? Yes or no, man! Yes or no! Think you these creatures angels?"

"It's hard to know the nature of anything."

Gomes slapped the arms of his chair. "You speak the nonsense of John Locke, sir! I ask you once more: do you believe the creatures divine? Answer, before I bring the executioners here and put your feet to the coals—or would you like that? Would you be a martyr for debate! Hah! I think you have not the stomach. Soon I'd hear you warble, as I did that cheeky wench with her Marian apparitions."

Down to truth, then; and it would have to out, for truth was an unavoidable sort of thing. Pessoa said, "They do not look like angels such as I would imagine. I have never myself, personally, felt a divinity from them.

And that is the end of my statement, and it must suffice or you yourself be damned. Put my feet to the coals and I will say the same. Never having seen such creatures before, I cannot—like you—make absolute claims as to their nature."

Pessoa, expecting rage, was unprepared for the crafty smile. "But not certain of their holiness?"

O, dear God. Gomes was more clever than Pessoa had realized. He had fashioned a snare to trap men of conviction—and Pessoa was not one of those. "No," Pessoa said, leaving the seven to their fates. "Not certain."

A commotion at the door brought in a blustery draft and the smell of rain. The guards entered, shaking the wet from their cloaks. And then came Soares, frail and sodden and confused.

"It has been decided," Monsignor said, "that the creatures are not angels at all, at least not holy angels. And so to declare them holy now would be a most grievous heresy."

Soares paled. Pessoa started forward to steady him, but the old Franciscan backed to a chair and collapsed into it.

Then Tadeo was on his feet, and saying with false cheer, "Father! Let us have you sit closer to the fire. Good, good, that is it. Isn't that better?" With an encouraging smile and a pat on the back, he exclaimed, "Look how wet you are! Give me that damp cloak before you catch your death. What an afternoon, is it not? And indeed, an entire season disturbed, summer too soon turned winter. Guard! Bring the father something dry to wrap himself in. And a coffee with brandy."

Pessoa watched the guard march out with the wet cloak, and then looked to where Soares sat, trembling and bewildered. Pessoa's eyes sought the refuge of the snapping hearth. Behind him came Monsignor's abrasive voice. "Father Soares, I have called you here—"

"Mary and Joseph!" Emílio cried, standing up of a sudden. "Where is that dry cloak? Guard! Are you deaf! Guard!"

Like spark to tinder, Emílio started up heat and action. Servants bustled in. Guards came. A cloak was brought, and Soares wrapped up in it. A servant put a porcelain coffee cup into the Franciscan's hand.

Porcelain, thin as eggshell. How much would that cup have cost? The green marble and gold clock atop the mantel? The silver coffee service? And then Monsignor was saying, "Father Soares? I ask you, do you still believe the creatures cherubs?"

They would take the house and its riches, but Pessoa would let the Holy Office have aught else. "Luis!" He caught Soares with his mouth open to reply. "I think you should know how the tribunal decided today."

Monsignor snorted. "How is that germane? Let him answer and hold your tongue."

Tadeo shouted, "No! Let Father Pessoa speak! Learn to hold your tongue yourself! Can you not? Can you not do that?"

Into the shocked quiet, Pessoa said, "The tribunal was unanimous in a relaxing to the state of two."

Cup rattled against saucer. "Who?"

"Marta Castanheda, to be strangled. Amalia Teixeira, to be burnt."

Soares blew out a breath. He held on to the saucer with both hands. The cup clattered and danced.

"However," Pessoa went on, "it is Monsignor Gomes's decision, over the advice of the rest of the tribunal, that all seven prisoners be relaxed."

Coffee splashed down Soares's brown robes. The saucer hit the carpet safe and intact, but the cup fell atop and shattered it. Soares lowered his head. "*Domine Deus.* Is there aught that I can do to make this right?"

"Yes, Luis," Pessoa told him. "You may forswear in your belief that the creatures are holy, for everything is lost for those seven, but I would not lose you."

"Now let him answer," Gomes said. "Father Soares, do you believe the creatures cherubs?"

Soares's fingers plucked at the chair arms.

Gomes's voice rose. "Have you caught the stubborn Jesuit disease? Answer me! Do you believe the creatures cherubs?"

Damn the man. Damn them both. Pessoa was nearly split asunder by frustration. "Luis!" he shouted, and still the Franciscan would not raise his head. "Luis, I beg you to tell him. Tell him, please, for God will know your heart."

Gomes pulled his bulk out of his chair. His tone was dangerously calm. "Father Soares, I am weary of your silence. I require an answer of you."

"Please, Luis," Pessoa said. "Please. When you peer into the cell where the creatures are . . . and I beg you to answer very carefully . . . when you peer into that cell, what do you see?"

Soares raised his head to the ceiling and squeezed his eyes shut. He whispered, "Nothing."

A N ICY PANDEMONIUM of stars clattered down. Rain came in blustery washes, like water thrown from a basin. Rivers ran the camp. Tents collapsed.

Afonso sat in his tent beside his bed and imagined Jandira with him. "I'm scared," he said.

He imagined that she laughed. *Why should you be frightened, sweetling, since you are not out in it?* The way she laughed scared him, too, because it sounded like a different Jandira; and Afonso wondered if she had swallowed Portugal's cabbage-and-codfish earth, and if that had made her bitter. He thought perhaps she was becoming something he did not want to know.

"God is dead, isn't He?" Afonso asked.

God all the time was dead, she told him. *And I did not see it.*

Thunder sent volleys booming through the hills. He tucked his fur-lined cloak more tightly about and put his booted feet closer to the brazier. He watched the damp lanterns smoke.

He was dead in Brazil, the new Jandira said. *He was dead when the white men orphaned me and the white fathers in their black robes captured me. He was dead when they brought me to Salvador de Sá.* And then she said, *Do not ring your bell any longer, sire, for I am free, and do not choose to come.*

"I love you," he said, and hoped that would stay her, for he knew that the jungles called and that she longed to go. He wished that she would let him ring the bell, for it had a pretty sound and made him not so afraid of the thunder and the stars falling and the rain. But he knew that it was he who had always liked the bell; and she had liked it not at all.

"Don't leave me." But the tent was empty. He ducked his nose into the fur. It smelled warm and clean, and he thought that he could smell vanilla there, too.

The captain came in from the rain and sat down beside him. He took off his gloves and warmed his hands at the brazier. "Bad night," he said.

"How far is Brazil?" he asked. "How long a trip?"

"O, I imagine two, three months or so, sire."

Would she find it? Afonso lifted his head. "Do you smell vanilla?"

The captain wiped rain from his beard. "Don't worry yourself, sire. The storm should be off soon. It never blows like this for long."

The side of the yellow-and-crimson tent bent. The rope supports twanged. The captain looked up dubiously at the tent's ceiling.

"I smell vanilla," Afonso said.

The captain slapped his gloves together. "Damn. Where is that priest?" Then: "Sire, I beg you. Please. I have not the skill for this." He cried out to the standing guard, "Bring me that priest!"

Father de Melo came, shivering and dripping. Before he could shake all the water from his cloak, the captain shouted, "You leave the king in such a state? Look at the boy! Look at him! And you without a care, traitor that you are, since his brother assumes dominion."

I love you betimes, Jandira whispered into Afonso's ear. *For you were passable kind and not like the others.*

"Don't leave me," Afonso said.

The captain squeezed his arm. "No, sire. I promised your father as he lay dying, and I promise you. Naught but death can send me away." To Father de Melo he said, "Shame upon you that you leave him thus. I'm a soldier, and rough-tempered, and no good with such things. Sit down, damn you, before I cut your legs off and make you sit."

Father de Melo found a blanket, wrapped himself up in it, and brought a chair to the brazier. "I know not what to talk to him about, captain. I've fair given up my arguments. I was never very good at it, not like that Father Pessoa, but then he is Jesuit-trained and used to such. I talk and talk myself into a state, and the boy does not learn."

You learn, Jandira told Afonso. *You have learned how brittle life is. How delicate is God.*

"He weeps for the slave, and I know not how to comfort him."

Father de Melo shrugged. "As he is apostate, I know not how to comfort him, either."

SOON AFTER DINNER, Monsignor called for him. Bernardo went, head lowered.

Such a friendless place Monsignor had made for himself. All about lay an ocean of dark, the solitary lamp an islet. It seemed to Bernardo that there were spirits there, but forlorn ones. The bed curtains were pulled to. Outside, branches lashed against the eaves. Hail clattered and rolled down the tile roof.

"Monsignor?"

The low howl might have been the wind.

Bernardo came closer. "Monsignor?"

The bed curtains twitched. Bernardo pulled them aside. Behind the velvet, Monsignor was plucking fitfully at the covers. His brow was pale and sweated. "The stone," he said.

Bernardo brought the lamp and set it by. He trimmed the wick and put back the tide of dark. "Better, Monsignor?"

Monsignor clawed at his belly. He stared fixedly at the ceiling. "I ate all the lamb you gave me for supper. You filled my plate and filled it, and now I die."

"I'll make the tea."

Before he could turn away, Monsignor trapped his hand. "Have the cook fix it. Do not leave me. Do you think this the stone come, Bernardo?"

Bernardo pulled away, went to the door, and called down to the guard to have the digestive tea prepared.

A weak summons: "Bernardo."

He went to the bed and looked down. He saw pain, yes, but no up-lifting transformation. He wondered if, agony continuing, transformation might come; or if some pains, like some souls, were stillborn.

"I feel such a cramping that it squeezes me, front to back. Do you think that this is the stone moving? O God, Bernardo. Do you think I die from it?"

"No." Bernardo found a chair and brought it to the bedside. He sat and regarded Monsignor. "You have felt the front-to-back pain before. You know that. And you have experienced pain worse than this."

"Yes. Yes, I have felt it before, have I not? Good, Bernardo. You are my perspective. There are no stones in the body. What are we, geese? Hah. I eat no stones, so where would they come from?"

A soft knock at the door. Cook came in with a tray and put it on the fruitwood table. Bernardo set Monsignor's pillows so that he might sit up and drink.

"Nonsense, really." He accepted the cup with both hands, blew on the top, and took a sip. "She was a lying witch, and deserving to be burnt. I'll think no longer on it."

Bernardo sat and watched him drink. Finally, through the noise of the tempest came a loud bleat of passing wind. Monsignor's jaw relaxed. "Yes," he said. "Just as I thought: easing now. *Lauda Dei.* Yes. Much better. Stones. What gibberish. Frightening tales for children. Quite right, Bernardo. I'll think no longer on it."

Bernardo poured him another cup of tea, and seeing that he was drowsy, started to the door.

Monsignor's whisper stopped him. "Think you so ill of me that you turn away?"

"Did you wish me to remain?"

Rain cascaded from the roof. A sapling battered itself against the side of the house.

That solitary room, that needy voice. "Not unless you want for company."

Bernardo put his hand to the knob.

"Bernardo?"

"Yes, Monsignor?"

"Will you not even look?"

Hand on the knob, Bernardo turned.

Monsignor was regarding him, sad-eyed. "Can you not understand that I am become a God-struck prophet, and not of my own choice? *Jesu pie.* I thought that you, out of all the world, would understand."

Bernardo asked, "Will that be all, then, Monsignor?"

After a silence Monsignor said, "Yes," and turned his face to the wall.

TADEO'S PEAR BRANDY made Pessoa deaf to the lashing wind and impervious to the pelting rain. It caused him to lose his footing in the rectory yard. He slipped and fell into Soares's young fig tree.

Behind him Tadeo and Emílio snickered and then shushed each other so loudly that they sounded like an entire flock of geese.

Pessoa thrashed about in the branches, wet leaves slapping him. Emílio, trying to help Pessoa, fell down as well.

"Shhh." Pessoa tried to tap finger to lips, but the night was too dark, so he tapped his nose, and all too painfully.

Pessoa and Emílio tangled limbs with each other, with the fig. Branches broke. Then somehow Pessoa was free of impediments. He fought his way upright. "This way," he hissed, and in the rain-driven darkness, ran into the rectory wall.

"This way, but without haste," he told them. Together, they felt their way along the wall. Pessoa found the front latch. He opened the door and they stumbled their way inside.

Soares was seated at the table, sobbing.

"O Luis," Pessoa said. Soares's weeping took the heart out of the seculars' merriment. It embarrassed Pessoa; it tore him in two with pity. How dare he cry? He who had never loved her, never kept private cameos of memory, never looked her full in the face.

Tadeo said, "Be of good cheer, father! We have a solution!" and he took the brandy bottle from out his cloak and set it on the table.

The rectory was for a while all wet cloaks being thrown off and cups being brought. Soares rose and quietly stoked the fire.

"Have some of my pear brandy, father." Tadeo poured them all a generous cup. "Well, not that it is mine, exactly, but belongs to Senhor Castanheda, who would no doubt give me an entire cask as reward."

The seculars toasted each other. Pessoa nudged Soares's cup closer to his hand. "Pay no heed to Gomes's decisions today, Luis. Marta and Senhora Teixeira are to be given to the state, of course, but the rest will be rescued." The brandy awakened some manic imp in him. His chest shuddered with repressed laughter, his lips twitched, and he clapped hand over mouth to still them.

Emílio reached into his pockets and withdrew a piece of foolscap. The paper came out so wet and so tattered, and with a piece of fig leaf stuck to one edge, that he went to holding it up to everyone's faces and shaking with breathless mirth.

Soares rose and fetched paper and quill. He set them on the table, and Tadeo took a seat there, dipping quill and scrawling. " 'To his Grace, Bishop Gastão Otavio Días, greetings.' " He looked up, all a-squint. "What now?"

Emílio sat beside him, peering at the handiwork. " 'We write you in—' "

"No, no! Not that," Pessoa said. " 'It is our sad duty to inform you.' "

"Sad duty!" Tadeo cried, gleeful. "Exactly so. Upon reading it, he will believe he is sent news of someone he cares for, and then upon seeing the rest of the message, he will leap with joy. Brilliant, father. Absolutely inspired." Then he looked up, all of an anticipation. "And next?"

Emílio: "Um. 'That Monsignor Gomes is become an asshole.' "

"Dear God! Will you not bend your mind to the task?" Tadeo complained. "I nearly put that down."

From Pessoa: " 'That Monsignor Gomes has, ah . . . surrendered to a loss of reason.' "

"Ah! Good!" Tadeo dipped his quill again.

Emílio: " 'And we, as devout guardians of the Church and the Holy

Office, find no choice but to' . . . Um. What do we find no choice but to do?"

" 'Write you,' " Tadeo suggested. " 'Write you to warn of . . .' "

" 'A grave injustice,' " Soares said.

Cries from both seculars of "Excellent, father! And now?"

" 'We beg you to recall Monsignor Gomes without delay,' " Pessoa said, " 'for if you do not act immediately, Your Grace, many innocents will die.' "

Tadeo wiped his nose with his sleeve. Emílio considered the foolscap.

Into the sudden pensive quiet, Pessoa went on: " 'He acts against all law, Your Grace, and overrides the dictates of the tribunal. The *auto* is to be held this Monday, thus time is not sufficient to beg help of Rome. We petition you, in your authority, to stay Monsignor Gomes's hand until we ourselves may win from the Holy Office a mercy for the unfairly condemned. We remain your servants, Tadeo Vargas, inquisitor, Emílio Cabral, inquisitor, and Manoel Pessoa, S.J., inquisitor.' "

Tadeo scripted the last of it and put down the quill. A pall had fallen. Rain peppered the window and shutters banged.

Solemn now, Tadeo said, "Yes. Good to remind him that you, too, are Jesuit. That might give us an edge."

Soares asked, "How do you deliver it?"

"King's messenger," Tadeo said.

Pessoa held up a hand. "No. Let us use our own inquisitorial guards."

"But how?" asked the seculars, looking at each other, "And under whose authority? They will not be guided by us. And certainly not by you."

Pessoa leaned across the table so urgently that he nearly fell down atop it. "The monsignor's own secretary."

"Excellent," Tadeo whispered.

Emílio said, "He is an odd, quiet boy. Think you we can trust him?"

Pessoa said, "Yes, yes. Absolutely. For he believes in the angels. Does he not, Luis?"

Soares was staring morosely at the fire. He shook his head. "How will it get to Lisbon?"

"Inquisitorial guard," Tadeo said, patience overtaxed.

"But how?" Luis asked. "Are you all so giddy with brandy that you fail to notice the rain? Do you? And do you not realize that the roads are certainly out?"

The room seemed suddenly darker, and bitter cold.

"O, then . . . " The seculars looked at each other.

How dare he? He who had never loved her. Pessoa said, "It will get through. The message will get through, and word sent back, and there is plenty of time to stop this. Two days, why, that is time enough." Into Soares's skeptical frown and the seculars' uncertainty he shouted, smacking the flat of his hand to the tabletop. "Damn your eyes! Did you not hear me? The message will get through!"

B ERNARDO RETURNED TO his room to find the dove weeping. "I want *pai*," he said.

Bernardo knelt before him, touching his face. "Your Heavenly Father is coming. Shhh. Do you not hear him? He chases all the demons out of the Abyss. I have brought you an orange."

The boy wiped his face with his sleeve. "I want *pai*."

"Soon." There, in the dove's warmth, a tender protectiveness bathed him. Bernardo pictured gathering the boy in his arms and felt demon Desire stir.

"I want *pai*," the dove said.

Bernardo told him, "Sleep. Perhaps he will come."

Then he told him that it was time for bed, and that he must lay his clothes aside for the morrow. He dared not lift hand to help, but watched the milk-pale skin be exposed, watched thighs quiver in the chill of the room, saw round buttocks blush in the heat of the hearth fire. His hands ached to hold, his chest, all of a seclusion, pained him.

"Wrap this blanket about yourself and crawl into bed, Rodrigo. Might I join you? For the night is loud and dark, and the day has been so strange that I find myself frightened of shadows."

The dove told him that he might, and so Bernardo went into the dark of the corner and removed his robes and his undershirt. Naked, he wrapped himself in a blanket. He lay down behind the dove, whose face was to the hearth. He put his arm about him and asked if he was warm.

Bernardo was warm all through himself, and he considered the angels, for the cherubs also had been led into temptation. How they, too, must have fought. Bernardo rested his head against the dove's and drank in his clean boy-smell.

"Are you still scared?" the dove asked.

Cupped together, wool between them, boy-scent in his nostrils, he said, "Not so much now."

He listened to the boy's breathing. "Can't *pai* come home? It's cold in the jail. It's lonely, because the angels won't talk."

"Still, Rodrigo. What a glory to be among angels."

"Not if they don't talk," the boy said.

Bernardo felt the pressure of leg against leg. He tested his resolve by slipping a hand under the dove's blanket and stroking the velvet skin of that arm.

The boy shrugged his shoulder. "Can't we go see *pai*?"

"Shhh." Down velvet arm to silken waist. Bernardo shivered and knew he dared go no farther.

"I want to go see *pai*."

His fingers ventured into dangerous and intimate warmth, down the swell of that small belly. "Tomorrow."

"I want to see him now. Please, father? Can't we see him now?"

He stroked that satin chest. "He is sleeping. As all good children should sleep."

The boy's body twitched—crying again. Bernardo stroked the length of his leg to give comfort.

"Please, father. Can't I visit *pai* now?"

He kissed the nape of the dove's neck. "We will hold each other," he told him. "For I must do battle against the demon if your *pai* is to be freed. Can you understand?"

The boy nodded.

"Then lie still, for I will not hurt you. Do not move, for if you move

I may forfeit mastery over myself, and the demon win, and your *pai* lost, and we do not want that to happen."

A small "No."

Bernardo pulled the blankets from between them and put a single blanket over them both. When flesh met warm virgin flesh, it stole his breath, nearly set the demon loose and howling. Bernardo buried his face in the boy's hair.

Into him poured such fellowship that wondered how he had lived so much of life in monks' cells, in lonely cots, in divine isolation. This was the answer, this being owned. For the dove owned him, down to the marrow.

God lifted the veil and showed him the other side of lust. Bernardo shuddered and held the boy tight. He opened his eyes a slit and saw that he had won: how in the reflected hearth fire, the room raged with orange brilliance, and black carnal imps danced death agonies between.

A disturbance started up at the door. Bernardo blinked, but was so blinded by visions of defeated Hell that he could not see its cause. Then came a shout of "God!" in Father Manoel's voice and the dove was snatched from out his arms.

Cold at the loss, Bernardo sat up. The door was open. How had that happened? The two seculars were standing agape.

The dove was weeping, and his sweet voice was high with panic. "The father there touched me, and I didn't like it, but he wouldn't stop. I said I wanted to go see *pai,* and he told me to lie still and said if I let him, he might let *pai* go."

Father Manoel wrapped a blanket about the dove. He understood, did he not? Bernardo expected no discernment in the seculars, but surely, surely Father Manoel could see.

Salus mea, Jesu. O, but the revulsion in his face.

P ESSOA WAS COLD and sober by the time he brought the boy back to the rectory. Soares was at the table, finishing the last of the brandy.

As they entered, Soares down his troubles as easily as he put down his cup. He held wide his arm. "O Rodrigo. Don't cry. What is it?"

The boy flew to that shelter.

Pessoa put down the boy's bag of clothes. "I found him together in bed with Monsignor's secretary. Bernardo is stranger than we thought." Then he held up a hand. "Not hurt."

Soares led the boy around to the hearth fire and sat him on a bench. He rummaged around in the bookcase, came up with an enameled box, and brought it over. The box was full of chocolates.

"You are a squirrel, Luis."

The comment won Pessoa a mischievous smile, then a more serious "And the message?"

"Emílio has some small acquaintance with the king's captain of the guard. He took a horse and rode out to the camp. He assures me that the man will help."

Rodrigo put a chocolate into his mouth and chewed listlessly. The boy was so exhausted that he looked dazed.

"And the secretary?" Soares asked.

"Jailed in the inquisitorial prison for now. Tomorrow to be handed over to the state. Gomes himself came downstairs, all agitated, and Bernardo weeping and trying to explain. But how to justify such as that? He will be hanged, I'm sure. Rodrigo! Time for bed. I've made the cot for you." The boy gave him such a look of suspicion that Pessoa snatched a blanket and withdrew completely from that side of the room. "I'll sleep on the floor."

"Go," Soares told the boy.

Rodrigo ran and threw himself on the cot with such boyish abandon that Pessoa feared it might collapse. Still clothed, he wriggled into the covers and, by the sound of the snores, was soon asleep.

Pessoa and Soares sat and drank together. The storm died, the wind growing quiet, the rain coming down in gentle showers.

"The rain ends," Pessoa said. "Sunny tomorrow. It will be no chore for a rider to get to Lisbon and back."

Soares yawned and said bleakly, "I am drunk."

Just as glum, Pessoa said, "I am sober." He drained his cup, took his blanket, and spread it by the fire. He pulled his travel bag to him and made of it a pillow.

When he looked around, he saw Soares seated on his cot, head bent, his fist slowly, softly, striking his chest.

"Luis," he hissed.

The old Franciscan lifted his head.

"Not your fault. Nothing is. Please forget that I ever accused you of it." A nod.

"Everything will end well, you'll see." Pessoa hiked the blanket and contorted his body until the warmth of the hearth unthawed his feet. A flagstone poked his rib. Something in his saddlebag jabbed his cheek. He peered over the bag toward Soares's cot. The Franciscan was practicing his *mea culpas* again.

"Luis!"

The fist paused mid-strike.

"What ails you now?"

Soares squeezed his eyes shut and covered them with his hand. "I denied them."

"The angels? *Salva me.* Of course you did. Better to protect your own flock. Besides, I coerced you into it. You did the wise thing, and if they are truly angels, they will understand the wrong that duty caused you to do."

"Not duty." Soares slammed a fist into the bedclothes. He fell back on the cot and slapped the blankets over his face. Through the wool came a muffled and remorseful "I did not want to burn."

Day 12

I N THE SILENCE OF THE NIGHT, IN THE HUSH OF HIS CELL, BERNARDO LAY
prostrate, seeking God in the flagstones. Once more he prayed, *"Sanc-*
tus, sanctus, sanctus." Once more it was not God who answered, but the
cold.

"Dominus Deus Sabaoth." Bernardo would never have hurt the dove;
and if Father Manoel could not see that Bernardo had conquered sin and
thus been unfairly accused, surely God knew the truth—God, who looked
upon the heart.

Bernardo's tears rolled quietly. *"Pleni sunt caeli et terra gloria tua."*

But Heaven and earth were so without comfort that Bernardo could
not bring himself to say the *Osanna.* He got up, dropped his habit over his
nakedness, then sat against the wall in the corner and looked about. He
thought he would possess the courage to face the gibbet that was to come;
yet demons were all arrived to greet him. Demons, for bars were no im-
pediment. They came for him in legions. They came in ranks. They ca-
pered amid the flickering shadows. They whispered in his ear but, as he
turned to catch a glimpse—o, so cunning—they concealed themselves in
the straw.

He held his rosary beads tight. *"Benedictus qui venit in nomine Do-*
mini."

Blessed is he.

Blessed is he who is not alone.

All the company Bernardo had ever needed was God, yet what had that adoration got him? By his hip was a crack in the floor, in the corner where he sat, in the solitary reaches of the cell. A crack which opened to a black and opaque Nothing. Bernardo could feel a dank, beguiling draft rise from there.

What had he done which had so offended Him? Had damnation lain within him all along, a puzzling flaw like the crack in the stone? While he stood and wrote his journals and practiced his mortifications and made himself busy, he could not see his sin; and now that he had so utterly fallen, it was close as a kiss, and far too late.

He looked across the cell. Guilherme Castanheda lay so far removed that Bernardo could scarce hear the man's snoring, could see aught else but a pile of blankets. The cherubs stood apart. The funeral candles around the fallen angel had burned to stubs.

I am so heartily sorry.

Would He not love Bernardo again? The radiant arms which had forever wrapped Bernardo had opened, nothing to sustain him but air. The little life left him gaped, as cold and hushed a void as absolution. How could one continue in such absolute silence?

He whetted his rosary's cross on the rough mortar, the silver turning more jagged than sharp. No matter. What would not cut, would tear. He wanted to say his Act of Contrition, but knew that Christ would not save him—he who had assumed himself easy to forgive. Before Quintas, it had all seemed so uncomplicated. Had he really marked others' iniquities in his book? So many flames for gluttony. So many for pride. Was that it? Had hubris damned him where lechery could not?

The wanton weakness of women, that foul, dank bunghole of temptation. With the Pinheiro woman, he had considered falling; and then with the dove, he mastered lust. Or had he?

Why did God—who knew All—look into Bernardo and find him detestable?

Bernardo dug the cross into the blue pathways of his left wrist. Mortification had toughened him to pain, and he went to his task with vigor, as was his habit with chores. He sawed into his unworthy flesh. Skin welted, seeped red. He labored until his muscles ached.

Of a sudden blood spurted up in a fountain. Ruby life spilled down his hand, so much life that he could never hope to stop it. All his warmth, spilling into the crack like ink into the mouth of a jar.

Alarmed, he clamped his wrist, but blood sought and found a way, overflowing the dam of his fingers and pattering onto the floor. *Jesu dulcis, suscipe deprecationem meum.*

Was this mistake? *O Jesu.* Such a careless one. But he determined to let God show him the truth of it and so into the darkness Bernardo poured his most dulcet and adoring prayer. He saw love sink without changing aught; subside as easily as his life sank into that headless, fathomless hole.

Bernardo's strength had ever been measured in ink-stained fingers, in the artfulness of a hand. Even the ruined and bleeding wrist had the power to open the other and let its wretchedness out.

Strange. Bernardo had always thought that death would hurt. Its numbness troubled him. His hands felt cold and foreign. His fingers lost their grip and the rosary dropped, chill climbing his arms.

The lethargy of despair was a surprise: downy as a bed, and as welcome. When he felt the touch, he found to his amazement that he was already dying—and so gently that he had not noticed. It was hard to open his eyes.

An angel was leaning over. He smelled of honey and flowers and his eyes were so wide and black that Bernardo could see his own reflection there.

No. He was wrong. What he saw was not his own reflection. Father Manoel had come. Bernardo had something to tell him, but he could not remember what he wished to say; and besides, the room was fogged and shadowy, and there was so little time.

No. The face was not Father Manoel's, but Christ's.

Ah, God had not turned His back after all. Even in despair, Bernardo had somehow been absolved. *Domine probasti me et congnovisti me.* For God knew him. And when Bernardo called, God had searched him out. *Tu,*

Jesu. Tu cognovisti sessionem meam, et resurrectionem meam. Christ knew all that was, knew where Bernardo had sat down, ah *Jesu dulcis,* knew without a doubt where he would rise up.

"I'm sleepy," Bernardo told him, and he spoke in a voice as weak and pure as childhood. He fought to keep his eyes open, but fought only for a while; for Heaven stretched, a wider and more measureless ocean than he had ever suspected, a deeper and more starry sea than he had ever dreamed.

He sailed, his cheek in Christ's hand.

A KNOCK AT the door woke Pessoa. His face was roasted, his backside cold. He rolled over, pulling angrily on the blanket, and saw that Soares and the boy were seated at the table having breakfast.

The second knock caught Soares already on his feet. Pessoa closed his eyes again. His back was stiff. His whole body ached. *Salva me.* Even his toes pained him.

From the door, he heard Soares's query: "Yes?"

And a stranger's voice: "Sorry to bother you, father, but something has happened with the Monsignor's secretary."

Pessoa sat up. One of Monsignor's jailers stood just inside the room, hat in hand. Soares said, "What?"

"Well . . ." The man shifted his weight from one foot to the other. "Happens that Monsignor is not awake, and no one has courage to rouse him, but it looks like a priest should come straightaway, for the creatures— whatever angels they are—are around that secretary close, and him all gathered into a corner. And he does not answer when his name is called, father. And that Castanheda, well, even being a soldier, he hasn't the belly to go see what's amiss. Can you come?"

Pessoa was already on his feet at the basin, splashing his face and shivering in the chill.

"Rodrigo? Stay here," Soares said. "Finish your breakfast."

"I want to see the angels," the boy said.

Pessoa scrubbed his face with a towel. "There is nothing to see."

"The angels did something to him. They could do something to my *pai.*"

Firm-voiced, Soares said, "Eat your breakfast. The angels did nothing." He picked up the satchel for the extreme unction.

Pessoa followed the two of them out the door. The morning was a dull gray, with clouds like fish scales. The wind blew, spitting rain into Pessoa's face. His cloak was dank, but better than the morning, and so he gathered the damp wool about his neck.

Everywhere lay the debris of storm. The cobbles were muddy and leaf-scattered. The oak tree inside the old rectory walls, the tree that had grown up in that spot where a priest had been crushed, was itself now dead—blasted by lightning, its top burnt, its trunk split in two. Soares crossed himself. Ahead, the pomegranate by the fountain was down, a laurel uprooted. Pessoa looked into the sky again, received an eyeful of rain for his trouble.

The day would turn fair, the message get through. What o'clock was it? Not yet seven-thirty, surely. Time enough for the sky to clear and the ground to dry. No. Tragedy was a thing that happened elsewhere, to others. It was writ in history books and studied in schools. As with the seculars, Pessoa's life was all of a sameness, potato-bland but for Berenice's olive oil and spices.

He thought of her and felt a mad jittering in his belly, an indigestion of dread. When this was over—for help would surely come—he would have her learn a little caution. He would be kinder and would bring her things. He would badger his brother for money. Did Pessoa not deserve it? And knowing João as he did, Pessoa knew he would have backed Pedro's winning side, and probably made a profit.

Yes, he would visit João, showing up as a surprise on his doorstep. *Ah, but I see you are prosperous,* Pessoa would tell him.

And João would spread his arms in a suspicious welcome, frightened, as they all were, as to the reasons Pessoa might have come. *And how goes the Inquisition?* he would ask.

Pessoa would see her dressed in warm clothes, for she spent too many winters sneezing. He would buy her something pretty, so that the village could not help but look. He would let them talk, for talking mattered not now. It mattered nothing.

They had reached the jail. Cândido was outside, shaking his head. Through the door, and past the guards muttering around their fire, and then down the steps. A blanketed mound waited in the women's cell, all alone. Pessoa turned and looked at the men's.

It was a scene of such impossible peace: Bernardo lay in a corner, the two creatures about him. One cradled the boy's head in his lap.

With a clang of keys, the jailer opened the door. Soares walked inside, Pessoa behind him—both of them walking into the smell of flowers and beeswax candles. The creature holding Bernardo's head looked up, its arms spread as if entreating them to look, as if it was offering that inert body, as if it was expressing that nothing else could be done.

Nothing could. From where Pessoa stood, even in the dim glow of the lamps, he marked the pallor of that face. He came forward and knelt. Bernardo's eyes were closed, his body curled. Pessoa reached to touch that marble forehead, but a hand seized his own.

Soares: "Look at his wrists."

They were torn apart, with wounds opened like bloody screams. Such a violence done, how could he rest so sweetly?

Pessoa crossed himself, then kissed his fingertips; and despite the sin of those wounds, he touched Bernardo's chill brow.

Behind him, Soares said, "I will go awaken the monsignor, since no one else has the fortitude for it."

He heard Soares's footsteps recede, then heard the door clang shut. He sat as the creature held its burden and the other sat close beside. The message would certainly come, but for Bernardo, all too late. "Lie nakedness to nakedness," he had told him, yet when the boy obeyed, Pessoa found his choice unpardonable.

In Bernardo's lap sat a rosary. Pessoa took it. The beads were gummy with blood.

Pessoa was halfway through an unspoken prayer for the dead when he heard Monsignor's booming voice. "God! Fool that he became, he compounded it."

Pessoa thought the comment directed at him, until he turned about and saw where Gomes was staring, saw the unexpected grief in his face. "Damn the boy! He throws away salvation! He abandons me!" Then he whirled to the jailers. "Take his body up, do you hear? Take him up and put him in a potter's field straightaway. O, this place is a glut of unconsecrated graves." And with that, he rushed from the room.

The women were staring. Berenice, all sleep-rumpled, stood at the bars, and so he looked quickly away. With a rustle of robes, Soares knelt at his side.

"It is Sunday," Pessoa said in surprise. "Isn't it? Already Sunday."

"Yes. I must leave for Mass soon."

Pessoa nodded. "The homily of the Watchman."

"Twenty-third Sunday, Ordinary."

Pessoa remembered Soares preparing the sermon, eating the bowl of figs. *I have appointed you Watchman over the house of Israel.*

"I must go, Manoel. I fear the church roof has lost tiles from the storm. It may be leaking."

I have appointed you. Pessoa saw the creature's bony hand resting atop Bernardo's shoulder, saw how the hand of the other lay atop the point of the boy's hip. "How do I convince them to give him up?"

Soares rose, patted Pessoa's shoulder. "Ask."

Then he was gone. Pessoa heard a low rumble outside, and hoped that it was distant Spanish cannon, for even war would be more welcome; but he knew that it was not. Thunder rolled again. Rain splattered the sill.

The jailers came and stood without the bars. They told him that the grave was ready. "Not as it is fancy, father. But we found a nice place for him all the same, nearby an apple orchard."

They stood waiting, one with the grave cloth folded over his arm. Pessoa looked into the creature's ebon eyes, felt aught but a prickle at his nape. "Will you give him up?" Neither of them moved until he explained softly, "I am the Watchman."

They put Bernardo down then, and retreated to the damp at the back of the cell. They stood in the mist from the window. The guards came, opened the rectangle of cloth, and laid it on the straw. One took Bernardo by his habit's shoulders, another by his hem.

Dear God. The boy was unshod. Pessoa had never noticed, not last night when he stood before them weeping and shamed, not even when they had marched him down the cobbled street to the jail, and Pessoa was so imbued by righteous anger that he had forgotten, too, to offer the comfort of a blanket. But should not a Watchman remember? Those poor bare toes, the clean and tender instep.

The guards seized the edges of the cloth and bore Bernardo up—his body sagging in the unbleached cotton—his pallid, serene face at one end, his cold naked feet out the other. Pessoa took his missal from his pocket and held it to his chest. He followed them from the cell, followed as they grunted their burden up the stair, the boy's corpse swaying.

He will die, and I will hold you responsible.

No choir marked their passage. Not even the guards huddled about the fire stood. Under his breath, for no one must hear him: *"Kyrie eleison."*

Outside, blowing rain wet his face. Droplets crawled his scalp. The two guards steadied their burden with one hand and adjusted their cloaks with the other. A small boy, really.

Sicut cervus. Like a hart which yearns for springs of water. He remembered the longing he had seen on Bernardo's face—the passion of Jeremiah. *"Christi eleison."*

Love like a burning fire.

Pessoa looked at those bare toes and knew that the boy had found it, if only because he had sought it so diligently. What had he said of him once? A secretive and moated nature? Little humor, hurtful joys? Yet ruthless ecstasy fed him.

Pessoa ducked his head into his collar and walked on. *"Kyrie eleison."* They trod the dank street, passing through the litter of last night's garbage. In a house window, a woman looked down at the procession and crossed herself.

The Watchman fallen asleep at the gate, the Enemy overrunning.

A FONSO TRIED TO dress himself, but became tangled in the legs of his pants and twisted the arms of his jacket into bewildering knots.

Jandira laughed at him. *Ah, sweetling. You can scarce do without me.*

In a tempest of failure, he threw down his jacket and stamped on it. "I want you back!" he cried. "Why won't you come back?"

She was stubborn. He called her; he begged and cajoled, as was unbefitting a king.

It matters not to me that you are royal.

"It should."

You climb the trees, sire.

"Do not!" he said, for she knew that he meant he was become monkey and looked for God in all the wrong and high places. But Afonso did not, for he had seen God in the fallen acorn, and had talked to Him there.

Afonso pulled off his breeches and threw them down; then he sat in his chair and glowered at the carpet. "Do not."

The same cook's boy came with breakfast. He remembered a little how to dress him, but did not remember as well as Jandira, who remembered everything.

"Father de Melo said that he must speak with you," the boy said.

And Afonso told him, with the gravity that was proper, "You may send him in."

The boy left. Father came. "I see you dressed in white today," Afonso told him. "Sunday? Is it Sunday? Well, I will not ask for the *Corpus Christi,* for you are probably stubborn and will not give it me, and I have begged enough of servants today."

Father drew two chairs together. He sat down on one, patted the seat of the other. "No, sire. No *Corpus Christi.* I come from the soldiers' Mass."

Afonso perched on the edge of the seat.

"Do you know what the homily was today, sire? No? It is about how when someone is in grave sin, it is our duty, as good Christians, to point out their failing. Do you see?"

"No."

Father scratched his head. "Ah. Well, then. This is as the Inquisition does, sire. The duty of the Holy Office is to point out failings, and if necessary, to cut the spot from out the apple. Do you see?"

"No."

Father lifted his gaze to the roof. He sighed. "The Bible says that we should advise our brother, and if he does not listen, we should take the cause to others. And if he still does not heed, we should take it to the Church. If he does not listen to the Church, well . . ." Father spread his hands sadly, as if letting a sinner drop.

"No one gives me spotted apples, and if they do, I would throw them back."

Father took Afonso's hand and held it. He regarded the carpet. "Tomorrow," he said, "we must go to town and attend a short Mass that is to be held in the square—a low Mass. It will be over quickly."

"I don't want to go to a Mass outside. It is wet."

"I understand." He nodded. "There is no choice in the matter, I'm afraid. If there is rain, your soldiers will hold a canopy over you." He squeezed his fingers. "It will not be very long. You will dress in your black velvet and wear your gold crown, the small one that we have brought. You must behave yourself and say nothing."

"What will your homily be?"

"I will stand by the altar, but Monsignor Gomes will celebrate. All the priests will stand by the altar. So you must be very quiet, and not hold yourself in the shameful place nor laugh out loud nor stand up when you shouldn't."

Afonso tapped his foot. He peered out the door of the tent, into the rain. "I cannot keep myself from laughing out loud when the fat priest speaks. It looks like he will spit turds. I want my breakfast now."

He started up, but father pulled him down again. The look on father's face scared him.

"You must not laugh during Mass, sire," he said. And then he took both of his hands. "When the Mass is over . . ."

"I'm hungry. The sausages get cold."

Father held him so tight that it hurt. "When the Mass is over, sire. Listen to me, I beg you, for this part is hard both for me to say and for you to hear. Are you listening? Good. When the Mass is over, we will all go out beyond the town, and there will be those there wearing black shifts with flames and carrying unlit torches. And I will be present, although not near you, and many of your soldiers, and the captain. Monsignor Gomes will be there, and other important people. But you, sire, will be the most important of all. And we will walk. Not ride. We will walk, even if it is raining. And we will not speak nor laugh nor wave at the crowd. We will not smile."

The press of father's thumbs made his hands ache. He twisted and wriggled, but father held him tighter.

"They will set those dressed in black afire, Your Majesty. The executioner will put them atop wood pyres, and they will set the wood aflame. And some will be strangled before, and some will not, and those who are not will scream most piteously."

Afonso snatched his hands free and jumped to his feet. "No! I will not wear black! Never! You will see if I will not wear black!"

"No, no, no . . ."

Father tried to catch him, but Afonso wrenched away. "I will wear the red or the purple!"

"Not *you*! It does not matter what you wear, they will not burn you!"

Afonso walked to the little table where his breakfast lay, but he was too anxious to eat, too anxious to sit. He walked to the door of the tent and went out. He would walk to God. He would walk to his castle and lie down on his bed there, and pull the covers up over his head. He would have Pedro find him another Jandira, for Brazil was full of them, and the new Jandira would put his head upon her shoulder, and hold him, and tell him a story, and sing him a song that had no words.

Father de Melo caught his arm. "Your Majesty, come out of the rain."

"No."

"Come. You have no cloak with you, sire."

"No."

"Listen to me, then. You are to watch the burnings, Your Majesty. That is all I meant to say. There will be diverse executions, and you must stay for them all and be a good and quiet boy, and I warn you that it will be arduous, for to see them burn will be a ghastly sight."

Afonso put his hands over his ears and let the rain slide down his forehead, his cheeks. "No! Not executions. Executions are where heads are struck from bodies and the bodies twitch, but not as bad as chickens, and blood comes all out in a gush, and they have sawdust to catch it. Executions are where necks are tied with rope, and the person pushed off a high place. That is executions."

Father de Melo pulled Afonso's arm down. "These are the executions that the Holy Office orders."

"Then they must learn how to do them right. So we will tell all those people not to wear black, if that makes the Holy Office angry. We will put them in happy colors like pink and red and green so that the Holy Office cannot find them."

"Your Majesty . . ."

"We will not let anyone wear black, ever. We will make a decree: no black."

"Sire . . ."

"And we will teach them executions. The rope, for that seems sudden and pleasant, although sometimes they dance a funny jig, and shit their pants or sometimes they wet themselves, and I do not care for that overmuch. So we will not attend the Mass in the morning, for it is a low Mass, as you said, and not worthy of a king. And we will not allow the walking afterward. Everyone shall stay in town, and all the black clothes be taken up, and then we shall see what next, is that not clear? We shall decide then. For I am not of a deciding this morning, having already had to think about clothes and chamber pots."

"Sire . . ."

Afonso saw the look in Father de Melo's face and heard the regret in his voice; and he knew this was to be like attending his own father's funeral or his own coronation or like sitting through the tedious meetings of council. He shivered, for the rain chilled him. "I will not go," he said. Still, he knew he must.

TADEO MET PESSOA on the road. The rain had stopped, and the morning sky, already past sunrise, was an unlikely rust color, the hue of long-spilled blood. Pessoa opened his hand and looked down. Bernardo's blood still stained his palm. So simple a prayer: *Fac me plagis vulnerai.* That is all that the boy had asked for, to be wounded with His wounds.

"I'm bound to Mass," Tadeo said, and hiked his cloak about his neck. "But I came to warn you: Monsignor Gomes is a bear this morning. He will not be comforted, and will not be reasoned with. I heard about the boy."

Cruce hac inebriari. Drunk with the cross, that was Bernardo.

The gentleness of the secular's touch surprised him. "Buried, then?"

Pessoa nodded. If God existed, Pessoa would forever be damned, to so beguile such a poor drunkard.

"Are you all right?"

Forever damned. He said, "Yes."

"Monsignor instructs me to tell you to inform the condemned without delay so that they may have time to make peace with their fates. Emílio and I will be glad of going with you, for we have experience in such things, not in the informing so much, for that is a cleric's job, but in instructing the condemned how to die well and quickly. That may be difficult for you to do, seeing as how . . ." He looked about, as if seeking guidance from the morning.

A freshening breeze spanked Pessoa's cheek, tousled his hair. It made the hem of his cassock flutter like a flag. Rain coming. Once again, rain. Pessoa would believe in God if He stilled the rain. If He got the message through.

Tadeo cleared his throat. "I have been told by an executioner that the air becomes rarefied above the flames, and that if the condemned breathes deeply, they will breathe in not only heat, but smoke as well. He says, and I have seen it happen, that the burned then die with less struggle. He says that pitch gives off a poison. For he himself had often become light-headed standing about the fires. Thus it is best to lean toward the flames, instead of away, as the condemned feels compelled to do."

The wind blew. The tops of the trees bent. Tadeo looked up into the sky. There was a bloody cast to the stucco walls, to the wet cobbles. "I'll tell them," Tadeo said. "After Mass."

"You'd best hurry," Pessoa told him.

Tadeo nodded. "And you? Co-celebrating?"

"No." He could not. The palm of his right hand was not clean.

"To the jail, then?"

"They need someone with them."

"Easier for me to go with you, father. For if you have never had this duty, I warn you that it is more a hardship than you can imagine. And worse if you have any sort of affection. God does not ask you to do it all."

Rain began to fall in huge battering drops. They stung Pessoa's face. They struck the cobbles in dull smacks, like the sound of fists. They left craters in the mud the size of ducats. Tadeo drew him into the shelter of an overhang. Pessoa would believe in Him, if God would only stop the rain.

"Damn the weather," the secular said. One squeeze of his shoulder, and Tadeo was gone, ducking through the driving wet. The street was empty, lit by the morning's *dies irae*. Echoing through the close-stacked houses came the clang of the church bell. Pessoa walked, letting the rain pelt him. Simple, really, for a God who had parted the sea.

A paltry guard stood ready at the jail, most gone to Mass. He took the missal from his pocket and held it in one hand, his rosary in the other. He took a breath and walked down the stair, going first to the men's cell, not daring a look toward the women. He stood silent at the door until the jailer brought the keys.

Castanheda was sitting against the wall, a blanket over his lap. He looked up.

"Guilherme," Pessoa said.

It must have been the manner in which he said his name, or perhaps it was merely because he was a tall black figure in a dimly lighted place. Castanheda knew. His eyes filled, and he bent his head. Pessoa knelt down, took the man's hand in his own. The fingers were trembling.

"Guilherme," he whispered.

The broad shoulders shook.

"We tried to stop it, the seculars and I. But Monsignor . . . and we have sent a message to Bishop Días. I want you to have faith, Guilherme, that the message will make it through. Can you have faith for me?" he asked, who had no faith at all.

Castanheda did not lift his head, but still he nodded. His fingers tightened around Pessoa's hand. "My daughter?" he asked.

"To be strangled. No, no. Listen to me. It is a quick death. I have seen it. The executioners are skilled. Her soul will leave in a blink."

His grip tightened so, Pessoa feared his fingers would break. "And me?"

"Burnt." Pessoa told him, "Pray with me. Not an Act of Contrition, but a happy prayer, for I do not accept that you will die. *Gloria in excelsis Deo.*"

There was a hesitation before Castanheda joined in. *"Et in terra pax hominibus."*

"Bonae voluntatis." The men of goodwill all in Lisbon, and between there and here, the rain.

"Laudamus te, benedicamus te, adoramus te, glorificamus te."

Through the *Gloria*, Lamb of God and Son of the Father, and then Amen. Castanheda loosed his hand and Pessoa got to his feet. Over him, he made the sign of the cross. "One of the seculars will come in a while. He will instruct you what to do if the worst happens. Can you trust in God for me?" he asked, and seeing the nod, Pessoa went out.

Then he went to the women's cell, and toward that solitary figure in the corner, huddled as motionlessly as Bernardo that morning. For a moment Pessoa was terrified that she was dead; hoped beyond hope that she was.

I will believe, he promised. *If You will only kill her well.*

At his footsteps, she looked up. She looked up, and she knew. He sat, put his missal and his rosary in his lap, and took her hands. "We've sent a message to Lisbon that this be stopped."

At the window, that red morning, and rain falling faster. The smell of beeswax, the candles now burnt out. All through the room was the dry odor of straw. If he lost her, he could never again pass a marigold, never smell lavender.

"When?" she asked.

He said, "Tomorrow."

She was stronger than Castanheda. Berenice said, flat-voiced, "They will burn me."

There was no way to soften it. "Yes. That is Gomes's judgment. But the message will get through. If perchance it does not, though, I want you to abjure yourself. Kiss the cross when it is presented to you. Do all the things that the Holy Office expects. In any case, I will be there."

"He will be with me." A single tear dropped, as if in error, from out her eye. "He is waiting. If I looked about the room now, and had the sight of the dying, I could see him."

Pessoa took his hands away and put them, all lonely, in his lap.

She wiped her cheek. "I should not be frightened. Death is nothing to be frightened of. I know that. And I feel that I fail him when I am so frightened, that I should have more faith. But it is more the pain, Manoel. It is the walking to the pyre. It is the wait. It is watching the wood be set alight. . . ." Her voice trailed off and she stared up to the window. "The wood will be wet."

"Gomes bought from a smokehouse. The wood is in sheds. No. He is experienced, and has planned well, I'm afraid."

Without looking at him, she said, "See to my burro."

"I shall."

She reached out and briefly clasped his hand. "Go to the others. They have need of you."

She left a chill on his fingers. He looked down. She had returned his gold cross. He got to his feet. "Are you hungry? Is there anything you need?"

"No." And so he left her looking at the blank, moisture-weeping wall, awaiting her lover.

He sat by the three other women. He held their hands and prayed with them. Marta wanted the *Stabat Mater.*

At the *"Vidit suum dulcem Natum morientem, desolatum,"* Maria Elena came to herself and began to cry—not for herself, Pessoa knew, but for hurtful words again—imagining her own son forlorn in death.

". . . fons amoris . . ." Font of love. He saw it in Senhora Teixeira, who would ascend the stake imbued by her own hard sort of affection.

At the end of the prayer, at the *inflammatus et accensus,* when the mention of leaping flames made the Teixeiras both lose their voices, Marta's became strong. *"Per te, Virgo, sim defensus."* Did she yet imagine that Mary would quell the flames? That the Blessed Mother would stay the garrote?

Marta tolled the last of the petition, loud as a challenge: *When my body shall die, see my spirit to Paradise.*

A FONSO WENT OUT into the rain and saw that the acorn had shifted in the night, the mud slid from underneath it. The door was pointed upward now, and the light inside still shone. A soldier standing at guard stopped him, although regretfully.

"Captain's orders, sire."

"But I can stand outside and shout to Him. Captain said nothing about shouting."

The guard stood beside Afonso, shoulder to shoulder. Afonso cupped his mouth, leaning farther into the light. "Hallo!" Afonso called. "Hallo!"

Not even a whisper of an answer reached him. Below the acorn, his soldiers were digging in the mud, God's grave yawning. It was probably best that He did not know what was to come.

Afonso went back to camp. He entered his tent, took off his cloak, and threw himself into bed. He pulled the covers around him and closed his eyes. He thought very hard, and imagined Jandira, who came and laughed at his distress. Since Jandira could not please him, he thought again, and this time he saw God.

The rare and improbable pink of some flowers, the brilliant green of mosses. Afonso pictured those colors sparking under earth.

Who are you? God asked.

"Afonso, the king," he told Him. "I have been coming to see You, and I would still, but the fat priest fears You, and something has happened with my brother, and the captain says that I cannot come see You anymore."

I forget, God said, but Afonso knew that He remembered the void. God's thoughts were dark—not the dark that is evil, nor the dark that is dull, but a ferocious dark, like the dark of a doe's eye or the dark of a jet-black horse.

He saw that God's thoughts were of emptiness, too; but it was the emptiness of expecting—like waiting to open a gift. For life was. God told Afonso so. Life was everywhere, in the dust of the stars, in bitter clouds around poison worlds. Life spewed out in a gladness and could not be quenched. Even Death begot it.

Comets and falling stars rained life down. It fell gently. It struggled, and ate itself, and teemed.

Afonso called for Jandira to come see.

Life is not remarkable, sweetling, she said.

Everywhere, in all the universe, in sulphur pits and lakes of frozen gasses, life burst out and multiplied, it killed, was murdered and reborn.

She whispered, *It is the only miracle we can touch.*

T HE SIGHT OF her empty house. The smell of the herbs. Pessoa sat by the cold of her hearth until he stopped trembling.

When he finally rose and pulled back the curtain, her burro whuffled, happy at the company. He dipped his velvet muzzle into Pessoa's hand.

Pessoa loosed the halter lead and, clucking, enticed him out into the threatening noon.

He led him up the hill and down, then past the old rectory and the church. Mass had ended, and the congregation already fled the muddy yard for home. They went through a meadow to the stable, where Felicidade put her head over the stall door to see who had arrived.

Pessoa went to the rectory next, but it was empty. He hurried out and rushed back the way he had come. The rain had started up again, and the sky now was a frightening green. Lightning played in the distance. Thunder boomed like coming war.

The church door was so heavy and he so tired that he could scarce open it. It groaned against its hinges; he fought his way inside. At the font, he dipped his fingers and crossed himself. Through the next door he could see the length of the church, down the line of niches and their candles to where the sanctuary lamp was burning. Other than Mary and a crucified Christ, the church was empty. He turned left.

The confessional stood mute and waiting. He entered the penitent's box and quietly closed the door. It was dim inside—ashen light filtering though the door's lattice. By where Pessoa knelt was a silken rope, its tassels palm-soiled. He pulled it, and heard the bell chime through the nave, the sanctuary, until it died somewhere near the altar.

He had left already. Gone to the jail, perhaps. Perhaps out to visit the sick. Pessoa started to rise, but heard a cough and approaching footsteps, a pause that signaled Soares's stop at the font. Then the footsteps resumed, the neighboring door creaked, and the grille clacked open.

From behind the woven cane screen came another cough, the sounds of a body moving, and the play of shadow.

"Forgive me, father, for I have sinned."

He heard Soares stir, recognizing his voice; then heard duty quiet him.

"It has been three months since my last confession. Father, forgive me the sin of pride." His voice trembled. He took a breath and waited until he had mastered himself. "Because of my pride, others will suffer."

From that faceless silence came the anonymity of the reply. "Your penance is to watch the suffering, my son. God demands aught else. Is there anything else you wish to confess?"

Pessoa listened a while to their duet of breathing.

"The sin of fornication, although I will not sincerely abjure that, for I lay with the woman in affection and not in lust, but in telling that to a boy, I killed him. At least telling him that I loved her—that much was the truth. So forgive me, father, the sin of murder."

A priest-whisper came in reply, so little of Soares in it. "If you find yourself not punished enough tomorrow for your sin, come to me and I will order penance. And as to the fornication, I absolve you, for you were right to show her honest affection and care for her, when no one else was willing."

Pessoa sat back. The place smelled like all confessionals. It smelled old. It stank of a parade of bodies. It held in its air years of candle wax, of furniture oil, of incense.

"Forgive me the sin of despair."

From the dim space beyond the screen came a breathy sigh.

"I've tried, you see. Thinking on it, I cannot imagine life continuing."

Pessoa caught a glitter of eyes through the weave of the cane. "Manoel . . ."

"Not suicide. It is just that I have no imagination, you see? No fantasy to hold on to. I keep trying to imagine myself leaving after the *auto,* continuing my rounds, and coming back here when the time is due. I try to picture arriving at the rectory, what we would say to each other. I try, really. I try to imagine your cats, seeing the streets, imagining how people might greet me. I try to imagine never going to her house again. Ah, God, Luis. I think I cannot come back."

"What will you do?"

He drew his cloak about him. The cloth was so damp as to be useless. "Flee to England," he said. "Leave behind my mission and my vows and my priesthood, for if she is to die because of me, I would have had enough of it. Another thing: I know where Guilherme's gold is hidden. And before I leave, I shall steal it. And I will not ask penance for that, either, for I will donate most to the poor; but keep some, for unfrocked, I will be as poor as any. I must take the money. Otherwise it will fall into the hands of Gomes and the Holy Office, and I would have them win naught else."

A grunt, then: "Even though you do not ask for atonement, I order you to make a restitution. For otherwise your soul will cause you torment."

"What?"

"If you take the gold and leave, you must take Rodrigo Castanheda with you."

OOMING, HOWLING DARKNESS woke Afonso. The wind pummeled the world like a teetering, drunken bully. Under the savagery, the tent ripped down its belly. Water poured in, drenching the lamps, bringing a blind and confusing night.

There was a frantic bustle at the door, and the captain came in, pulling Afonso off the wet bed and into the cubbyhole between the foot and the dresser. He shoved Afonso's head against his chest and wrapped his arms about him so hard that Afonso could feel the man's heart pounding.

He shouted, "Hold those tent poles!"

A panicked voice spoke out. So close was it, and so loud, that it hurt Afonso's ears. "The men want to dig the acorn back up again, sir! Permission?"

"No."

"But the storm started just as the dirt topped it, and that light still burning down there. Mary and Joseph! I've never seen aught like this, sir. Wind blew the wagon off the hill. It blew the wagon plain off, horses with it!"

Afonso wanted to go see the fallen horses and the wagon. He wanted to see the rain wash God free of His grave. He lifted his head, but saw only lightning-struck darkness, and then the captain pushed him down again.

"It will blow over directly, man. All storms eventually do."

"Pardon me, sir, but that's what you said yesterday. And yet God's peevish."

Afonso popped his head up from under the captain's arm. Close by stood a man-shaped shadow. "Tell Him."

The shadow moved. "Sire?"

"Go tell God. If you go stand by His grave and say that it was not you, but that fat priest who ordered it, He will stop the storm."

Nearly lost in the tempest's outraged bellows was the soldier's grateful "Thank you, sire. Thank you."

Afonso ducked his head again, and let the captain hold him. The captain wasn't as soft as his nanny or as warm as Jandira, but his heartbeat was strong and steady, and his arms gave a muscular sort of comfort.

Then Afonso noticed that he could see, for the day had brightened. And he could hear, too, for the wind had died. The striped tent fluttered, fluttered again, and went still. The captain unwrapped his arm from Afonso and stood.

Afonso got up with him. The tent was all a wreck of drowned lamps and lifeless candles and loose papers and bedclothes. An end of the tent sagged, weighted down by water. From the rent in the canvas side, rain dripped, a steady beat like a drum.

"The storm quit," the captain said.

"Yes."

"Sweet Mary," the captain whispered. "One instant to the next, the storm simply quit."

PESSOA ARRIVED AT the Castanheda house when the storm was passed, and the sun out, and still all was lost. He came as the rivulets about the town swelled to muddy rivers, and once peaceful streams washed uprooted trees down their cascades. He arrived with his saddlebags empty, and met Emílio and Tadeo on the stoop just as they were leaving. They looked at him strangely.

"What do you do here?" Tadeo asked.

"Come to find clothes for the boy, and a trinket of his father's to re-member him by."

The seculars nodded. "A bad ending." Emílio looked about hope-lessly at the sopping litter in the street.

Tadeo said, "I assure you we will petition the Holy Office on the boy's behalf—but true—best you save mementos for him now before some sticky-fingered inventory."

"Well." Emílio shrugged, held his hands palm up. "My conscience is clean, and I have need of a brandy. We sup at the inn tonight. Why do you not gather the boy's clothes and come with us, father? Monsignor has de-clared a day of fasting and prayer. He even dismissed the servants, can you fathom that?"

That evoked a sharp bark of laughter from Tadeo. "Well he might, for he has a year's surplus of food stored in that belly. Come to the inn with us, father. We would have your company."

"Come," Emílio urged. "For we have gone to instruct the prisoners, and it leaves a bitter taste in our mouths."

Pessoa took the saddlebags from off his shoulder and folded them over his arm. "Perhaps later."

"Yes, yes," Tadeo said. "Later. Please do. For it will be a long night without the succor of wine. We have ordered up brandy for the prisoners, all that they will take. And whatever food they wish, although it has been my experience that the condemned do not eat."

Emílio said, "Best they don't. I have seen some eat wantonly, then vomit all about. The *auto* is to be held in the afternoon, so mind you break your fast, father, for you will need your strength. But do not eat after, for I have seen priests and witnesses disgorge their luncheons, too."

"Enough, Emílio, with your morbid attractions! Yesterday the crea-tures' offal and vomit today."

Still bickering, the seculars made their way down the stair. Pessoa watched them go. When they were out of sight, he went into the house and made his way to Rodrigo's room. He packed two sets of clothes, a night-shirt, a brightly colored ball, and a wooden soldier. Would he need of aught else? His boy? His. The irony of it, a vow of chastity, failed seed; and at age thirty-nine, fatherhood come upon him.

He went downstairs. The house was empty, the servants gone. He walked to Castanheda's study and took the shield from off the wall. The chest was still there, and the money. Pessoa wrapped the coins in Rodrigo's clothes so that they would not clank. He set the chest back in its niche, placed the shield over it.

That military study. What did Castanheda remember there—the glory? The noise? The murder? Pessoa took from the wall the green sash and the sunburst medal. He folded it and put it atop the clothes. When he boosted the saddlebags over his shoulder, he was unprepared, and staggered under the weight.

Then—bracing himself, back straight—he walked out of the study and toward the door. He would hide the bags in the rectory and tell Castanheda of his plans tomorrow. He would give him at least that hope. Too, he would take the boy to the jail for a farewell. Everything must be done properly, for Pessoa intended to be a good father.

What do you know of milk puke?

Nothing yet, but Pessoa would learn.

He put his hand to the doorknob. "Why are you here?" Monsignor's voice boomed from the stair.

Pessoa turned, his pulse in a fright, his thoughts turned vapor.

He saw a fat hand on the banister, and watched a huge form descend into the entranceway's light. "I asked why you have come."

"Clothes."

Monsignor stopped. "But the boy's room is up top."

"Something of his father's." Pessoa, fumble-fingered, opened the saddlebag, brought out the sash, and offered it up.

Monsignor took the sash, opened it. He stared down at the medal. "Looks like gold."

The lies were like walking along a precipice—a miracle of one foot, then another. "Won in battle. I thought the boy should have it. Given by the queen's regency after João died."

Monsignor grunted and handed the medal back. He came down the rest of the stairs and walked past Pessoa to the dining room. "Come with me."

Nothing to do but follow. One foot, then the other, through the dining hall and into the warm kitchen, where the hearth fire was still lit.

"I have declared a day of fasting and prayer, but yet we may have a coffee," the man said. "Sit." He gestured to a rough table, scarred by the cutting of game and potatoes. The table where the servants dined.

Pessoa took a three-legged stool and put his saddlebags down, O so carefully, beside him. Monsignor stoked the fire higher. He rummaged among the shelves until he found the coffee. He pried off the top of the box and sniffed. "Brazilian." He smiled, and held the box out to Pessoa. Dutifully, Pessoa lowered his nose to it. "I like Brazilian coffee," Monsignor said.

The man made coffee in the country way, dumping a handful into a pot of water and putting it on to boil. Then Monsignor stood, his back to Pessoa, watching the flames. "Buried?" he asked more softly than Pessoa thought possible.

"A pretty spot with apple trees and a board fence."

The broad back bent. He leaned an arm on the wall. "Flowers come spring."

"I would think so. Buttercups and primrose."

Monsignor took in a long breath. He whispered, "Bernardo was my best boy. Best boy."

That odd heartfelt eulogy, one which, without Monsignor ever realizing, skirted the edges of disdain. "Best boy."

The water began to boil. The room filled with the smell of coffee. Monsignor pulled the pot a little off the flame and let it simmer.

A knife rested on a peg. A butcher's knife, broad at the base for sawing bone, narrow at its end, but stout. Pessoa could kill with such a knife. Anyone could. And the servants not home.

"I had had other secretaries, you know. But none so utterly willing."

A hatchet, too, chicken blood still on it. A hatchet. And only an arm's length away.

"He was a somewhat intense-natured boy, Bernardo was, but dedicated to service." Gomes was staring sadly at a ham that was sitting on a marble sideboard. "I shall not find another like him."

For an ice-bellied moment Pessoa thought the man would ask, and that the tribunal in Mafra and the Holy Office would agree, and that he would be sent to Lisbon for a life of candle-weakened eyes and ink-stained fingers. But no, he would to England, would he not? For he had the money. And the boy. He must not forget the boy.

Monsignor had turned and was peering at him sharply. *Miserere mei.* The man had asked a question.

"I'm sorry?" Pessoa said.

"I asked if you did not find that that which we love the most often destroys us?"

That hatchet—which had already tasted blood. If not for Berenice, then for six others.

"The boy so loved his angels. A bit God-struck. I thought ill of him yesterday, and accused him, and I bear the guilt of that today, for thinking that he meant to hurt me. But it was an excess of affection, bringing me food and yet more food, and that was not good for me, true; but when I was in distress, he would ever rub my back. He would read to me. Who will be there now to see I get the poppy? I tell you: there was not another like him. Did you know him well?"

Led him into temptation. Murdered him with ideas. He remembered the desolate sound of Bernardo's corpse falling into the wet grave and how the grave cloth had flapped open—*I am the Light of the world*—the dull thud of clay clods, and the sight of a pale boy, his eyes closed, fast asleep in a low and narrow bed. "No," Pessoa said. "Not well."

"He would not do such a thing—hurt a child. Not Bernardo. It is this place which ruined him." To Pessoa's shock, tears welled up in those pitiless eyes. "I should not have brought him here, for he was a sweet boy and ever besotted with angels."

Monsignor looked away quickly, took the coffee from off the fire, and found cheesecloth and cups. The wink of the blade. In the back and of a sudden, so that pleading could not stay the blow. But then it was too late,

and Gomes had turned, and had set a cup by Pessoa, and had sat on a stool
across the table.

He blew on his cup. "I know that you do not credit it . . . What is your
given name again?"

"Manoel."

"Yes. Manoel. Just so. I know that you do not credit it, but I defend
God here. I alone, for God has set me that burden. And so I take the sin and
the blame from off your shoulders, do you not see that at least? For I am
not so dull-witted as to think that the Holy Office will not censure me. Neither am I all abandoned of kindness."

No, Pessoa could not kill him, even though it meant saving seven innocents, even though he doubted the murder would count as sin. Instead,
he sipped his coffee and found it surprisingly good.

"Quiet, is it not?" Monsignor asked, and it seemed that something in
the silence frightened him.

"The storms are over."

"Over," Monsignor said. He put the cup down on the table. Unseeing,
he stared at the wall. When Pessoa arose, he did not seem to notice. He did
not try to stay him when he took up the saddlebags and walked out the
door.

Day 13

THEY CAME IN THE MORNING, THE COOK'S BOY AND TWO FOOTMEN. They dressed Afonso in his black and rested the circlet of gold on his brow. When he was fully dressed and very splendid, Afonso put Mario's dagger in a silken cloth. He placed five gold pieces in it and tied the ends. Then he ordered that a scribe come to the tent, for he wanted someone to take a letter down.

"Tell Mario that I thank him very much," Afonso said. "Tell him that his dagger was nice, and that I liked it. Tell him I should have returned it before, but that I remembered him by the dagger and so did not wish to give him up." Afonso asked the scribe to sign the letter and to see that it was delivered. Then he put on his cloak and walked outside.

The sun was a brightness, the sky a wide deep blue. The camp was in a clutter, with banners fallen, and tents collapsed, and soldiers working to set it aright.

Afonso splashed his fine black boots when he walked, but he did not care. He walked to where he thought the acorn should be, but it was there no longer. Down the hill was a lump of earth where soldiers were planting grass. In a crevasse between two hills was wedged the splintered remains of a wagon and two dead horses.

The captain came to him and bent his knee. He looked like a noble, in his cobalt velvet and gold chain. "I ask you to come, sire, and stand by me, for I have selected those guards who will accompany us, and I mean to address them. I think that you should hear what I have to say."

Afonso followed. When he arrived in camp he saw that yet another group of soldiers had assembled; and they looked handsome, too, with their uniforms brushed and clean, their swords and breastplates polished to a dazzle.

The captain helped Afonso up onto the bed of an open wagon, then he climbed up after. The captain called out to his men, "At midday, we ride into Quintas, there to attend what I am told is an illegal *auto-da-fé*. There will be a Mass before, with all the priests in attendance. The Host will not be offered to your king. And, as the Inquisition means to thus shame him, I will refuse the Eucharist when it is offered. I may not ask so of you, for I would never require aught which might imperil your souls. But it seemed to me, days or weeks or years later, men, when you are asked if you attended this *auto*, it would be good to say that you had, but that you did not participate, nor did you lend any aid in the murder of innocents, except to do that which was ordered directly by the Holy Office. When we reach Lisbon, I will stand together with those inquisitors who have argued for clemency. As God is just, I will see the inquisitor-general jailed."

The captain thanked his men and dismissed them. When they had wandered away, he helped Afonso down from the wagon. "Will you have something to eat, sire? Best that you eat now, rather than later."

Because the captain wanted him to, he sat outside in the sun while his tent was set in order. He ate a loaf with ham. The captain sat with him and ate an apple with cheese.

"It will be hard, this thing," the captain said. "But I will not leave your side. Has Father de Melo explained what is to happen?" The captain stared hard at the table as he spoke. Afonso leaned down to catch his eye and wriggled his fingers at him.

The captain raised his head. "Well, sire? Did he?"

"He talked of a Mass and those dressed in black who would be set afire, and so I do not think I will like it."

"No, Your Highness," the captain told him. "I think that you will not."

THE DAY WAS far too bright, the sun hurtful. Pessoa walked to the square and found the podium ready. In his alb, Father de Melo was laying the corporal atop the three altar cloths, white on white on gleaming white: falls of tepid, sacred snow. Pessoa stopped, but de Melo was intent on his work, and did not see him.

Pessoa walked on, following the path the condemned would take, down a wide street, then a narrow lane where housewives were sweeping steps. The litter gatherer, as he always did, was scraping up the night's garbage for his pigs. Sunlight sparkled on the cobbles, and heat chased the damp.

He walked past the last of the houses and around a corner until the sight of the pyres stopped him—four were already built, and they stood stark and black against the gaiety of the morning. Yet there was an every-day bustle about the place: hammering carpenters, soldiers bearing pitch, the three executioners barking orders.

He should not have come here, not seen this. He hurried back the way he had come, hurried so fast that he stumbled, not knowing where to seek for safety. He rushed past the square, and de Melo at the altar. Head down, he went past the jail, then to the church, and yet that was not good enough, either, and so he went on; by the old rectory, through the muddy meadow, past the wattle fence, until he was at Soares's cottage. There, in the refuge of its shadow, he stopped.

Yet it was a shock to hear Soares's voice raised in anger. To hear someone else, too, shouting beyond that closed door.

". . . care not for this!" Soares cried. "And you may leave my presence!"

Magalhães's reedy "He will not pay! So someone has to, don't they? And me with nine *sanbenitos*!"

Pessoa put his hand to the stucco wall. Nine. The wrong count, and Bernardo never corrected it. Nine. He had the wild, senseless hope that, for lack of a *sanbenito*, Berenice would be saved.

"Take them all back on account and have done with it."

Magalhães was outraged. "Gomes *seized* them. He had those king's guards there, and those Inquisition guards, and he seized them! Said as to illegality, the Holy Office might charge enough crime on his head for a lifetime in prison, didn't he? So punishment for such a petty debt would give him no terrors. He said as how I should go begging for it. Me! Go begging! When I fair put my eyes out painting those flames. So . . . no! Don't turn away from me, father, unless it is to get the strongbox. I saw how money was taken up this morning, and I mean to have it."

Pessoa put his hand on the latch, and then heard Soares say, "I will go to Gomes with your heresy."

Such a soft reply issued from Magalhães that Pessoa could not distinguish the words.

"Think you I will not?" Soares asked. "For you laughed at her, and said even as I chastened you, that a rape of a witch was no sin. That would be two of the same, my son—like the heresy which got you a *sanbenito*. A statement well worth a burning."

Angry footsteps approached the door and Pessoa shrank back against the rectory wall. Not Castanheda. No one handsome or of importance. No one she could love. He saw the door open and Magalhães emerge, a man not of a grand ugliness, but only a sad mediocrity. To ever have such beauty, he had to force his way. And the shame of it—Magalhães seeing no closer than the end of his cock—the rape's pathetic nature. He imagined Magalhães throwing a cloth over her face and forcing her down, flinging himself atop her, hurrying, breathless, terrified and excited all at once, hurrying it, fast and over with as quick as a rabbit, no romance, no kisses, lest someone see what he was doing and tell the wife. Magalhães, not Castanheda, shoving his old and wrinkled worm inside.

The tailor glanced to where Pessoa stood, and the man's eyes widened. He started away, but Pessoa caught him.

He was not a large man, but he was strong, and Berenice so ill. No one there to love her. Dying, and no one there to bring her water. Pessoa whispered, "A very dangerous heresy, José Filipe," and saw the tailor go fishmouthed.

Magalhães tried to pull away. He stood tiptoe and Pessoa felt the urge to batter and to squeeze, a craving so strong that it felt like lust. He hungered for savagery. He wanted to tighten his fingers and watch that face go purple.

The tailor must have seen murder in his eye. He panicked and began to flail. They staggered, locked in eerie silence, until they fetched up against a low stone wall. There, Pessoa knocked Magalhães to his knees. He pummeled him again. Struck him, struck him until blood spurted.

He should kill him. Right here, right now. Leave the judgment of Gomes to God, but this? This was a small thing. A thing not worthy of continuing.

"No, father!" Magalhães was bleeding from the nose and mouth, all hopeless and weeping. "I have a family, don't I? What will my children do?"

Pessoa had not counted on his begging, had never expected that. He had not counted on his own sympathies, either, for his hands felt incapable, yet still impassioned, as when lust fails.

The tailor crawled away, sliding in the mud, whooping for breath. Pessoa watched him go. When the man reached the end of the rock wall, Pessoa called after, "An hour, José Filipe, and I will go to Gomes. He will not have to pay for the *sanbenitos* then."

The tailor staggered up and fled, arms windmilling in alarm. Pessoa sat in the wet grass and watched the sun climb the trees. He sat, and had still not tapped his rage. Left inside, it would burst him, like a cask of green wine. He began tearing the wall apart, stone by deliberate stone. He worked until he was bathed in sweat and his body trembled.

He raised his head to the sky. The sun was nearly overhead now, the stone wall a ruin, like a fortress that had been sacked. Trembling and exhausted, he went into the cottage.

Soares was seated at the table, his elbows propped, his fingers interlaced, already dressed for Mass. He said blandly, "Best to change cassocks. The alb won't hide all that."

Pessoa looked down at himself, at the streaks of mud, the sweat, the bruised and bleeding knuckles. Arms and back aching, Pessoa stripped off his cassock. He washed himself as well as he could in the basin.

When he heard Soares's voice again, he heard the wry fondness in it. "Something I've noticed in you, Manoel: a morning ill-temper."

A T NOON, THE captain came, leading Doçura. "Are you ready, sire?" Afonso said, "They are packing the tents."

"Yes, Your Highness, for when the *auto* is over, we will start for home." The way the captain said it, Afonso knew he was left with no choice. And perhaps the captain was right; it was time to leave the meadow.

Afonso stood straight as a king and nodded. "Then I will go to God's grave and say good-bye. I will ring my bell once more for Jandira."

He walked to the rise where the acorn had once been, and where only a pile of dirt and a pair of dead horses were now. He looked down at the grave. He told God, "You look very ugly, but I suppose the grass will fill in. For now, though, You are all molting, like a fledgling bird."

He could not see the light under the bank of dirt, but he felt the light's vibration. *You look very fine,* God told him.

"I must look fine," Afonso told him. "For I am the king. They will make paintings of me, and tile murals, and I will be shown holding a sword, although I did rarely; and I will be astride a rearing horse, although horse never reared for me, either." He looked at God's grave this way, then that. "It's all right, really. The grass will probably grow in."

God asked politely, *Do I know you?*

"Yes. For I came to visit You often while You were becoming. Now that You have become, You seem not to know much of anything."

I am sorry that I do not remember.

Afonso said, with the courtesy one monarch shows another, "Well, think no more on it. All in all, You did not know me well."

He should have gone straightaway back to camp, but instead he walked the long way around it, kicking his fine boots in the dirt, ringing his bell; and when he rounded the hill and looked down into a ravine, he saw an arm.

It was the same color as the clay it rested upon—the hue of Portugal's codfish earth. The linen grave cloth they had buried her in had gone sad and dull as well. It trailed away in dirty ribbons where she had tried to burst her brightness through.

"It is time," he said. "We must go."

He sat down and waited for her to come to him, but although he waited a long time, she would not rise; and so when the captain called his name, and then called his name again, Afonso at last got to his feet and waved Jandira good-bye.

A S PESSOA AND Soares walked to the jail the seculars stopped them. Pessoa told Soares, who was fretting about the time, to go on.

Emílio leaned forward to whisper, "I have had word from the captain of the king's guard."

Pessoa's heart leapt, and lodged itself, pounding, in his throat. Dear God. Done. The message from Bishop Días had arrived, and everyone was saved. *I believe.* Dizzy, Pessoa flung his hand out, grabbed the iron railing of Castanheda's steps. *Credo in unum Deum, Patrem omnipotentem.* He took a ragged breath, feeling such a gratitude that tears sprang to his eyes.

But the looks on their faces. Why the distress that he saw? Emílio had said, had he not, that he had heard from the captain? What else but the message?

Tadeo put an arm about Pessoa's shoulder, and what pity was this? What pity when the message was come? He shrugged Tadeo off, for Pessoa was the giver of comfort, not the taker. Solace was his place, and he would accept sympathy from no one. Besides, this was a private matter: the message a promise between himself and God. Pessoa would make good on it. *I believe, for He has seen fit to save them.* God over Heaven and earth, mover of mountains. *Factorem caeli et terrae, visibilium omnium, et invisibilium.* Ruler of the visible and the not.

"He has sent another after. Just a note," Emílio said, "writ by him and in his own hand and sent to the regent begging that he stop this thing."

Tadeo said with frightening compassion, "Father? Are you all right?"

Pessoa looked from Tadeo to Emílio, and Emílio was speaking, the words not important now, because Pessoa knew that hope was lost, that the messenger never made it back.

". . . likes him not, Gomes. He laughed to near bring the walls down when I told him that Gomes now fears to eat. Terrified of any food, that glutton! Can you believe? At any rate, the captain said he sent the second message last night when the storm blew off. Sent his best and bravest man, and on his stoutest horse." He gave a sympathetic twist of his mouth. "Yet he could not beg of the bishop, as he does not know him. But he knows that Afonso's brother is kindly, and owes much to the captain, and so I think . . ."

Light dazzled on the damp tile roofs. Pessoa looked away. He gathered his alb so that it would not flutter, so that its lace hem would not catch the mud.

"Father?" Tadeo called after.

Pessoa walked and did not stop until he reached the jail. There, Cândido asked him a question, one which Pessoa did not hear, and so begged him to repeat it.

"The thing's gone wrong," Cândido said. "Sending Guilherme up, and that poor Maria Elena and those imps with him. So, I'm asking to be released from your service, father, and no debt incurred. Don't know where you'd get the money to pay me at any rate, as you're left wretched as a two-legged dog."

"Yes," Pessoa whispered. Ten stones were set into the arch above the old inn's door. Ten stones, like ten *sanbenitos* needed. Ten, an Apocalyptic number. And just beyond, one of Gomes's guards was holding a Trinity of pikestaffs. Twelve stones above . . .

"Father? You hear me?"

the fireplace. Twelve stones, a gathering of Apostles.

"Father?"

He reached out, patted Cândido's arm. "Do not worry yourself. Everything will be right." He walked inside, past the guards, and down the stair. In the men's cell was an agitation. Three guards and Soares were gathered around the dead creature, and the prisoners already with their *sanbenitos,* Guilherme Castanheda looking absurd in the knee-length shift as he was meant to, for who cared when fools burned? Rodrigo was solemnly holding his father's hand. And beside him stood the guards and Soares and the two straw effigies, only one of them dressed. The creatures looked foolish in their *sanbenitos,* too, and the dead one all sunken in.

"I touched him," Soares said. "I merely touched him. And the flesh liquefied."

A guard was trying to fit an arm into the shift, but the arm was warm wax.

"I merely touched him," Soares said.

Pessoa straightened. He ordered a guard, "Go bring Cândido Torres to me straightaway. He was just outside. Tell him I have a need."

He waited, not daring to turn around. He could not bear to see her dressed to wed fantasy, her hands not gripping flowers, but an unlit torch— become a bride of ridicule.

When Cândido came down the stair, Pessoa stared at the wall and said, "Take the boy Rodrigo to the rectory. Do not leave him. Do not put him in another's care. I will come for him directly."

Rodrigo started to weep. "I want to stay with *pai.*"

Cândido picked the boy up and left. Pessoa went to Guilherme and very quietly said, "I take as my penance the raising of your son. I will leave the Church and the kingdom. And also as penance, Guilherme, I will do as you begged me once. I will take your money."

Castanheda took a deep breath. He raised his head to the ceiling. Easier to leave his side now, having said what he must, yet a novena of bars across the window caught Pessoa's attention. Nine. The ninth Station, in which Jesus falls for the third and final time.

An inquisitorial guard called down for the prisoners, and the one below called up, saying that the dead creature was become a puddle, and then it was all too late, all gone too far now, for the guard atop was saying, "Monsignor's ready for the Mass and will not be delayed! Bring him, anyway." The man below flapping his arms and saying lamely, "But all that would hold him is a bucket."

Soares took Pessoa's arm. "Manoel?"

Too much sympathy in the touch, so Pessoa pulled away; and there she was in the other cell, standing in her *sanbenito.* Was that the way he would remember her? And yet she did not look the fool, but seemed small and lost instead—meeting no one's eye. Berenice, drunk with her man of light. Pessoa, a man of dark nature, dressed in dark wool. How could he have imagined that she needed him?

He clutched his missal as he watched a guard open both cells wide. Soares took up a staff-length cross and said that he was ready.

Exiting in the order of their deaths: Senhora Teixeira, holding her unlit torch loose-handed, helping Maria Elena up the stair. Then Marta, who stood, but could scarce walk in her burnt and wounded feet, even with the guard come to her aid. Behind Marta came Guilherme Castanheda, as stuporous as the demented little Maria Elena. And as they went, the walls of the prison closed in. Soon Berenice would leave, and it would be best if she walked where he could not see her. Yet on the steps he looked back once, not Lot's wife punished, but gifted instead, seeing Soares gently guiding angels.

Upstairs, Maria Elena's grip failed, and she dropped her torch. Pessoa got to her before the guard's anger did.

"Hold it tightly, Maria," Pessoa told her. "Holding on to something will give you a comfort."

It seemed that she had not heard him, or at least that she had not understood; and yet she took the cold torch when it was handed her. Her bruises were healing. Six bruises. The sixth Station, Jesus meets with Veronica, and the "O Lord, imprint Your image on my heart, so that I may be faithful."

Berenice walking behind him, and he wanted to turn, yet he could not. Besides, it was not needed, for she had the bright fantasy to hold. But he . . . how could he see marigolds? How could he smell lavender? Never had he been unfaithful to her except with the Church. And why? He did not love it.

It was a strange silent procession, with no chants, no banners, the condemned's stocking feet on the cobbles. He walked shoulder to shoulder with Maria, Senhora Teixeira suspicious and peering back. *"Agnus Dei,"* Pessoa prayed. Maria, tractable as a lamb, responded. *"Qui tollis peccata mundi, miserere nobis."*

From behind him came Marta's voice, squeezed and breathless with pain. *"Miserere nobis."*

They went out of the prison and into the sunlight, where mercy was not.

Townsfolk peered from behind lace curtains. He walked, hearing Marta limp and stumble and whimper behind him. He clutched his missal tight, for holding was a comfort; and soon they arrived at the *praça,* which should have been full of villagers and yet was empty. Empty, but for Tadeo and Emílio and a handful of inquisitorial guards. There sat the benches for the accused and the podium for the Mass. Atop it stood Gomes in his surplice and chasuble, the purple stole fluttering. De Melo was straightening the pall atop the chalice. Across the way, the young king was sitting, his captain standing beside him; and ringed all around, brilliant in their crimson, were ranks of king's soldiers, nothing in their faces but duty, pikestaffs in their hands.

Maria Elena, who might have remembered Spaniards, halted in her tracks. An inquisitorial guard barked an order, but Senhora Teixeira whirled about and seized her daughter's hand.

"Not allowed," the guard said. "You go to the Mass and then to the pyre by yourselves. Holding hands is not allowed." He tried to separate the two women, but Senhora Teixeira pushed him back.

"So burn me," she cackled.

Pessoa said to the guard, "The girl is frightened, can't you see? And insane. She could cause a furor. Let her mother help."

The guard shrugged. All about, sun glinted off breastplates. There were too many soldiers to count. Pessoa looked up, saw the cloud white of Gomes's surplice, the virginal white of de Melo's alb: two ghost-pale priests. Two. And at the second Station, Jesus took up his cross.

Somehow Senhora Teixeira was already seated and Maria Elena was genuflecting, passivity returned to her face. Soares whispered in his ear, "Up to the podium, for we will be altar servers, or so I've been told. Come, Manoel. Stand and look prayerful, and I will handle things."

The miracle of one foot and then the other, the ascension, Gomes turning to them, still wearing yesterday's grief. Then it was time, and Gomes was kneeling and kissing the altar, then rising up and turning, his hand already uplifted. *"In nomine Patri, et Filii . . ."*

The benches of the condemned were quiet. Motionless soldiers stood at the borders of the plaza. Time was waiting, its breath pent. The two creatures had dropped their torches, but no one seemed to care.

". . . Spiritu Sancti."

Pessoa saw the king say something to his captain, saw the captain bend down.

All about them, soldiers said, *"Amen."*

"**N**O ONE TOLD me they would burn angels," Afonso said. The captain told him, "You must try to be quiet, sire."

It had not been much of a procession. Afonso had seen many which were better. And not many people were come to Mass. The fat priest was saying something.

"God will not like it," Afonso told his captain.

The captain looked straight ahead, and together with the others in the *praça* he said, *"Et con tuum."*

Afonso was used to taking the *Corpus Christi* alone and hearing Father de Melo's homilies. He did not know Mass well. Still, he stood when the others stood, he sat when the captain whispered for him to sit—which was a rare thing, for sitting was not much a part of it. Besides, only Afonso and the people in black had chairs. Afonso knelt as well, and much too often. No one had thought to bring his prayer cushion, and the floor was hard.

He heard the fat priest say *"Kyrie,"* and Afonso knew to repeat it, too, as Father de Melo had taught him. The *Kyrie,* the *Christie eleison,* then again a *Kyrie,* and still they were not done. The *Gloria,* and sit, stand, kneel, sit.

Afonso was tired. He was bored, too, and wanted to hold himself, but knew he couldn't. He tugged on the captain's tunic. "Does the fat priest know that God will not like us burning His angels?"

The captain tapped his lips for silence.

On the altar, the priests were busy with plates and cups and towels and the fat priest was washing his hands. Everyone knelt again. Afonso watched the fat priest play with the Host, lifting it up, bringing it down.

He whispered to the captain, who was kneeling beside him. "Will it be over soon?"

"Shhh, sire."

The fat priest took bread and wine for himself, and Afonso wondered if he would take all the bread, the way he had taken Afonso's chocolates. The other priests took the *Corpus Christi,* one after the other, and Afonso had to kneel through that, too.

Two men who were guarding the people in black finally got up from their knees, and Afonso started to stand as well. The captain pulled him down.

"But they're standing." Did the captain not see how wrong it was for two commoners to stand while the king knelt?

"Shhh," the captain said.

"My knees hurt," Afonso said. "And it is not right."

The captain smiled. "Watch, sire."

Why? There was nothing to see, except that now there were three men who had gotten up and gone to the rail to take the *Corpus Christi.* A fourth stood, peered about, and then knelt back in his place.

Would the whole world but priests forfeit the use of ass and feet? Afonso did not make courtiers or even commoners kneel so long.

The fat priest gave the three at the rail the *Corpus Christi.* Then he waited some more.

"He will never let us up," Afonso said.

The captain seized his arm. "O, but look at your men, my liege. Is that not fine?"

Why fine? And what was there to see? The soldiers were simply kneeling. Everyone but the priests was kneeling, for the three who had taken the *Corpus Christi* had gone back to their places and, to Afonso's dismay, had knelt again.

It was indeed a low Mass, with everyone on their knees, with the fat priest not doing much of anything. But then Mass started up, the fat priest speaking, and only a little while later Afonso heard the *Dominus vobiscum.*

He remembered his *"Et con tuum."* His knees hurt. The day had been long, and Afonso was ready for cakes and coffee. He turned to the captain and said, "I would like to go now."

The captain looked hard into his eyes, so hard that Afonso became troubled by it. "Yes, sire," he said. "Now we go to the pyres."

Gomes WALKED IN front, head bent, requiem-purple stole fluttering. Behind him came the executioners, even more frightening today—three big men, faceless in their masks. As he walked, Pessoa took hold of Maria Elena's hand. She smiled as if somewhere, either beyond or inside him, she had seen something beautiful.

"Maria Elena?" He inclined his head to her, and in that one act, Pessoa banished all else. There were no soldiers, no executioners, no approaching pyres, just himself and the girl, her need and the sunlight.

"Yes, father?"

He squeezed her fingers. "Would you care to repudiate your sin and beg God's forgiveness? Would you like to do that now?"

"I have a sin, father."

He leaned closer, so close that her hair tickled his cheek. She smelled of the *sanbenito*'s paint, and of the straw she had lain in. "Yes?"

"I do not know what it is, father. But still, it caused me to lose my baby, and I am very sorry for it all the same."

He made the sign of the cross over her. "I want you to say a good Act of Contrition now, Maria Elena. And in a little while, when you are asked if you abjure, I want you to say that you have, and have begged pardon, and have asked me to intercede in your behalf. Do you understand?"

Behind him, Marta began to sob. He turned to see that she had stopped. The entire procession had stopped there in the narrow street where the women had swept their porches and the litter gatherer had collected garbage for his pigs. Above them was a lace-bordered window and pink geraniums, with a single pallid face looking down.

Little red footsteps trailed a path down the cobbles. Marta was weeping. "I can't."

An inquisitorial guard pushed Guilherme Castanheda back. "Don't touch her!"

Another guard came, appraised Guilherme's size, and clapped his hand to his sword.

"Walk! Walk!" the first guard ordered.

Marta said, her voice small, "I can't."

"We will walk slower," the second guard told her. "Sit down for a while if you must."

She could not manage that, either, and so the guard helped her down to the cobbles. He turned to Guilherme. "No one cares to see her cry, but there are rules, sir. And she must do it alone. We will walk if it takes all day; and if she must sit down every few meters, we will do that."

Two guards stood by the two condemned. Four altogether. The fourth Station, in which Jesus meets his mother. *Grant me a tender love.*

Suddenly Tadeo was there, shoving both guards back. Emílio plucked the torches from out Marta and Guilherme's hands. "God! Where are your hearts! Can you not let her father carry her!"

Marta was a small girl, no challenge to lift. Pessoa himself could have done it. Beyond the father with the daughter snug in his arms stood the two creatures, Soares holding their torches. Next stood Berenice—too hurtful to look at.

The procession started up again. Pessoa walked quickly to catch Senhora Teixeira.

"Maria Elena abjures," he said.

She grunted. "Good. For I would have asked her to if you hadn't, and so she would have done."

They rounded the corner. Ahead were the pyres, a stark and pitch-laden black against the azure sky. He could leave now. Nothing held him. He could walk away today, for tomorrow he surely would. It was best not to see this. Then he could live in England happy, imagining that the message had come.

The crooked smile on Senhora Teixeira's face surprised him. "We have had our disputes," he said.

She laughed.

He said low enough so that neither executioners nor de Melo could hear, "But I beg you now, whatever hatred you harbor for God or for me, say that you abjure your sin, and sincerely repent, for otherwise you will be burnt to death in your daughter's sight."

She said, "Hatred for you, Father Manoel Inquisitor? Not anymore, and no hatred special, except for your manhood. All I regret is having to die first, without watching you lose that prized dignity when you send your own bitch to the fire. Or will you even then?"

"I care not that you burn," he hissed back. "Not you. But when the flames touch flesh, you will scream Hell's door open. Do you want your daughter to hear that? Do you? And then her having to climb the pyre herself, little understanding that she will not have to burn as well?"

It was uncanny, that look, as if she saw inside him, saw the small mean thing Pessoa was; while her daughter had looked in him and seen grace.

"I will not scream," she said. "I will lean into the fire, and drink it, for it will taste better than this, and smell better than you, and I will have a kinder ending than husband would ever give me."

A FONSO WANTED TO talk to the herbalist, for he quite liked her. He wanted to tell her that Jandira had burst her cocoon and was finally becoming, although he knew not what. The captain held him back.

He would have spoken to the angels, too, and wanted to tell them to take off their silly black robes. They could wear red, like the pretty crimson footprints he had seen on the cobbles. Or blue like the wide sky. Or green like the weeds which grew oftimes between the walls of the houses and the cobbles. Green. That was a happy color.

It was a strange parade, with the angels wandering and having to be herded, with the weeping man carrying the weeping girl, with the people in the windows peeking between their curtains as if afraid to be seen, and him not able to wave. But of all of them, the fat priest, the executioners, the people dressed in black and flames, he was the most important one. So he walked importantly, with his chest out and his chin up.

Just outside the village was a meadow, all happy and green from the rain. And there were marigolds in plenty, and late daisies, and large stacks of wood that were nearly thrice the height of a man. Two of the stacks at the very end were tiny—angel-sized. There in that meadow the procession stopped, and the fat priest spoke, and the people who were in the silly black dresses that barely reached their knees all listened, and more of them were crying now. A soldier brought Afonso a chair, and the captain bade him sit down.

"Will it be long?" he asked.

"A while, sire."

"Will we have dinner here, then?" He thought a dinner on the grass might be pleasant, for the sun was warm and the breeze brisk, the meadow so pretty, and the daisies fresh-faced.

The captain shook his head. "No. Look there, Your Majesty. See? This part is easy to watch. The effigies first."

The little wood stacks were not meant for angels, but for two straw figures which were quick to burst into flame.

"It is all most carefully planned. They set the easternmost ones first, sire," the captain said, "for the afternoon wind is west to east."

Afonso watched the wind pluck at the straw men and carry bright pieces of them away. "I see Father de Melo."

All the priests were standing about a woman who should not have been dressed in the short shift at all. Her legs were knobby in some places and fat in others, and her hair had come loose from her bun and stuck up on her head in a fright.

"Do not wave, sire. Father is busy. Now, when the pyre is lit, you may hold on to my hand, if you wish. But do not rise up out of your chair. Nor should you make any outcry, nor a protest of any sort. If you feel the need to vomit, do so to the side there."

The woman was angry and shouting. "Those priests should stand back," Afonso said, for she seemed very furious.

A masked executioner came to help her up the stack of wood, but she slapped at him. She hiked her skirt above her skinny shanks and walked up by herself. All the priests below were waving their crosses, waving their crosses, and her laughing down. The executioner tied her about the stake, hands and legs, and then he left her, and she was all alone there, shouting.

The priests hushed their prayers, and Afonso could hear what she said. ". . . all men murderers! For I look down and see not a woman among you! Cock-proud, cock-stupid. You had best fear me, hadn't you? Hadn't you? And do not dare sleep. For I'll come tonight in your dreams and suck the life out from between your legs!"

Afonso told the captain, "I like her. She is funny, and she reminds me of Jandira."

On the other side of the wood, the executioner was setting the wood alight. He raced to the front and set that afire, too. Afonso saw the woman look down once before the tinder caught.

The woman's shouts went shrill. A wall of fire rushed up. She tried to lift herself, she tried in a frenzy, but her legs were bound tight. Her black shift caught, and made the painted flames a radiance. Her hair caught, too, and she screeched loudly and very long. The meadow hushed, and for a while it was only the deep-throated roar of the fire and her screams.

"The priests need to be careful of her," Afonso said, for it seemed that when the ropes burned through, she would climb down and strike them.

She did not come down. She bellowed. She struggled. And it was not Afonso who sought the captain's hand; but the captain who sought his. Afonso thought that the burning was not so terrible. True, the woman screamed, but she laughed, too; although it was a laugh that hurt to hear. And then the flames shot up high of a sudden, and the laughs and the screams went quiet, and then it was only the noise of the fire and the whisper of the wind.

He could see her, at times, amid the bright flames: a dark, still figure. The shift had burned off her, but that did not matter, for she had no true nakedness, really, and was a woman no longer. She had changed. All of her was a sort of charcoal; and then that, too, was gone, the hinged floor dropping open, the charred body falling through the embers.

The captain cleared his throat. "An angry old hag," he said. "Probably nothing could have been done to save the bitch. Let us pray that the rest are not so damnably obstinate."

Afonso looked up and saw him staring blank-faced and straight ahead. His hand was hot and sweaty. He held Afonso's fingers tight.

D E MELO EMBRACED Maria Elena and welcomed her back into the Body of Christ. She kissed the cross when Soares lifted it to her. She held on to the sleeve of Pessoa's alb.

Pessoa told her, "We will go up the pyre together, Maria Elena. You and Father Soares and I."

They had to, for she would not let go his sleeve. He put his arm about her and helped her up the first log, then the next. On one side was the low crackle of her mother's pyre; on the other, Soares, intoning a Pater Noster.

Then they were at the stake. Below, were Gomes and de Melo, a bright ring of soldiers, and the meadow stretching emerald and wide. The air smelled of wood smoke and pitch and the sweet sick stench of her mother's burnt flesh.

Soares prayed, *". . . panum nostrum da nobis hodie . . ."*

Maria Elena looked down at the gathered soldiers, the waiting priests. The crowd below, all looking up. She held Pessoa tight. "Please, father. Tell me about Heaven."

What could he say except that it seemed they were already ascending? The meadow was so achingly beautiful, the sky above them wide and waiting, the soldiers below so small.

Soares leaned to her. "Christ waits for you there, for you have been a good girl, Maria."

Now she gave Soares her desperate longing. "Have I?"

"O, yes." Soares patted her hand. "A very good girl."

She looked at Pessoa again. Why? He had naught that would help her. Yet she held him with her clinging, demanding fingers. "And my baby?"

Pessoa said, "I believe that your baby is most likely in Heaven, too."

"I'm afraid of Purgatory, father." Her fingers squeezed his, so that bone grated bone. "I do not understand it. Hell is something at least, but Purgatory has always seemed to be an in-between place, somewhere that God might lose souls. I think sometimes—just before I fall asleep—it seems to me, father, that I am lost there. I think I will wander, my baby gone to Limbo, for the sweet was never baptized. I might bear Purgatory with my baby with me, but I am so afraid to be alone."

Pessoa took hold of her wrists. "Listen to me, Maria." Easier for him to say it than for Soares to lie. "I promise you: you will not be in Purgatory today, nor your baby in Limbo."

"And I can hold it?"

He sensed the oddly gentle, uncannily silent approach of the executioner.

"Not yet," Soares told him, and then plaintively asked the man, "Must you tie her?"

Pessoa said, "Look at me, Maria. Look! And listen to me carefully. I promise you: in just a moment you will be in heaven. And once you are there, you may hold your baby."

The executioner took hold of her hand, but she gasped and snatched it back. Then suddenly she went wide-eyed. "Hold my baby!" she cried. "He can't take me! I want to hold my baby!"

"Yes. Very soon now." Pessoa caught her wrist and fumbled for the other, but Soares already held it tight.

The executioner slipped the garrote about her neck, and let the rope rest gently as a length of velvet ribbon.

"Say your prayers, Maria Elena," Soares said. He looked to the executioner.

"*Pater Noster, qui es in cae—*"

Such merciful violence, that quick twist of the handle. Pessoa held her struggling wrist, held her. He could not look into her terrified face; and yet to be kind, he must. She shuddered. She held the lace of his alb in her fists. One last heartbeat, then the feverish yearning in her eyes went out. She fell limp, Pessoa falling with her. Soares went to his knees, praying.

The executioner pulled the body away, and Maria Elena's fingers came loose, leaving handprints, sweated furrows in the cotton. When he looked up, Pessoa saw her already being tied to the stake. Her head was hanging down lower and more helpless than it ever could in life. Still, the executioner, a cautious man, put his hand over her mouth to check for breath.

Someone plucked at his sleeve, and he thought—O God, he feared— that it was Maria Elena.

Only Soares. "Come down, Manoel. He is ready to set the wood alight."

A FONSO DID NOT like to see the girl set ablaze, for she was just Pedro's age. Executions were for grown people, for murderers and Spaniards. They were for those who plotted against the crown.

He fidgeted in his seat. The captain gave a cautionary tug to his fingers. "Sometimes it helps to think of something else, sire. A novena, perhaps. Or counting. That always does well for me."

Next to burn would be the man and the girl. They sat together at the base of a stack of wood, and there the priests stood in a knot with the executioner, arguing. Afonso wanted to leave the meadow for home now. He very much wanted his own room, the damp mildew smell of the castle, his window which looked out on the Alfama. He raised his head to the sky and tried to think of something else. He tapped his foot. He counted, but too soon reached the end of his numbers. He counted once more to five.

Perhaps a novena. "Sacred Heart of Jesus, I trust in Thee. . . ." He stopped, confused. Somehow he had begun in the middle of the prayer, and could not remember the rest.

The captain bent down to him. "Sire?"

He could not count well, but he knew how to mark his fingers. Nine. All the fingers but his left thumb. Afonso held down his second finger and said, "Thy kingdom come."

THE EXECUTIONER COULD not pry Marta out of her father's clutches. "See why we do not allow the condemned to touch?" the man asked, exasperated. "Look you! We have this, father! And what good is this?" Behind the mask, his eyes gleamed, less with fury than frustration. "Worse for them, that they become willful, and cannot be managed except to hurt them!"

Soares knelt by where Guilherme sat, cradling his daughter. "Let her go, Guilherme," Soares said. "It is time."

Castanheda shook his head.

Pessoa told him, "I beg you, Guilherme. I would not have the guards hurt you." That hand, a huge soldier's hand, was tangled in her loose, brown hair. Five fingers. At the fifth Station, Jesus was helped by Simon. *Lead me through my daily trials.*

Guilherme's huge body twisted in a child's posture of woe. He lifted his tearstained face. "Take me first."

Soares touched his shoulder. "We cannot."

"Please. I cannot watch her die."

Soares said, "Then she would see you die, instead, and that would be more cruel."

Little Marta curled in his lap as if she slept, her face hidden against her father's broad chest, her bloody feet tucked under her. She was—no, all of them—they were all of them so tired.

Pessoa, who was weary, too, bent down and said, "If you die first, who would carry her up the pyre, Guilherme? And her feet hurting her so. Go ahead and carry her up. They will let you do that." He rose, turned to the executioner. "Let him do that."

The executioner, job all unraveled, shrugged. He went up alone.

Soares took Castanheda's arm, Pessoa the other. They went up the logs—the miracle of one foot and another—until they were at the top, and Soares was saying, "Guilherme, you must put her down."

More difficult a duty than Maria Elena's, even though it was not Pessoa that Marta clung to. She wailed piteously when guards came to lead her father away.

"Be strong," Soares commanded her. "Listen to me! Do you understand, Marta? You must be brave for your father."

Her small hands. Pessoa had not noticed that she clutched a rosary. Five fingers. Five. The fifth Glorious Mystery, when Mary is crowned Queen of Heaven.

The executioner took her wrists and bound them to the stake.

"Not so tightly," Pessoa said.

He caught a wry glitter in the eyeholes of the mask, then the man sighed and shook his head. "She'll fight the garrote."

Marta peered anxiously at the executioner, first over one shoulder, then over the other.

Soares bade her kiss the cross, and she did. He opened his missal. The executioner knelt to tie her legs. Pessoa bent with him. "When I clench my fist, thusly," he whispered. The man nodded and Pessoa arose. About the meadow were gathered flowers and soldiers, the sweet-faced daisies all looking up, and marigolds, too, as bright as candle flames. Pessoa heard the crackle of Maria Elena's fire, but above him was that wide deep sky, and there perhaps Maria Elena held her baby. The fourth Glorious Mystery.

Pessoa heard Marta praying, and realized he was not hearing Latin.

The garrote was already about her, the rope loose enough for her to pray. ". . . protection of the living and the salvation of the dying. Purest Mary . . ."

Not an Act of Contrition, for that had come in the jail. She instead sought comfort from a simple novena.

Her voice trembled. ". . . sacred name, Mary, Mary. What a consolation, what sweetness . . ."

Pessoa looked at the executioner. He clenched his fist.

B EFORE HE EVEN went up the pyre, the man in the black began screaming and shaking his head as if the flames on his shift were burning him. And though he and the two priests walked up the wood together, he cursed them as they went. He cursed Father de Melo. He cursed the fat priest, too, which Afonso very much liked.

"He is a nice man, I think," Afonso told the captain.

"Yes, sire. I am told that he was a soldier, and was awarded a medal by you for great bravery."

"Did I give him a medal?" Afonso peered at the man this way and that. "I do not remember."

"No, sire. But it matters little now."

Shouts from Father de Melo, from the fat priest, and still the two other priests were praying and one was trying to get the man to kiss the cross. The more the priest tried, the more the man turned his face away, and the louder he cursed. The fat priest began barking orders. Two guards climbed the pyre and led the priests away.

"Will it be over soon?" Afonso asked.

The captain nodded vaguely. "You know? It is interesting that I can still recite *The Lusiads,* and I learned it, O, years ago now, in school. Is that not strange? Do you remember your Camões, sire?"

When the priests climbed down, the man on the stake grew quiet. He looked about him. Afonso caught sight of the executioner standing behind the pyre with a torch.

The captain cleared his throat. "First canto: 'This story is of heroes who left Portugal behind. Who opened a passage to Ceylon and crossed seas where no man had yet sailed.' "

Such a silence across the grassy meadow. The white knot of priests, and the man in black on the stake, peering anxiously about.

The captain's words came in a lunatic and unsteady gallop. " 'This is a story of kings who progressed beyond faith and empire, who struck fear among the heathens of Africa and Asia.' "

The executioner disappeared behind the mound of wood.

"And . . . and something, something, something," the captain said. "My memory is imperfect, I find. O! O yes. How stupid of me. O yes, I know. 'So let us hear no more of Ulysses and Aeneas and their travels, or Alexander and Trajan and their victories. I speak of the courage and repute of the . . .' "

The wood at one corner went up in a rush. The executioner quickly ran the other three, touching torch to kindling. Even before the flames had touched flesh, the man started to scream.

The man fought the ropes as if he would climb the stake and make an assault on Heaven. He fought so, he kicked his leg ropes free. His shouts were terrible, first hoarse, then, when the flames reached him, going shrill as a woman's. And even higher, until they were thin and sharp as a trapped stoat's. The man danced atop the wood, in that bright inferno. He raised such a clamor that Afonso could not bear to hear it. He could not bear to see him twitch. "No!" Afonso said. "No!" They must bring the man down, for it was not right for anything to scream thus. He clapped his hands to his eyes, then to his ears, and then to his eyes again, slapping himself so fast and hard that his head rang; and still he could hear the man shrieking.

PESSOA THOUGHT, *If God is good* . . . But how could He exist in Guilherme's unbearable screams, that pain so near to Heaven? It would break any father's heart.

Soares stood next to him, praying in whispers, and what prayers were worthwhile? Best to kill Guilherme where he stood, wrapped in flame, howling. A musket. Pessoa whirled, saw only pikestaffs. Of course no muskets, for either God was not, or He was of a mean and waspish nature.

Then mercifully the screams were over, and the day was almost done. Gomes was standing apart, a solitary figure, his gaze cast not to the pyres, but to some distant spot across the meadow. Weeping again, as he had at Communion? And not weeping in pity for the condemned or even for the affection of a best boy. Pessoa knew that the man mourned private griefs: the loss of gluttony's delights, the humiliation to which the king had put him.

Pessoa looked down the dwindling line of pyres and saw her sitting, head cocked, as if listening for whispers. She had never heeded Guilherme's shrill cries. She was selfish, like Gomes, building all her walled gardens, her private dungeons.

Pessoa had had enough of the afternoon and the flames. He would have left, but Pessoa was of a truer nature than she ever was, she who cared for no one. He would be priest for one more day, and his vow was to give comfort. Pessoa had seen his lambs to the flames. There was one more duty to consider. He could have walked out and left everything if it had not meant abandoning her.

"I THINK THAT God will not be happy," Afonso said as he watched the two cherubs be led to their stakes. The angels went where the executioners told them to go. They let themselves be tied. They complained of nothing.

The old priest climbed the pyre and offered the cross. The fat priest, who had mostly seemed asleep, came to himself then. He shouted for the other priest to put his cross away. "You will not sully the crucifix for those demons! I will not have their lips against it!"

An executioner led the old priest down. Once the pyre was clear of everything but angels, the fat priest ordered in a loud voice, "Burn them without delay!"

The executioners touched the angels' unlit torches to the brazier. When the pitch-soaked ends had caught, they put them to the kindling.

"God will not like this," Afonso said.

It was just a little fire at first, then the wind snatched at it. Flames swept up the wood. The angels said nothing as the blaze approached. They did not cry out even when the flames touched their hems. They looked about, at the sky, at the soldiers, at the meadow. Then one's eyes met Afonso's and the world vanished.

Come with me, the angel said.

The vapor that was Afonso flew through bright Heaven and into the part that is forever dark. He and the angel flew so far, they reached that border where emptiness turns back on itself. There Afonso came to understand that the angel loved the void, loved it as much as God did. And Afonso knew that emptiness was the place angels went to die.

It was peaceful there, the angel at his side. *You are dying now, aren't you?* he asked.

In eyes as dark as the place it had been born, Afonso sensed laughter spark. *Yes.*

Afonso was sorry that God and His angels had to fall all that way to teach the shod people, and he was sorry that, for their trouble, no one had learned much of anything. Still, he looked around Heaven and thought how nice it was to float there, the answer to everything within arm's reach.

Worlds and answers were as close as plucking oranges. *Take one,* the angel said.

The secret of the colors. That was what Afonso picked. And when he had taken the ball of the colors down and had opened it, he saw that the answer was empty, for all colors were one, and all lives one as well, and the answer was so puzzling and the emptiness so huge that it very much scared him, and he wanted to go home.

He turned around and around, floating there in the void, but the angel had left, and Afonso could not see God. "Hallo! Hallo!" he cried, but his voice found the border and bent back.

Afonso was terrified to be alone. He seized another answer, the answer of home, but that was empty, too. And the emptiness, which had no real voice, explained that the void was part and parcel of the whole, and that it stood behind everything, behind hills and skies and cities. Afonso knew that the dark, just like the angel, was trying to teach him something; but Afonso did not care to learn.

I want to go home now. Let me go home.

The darkness told him that the void was home, and emptiness embrace; but Afonso needed comfort that he could touch, and so he screamed for someone to come save him.

The dark absorbed his pleas. It gave him back joy. Afonso did not want it, for the pleasure that the void gave was strange; and so he took another answer and cast it down and burst it, and then he dashed another, and again another, and the third answer was the captain's face.

"Sire?"

The captain was kneeling at Afonso's feet. Over the captain's shoulder, Afonso could see that the pyres were burning down, the angels all turned to string and liquid.

The captain's face darkened at the edges, for the void had claimed Afonso, and was not about to let him go. He clung to the arms of his chair, fighting to keep the world.

Yet the meadow faded, the sky went black. Angels were calling. Ah. Angels calling, and the dark was so ruthless a joy that at last Afonso gave himself up to it. The void took him gladly. Its arms were huge, yet warm in their own way. And the dark held an ardent brightness of its own. The answers were so easy, really. Why had he not seen before? There in the void Afonso came to understand everything, all within the space of a heartbeat. He understood not just the edges of things, but the invisible within.

P ESSOA SAW THE king fall in a twitching fit, saw the guards and the executioners back away from the pyres, crossing themselves. The soldiers went restless.

They must stop the *auto* now, for Death had claimed enough of the day. Could Gomes not see the king on the ground convulsing, Soares weeping, and all the king's soldiers dazed?

Berenice, terror in her eyes, stood only two meters away, ready to mount the pyre. So soon? When had that fear come upon her? And why had Pessoa not noticed? Why was it not him, but Soares at her side?

Soares would not know how to give her comfort. Pessoa heard the old priest trying to lead her into an Act of Contrition. He shoved him aside. "Stop! Stop!" He pushed Soares so hard that he nearly knocked him down.

Berenice seized hold of his alb, her fingers taking the place of Maria Elena's dying hand. "I look and look for him, Manoel." Her breath came fast and shallow. "And he does not come."

Fantasy had abandoned her. Pessoa had known that it would, for the man of light was of a nothingness. Only Death was tangible.

"I call him. Why does he not come?" Her lovely intelligent face was turned witless with her panic.

Pessoa did not know faith, but he knew faithfulness. He knew touch. He seized hold of her fingers. Too soon the executioner was beside them, saying that it was time. The man pulled her up the logs, Pessoa together with them. Hand in hand, he and Berenice would walk up the hill of wood, then down the other side. They would set out across the meadow. They would leave the hills of Estremadura, walk the pine forests of Tras Os Montes, go beyond the kingdom, to fog bound fishing villages where only Basque was spoken. Together they would walk until they reached England. And there he would buy her a warm cloak; and she would be so beautiful that the English would feel privileged just to look her in the face.

Her mouth was moving. He bent his head, thinking she meant to tell him something. But bewildered, she was telling the pyre, the stake, the very air, "He does not come."

A restless stirring among the soldiers below. Was the king dead? He was lying so limp in his captain's lap.

Pessoa heard her whimper, and saw that the executioner was already tying Berenice's hands to the stake. "God!" Pessoa pulled him away. The man slipped on the logs and fell at Pessoa's feet, his arm over his head lest Pessoa strike him.

"Get him down!" Gomes shouted. "Get the fool down and let us have this over!"

A second executioner mounted the pyre, but Pessoa would not leave her. Let the man run him through. Let them all see a priest's blood spilled. The man caught Pessoa's arm. Behind the mask, his eyes were shocked. "Please, father," he said. "Please do not hurt him. We have all of us seen the trials, and we know a little law. We do not agree with the verdicts, either."

That voice. Those eyes. This was Maria Elena's executioner, the one of the merciful strength. "Will she not kiss the cross?" he asked.

That wide sky. The marigolds and the meadow. No, she could not die here, not with the breeze so agreeable and cool. Pessoa made his way around the pyre to where she was tied. Her eyes were lifted to cloudless, comfortless nothing. Her breath came as quick as a startled rabbit's.

He made the sign of the cross over her. "Berenice." When she would not look at him, he raised his voice. "Berenice! Say that you are heartily sorry for leading others into heresy, for you knew not what you did. Say that now that you are made aware, you are made ashamed, and say that you beg God's forgiveness. Damn you," he hissed. "Say it."

She was so small. And from where he stood, there by her side, he could see how fretful her hands were as they worked against themselves, needing something more than air and light to hold.

"Say it. 'I am so heartily sorry.' Say it!" he shouted. He would have struck her down, had she not been tied to the stake. He would have beaten her as he beat Magalhães, until she said the words. " 'I am heartily sorry!' Damn you! Say it!"

Someone touched his arm. "Time, father."

"She abjures. I heard her. She said it just now."

"Please. Come away."

Since he would not go, the two executioners forced him, and they went stumbling down the pyre, traveling so far from Heaven, the freedom of the meadow grown small in perspective. Then his boots were on the soft ground and Pessoa saw the third executioner. Berenice's torch was already lit, and fire was quickening in the pyre's furthermost corner.

Pessoa broke free and started up the pyre toward her, crawling. It was not too late. He would loose her bonds. He would strangle her with his own hands before the flames could make her shriek.

The wind changed. Smoke choked him. Through the billowing pall came the strange, quiet crackle of the inferno. A sudden blast of heat whipped the hair back from his face and set his cheeks, his alb, aflame. He fell where he was, squeezing his eyes shut against it, and yet, evenso, all he could see was brilliance. The heat took his breath. There was no air, and so he could not tell if he was screaming, did not know if he could. Such a brightness was it that he could not know up from down, knew aught except that he had erred, erred so badly, and that he would die there.

Hell stood all about, dark as choking pitch, yet through it came a furious dazzle and a voice. "You idiot whoreson Jesuit!"

Such agony scalded his right side that he was certain this time that he had cried out. A force jerked him back, if not God, then the devil, for Pessoa was tumbling, sparks whirling up in a mad splendor, logs rolling.

He hit the cool mud as the burning logs did, as the executioner fell atop him, still cursing. Then it was all a tangle of logs and legs, his alb burning, and the executioner splattering mud to put him out.

Another voice shouted, frantic. "Pull him away! He will make a mess of it!"

But Pessoa was still afire, his arms and hands in a hot torture, his alb in blackened tatters.

"Pull him away!"

His hands were burning. No, not so. His skin was but reddened. He found himself jerked roughly to his feet. Pessoa saw what horror he had done. One side of the pyre was burning cruelly, Berenice striving to lean away. She could not flee, and it would take the fire so very long to catch her.

"Idiot!" The executioner who had saved his life threw Pessoa back into the mud. "You will make her suffer worse!" The other executioner ran, hurriedly lighting the other corners, but not running fast enough.

Nothing would be fast enough. Pessoa's skin from hands to elbows was scalded, a miser's share of her coming agony. Then Soares knelt beside him, pulling Pessoa's face down hard against his shoulder. In Pessoa's nostrils was Soares's familiar smell: powdery age and wool and something oddly cat-clean.

Even though his arms were torment, he grasped Soares close, embraced him until he realized how quiet the day was, and how she had died without a sound.

He raised his head. The executioners were staring upward in awe, guards and soldiers alike gaping in wonder. Gomes was standing, consternation in his face. Berenice stood alive atop the pyre, backlit by radiance like a saint in a stained-glass window. In the tender hush of the meadow, the breeze was dying.

He started to his feet, knowing not what he intended. Soares pulled him down again, crooning in his ear, and Pessoa was confused as to why. Why was Soares trying to shush him? The day was silent, Berenice not screaming.

She had turned to look beside her, but nothing was there. Nothing. So what pleasantry was she peering at, and so intently? Would that she had ever looked upon him that way. Would that she had cared for Pessoa thus—caring enough for the invisible that she would die trusting.

Next to her was a parapet of flame. She had to see it. Yet her man of light must have shone even more brightly. Then a gust of wind whipped east, and she died swallowed by splendor, in the remarkable silence of angels.

Soares rocked him, whispering in his ear, "Be strong."

Of course Pessoa would be strong. It was over, was it not? And though God deigned not to save her, Pessoa must believe now, for this tranquil death was miracle enough.

It was only when the ropes burned through, and her body had fallen dark as mystery down through the flames, that he realized how loudly and how without shame he was weeping.

He sobbed and let the old priest rock him, for faith brought not the comfort of holding. Berenice had died knowing that. Faith had never been the comfort of holding. Ah, sweet God. It was the comfort of being held.

Day 22

HEN BLUE TWILIGHT WAS SETTLING OVER LISBON, PRINCE PEDRO kicked his stallion through Castle São Jorge's gates. The Count de Ericeira trotted his long-legged English mount behind.

"Sire!" the count called.

Pedro had had enough of councils. He wanted a gallop. He wanted to see Afonso's eyes go alight when he gave him the present.

"Sire!"

Pedro finally reined his gray. The stallion crab-stepped across the cobbles. "Not 'sire.' I will not have you call me 'sire.' Especially not in my brother's presence."

The count inclined his head. "My prince." The man was already out of breath.

Pedro stood up in his saddle. All around the seven hills, lamps shone in windows. From where he sat he could see the quay and the fish sellers, now closing their awnings against the night. "One day I will build a palace there by the Tejo."

The count hiked his cloak about his shoulders. "Consider textiles, my prince."

Pedro laughed. "Yes, yes. Textiles."

"And after we see your brother off, we will to the merchants, then?"

Down by the quay, the royal caravelle was docked and waiting, its lanterns aglow. Pedro spurred the Barbary. It danced nimble-footed down the hill, the count's "It was his own fault, you know!" following.

Pedro took regret with him down the narrow streets. He raced anger and left the count and his guards behind. The stallion's hooves rang among the close-packed houses.

At the docks, the captain of the king's guard was waiting. When he caught sight of the Barbary, the old soldier started to his knees. Pedro leapt off his saddle and motioned him up.

"I have brought him a present," Pedro said, holding out the statue.

"Good of you." He smiled, but with such a melancholy.

"Was it so bad, then?"

"Harder for me, I think."

The quay smelled of tar and salt and fish. From someplace nearby, just beyond the Baixa, came the clang of a solitary church bell. "Captain, there is no need for you to accompany him into exile, if you do not wish. I could—"

A sharp and too curt "No."

"Well." Pedro hugged Afonso's gift to his chest. "A year or so. Then he can come back. The Inquisition will busy themselves with other matters and forget him."

"My prince," the captain said, "with what His Majesty has seen, the Inquisition can not afford to forget him. Your brother not only saw terrible deaths, but also witnessed a great beauty."

The captain's words caught Pedro off his guard. He was so confused by them, in fact, that they made him feel irritatingly callow. He dared not ask the man's meaning. Instead, he took his leave and went up the gangplank.

The Tejo's torpid swells rocked the boat like a cradle. In the light of the lanterns, the ship's wood gleamed. As Pedro boarded, fighting for his sea legs, the shipmaster bowed.

Along the quay came a clatter of hoofbeats. The count had finally arrived. He called up, "Soon, my prince! We are to meet them soon!"

Pedro asked the shipmaster, "Where?"

"Down in his cabin, sire," the man said. "Waiting."

Pedro took his unsaid objection below. Father de Melo stood at the foot of the stair.

"I brought him a present," Pedro said, showing him the statue.

De Melo clapped his hands together. "O, how nice that you thought of him, sire, for I know how busy—"

"Not 'sire.' Afonso is king," Pedro said. "I am prince regent, and I ask you to please remember that."

"O! Yes! Of course. How silly of—"

"How is he? I have heard diverse stories, and do not know what is true. I would have visited earlier, but I had not the leisure."

De Melo's voice lowered to such a sugary confection that it set Pedro's teeth on edge. "Well, of course you could not, my prince. Affairs of state, and . . ."

"What is the truth of it?"

"Ah." De Melo sought for help on the ceiling.

Around them, lamps flickered. A door nearby stood open: the ship-master's cabin, its desk littered with charts and an astrolabe. An ordinary room, but beyond it, waves slapped, water gurgled, spars creaked. Pedro remembered how afraid Afonso was of the sea.

"He is of a stubborn nature, as you well know, and at the present he apparently does not wish to discuss things."

Pedro pushed de Melo aside. "He will talk to me." He opened the next door, the one with the crown carved into it. The stateroom felt stuffy and close; the curtains were drawn over the dreary day. Across the room, Dr. Sales was seated in a chair. And next to the doctor was a bed with a shadowy figure upon it.

"Can we not have light?" Pedro snapped.

The doctor quickly trimmed the lamp, and Pedro could see that Afonso was drawn up into a corner, his knees to his chest, his face to the wall.

"Afonso?" He mounted the bed, crawling over covers to greet him. "Look, Afonso. I brought you a present."

When Pedro was closer, he heard Afonso singing. That surprised him. And, although he listened hard, he could not make out any words. So unearthly had Afonso become that, when Pedro touched his brother's hand, he was surprised to feel that it was warm and firm. When he took his wrist, he was surprised to find a pulse.

"See?" He set the statue down. "It is Don Quixote, Afonso. Will you not look? Will you not even look at me?"

That wordless whispered song, those eyes that looked at the bulkhead, and yet somehow saw too far.

"It is not really a banishment, Afonso. A little while and then you can come back. I would have you with me, you know that, do you not? Do you? And the Azores. Why, you will like the Azores. It is so beautiful there."

God. What had he done?

"Afonso? Was it the acorn? Was it the burnings? I could not stop them. Not and keep the kingdom."

Such a brutal and remote peace rested in him—the tranquillity of a saint forced face-to-face with God.

Pedro put his ear to his brother's chest. Gentle and steady as the slap of waves, Afonso's heart beat. Air went in and out the lungs. Pedro wrapped his arms about that still-warm body and took what comfort he could.

"Please," he whispered. "Tell me about the windmills."

Afterword

The historical Afonso, who was most likely retarded but not—I suspect—as good-natured as I have drawn him, spent fifteen years of royal exile in the Azores. He never returned to Lisbon. Prince Pedro married Afonso's little French princess and, upon his brother's death, ascended the throne. He reigned another twenty-three years.

This book takes liberties with Portuguese history, particularly with the character of Count Castelo Melhor, who suffers from the author's playfulness. I tried, however, to portray the young Pedro as he was: a good king, and a forward-thinking one. Although he ultimately failed, Pedro attempted during his thirty-eight years of rule to bring Portugal into the Industrial Age. He was thwarted at every step by the Inquisition.